The Kindled Flame

Sally Laity
&
Dianna Crawford

Tyndale House Publishers, Inc.
Wheaton, Illinois

Scripture quotations are from the *Holy Bible,* King James Version.

Library of Congress Cataloging-in-Publication Data

Crawford, Dianna, date
The kindled flame / Dianna Crawford and Sally Laity.
p. cm. — (Freedom's holy light ; v. 2)
ISBN 0-8423-1336-2
1. United States—History—Revolution, 1775-1783—Fiction. 2. Man-woman relationships—United States—Fiction. I. Laity, Sally. II. Title. III. Series.
PS3553.R27884K56 1994
813′.54—dc20 94-5907

Printed in the United States of America

99 98 97 96 95 94
6 5 4 3 2 1

This book is dedicated to our families
and friends who patiently encouraged
and supported us with prayer and love.
May the Lord bless them all richly.

The authors gratefully acknowledge the generous assistance provided by:

Philip Bergen, librarian
The Boston Historical Society
Boston, Massachusetts

Joan Diana, head librarian
Pennsylvania State University, Wilkes-Barre Campus
Lehman, Pennsylvania

These individuals helped us gather necessary period data and maps, shared their extensive knowledge of various settings, and forwarded biographical information on prominent figures who played a part in colonial America's fascinating history.

Special thanks to fellow writers and friends:

Sue Rich
Jo Frazier

Dear Reader,
We highly regard your interest in our trilogy, and would be pleased to receive your comments and answer any questions you might have.

Sally Laity and Dianna Crawford
P.O. Box 80176
Bakersfield, CA 93380

P.S. Your self-addressed stamped return envelope would be appreciated.

Rhode Island, June 1772

The sun slipped behind a crown of trees on the western horizon, gilding the edges of faraway clouds and tinting the sky in muted shades of rose. Ever-deepening shadows clung to the rolling landscape as the hush of evening settled over Pawtucket.

Emily Haynes was enjoying the glorious display when her eye was caught by a sudden movement. Shocked, she watched as Ted Harrington's uniformed arm yanked her sister Jane out of sight around the corner of the house. After an entire evening of her sister's scandalous flirting—and right under the nose of their overly proper mother, no less—his action was more than predictable. But when Jane's delighted giggle ended abruptly in a smothered sound, Emily felt her own cheeks warm.

She glanced up shyly at the tall British officer standing beside her on the bottom porch step, and her heart gave a nervous flutter. Surely Alex wouldn't be as bold as his chum, would he? He really was, she had to admit, rather dapper—for a wretched lobsterback. Tall and lean, he carried himself with the grace of the aristocracy. And a rakish grin softened his long face and complemented his refined features.

She watched as Alex Fontaine's gray eyes twinkled with devilment. He obviously was fighting back a smile. He removed the tall black hat cradled in the crook of one long arm, situated it atop his white military wig, and fastened the chin strap. Then, taking one of Emily's hands, he raised it lightly to his lips. "Don't fret, my fair green-eyed kitten. I shan't take such liberties. Not with the youngest daughter of the house, to be sure."

The lieutenant thought her little more than a babe-in-arms! Emily glared at him, but he merely chuckled. With a grimace, she shifted her attention back to the edge of the two-story white house, where an angle of dark shadow effectively shielded her sister and the other officer from view. But Emily could hear Jane's soft whispers and laughter . . . interspersed with moments of heavy silence. She drew a deep breath and forced her thoughts elsewhere.

Alex inclined his head and offered an arm.

With a polite smile, Emily threaded her hand into the curve of Alex's elbow and stepped with him onto the stone walkway.

"I say, 'twas an enjoyable evening," he said with a friendly tap on her fingers as he drew her toward the arbor at the edge of the lawn. "It was most hospitable of your family to provide such a delightful meal upon our arrival from Philadelphia. Their kindness is most appreciated."

"Even more by your friend, I'm sure," Emily blurted out, still stewing over Jane's disgraceful behavior with Lieutenant Harrington. Alex shot a fleeting look in that direction, and she clamped her lips together. When would she learn to hold her tongue?

Much to her relief, Alex laughed—a hearty sound that carried easily on the summer night air. The laugh echoed back from the rambling, weathered barn that housed many of the prized Narragansett Pacers raised by her family. Emily found herself joining in with his merriment.

Finally her sister reappeared, coming toward them arm in arm with Lieutenant Ted Harrington, the beau she'd lured up from Philadelphia. The rosy glow on Jane's face heightened the sparkle in her wide brown eyes, and she seemed unable to stop smiling. As she walked, her billowy russet skirt, the same shade as her hair, swayed like a bell.

Ted's blue eyes beamed at Jane from beneath straight brows. He was neither as tall nor as lean as Alex, yet his muscled frame showed the discipline of military training. His demeanor seemed consistently pleasant, and fine lines beside his mouth gave evidence of an easy grin. But Emily noted that it held a tiny flicker of guilt.

"What were you two laughing about?" Jane asked as they neared. "Or is it a secret?" Her expression reminded Emily of a satisfied cat beside an empty birdcage.

"Not at all," Alex answered. "I was merely having a chat with this delightful sister of yours. A charming little thing she is, I must say."

Emily clenched her fists. She had endured enough for one evening. "Oh, my, it's way past my bedtime," she said icily. "I must get tucked in, before the nanny discovers I'm out past dark." With a swish of raspberry taffeta, she turned and flounced toward the house, her blonde curls bouncing as she went.

The chorus of laughter that followed her theatrical exit only added fuel to her already smoldering temper. Emily plopped down on the steps and watched the two king's men mount their horses. She wasn't a baby—not at seventeen. She just had never particularly fancied having boys making moon eyes and fawning over her.

From her perch, she watched Ted bend to kiss her sister's hand. "Till tomorrow, my sweet," she heard him say as both his gaze and his hold lingered.

"See you on the morrow, little missy," Alex called out with a jaunty wave. He and Ted nudged their mounts forward.

Emily gave a slight nod. To be fair, she had to admit that Lieutenant Fontaine was nothing like the other boys who came around. Not only was he a few years older than the neighborhood swains, he was also sophisticated and extremely polite. She just didn't happen to share her twenty-year-old sister's fondness for lobsterbacks. Releasing a sigh, Emily rested her chin in her hands.

Jane drifted backwards up the walk, as if unwilling to relinquish the last glimpse of her uniformed soldier until he and Alex disappeared over the rise. "Isn't he just the handsomest thing you've ever seen?" she breathed dreamily. "I just adore his eyes, his smile, that tiny cleft in his chin, . . . and I could listen to his accent forever. He makes me feel so special. So beautiful." Grasping her satin skirt in one hand, she dipped and curtsied, her shapely form graceful and fluid as she danced an imaginary minuet over the grass.

Emily swept her eyes heavenward. "I think you were quite brazen, if you must know. Batting your eyelashes and gushing over him all evening. *'Why, Ted,'*" she mimicked in an overly sweet voice, "*'how gallant of you to say such things.'*" With a ridiculous titter that exactly duplicated her sister's, she doubled over with giggles, then sobered. "Mama would have had the vapors if she had seen you disappear with him that way."

Jane shrugged. Fingering a coppery ringlet, she raised her chin. "Oh, well, you're just a child. How would *you* know how to catch an eligible bachelor, anyway?"

"Is that what you call it?" Emily asked, ignoring the barb.

"Of course. What else? Now that Ted and Alex have at last been reassigned to Boston, I'm positive Ted will get around to asking me to marry him. And very soon." Jane extended a hand and spread her tapered fingers, pretending to admire a ring. Her full lips softened into a smile. "And I shan't be a bit sorry to leave this tiresome place, either."

Leaning forward slightly, Emily wrapped her arms around her knees. "I don't care what you say. I like it here."

"You would."

Emily bristled at the bitterness in her older sister's voice. "I'm not certain exactly what you mean by that, my being a *child* and all. But one thing I do know. I would absolutely *hate* being married to a redcoat—especially if we had to live in Boston under the thumb of those king's puppets."

"Well," Jane answered, regarding Emily with cool indifference, "*I* would adore it! Do you realize the advantages I should have there, and the status, being the wife of a distinguished officer of the Crown? No doubt we'd be provided a charming home of our own and be expected to attend all sorts of important functions. Why, with his friend Alex's own mother a cousin to Lord Hillsborough, the most important man in the Colonies, I shouldn't be surprised if Ted and I were extended an invitation to dine with the governor himself." Arching her eyebrows, she gave a nod of emphasis.

"The governor himself," Emily said dramatically, shaking her head in feigned amazement.

The staccato sound of approaching hoofbeats carried from the dirt road on the rise. Half expecting to see Ted returning for another kiss, Emily stiffened as Jane moved up a step. They looked toward the rider.

"Oh, it's just that freckle-faced Tommy Martin," Emily groaned, recognizing the storekeeper's pudgy son.

"Well, let's go see what's brought him by." Holding out a hand, Jane drew Emily to her feet, and together they walked to the gate of the picket fence, where they waited for the young man.

The lad stopped near the arbor, but remained in the saddle as his mount pranced nervously in place. The buttons of his brown waistcoat strained over his belly. He nudged his tricornered hat back with a thumb and bestowed a crooked grin on Emily. Even in the near-darkness, the abundance of freckles on his face stood out in mottled glory. "Saw your brother Dan and his wife in Providence awhile ago, just as they arrived on the packet. Asked me to let you all know."

"Oh?" Emily said, elated. She hadn't seen her favorite older brother since he had married Ted Harrington's sister.

"Yep. Said they'd be staying there the night. They'll be hiring a wagon first thing tomorrow to bring 'em the rest of the way, them and their things. Should be here by midmorning, I'd expect."

"Well, thank you for coming by, Thomas," Jane said, absently twisting the lace handkerchief she held. She turned and headed toward the house.

Emily started after her, but stopped when Tommy spoke again.

"Sure is a looker, Dan's wife. Said it's the first time she's been to Rhode Island. Found her in Princeton, didn't he?"

Stopping, Emily turned and gave a curt nod. "Dan studied for the ministry at the college there. In fact, he was just recently ordained. He's been asked to assist the pastor of a church in Boston, so he will probably take that charge."

"Say, that's wonderful." Tommy's voice cracked, and he cleared his throat and swallowed. "They won't be far from here."

"Yes. We're all very happy for them."

"Speaking of not bein' far," he continued, "I just passed a pair of lobsterbacks. First I ever seen east of Pawtucket."

"Thomas Martin!" Jane scolded from the porch. "I'll thank you to keep a civil tongue in your mouth. Those gentlemen were our guests for supper this evening, and I expect you and that lot who hang out at your father's store to treat them with due respect."

"Yes, ma'am," he muttered, abashed. "Didn't mean anything by it." Then with a grin in Emily's direction, he kicked his horse into a trot, wasting no time in his hasty retreat.

Jane's wide chestnut eyes flashed as she stared after the boy in disgust, hands on her hips. "I shall be so glad to get away from these provincial buffoons."

"And no doubt they'll share your joy," Emily murmured, going inside. She wondered how her mother would take the news of the impending visit of the daughter-in-law she had never approved of.

Following right behind, Jane brushed past to be first into the parlor. "Mother, Papa, Mr. Martin's son just stopped by on his way home from Providence. Dan and Susannah will be here in the morning."

Their mother's shoulders sagged, and her embroidery hoop dropped to her lap. She raised her regal head with a frown. An expression of irritation flared in her eyes. "In the morning?"

"Splendid!" Their father slapped his knee with a work-roughened hand and grinned, displaying straight teeth. As he smiled, some of the care lines left his tanned face, and Emily noticed how much her father looked like an older version of Dan, with his softly waved hair and brown eyes. "They must've had some fair winds. I didn't think they'd get here for another couple of days."

"Yes," Emily added with delight. "Tommy says they'll hire a wagon first thing."

"If Daniel were alone," Mama challenged, "he'd be here now, instead of sending that boy. It's only four miles, after all. His wife is obviously creating difficulties."

"Now, Sophia," Papa said, his tone placating. "The fact that Dan has married does not mean he loves you any less, you know. Just that he has more trunks. After all, you more than anyone emphasized the fact that he had been of age for some time and had a responsibility to settle down."

She sighed, stroking absently at the maroon brocade on the arm of the upholstered chair. "That's true. But I had such high hopes for Daniel as our firstborn son. Why did he have to choose *that* woman? He could have done so much better. And you know that as well as I."

"Sophia—"

"Well, really, Edmond," Mama said with a sniff. "Any young woman who would deliberately sign herself into servitude so she could prey upon a college full of innocent young men. . . ."

Watching her parents' exchange, Emily couldn't help smiling at the ridiculous notion her mother so stubbornly held. "Oh, Mama," she said. "Dan already loved Susannah. He married her before he even returned to complete his studies, remember?"

"Yes. But still, it didn't stop her from continuing to work in that inn—claiming she had a responsibility to those people. And she even wooed our son into staying there with her."

Laying her sewing upon the lamp table at her side, she plucked a few stray threads from her skirt and stood. "Even Susannah's own brother, that nice, respectable Lieutenant Harrington, can't condone or explain her actions. I'm surprised, Jane," she said, transferring her attention to the older daughter, "that you were able to convince him to stop by here on his way to Boston to welcome them home. And Alex . . ."

She paused. Her gaze moved to Emily, and her voice softened considerably. "I think Lieutenant Fontaine might possibly have had a more pressing reason for accompanying Ted here than just mere loyalty."

"And to think he's an aristocrat," Jane added. She peered sideways at Emily. "But what he could possibly see in a tomboy like Emily, I'll never know."

Emily glowered at her sibling. "Perhaps he appreciates the fact that when he's around me he can breathe a bit of fresh air, instead of choking on the smell of all that horrid perfume you wear."

"Well, he'd better not get too close to you," Jane retorted. "He might notice that the *fresh air* around you is laced with *fresh* horse manure."

"Girls, girls!" Lamplight danced over silver strands in Mama's auburn pompadour as she shook her head. "Such talk."

Emily watched her father cross the room and put an arm about her mother's shoulders. "Well, ladies—" His glance included all of them. "—enough of this chatter. I think it's time we retire. Don't you, my dear?" he asked, walking Mama toward the stairs. "I'm sure you'll want to be up early to help Tillie make all of Dan's favorite dishes."

Emily headed for the nearest parlor lamp.

"And Ted's, too," Jane gushed with a smile. "Oh, Emily," she tossed back, "you could make some of Alex's."

Poised over the glass globe, Emily seethed as her sister dashed laughingly up the steps behind their parents. She quickly blew out the flame, hoping Jane would stumble in the dark, but heard no such mishap.

Oh, Emily, she mimicked silently, cocking her head back and forth with a pout. *You could make some of Alex's.* "Hmmph. One lobsterback in the family would be bad enough," she muttered, moving to lock the front door. She reached for the bolt but then changed her mind and opened the door instead, stepping outside into the balmy night.

The silver-white light from a three-quarter moon outlined the bushes and shrubbery bordering the neat lawn. The glow illuminated acres of fences and split-rail paddocks, making them appear delicate, ethereal.

The lonely hoot of a barn owl joined the cacophony of night sounds made by crickets and tree toads. Inhaling the intoxicating fragrance of her mother's roses, Emily moved to the edge of the porch and rested her hands on the banister as she watched a pair of fireflies playing hide-and-seek. She smiled and turned, noticing a light still burning at Tillie and Elijah's cabin, to the right of the corrals. Perhaps she should inform the hired Negroes about Dan's coming. They had been part of the household forever and would be pleased to hear the news.

Maybe later, she decided. Descending the steps, she linked her hands behind her back and strolled leisurely up the fence-lined lane toward the barn. On either side, several sorrel-colored horses wandered up to gaze curiously over the rails, their coats glistening in the moonlight. "Hello, Foxfire, old girl," she breathed, veering toward one of them. "How are you doing?" She stroked the velvety muzzle and gave it a soft kiss, then patted a crowding gelding, giggling as he nuzzled her fingers. "You're looking lonesome, Star. I've been neglecting you, haven't I?" The animal pressed its nose against her hand, and she reveled in the warm softness.

The past several days had been busy at the house, baking and preparing for the visit from the two young military officers and her brother. She hadn't had a moment of solitude. On impulse, Emily hiked her skirt, scaled the fence, and slid onto Star's back. Guiding him by the mane, she nudged him to the gate, opened it just enough for them to go through, then shoved it closed again.

With her knees she urged the horse into a gallop down the lane toward the road. Wind loosened the ribbon tying back her long curls. Pulling off the velvet strand, she let it drift recklessly from her fingertips so her hair could fly free. When she rode horseback there was no one around bossing her . . . or trying to marry her off to some tin soldier who would undoubtedly take up where her family left off. She filled her lungs and felt the heady sensation of independence.

Turning east, she guided Star toward her special hill. From the clearing there she looked toward Providence Town. In the distance she could see Narragansett Bay, dotted with its numerous islands. She couldn't wait to see Dan again. On his last visit, more than a year ago, he had informed their brother, Benjamin, that because of his marriage to Susannah he would be giving up his postriding job. And he had come to fetch Ben to Boston to take his place. Emily sighed. Boys *always* got their freedom sooner or later.

Leaning forward as the horse began to climb the knoll, she looked skyward. *Dear Lord, why, why did you have to make me a girl?*

Upon reaching the small plateau, Star wandered to a stop. Emily's gaze jumped past Pawtucket's little cluster of lights to the thousand sparkling diamonds called Providence. *If I were Ben, I'd be riding the post roads this very minute, delivering mail, or perhaps—* Her attention stretched farther to Narragansett Bay and then to the horizon where the vast Atlantic lay. *—perhaps sailing the high seas.*

The hoot of a distant owl drifted on the June breeze. Emily exhaled heavily. "But what good are all my grand dreams? I'm to be married off and locked away somewhere. That's my fate. And if it must be . . ."

She straightened and looked again to the lights of Pawtucket, only a mile away, where the two British lieutenants had secured rooms in Pidge Tavern. The last few times Jane had convinced Papa to let her and Emily go to Philadelphia on the pretext of visiting Cousin Charlotte, it had really been so that Jane could see her handsome officer posted there. And on those occasions, Alex never seemed to mind escorting Emily. In fact, he had always seemed quite amused by her, for some odd reason.

Emily looked despairingly down at her slight curves. Her figure had shown real promise at fifteen, but somehow it hadn't progressed much beyond that. No wonder Alex treated her with cheerful tolerance. She *did* look like a child. She grimaced dejectedly. Of course, she had never really encouraged him, either. But if her lot in life was no more than to be someone's wife and the mother of his children, perhaps she should make her parents happy and marry well. A rueful smile tugged at her lips. If nothing else, Alex Fontaine could easily afford to buy her a spirited horse of her own. "Yes," she announced. "One of those English hunters. There'd be quite a measure of freedom in owning a swift, long-legged steed."

Star perked an ear her way and snorted.

Emily laughed and patted his neck. "I do sound like a silly goose. It would be harder for me to find myself accepted by that aristocratic Fontaine family in England than it would be for you, my dear friend, to be stabled among their fine horses." Her attention drifted again to the lights of Pawtucket. "But neither of those things would be half so difficult as it's going to be for Dan's wife, the indentured servant, to be accepted by Mama." She sighed. "How fortunate Dan has obtained a position at a church. *Fortunate* . . . there's that faithless word again. He'd be the first to remind me that fortune had nothing to do with it, that God is simply taking care of him."

Picking up a strand of Star's mane, Emily began braiding it. "I would trust God myself . . . if I could ever once get what I wanted. But that'll never happen, I'm sure." An unexpected sob clutched her throat at the truthfulness of those words, and she quickly swallowed it down. She hadn't come up here to bemoan her bleak future. She had come to dream of distant lands and exciting adventures.

Lolling back, she pillowed her head on the horse's rump. Overhead the sky glittered with a million stars. She picked out Ursa Major, then the North Star, the point that sailors had used for hundreds of years to chart their courses.

"Ah yes, my life lies open before me. Where shall *I* sail?"

From a second-floor window at the King's Crown Inn in Providence, Daniel Haynes surveyed the bustling port.

"'Tis as lovely as you said it would be," Susannah murmured from within the crook of his arm. "Look how the lights from the ships dance over the water like so many fireflies. I shall hate leaving all this beauty and peace on the morrow."

Dan tightened his hold on his wife's slightly thickened waist, his fingers resting on the gentle swell of her abdomen. He would never tire of the melodic sound of her British accent or of having her near. Unceasingly, he thanked the Lord for the treasure of her love. With his free hand, Dan took her clefted chin between his finger and thumb, turning her face toward him. How could it be possible that she had grown even more beautiful since their marriage a year and a half ago? His gaze wandered over her tawny glowing hair, that satin skin, those incredible gray-blue eyes, then moved to the expressive lips he always ached to kiss.

Inhaling a long, slow breath, he wrapped his arms around her, feeling his pulse thundering in his ears. "Please, love, don't be nervous about meeting Mother. I'm sure that once she gets to know you she'll love you as much as I do. Almost, anyway," he added, pushing aside a silken curl so he could nibble her tender neck.

Susannah's enchanting laugh washed over him. "I only hope you're right. I do so want to have close ties with your family. But since the night when that very public announcement of my indenturement caused such scandal, they've barely even communicated with us by post. My heart flutters at the mere thought of actually meeting them."

"I know. I think I can hear it." He straightened a fraction, cocking an ear toward the street. "No, wait. That's a drum. Listen. I wonder what's happening." Releasing his hold on Susannah, Dan leaned out the open window.

The throbbing beat grew louder by the moment. Dozens of men poured out of the buildings all along the street, some still buttoning their shirts and waistcoats, some tugging their boots on as they, too, looked toward the commotion.

A slight youth of about fourteen came into view, the leather strap of a drum slung over one shoulder. As he marched, he pounded out the cadence to his steps. Behind him followed a parade of men of all ages and manner of dress. Reaching the bright glow from a multi-paned shop window below, the lad stopped, and beneath his cap a thatch of white-gold hair caught the light. With a few more whacks of his drumsticks, he ceased abruptly. "The *Gaspee* has run aground off Namquit Point," he shouted.

The bystanders let out an enthusiastic cheer and thumped one another on their backs.

Dan strained to hear the boy's next words.

"She won't be able to get free till after midnight!" the drummer added jubilantly. "You're all cordially invited to join Mr. John Brown at the public house across from Fenner's Wharf. *If* you feel disposed to go and destroy that troublesome vessel."

"Try to stop us!" came one loud voice.

Another cheer went up. "Lead the way, lad."

The boy began pounding the drum again and strode out into the street. To a man, all present fell into step and marched behind him, talking excitedly among themselves.

As the merry mob passed beneath Dan's window, his eye caught sight of a familiar form among the crowd. "Yancy! Yancy Curtis! Wait!"

The lanky redheaded sailor cocked his head and stopped, nudging back the brim of his sailor cap with a calloused hand. A wide grin spread across his weathered face. "Shiver me timbers. Dan Haynes, it is. Comin' with us, mate?"

"Just give me a minute." With a wave, Dan turned.

Susannah caught hold of his arm and stopped him. "Surely you can't be thinking of going down there, Dan, and joining that mob." She searched his face.

Dan ran his fingers down the side of her cheek. "I just want to find out what it's about, love. And I've got to say hello to my friend Yancy Curtis . . . you remember him."

"Who could forget him?" she asked with disdain. "A man who resorts to dressing up as a woman in order to smuggle goods right under the noses of the customs agents!"

"Now, don't go making that sound like a crime," he said teasingly, as he coaxed her frown into a smile. "Where would the Colonies be without its smugglers?"

"Oh, Dan—"

He cut off Susannah's words with a quick kiss. "I won't be long. I promise." Turning, he crossed the room and opened the door, then stopped. He grinned sheepishly at her. "In Rhode Island, smuggling is considered quite an honorable profession, as you'll soon find out."

Susannah shook her head as Dan closed the door behind him. Moments ago she had been thanking almighty God for giving her such a loving and considerate husband and for the pleasant time they had been having since they'd left Princeton for a visit to Rhode Island. Now his eagerness to leave her side and become part of some dreadful activity filled her with foreboding. He had survived many dangers before their marriage, when he had been a postrider aiding the patriots in Boston, she reminded herself. But it had come as a relief to her when Dan passed his responsibilities on to his younger brother, Ben, and finished his studies for the ministry, where his real calling lay. The sight of him behind a pulpit, strong and commanding, his countenance filled with fervor, always made her heart leap. She breathed a quick prayer that God would grant him wisdom.

Outside, Dan barely set foot onto the street before Yancy grabbed him with a hearty laugh, enveloping him in a bear hug. Then, clasping one another's shoulders, they drew apart.

"It's mighty good to see you, Yance. It's been ages."

"A good spell and more, that's for sure. But I run across that kid brother of yours now and again. Says ye went back to that school in New Jersey to learn preacherin'. And that ye hopped the broom with that little English lass ye was so set on, to boot." His blue eyes sparked with merriment.

"All true." Straightening, Dan tucked his thumbs under the lapels of his frock coat with a mock-serious expression and rocked back on his heels. "So I'll be expecting the respect due my new, distinguished station, of course."

"Aye, aye, sir," Yancy said with a salute. Sturdy white teeth flashed in an infectious grin. "Next time we're doing some midnight ship unloading, I'll be sure to say *please,* sir, 'fore I toss ye a chest of tea. Right, mate?"

"As much as I can expect, I'm sure."

"Ye and the missus back in Providence to stay?"

"No, just on a visit. I've been offered the assistant pastorate at the Long Lane Church in Boston, and we'll take up residence in the Bradley house on Milk Street. Personally, though, I think President Witherspoon thought I might be of more help there in the cause for freedom than in merely assisting the aging Reverend Moorhead."

"Could be right," Yancy said, nodding in thought. "Well, at least in Boston ye won't be far from your family."

"No, not at all. On one of our good pacers, I could be back here in a hard day's ride. So, if they ever need anything . . ." He finished with a shrug. Then noticing that the noise from the crowd had diminished in the distance, he lowered his voice a few notches. "What's going on? I never saw a crowd so eager to row out and destroy a ship in my life."

Yancy chuckled. "Ah. I take it ye ain't heard tell of His

Majesty's haughtiest pirate, Lieutenant William Dudingston. The insolent blackguard come sailing in about three months back and set anchor on our flourishing enterprises."

"And?"

"He's threatened to sink any ship entering the bay that don't give him permission to come aboard an' search for contraband. Besides bullying the ships' masters, he also helps himself to sheep, hogs, poultry, whatever catches his fancy. And if he finds something the least bit suspect, he seizes the ship."

Dan groaned and shook his head.

"But that's not the end of it, mate. That shark's even set the farmers to plucking their chickens . . . for the tar-and-feathering party they're planning for him. He's been sending his crew ashore to raid their storage bins and take their livestock. He's even been cutting down their fruit trees for firewood. Yessirree. One of King Georgie's finest, come to protect all us ignorant colonials. 'Tis a wonder we ever got by without 'em."

"So you're all intending to destroy his ship while it's stuck on a sandbar?"

"Seems a far sight better'n sitting on our hands."

Dan nodded slowly as the seriousness of the situation became clear. "Well, be sure you sneak up real quiet, Yance. He sounds like the sort who'd blow you clean out of the water just for thinking about it."

Yancy frowned. "Ye won't be coming with us, lad?"

"Don't think I'd better. I don't want to leave Susannah alone. She's in a family way. We've only just arrived here, and she's anxious about meeting my family for the first time tomorrow morning. And I know her being with child has also unsettled her. And losing her best friend in childbirth hit her quite hard."

"She's with child, ye say? Well, I'll be a drunken sea rat!" Grinning, Yancy stepped farther out into the street and looked up toward Susannah, who watched from the window above them. He whipped off his hat and bowed with a flourish. "Congratulations, Miz Haynes. Netted yourself a fine husband here. But if he don't look after ye right and proper, I'll see he walks the plank. Be sure of that."

At the sound of Susannah's light laugh, he stepped nearer to Dan again. "Well, I'd best catch up with the others. Those longboat oars need muffling before we row out."

"Godspeed, Yancy."

The rawboned redhead grinned, tugging his seaman's cap on again. "I'll be counting on ye praying us through, mate."

"How about if I pray that God's will be done?"

"One and the same, mate. One and the same."

"Perhaps."

Yancy gave a nod, then began striding away.

"We'll be at my family's farm for the next few days," Dan called after him. "Come for dinner."

"Aye, I'll do that," Yancy said cheerfully, then stopped and turned around. "Any of those pretty sisters of yours still home?"

"Two."

"Count on me tomorrow, mate."

Watching his friend trot off toward the wharf, Dan chuckled to himself.

❦ ❦

Young Robert MacKinnon felt the dark icy waves of Narragansett Bay close over him. He struggled to get his head above the water again. Only hours ago the shore had looked so close, before darkness had shrouded it . . . before he had dropped the rope over the side of the *Gaspee* and managed to slip down undetected.

Treading water while he caught his breath, he realized he hadn't yet gone half the distance he needed. He had learned well how to swim in the frigid current of the Ayr River back home in Scotland. But the heaving swells of this bay pulled at his clothing and shoes, sucking him under. He'd have to discard them if he ever hoped to make shore.

But how could he do that? Once he reached land he'd need his clothes. They were all he possessed beside those few pounds he and his father had spent five years scrimping to save, oil-wrapped and tucked deep inside the pocket of his coat. The woolen over-garment weighed him down the worst. Perhaps if he sacrificed even that much . . . it was summer-time, after all. Digging deep, his stiff fingers closed over the packet, and he put it in his teeth while he shrugged out of the soaked coat and let it sink.

His arms still felt like lead. He stuffed the packet of money into his shirt pocket and rolled over onto his back to rest for just a moment, trying to steel himself against a cold so invasive it felt like the first spring run-off.

So far, so good. No one on the ship seemed to have noticed his absence. He had been careful not to mention his plan to anyone.

From across the swells, a faint cough bounced toward him, an eerie sound in the watery darkness . . . and all too close. Robby's heart gave a lurch. Had he not made good his escape after all? Struggling to keep quiet, he let his body sink down until only his nose and the top of his head rose above the water. Revolving slowly, he searched for the source of that sound.

Within seconds he found it. The dim silhouette of a long-boat, slicing silently through the waves, bore down on him . . . *coming from shore.* It passed him with only a few yards to spare. A dozen men bent into their oars, propelling the craft. Just about to exhale with relief at not having been sighted, Rob noticed another ghostlike longboat, then a third. He counted seven in all—all apparently heading for a surprise visit to the *Gaspee.*

One healthy yell would easily carry to the ship and alert the crew, he knew. But Robby had no intention of doing that. He felt his cold lips widen into a bitter grimace. That tyrant, Dudingston, rated no warning. He deserved to be skewered on a lance and sent straight to Hades.

Teeth chattering, Rob ignored a twinge of guilt that tickled his conscience over the fate that certainly awaited his ship-mates. But he stiffened his resolve. They were on their own, just as *he* had been since the Almighty had forsaken him and allowed him to be snatched off the Bristol docks and impressed into service all those months ago.

With grim determination, he put renewed effort into the long strokes he hoped would get him far enough away before the melee broke loose. At least he had managed to escape before that small army of angry Rhode Islanders—no doubt well armed—swarmed the vessel. Without bothering to glance back in that direction, he pressed steadily onward.

Rob peered up at the sky to check the position of the stars for a bearing. Then, harder and harder, he pushed on for what seemed an eternity. His knee finally scraped bottom. *He made it!*

As he came to his feet in the shallows, the evening breeze sliced through his dripping shirt and trousers. Goose flesh covered him from his head to his toes. Wrapping his arms around his thin, shivering torso, he sputtered into a victorious chuckle. What was a little freezing? He was free . . . about to stroll onto a new land . . . and into a new life.

He knew he should start moving at once, get as far from the bay as possible before daylight gave him away. But he paused, relishing the feeling of solid ground beneath his feet. He patted his pocket and felt his hoard of money beneath his fingers. Thanks to Dudingston he still had it all. It had been intended for purchasing the price of the voyage—and it would have been if that villain hadn't kidnapped him to serve as cabin boy.

The stretch of sand surrounding him looked uninhabited and lonely, and not at all familiar like the rocky shores of Scotland. But not far away were lights. Buildings. In the past months, he had memorized every nook and cranny of the Narragansett waters from the rail of the ship. But Dudingston had been no fool. He caught the longing on Rob's face in an unguarded moment and never permitted the lad to go ashore.

Making his way slowly toward Providence, Robby looked out over the black water to the lantern lights of the *Gaspee,* listing to one side, its deep hull grounded on a sand spit that, at low tide, was only a few feet below the surface. He raised a hand to his bare head in mock salute. "I bid ye farewell, Lieutenant Dudingston. May the devil himself awaken ye tomorrow."

At that moment he heard the distant shout of the ship's sentinel. The call split the eerie quiet of the night.

"Who goes there?"

❦ ❧

In one of the longboats, Yancy Curtis's heart plummeted. They had been sighted!

But the attack party had already crowded close enough to the *Gaspee* to be below the range of the cannons. He looked to the bow of his craft, and to Captain Whipple, a seaman with unerring knowledge of the Rhode Island waters, who had piloted the expedition along with another local sea captain, John Hopkins.

Whipple bravely stood, but made sure of his footing in the wobbling boat before giving an answer.

Someone leaned out over the railing, holding aloft a lantern. It was Lieutenant Dudingston, easily recognized by his jib-shaped hat. "State your business," he ordered as other crewmen came and lined the rail on either side of him.

Captain Whipple puffed out his stout chest. "I am the sheriff of the county of Kent," he lied with equal authority, embellishing his reply with a burst of profanity. "I have a warrant to apprehend you. So surrender."

A gunshot cracked.

Ducking, Yancy searched for the origin. His eyes flared wide when he saw Dudingston drop the lantern and slump over. A nearby sailor caught his limp form as it slid to the deck.

"I've killed the rascal!" Hotheaded Joseph Bucklin, one of Yancy's fellow crewmen, waved his now-empty musket.

Yancy couldn't believe the fool's thoughtless action. He shoved past the man to reach Whipple, who stared at the deserted *Gaspee* rail with disbelief. "We must go aboard, sir, before they've time to unlock their arms and pass them out."

"Right." The older man drew a pistol tucked in his wide belt and held it high. "Drop down your ladders," he shouted, "and let us board before any more harm comes to you."

Yancy regarded the man in astonishment. *Did Whipple really think his command would be taken seriously? No seasoned man-of-war sailor would give up without a fight.* He reached for the nearest coil of rope with a grappling hook attached. But before he could gather its length, he heard several loud thwacks against the hull of the ship. The seamen had actually complied with the order!

John Brown, a merchant who had gained prominence in the trade of smuggled goods and had outfitted the expedition, stood up in the next boat that bobbed against the ship. "Is Dudingston alive?" he called upward.

"Yes, he's still breathing," came a reply.

Brown faced the small flotilla. "I need a longboat. You," he said, indicating his choice, "row back to port for a surgeon. All the rest of you men come with me." He reached for the rope ladder and began to climb.

Yancy waited for Captain Whipple to go first, then followed, fearing all the way that the enemy would retaliate and open fire on them. He tried to keep as near to the ship's hull as possible, using its angle as a shield.

Yet to his utter amazement, when he reached the deck of the *Gaspee,* he saw her seamen—this band of marauders who had been the scourge of Narragansett Bay for the past several months—meekly standing back. Yancy studied the members of the crew as they stood together silent and unresisting, and for a fleeting moment he wondered if the expression so evident in their eyes was actually guilt or remorse for their arrogant pillaging. Whatever it was, it was truly unbelievable.

Yancy sent a thankful glance heavenward. Perhaps there was something to that prayer business after all. At any rate, Daniel Haynes sure must know how to talk to the Almighty!

After the returning men left the longboats and went their separate ways, Yancy lingered on the wharf to look one last time across the water at the glow of the burning ship. Growing dimmer by the minute, soon there would be nothing left of the *Gaspee,* the menace of this free-spirited port. Of course, when Dudingston and his crew reported the incident to the authorities, there would be the deuce to pay. But it had been worth it.

With a satisfied smile, Yancy tucked his hands into his pockets and started toward the side street where he had rented a modest room for the night. As he walked, a tune that a sailor friend had taught him some time ago came to mind, and he began singing softly under his breath:

'Twas in the merry month of May,
When all the flowers were bloomin',
Sweet William on his deathbed lay
For the love of Barbara Allen. . . .

Puckering his lips, he whistled a few more bars. Tomorrow he would be going to supper at Dan's. Four or five lovely lasses had once lived there, as he recalled. But now Dan said only two sisters remained. Yancy hoped one of them was the copper-haired beauty he'd seen riding behind Dan into Providence a couple of years back. There'd been something quite fetching about that wee minx—a spark of mischief in her big brown eyes that set her apart from the usual colonial lass, and she carried herself with grace. Of course, she had pretended to ignore him, but he'd caught her stealing peeks through her lashes more than once. Aye. More than once. He smiled to himself.

"'Twas a great, grand bonfire ye had goin' oot there in the bay," came an unmistakable Scottish brogue from the darkness nearby.

Startled, Yancy stopped, straining his eyes to make out who had spoken. "Liked it, did ye?" he asked tentatively.

"Aye. That I did." A young man moved from the deep shadow of a building. He appeared to be about eighteen, a whole head shorter than Yancy, and all skin and bones. In just his shirt sleeves and sodden trousers, he shivered, holding onto himself for warmth. "Disappointed I was to've missed it. But I'd already set me heart on seein' this new land of yers. I parted from that fine ship and that *kindhearted* officer not fifteen minutes b'fore ye sent him your greetin'."

Yancy chuckled at the lilt in the young lad's speech. "The lieutenant will be sending some greetings of his own, no doubt, once he's mended."

"Nay! Ye canna' mean ye set him free already! The mangy cur will have ye all arrested b'fore mornin'."

"Oh, he'll try. Make no mistake of that." Yancy pulled off his navy seaman's coat and tossed it to the newcomer. "Here, put this on, before the clacking of your teeth wakes the dead."

"For just a minute, till I warm a wee bit." Nodding his gratitude, he shoved shaking hands into the sleeves.

Taking off his worn black cap, Yancy plunked it on the damp head for good measure.

"Ye shouldna' be givin' me yer own hat, too."

"I'd say you're needing it a sight more'n me, right now."

"Weel now, I canna' dispute that. But 'tis best I be on me way, soon, or he'll ha' me in irons, too." The young man stomped his feet and rubbed up and down on his arms. "Could ye be pointin' me to some oot-of-the-way corner where I might dry oot an' tuck meself away for the night? An' perhaps ye could tell me aboot some kind wheelwright or farmer who might be of a mind to do some hirin'?"

Yancy grinned. "Ye really did jump ship, lad?"

"Aye. I owed no allegiance to a kidnapper." The bitter words came out in a rush.

Yancy gave a snort. "Ye were pressed into service against your will, eh?"

"Aye, but I'll na' be such a fool again."

Yancy knew from his own similar experience some years ago that the practice was a common occurrence on the English docks, and in his travels he had come across a number of sailors as unfortunate as this lad. "Grabbed ye while your back was turned, did they?"

The young man nodded, causing the big cap to wobble loosely on his head. "Right off the Bristol docks. Weel, 'tis a pleasure talkin' wi' ye. But 'twould be wise, methinks, if we got off the street b'fore Dudingston rallies a force an' comes lookin' for the likes of us."

"That'll take him a smart spell, in this town," Yancy said dryly. "Aside from the fact he took a musket ball in his hip, it'll take quite a lot of talking before the sheriff feels pressured into taking action." He looked the lad up and down. "Tell ye what. I've some spare clothes in my room on the next street. Looks like ye could use a bit of rest anyway."

"Ye'll na' think me too much trouble?"

"Nay. Been falling behind in my good deeds lately anyway. Yancy Curtis is the name." Grinning, he held out a hand. "And ye're—?"

The lad took it with a firm shake. "Robert MacKinnon, sir, of Ayr, Scotland. An' I'll na' be forgettin' your kindness."

❦ ❦

A few hours later, as the first glint of morning appeared at the edge of the dark eastern sky, Yancy left Rob hiding in the shadows while he rousted the livery boy out of his sleep long enough to saddle a horse. He quickly chose a local breed from the animals available, knowing the sturdy pacer would easily carry two men on its back.

After leaving the settlement at Providence behind, Rob bounced along in back of Yancy for the good part of an hour before venturing to speak. "This lowland country looks rich for farmin'."

"Aye."

"D'ye know if there's land for sale, here aboot?"

Yancy narrowed his eyes against the early morning light and took in the lush green surroundings. It probably looked enticing to a newcomer, with livestock growing fat on its rich grassland and wooded rolling hills off in the distance. "Can't say. The sea's always been me life."

"Seems in such a vast land, a man might be able to have both, would he na'?"

With a smile, Yancy considered the young man's words. "Ye could be right, lad. But with so many years still ahead of me, I ain't given much thought to settling down." A picture of a shapely young woman flashed to mind, one with rust-colored hair and rich brown eyes. He blinked in surprise.

"Hm. Choosin' to wait. That's good."

Yancy swung around with a scowl. The black-haired lad looked as though he'd barely begun to shave on a regular basis. "Ye don't think I'd make some lass a fit husband?"

"Eh?" Rob's boyish face reddened. "I dinna' say that a'tall. But back home, if a man wants to get ahead, he must spend every wakin' moment tryin' to make a spot for himself first. Wi' the lairds ownin' most of the land, there's na' so much left to go around."

"Aye. I see what ye mean." Approaching the road that led to the Haynes farm, Yancy reined in the mount. "We're just comin' up on me friend's place, Rob. An' I don't—"

"Ye dunna' think I'll be welcome?"

"Well, ye would by Dan, that I know for certain. His loyalty's with the Sons of Liberty. But he's not here yet and won't be for a few more hours. Perhaps ye should keep out of sight till I find out how the rest of the family feels about things."

"Aye. That might be wise." Before the words were completely out, Rob had dismounted. He raised his brows hopefully as Yancy glanced toward the farm just in sight through a line of trees.

"Head on over in that direction," Yancy said, indicating a patch of woods with his finger. "Soon as ye see the back of the house, make your way as quick as ye can to the springhouse and hide there till I come for ye."

Rob gave a nod and skirted the grove as he had been instructed. Yancy watched the lad go—a fine-looking young man whose broad-shouldered frame would soon fill out, once he ate proper. The legs of Yancy's seafaring trousers had been a touch long for him, but the blue homespun shirt fit reasonably well. Nudging the horse onto the lane, Yancy rode slowly toward the Haynes home.

Dan's father came out of the barn.

"Mr. Haynes," Yancy said, dismounting.

"Yes. Good day," the man said with a puzzled frown. "Curtis, isn't it?"

"Aye."

"Thought so, once I saw that carrottop of yours." With a grin, Mr. Haynes wiped his palms on a handkerchief from his back pocket, then offered a warm handshake. "What brings you out to our neck of the woods?"

Yancy watched beyond the man's shoulder as Robert MacKinnon moved stealthily to the squat outbuilding and unlatched the door. It gave a low squeak, and Yancy coughed, then cleared his throat. "I saw Dan in Providence last night, and he talked me into coming out for a visit. Hope ye don't mind, sir."

"No, not at all. His friends are always welcome here."

"He says he'll only be here a couple of days, him and his new wife, before takin' up his post."

Mr. Haynes nodded and grinned. "Makes me smile every time I think about it."

The back door of the house slammed shut, the sound echoing off the barn.

"Why's that?" Yancy asked, trying to remain casual. *Don't let it be someone heading for the springhouse,* he thought, but he kept his expression even. His pulse accelerated as a slight, fair-haired lass headed right for that very structure. This couldn't be happening.

"Oh, you know. The idea of the son of a good Rhode Island Baptist and a loyal Anglican from Pennsylvania becoming a Presbyterian minister in Congregational Massachusetts." Mr. Haynes laughed and shook his graying head. "Unbelievable!"

Dan's mother belonged to the Anglican church? The Church of England? Yancy called himself all kinds of fool for not remembering that particular fact. He'd heard talk that her loyalties had never been with her husband's people. His gaze slid to the springhouse . . . where one of the woman's young daughters, at this very moment, was opening the door.

Emily shifted her pewter pitcher to the hand holding the basket, then reached for the latch, noticing absently that someone had forgotten to set it properly. She groaned with impatience. Jane's mind was far too occupied by a particular British lieutenant for her to be of much use around the farm of late. It would give Emily great pleasure to remind her bossy older sister to be more careful. Opening the door, she stepped inside and set down her basket as she closed the door behind her.

The fine hairs on the back of her neck bristled. Sensing she was not alone, Emily whirled around. Her breath caught in her throat at the sight of a dark-haired young man. "Wh-who are you?" When he did not answer, she opened her mouth to scream.

His hand shot out and clamped over it as he yanked her to him. "Shh. No need to be yellin'. I'll na' be harmin' ye, lass," he said in a distinct Scottish accent.

Squirming loose, she jabbed him in the ribs with her pitcher.

"Oof!" He knocked the weapon from her hand and pinned

her arms at her sides. He pulled her back. "I said I'll na' hurt ye," he whispered against her ear.

Trapped against the stranger, Emily noticed a strong smell of the sea about him. She knew her father was at the barn. She opened her mouth a fraction.

"If ye promise ye'll na' cause trouble, I'll—"

The door crashed open, admitting another intruder—a tall redhead. Emily's fear doubled, until she saw her father right behind him.

"Papa? What's happening?" Even to her own ears her voice sounded high, frightened.

The other man barred her father from coming to her rescue. His face seemed familiar. She took a closer look. "Aren't you Yancy Curtis, Dan's friend?" she asked in amazement.

"Aye," he answered, a disconcerted grin bringing a twinkle to his blue eyes. "'Tis all right. 'Twas me sent the lad in here to hide."

"You?"

"I needed a chance to talk to your father about him first," Yancy continued.

"Is that so?" came her father's astonished voice. "Did you also tell him to maul my daughter while he waited?"

The stranger released her immediately and stepped away.

"Please, Mr. Haynes," Yancy said, raking freckled fingers through his wild curls. "My apologies for causing this whole mess." He gestured with his thumb toward the younger man. "This lad is Robert MacKinnon. He escaped the *Gaspee* last night and needs to hide out for a spell."

"Now, wait, Seaman Curtis," Emily heard her father say. "One thing we do not need around here is to have the authorities crawling all over this farm. It's bad enough that they gave Dan problems in the past and are now harassing Ben at every turn along the post roads. I'll not stand by while they haul the rest of us off."

"Aye, I understand your thinking, sir. But the lad was serving against his will. He was pressed into service right off the docks when he went there to buy his passage to America! He just wanted to be free of that plaguing ship. And he deserves a chance to seek his fortune here like the rest of us."

"I'll na' be causin' ye any grief, me good man," the young man said quietly. "Ye've me word on it. I'll be leavin' post-haste. But I'd be thankin' ye if ye could perhaps direct me to some farm or a wheelwright where I might be findin' work."

Listening to the pleasant roll of the lad's words, Emily studied Robert MacKinnon. He was easy enough to look at, with thick black hair brushing the top of his collar and just beginning to curl upward near his ears. His dark eyebrows matched the beginnings of a mustache. His hold upon her, though firm, had been somehow gentle. And he had the most compelling blue eyes she'd ever seen. As his gaze turned her way, she lowered hers and studied the packed dirt floor.

"Off the *Gaspee,* you say?" Papa said thoughtfully, looking from Yancy to Rob. "Well. That does cast a different light upon the situation. Anyone who has mind enough to bid farewell to that devil ship is most welcome to stay here till we can find you a fit place."

Yancy cleared his throat and shifted his weight to his other leg. "Then, uh, you've not heard the worst, I'd venture."

"The worst?" Papa said, a guarded note in his tone.

"It, uh, seems the *Gaspee* . . . well, it caught fire and burned last night." A wicked grin made its way across Yancy's seasoned face. He tried unsuccessfully to wipe it away with his hand.

Her father's hearty laugh filled the springhouse. "You don't say."

"Not by my hand," the Scot quickly added.

Suddenly footsteps sounded from just outside, and Jane burst into the springhouse. "What's taking you so—" Her chestnut eyes darted wildly about the interior, taking in the unexpected crowd.

Emily glanced in Robert MacKinnon's direction. A moment ago he had appeared quite relaxed, but now he seemed tense, uneasy. She lifted her nose Jane's way. Knowing her sister's loyalties lay with the British—especially now that she had Lieutenant Harrington dancing on her string—it would be impossible to expect her to harbor a deserter willingly. Did Papa know that? She looked his way.

His expression indicated that he did indeed.

"Ah, the fair Miss Haynes," Yancy said with an exaggerated bow, drawing Jane's attention to him. "'Tis always a delight to see ye again." His blue eyes gleamed.

Jane brightened and nearly smiled, then quickly composed herself. She turned to her father. "Isn't this a strange place to entertain guests, Papa?"

"I . . . uh . . ."

Yancy stepped toward her and gave the door a shove with his hand. "'Twas my own doing, Miss. As a friend of Dan's, and all, since he's such a patriot, I knew I could safely bring a deserter from the *Gaspee* here, and ye'd be willing to hide him fer a spell."

Jane's mouth gaped. "We most certainly would not!" She folded her arms with a huff.

"Now, young lady," Papa said, his serious expression unwavering. "As the God-fearing head of this household, I will not turn away from a man in need any more than the Good Samaritan did on the road to Jericho."

"I beg your pardon?" she said, her brows winging upward in haughty protest. "As I recall, Papa, that man had fallen among thieves."

"And there are many kinds of thieves," he returned, eyeing her steadily. "Some of them go so far as to steal young men away from their own families, as this lad was." He gestured toward MacKinnon. "I'm sure the Lord would consider him just as much a victim, taken as he was against his will and forced to serve aboard a ship."

"Nonetheless, he's bound to fulfill his term of service, Papa. The law says—"

He moved upon her so quickly she was forced to take a step back as he raised a finger to her face. "I will hear no more about the matter. Is that clear?"

Hesitating, Jane closed her lips and nodded.

"You will say nothing about any of this—to anyone," he said in a tone that allowed no dispute. "When the time is right, I'll inform your mother myself about our new guest. And that might be well after the welcome-home celebration for Dan and Susannah. Particularly after your guests leave." He continued studying her for a moment, then turned to Emily. "As soon as you can, my dear, I want you to take young Robert up to Ben's room and settle him in. From the look of the lad, I'm sure he could use a good rest."

"Yes, Papa." With a smile she started for the door.

"Wait," he said. "Why did you come in here?"

"Mama wanted some fresh butter and cream."

Nodding, her father bent and picked up the discarded pitcher. "I'll take them to her myself. I'll tell her I've sent you on an errand and keep her occupied while you spirit our guest upstairs." He smiled at Robert, then Yancy. "And I'll inform her we'll need another place for dinner."

Yancy followed as the three filed out of the springhouse. But at the doorway he stepped aside, gesturing for Jane to precede him.

With her lips in a tight line, she swung around to face him, stepping right into his path, her hands planted on her hips. Bright color blazed high on her cheeks, and sparks flashed from her eyes. "Whatever possessed you to bring that criminal here?"

Yancy had problems keeping a straight face. He knew Jane's feathers had been ruffled by her father and that she had been embarrassed at having been put in her place before not only a guest, but a stranger as well. But he couldn't help wondering if she knew how beguiling she looked during this little display of temper. He affected a look of innocence. "I saw Dan last night, and—"

"Oh yes. How thoughtless of me," she snapped. "You're that sailor friend of his. I should have remembered." Shaking her head, she made a helpless gesture. "This is just too much.

Papa can't possibly expect me to entertain two British army officers at the same table with a . . . a . . . smuggler!"

Yancy shrank back, raising his hands in mock horror. He hoped the feigned action would mask his uneasiness at the knowledge that there would be two lobsterbacks present during his own visit.

"Oh, *I* knew who was sending us all that tea during the boycott," she said disparagingly. "Don't think I didn't."

"Aye. But that didn't stop ye from drinking it, I'll wager." At his challenge a look of confusion crossed her face, and he smiled to himself. He had her now.

With a sniff, she started to retreat, but caught the heel of her slipper on an empty gunnysack. She fell headlong, sprawling unceremoniously in a flurry of yellow skirts.

On reflex, Yancy bent and plucked her from the floor. "Unharmed, are ye?" he asked with the most devilish grin he could muster.

Jane's face reddened, and for an instant she looked mortified as she stiffly brushed the dust from her skirt. But just as quickly the color faded, and she slowly looked up at him.

Ah, he thought. *Many a lass has wilted under the deadly charm of this particular grin.* And for that very reason he used it sparingly.

Suddenly Jane's expression hardened, and she tried to jerk away.

Yancy tightened his grip, drawing the pert lass close. "What's this? Not so much as a 'thank ye' from the lady?" he asked softly.

"Not when the *gentleman* refuses to unhand her."

So that's how it is. She considers me some sort of nuisance—and beneath her. He jutted out his chin and peered down his nose at her. "Ye prefer being held by some arrogant dog of a British soldier, is that it?"

She glared at him. "Well, at the very least, Lieutenant Harrington is a true gentleman."

"Ye don't say," Yancy returned as he pulled her, struggling, into his arms. "He'd never do this, then, would he?" Grasping the back of her head, he gave her a sound kiss, then released her abruptly.

She fought to regain her balance. *"How—dare—you!"* she gasped, delivering an ear-ringing slap. She whirled around to leave.

Ignoring the sting, he blocked the doorway with his arm. "Well, if ye don't want your arrogant dog of a gentleman to know just what *good friends* you and me are—" He gave a bold wink. "—I suggest ye keep your pretty trap shut about the unlucky lad upstairs."

Jane's mouth dropped open. Then she clamped it shut and shoved past him, storming out of the springhouse.

He watched as she stalked all the way to the house.

Chuckling, Yancy massaged his jaw and grinned. *Ah, but it would be fine sport to tame that one!*

Closing the door of Benjamin's room silently behind them, Emily turned and smiled at Robert with a self-conscious shrug. "I hope you'll be comfortable. We keep the bed made up in case Ben happens by. He's a postrider, but for some reason he doesn't have a regular route." She hated her tendency to babble when she was nervous, but she couldn't seem to stop herself. "He just pops in from time to time whenever he has the opportunity."

She felt Rob's gaze follow her as she moved to the commode, and from the corner of her eye, she saw him turning his cap around and around in his hands. "I thank ye, lass."

"Yes. Well, we do what we can." Emily poured some water into the enamel basin and placed a towel beside it. She felt the intensity of the young Scot's scrutiny as she crossed the room to the armoire and selected some fresh items of clothing. Trying not to let his stare unnerve her, she smiled again. "These should just about fit you. You're about the same size as my brother."

"Thank ye," he repeated.

"I . . . should be getting downstairs. If there's anything else you need, just let me know. I'll bring you some food when I can." At his nod, Emily reached for the latch.

"Lass?"

She stopped and looked back at him. "Yes?"

"I dinna' hear your name."

"Oh. I'm Emily."

"Emily. Has a bonny ring to it." A smile curved his mouth. "Ye bring me homeland to mind when I see ye movin' aboot, quiet as a highland breeze."

Emily blinked in surprise and felt the warmth of a blush. No one had ever spoken to her that way. She made an unsuccessful attempt to keep her heart from fluttering.

"Thank ye for givin' me a place to hide," he continued, "an' for goin' against the British dogs to do it, yet."

"I was under the impression that Scotland was a part of England."

He shook his head with a grimace. "Aye, so the Brits would ha' ye believin'."

Tilting her head slightly, Emily considered their young guest. "Well, you couldn't possibly have as much to complain about as we do here in the Colonies."

"Is that a fact?"

She nodded. "When your people have a grievance, you have representatives in Parliament who'll speak for you. Here we're at the mercy of all their greedy whims—as you must know, since you just left that despicable *Gaspee.* My papa calls it a devil ship."

"Aye. An' under the command of the devil himself, that Dudingston. A pirate, he is, wi' a license given to him by almighty Georgie Porgie."

Emily giggled at the irreverent reference to the king, then smothered the laugh with her hand. "Well, I'm afraid we'll be having two of the king's own for dinner today at noon . . . army lieutenants who happen to be friends of my sister. They should arrive soon. Please try not to move around too much up here. Perhaps you could sleep till they've come and gone. When it's safe, I'll let you know."

"Ye're a brave an' bonny lass, wee Emily. An' I thank ye from the bottom of me heart for your kindness."

At the young man's almost comical sincerity, standing there with his hand over his heart, Emily found herself speechless. "I . . . could do no less," she finally managed.

A gentle smile lit his sky blue eyes. "I ken."

"Well, I have to go now," she murmured. Leaving the room, she closed the door and leaned back against it to gather her scattered thoughts. Robert MacKinnon was so different from anyone she'd ever met before. He spoke to her as though he really knew her . . . actually cared what she thought, and considered her comments valid. Smiling to herself, she took a slow breath. Then, buoyed by an odd mixture of excitement, joy, and peace, she headed for the stair landing.

Susannah's fingers tightened on Dan's as the cart entered the lane to the Haynes farm. Her eyes made a wide sweep of the picturesque setting of fenced pastures that stretched forth until they met gently rolling hills. "Why, it's really quite lovely here, isn't it?" She hoped he didn't notice the ridiculous tremor in her voice. Her attention came to rest upon the spacious two-story house facing them across the way. Pristine white with forest green shutters, the structure was bracketed by large stone chimneys on either side and had a deep porch spanning most of the front.

Dan released her hand and put an arm around her shoulders, hugging her close. "Don't be afraid, my darling. There's nothing for you to be nervous about."

"I only hope you're right," she said with a sigh, still not convinced.

With a sudden tug on the reins, he drew to a stop in the middle of the lane. "Hey, love, I'm not bringing you here as some sort of punishment," he said on a teasing note. "I want my family to get to know you . . . and care for you the way I do."

Susannah smiled at the love shining from the depths of his sable eyes. "I know. I'm being terribly silly."

"Anyway," he continued, "Mother's been after me for years to produce a grandson and heir. Once she hears you're carrying my child, she'll welcome you with open arms. You'll see." Clucking his tongue, he urged the horse on.

Susannah tried without success to shut out the memory of the only time she had ever even seen Dan's mother, two Christmases ago. She shuddered, remembering the disastrous night it had turned out to be. To have had her own indenturement announced at a Christmas ball for all to hear, humiliating her escort and bringing disgrace upon his very prominent Philadelphia family, still caused spasms of anxiety. Her mortification had been so complete she had run from the ball in tears, and then left the manse the following morning before anyone else had even awakened. She could just imagine how aghast Mrs. Haynes had been to learn that Dan indeed planned to wed the object of that dismal incident.

Susannah's reverie came to an end as the cart rumbled up to the edge of the yard, the last few jolts only adding to her uneasiness. Dan stopped at a white lattice arbor covered with two varieties of roses in full bloom. Strawberry pink and dark rose, the two colors met at the top and intertwined, emitting a fragrance that brought back a brief childhood memory. Her own mother had grown splendid roses back in England, before asthma had drained her of the strength to care for them. Susannah inhaled a shaky breath and looked toward the house. Already, boisterous family members were pouring out the front door and hurrying toward them.

Dan jumped down and held his hands out for her, and when she stood and leaned into them, he swung her gently to the ground. "What God hath joined together. Remember, love?" he whispered, giving her waist a squeeze.

Susannah nervously smoothed her pink muslin dress, then stopped suddenly and looked up as a slight blonde-haired girl flew down the steps of the house in a flash of lavender dimity.

"Dan! You're here!" Without slowing, she threw herself into his embrace. "We've missed you so."

"Hello, Sis," he said with a grin. "It's good to be back."

When Dan raised his head, an older woman Susannah recognized as his mother reached him next. Clad in an olive silk gown with ecru lace trim, she still carried herself with queenly grace, but she looked somewhat more frail than she had two winters before. "Daniel," she breathed, closing her eyes as he drew her close in a hug. "Welcome home."

"Mother."

Susannah watched as Dan's father greeted him. The older man had the same carriage as his son, the same amiable, caring face, but with a smattering of fine lines about his kindly brown eyes. His thick graying hair must have once been the same rich chestnut shade as Dan's.

After Mr. Haynes came the copper-haired beauty Susannah knew to be Jane, then the sailor, Yancy Curtis. Last of all, waiting off to one side, stood an old Negro couple. Susannah watched the open display of affection and warmth with pleasure. *No wonder Dan himself is so loving, with a heritage such as this,* she thought.

The happy chatter died away as all eyes turned her way. Dan stepped to her side and wrapped an arm around her. "This, everyone, is my wife, Susannah," he announced with pride. "Sweetheart, I'd like you to meet my family." He gestured with one arm. "This beautiful woman is my mother."

"I'm most honored to meet you at last, Mistress Haynes," Susannah said with a small curtsy.

"Susannah." The woman's voice seemed pleasant enough, yet there remained a measure of reserve in her eyes and manner as she reached out a cool hand and gave Susannah's a perfunctory squeeze.

Susannah felt a chill wriggle up her spine, but fought to subdue it.

"This is my father," Dan continued, indicating the well-dressed man beside his mother. "He's been especially anxious to meet you."

She warmed at once to the genuine welcome in the man's smiling brown eyes. Up close she noticed the strong resemblance to Dan even more. "Pleased to meet you, Mr. Haynes."

"I believe you mean Papa," he said gently. Skipping the polite handshake, he pulled her into a hearty hug instead. "Welcome to the family, my dear. We're so happy you've come."

"Thank you," she whispered, still caught in his strong embrace. She felt sudden tears threaten and blinked them quickly away.

"Hey, that's enough, you two," Dan piped in with a laugh as they drew apart. "Over here are my sisters, Jane and Emily."

"Yes, I remember." Susannah held out a hand to the russet-haired girl who stood eyeing her with equal interest. "It's so nice to see you again, Jane. And Emily. Dan talks about you both quite often."

The older sister merely smiled with polite aloofness as she gave the barest hint of a curtsy, but Emily stepped forward and gave Susannah an exuberant hug. "I'm going to love having you for a sister. I have to hear what miracle you performed to make Dan give up that exciting life he had as a postrider."

Susannah laughed along with everyone else. "I'll be happy to tell you the whole story."

"Well," Dan broke in, "at least greet a few other special people first." He led her toward the beaming Negro couple a few feet beyond the others. "This is Tillie and Elijah Moore, who have been part of our household forever. You'll be eating some of Tillie's superb breads, I'm sure."

Susannah smiled. "I'm so delighted to meet you. I've heard so many stories about the two of you."

"Well, any wife of Dan'l's is part of this farm already, that's for sure," Elijah said with a grin.

His wife nodded. "We been lookin' forward to havin' you come."

Dan swept a glance around the group. "Well, that's just about everybody you *didn't* know. That leaves only Yancy, who you saw for a few minutes in town last evening."

The sunburned redhead grinned disarmingly from the other side of the arbor as they approached. He took Susannah's hand in his big calloused one. "Miz Haynes. From the first day Dan's eyes lit on you, I had a feeling he'd not be letting ye slip off the line for long. You're looking well."

"Thank you, Mr. Curtis," Susannah said. "I could say the same about you."

Dan clapped him on the back. "I'm surprised to see you here so early, Yance."

"Aye. Well, I was beginning to feel a wee bit closed in. Thought a ride in the country might fill my sails again."

"I see. Well, do you suppose I could impose on you to help me unload the cart?" Dan asked. "It has to go back to Providence later today."

"Sure enough. I must owe ye a turn by now for all the cargoes you've helped me with," he said with a mischievous twinkle in his eyes. "And I'll be glad to return the rig for ye when I leave. Lead the way." He lowered his voice conspiratorially. "I've an interesting mate to tell ye about."

"Susannah, love, why don't you go inside with Mother and the girls," Dan suggested, gesturing with his head. "I'm sure they'll be happy to show you around. Won't you, Mother?"

"Of course," the older woman answered.

Emily grabbed Susannah's hand. "You and Dan will have his old room while you're here. I fixed it up special once we heard you'd be coming. Wait'll you see."

"I'm sure it must be lovely," Susannah said, trying to keep up with Emily's enthusiastic tugging. She could feel Sophia Haynes's eyes boring holes into her back as Jane and her mother followed. But a scented summer breeze blew a comforting warmth across her face.

Within a short time, Susannah had taken the grand tour of the main floor of the house. The quality of the gleaming mahogany furniture and lush brocades did not come as a surprise, nor did the lovely crystal lamps and accessories. She glanced admiringly at the rich lace sheers in the parlor, then beyond them, to where Dan still talked with Yancy out near the wagon. *Would they never come inside?*

"How big will your house be in Boston, do you know?" Jane asked from beside her.

Susannah turned. "I'm afraid I've not been informed. But

I'm sure it'll be quite adequate . . . for the time being, at least."

Mrs. Haynes raised her perfectly arched brows.

"Maybe the home was built for a big family like ours," Emily said. "We have four bedrooms upstairs."

"And sometimes it still seems crowded," Jane piped up. "Like when we have guests. With you and Dan returning, and perhaps Ben, I'm back to sharing a room with the pest." She glared at Emily.

The younger girl tossed her head. "But *I* have to make the bed."

"Where *is* Benjamin?" Susannah asked. "It's been so pleasant seeing him the few times he has been able to stop at the inn and stay overnight. I've already grown to think of him as my younger brother."

"We do expect him, of course," Mrs. Haynes answered. "But with that *odd schedule* of his, we never know exactly when he might arrive."

"But your *own* brother should be here at any moment," Jane announced triumphantly.

Susannah felt the color drain from her face. "I beg your pardon?"

"Yes," Jane added with undisguised delight. "Ted and his friend Alex will be here for dinner."

A wave of dizziness swept over Susannah, and she put a hand on the lamp table to steady herself.

"You look pale, my dear," came Mrs. Haynes's voice, sounding fuzzy and far away. "Perhaps you should sit down."

She nodded. "Thank you."

Emily came quickly to her side, and with her help, Susannah moved to the nearest upholstered chair and sank to the seat.

"I'll fetch you some water," the younger girl said quietly.

Remembering the dreadful scene her brother had caused at the infamous Christmas ball, Susannah cringed. With regard for neither place nor time, Ted had disowned her for disgracing the family name by indenturing herself. He had stormed out of her life—for good, he had told her. How could he be coming here today, of all days? Noticing that Jane and Mrs. Haynes had also taken seats and now watched her closely, Susannah forced the semblance of a smile. "Please, forgive me for being such a bother. It's just such a surprise to hear that my brother is coming here. We've not been . . . close, of late."

"Oh yes, I know," Jane gushed. "But Ted and I have become such fast friends, and he's even managed to secure a transfer to the Fourteenth Regiment in Boston because of me. And I thought it high time he forgave your unfortunate choices of the past. Don't you agree?"

Staring at the presumptuous girl whose proud bearing bore the imprint of her mother's manner, Susannah's blood began surging once more, this time at full force. "Yes," she said evenly. "I suppose he should. And I suppose I shall also have to forgive his. It *would* be the Christian thing to do, would it not?"

Across from her, Mrs. Haynes's chin lifted a notch.

"Of course," Jane replied, a confused look on her face. "But I don't see what grievance you could possibly have against someone as wonderful as Ted."

"My *grievance* is quite a simple one, actually. And perhaps more for my dearly departed father's sake than my own. It was Father's dearest wish that Theodore would follow in his footsteps . . . get his credentials at Oxford and become a minister. It was his lifelong dream." She paused. "When I learned Ted had cast his schooling aside and, in its stead, used his inheritance to gain a commission in the army, it came as a great disappointment to me. But what's done is done."

Mrs. Haynes tapped a finger idly on the arm of her chair. "I understand how you feel. Sons have a way of doing as they please."

Susannah easily caught the double meaning behind the woman's seemingly supportive comment. She would have gladly risen and walked the four miles back to Providence, if not for Dan.

Emily returned just then with a glass of water.

Accepting it with a grateful smile, Susannah took several swallows, then nodded toward Dan's mother. "If you don't mind, I'd like to go to my room and rest."

Reaching the door to the bedroom that once had been Dan's, Emily swung it open and stepped aside while Susannah entered. "I hope you'll be comfortable. It's always been the quietest room in the house." She wondered suddenly if she had done well enough in readying it for Dan and his new wife. Regardless of Susannah's short period of indenturement in Princeton, the young woman possessed an obvious elegance. Emily had liked her since the first time she had seen Susannah at that Christmas ball in Philadelphia.

"Why, yes. It's most charming. Thank you, Emily. I shall appreciate a chance to rest after our tiresome week of journeying." Susannah set the half-empty water glass down and moved to the window. She parted the curtain panels. "What a lovely view. Dan promised to show me around the grounds and paddocks during our stay."

Emily crossed to her side and looked past her to the vast sprawling scene outside. The farm had always been her home, and she had taken its spaciousness and beauty for granted. But now, seeing it through Susannah's eyes, she looked at it as though for the first time. Recent rains had deepened the variegated shades of green in the trees and rolling hills, and a slight summer breeze stirred the branches and leaves, sharpening their contrast against strands of whitewashed fences. In numerous rectangular pastures, clusters of reddish brown

Narragansetts frolicked about. "See that horse in the corral nearest us?" she asked.

Susannah nodded.

"It's Star, my favorite gelding."

"How splendid. I never had a horse of my own," Susannah confessed. "But I had a very good friend whose family owned quite a stable. We had some delightful times. I shall pay close attention when I see Star close up."

Putting an arm around Susannah, Emily hugged her. "I'm really glad to have you for a sister." Then, noting fine lines of weariness around the gray-blue eyes as she met Susannah's grateful smile, she stepped away. "Well, I'd best leave you alone. We'll talk more later. Is there anything I can get you before you lie down?"

"No, thank you. You've been most kind."

Emily gave a nod and left.

Susannah loosened the top buttons of her muslin dress and poured fresh water into the basin from a china pitcher on the commode. She washed her face, then sank heavily onto the feather tick. If only Dan's whole family were as accepting and sweet as his father and Emily. But his mother and Jane apparently still held her *unpardonable sin* against her and would never forget the disgrace of her indenturement. Indeed, Jane had been almost gleeful in the announcement of Ted's arranged invitation for dinner today. After all these months, her brother had paid not the slightest heed to her existence. Susannah wondered how it would be when she came face-to-face with him.

With a sigh, she pushed aside the unpleasant memory of their last parting and instead looked over Dan's room. Sturdy mahogany furniture, which had no doubt endured a young boy's roughness, now stood polished and mute. The walls were painted a bland tan with dark green woodwork. The homey colors complemented the intricate counterpane done in matching shades. Lying back on the pillow, she closed her eyes and imagined Daniel there in various stages of his life.

Just knowing that her husband had grown up in this very house, this very room, gave Susannah a measure of comfort.

❦ ❦

Emily moved soundlessly away from the landing. Once she had made certain no one below seemed concerned over her absence, she approached Ben's room. After a gentle knock, she opened the door.

Rob MacKinnon sprang up from his relaxed position on the bed and swung his legs to the floor as she came in, alarm wrinkling his forehead. "Is there trouble, lass?"

She smiled and shook her head. "I was just checking to make sure you were all right."

"Oh." Emitting an audible breath, Rob ran his fingers through his thick black hair. "I canna' help bein' on edge."

She noticed he had changed into one of Ben's clean shirts, while his own lay neatly folded atop his other belongings on a chair. "I just brought my sister-in-law up to the room across the hall and settled her in, so if you hear anyone moving about you needn't be frightened."

"I thank ye." A disarming grin spread across his sea-tanned face, causing a twinkle in his eyes.

Emily felt his observant glance linger, and for the first time in her life, she enjoyed the experience. Determined not to act coy and shallow like Jane, she smiled back. But suddenly her hands began to tremble. She curled her cool fingers inward and struggled to remain composed.

The sound of approaching horses carried from outside.

Emily went to the window, then turned to Rob. "Our company has arrived—the two British officers I told you about. You must be particularly quiet while they're here."

"Aye. I'll na' be forgettin', sweet Emily—"

To Emily's dismay, she blushed at his boldness. Quickly she returned her attention to the arriving party.

"Nor shall I be the cause," he went on, "of bringin' an ill wind upon your kind family."

Conscious of her heightened color, Emily watched her

father, Dan, and Yancy emerge from the barn and walk toward the dismounting soldiers. Then she saw Jane rush out of the house, skirts and hair flying. She had better go back downstairs before she was missed.

Emily walked over to the door, then paused as she touched the latch and looked back at Rob. "Perhaps it would benefit all of us if you were to spend the afternoon in silent prayer for us."

A curious expression flashed over his face, then left as swiftly.

She wondered if it had been her imagination. "You do know how to pray, I presume."

"Aye," he answered, regarding her steadily, "though I canna' say that it's done me much good of late."

Considering the young man's predicament and the circumstances that had precipitated them, Emily could not help but agree. "It does seem that way at times, doesn't it?" she murmured wistfully. Then, going quickly out into the hall, she shut the door without a sound.

❦ ❦

Yancy felt threads of jealousy tangle around his insides like a mass of seaweed as Jane all but hurled herself at the lobsterback lieutenant tying his horse at the hitching ring near the gate.

"Well, I'll be," Dan remarked. "Looks like Susannah's brother, Ted, and that friend of his—Alex something or other. What could they be doing here?"

"Fontaine," his father supplied. "We've been expecting them for dinner. The two of them have been transferred to Boston."

Yancy watched a flicker of something akin to resentment register on Dan's face as his friend quickly looked his way.

"Yes," Mr. Haynes continued, "Jane convinced him to stop for a visit on the way to their new post. She is adamant about arranging a reconciliation between Ted and Susannah. Jane is far more eager than Ted is about the whole matter. Nevertheless, he is here."

"Hm," Dan muttered. "I for one would be more than happy if that were only possible. Ted was absolutely furious when he stomped out of Susannah's life. He never once considered the possibility that she might need him then as never before, or that the whole reason for her contract was one of survival when she was all alone in a strange land."

Listening only absently to the conversation as they drew nearer, Yancy kept his eyes riveted on the arrogant redcoated figure already standing a bit too close to Jane.

"This is an answer to prayer," he heard Dan say. "Ted is the only family Susannah has left in the world, especially since she had to leave the Lyons couple back in Princeton."

As they reached the edge of the yard and went through the gate, Yancy saw Jane approaching, a uniformed officer on each arm.

She smiled sweetly and glanced up first at one, then the other. "Both of you remember my brother Dan, don't you?"

Yancy cringed inwardly at her syrupy tone but tried to maintain his normal cocky demeanor. Why should it bother him who the little vixen set her claws into?

"Yes," the shorter of the pair answered. "Dan, Mr. Haynes." Giving each of them a polite handshake, he glanced toward Yancy.

"Ted," they replied as Yancy offhandedly took the soldier's measure.

The taller officer, whom Yancy deduced must be Alex, offered a more dignified response. "Good day," he said to Mr. Haynes with a click of his polished heels, then nodded at Dan.

"Dan," Jane continued, resolutely ignoring Yancy, "Ted and Alex are on their way to their new post in Boston with the Fourteenth Regiment. Isn't that the most amazing thing? Why, with you and Susannah going there to live too—" She focused wide-eyed innocence at Ted. "Oh, I forgot to tell you that, didn't I? Dan and Susannah will be moving to Boston themselves to assist at the Presbyterian Church. Oh, it'll be ever so much fun. I'll come for long visits, and of course we shall all attend every military ball and only the best parties."

The very idea made Yancy seethe. Apparently, Jane didn't bother to notice her brother's lack of enthusiasm or his hesitance in responding. Dan would be as out of place hob-nobbing with British sympathizers as he would be himself. With mild disdain, Yancy regarded Dan's sister going through her little routine, her dark eyes sparking with mischief. She did look rather bewitching in taffeta ruffles the color of daffodils, and her floral perfume had an enchanting scent. Casually, he eased between Jane and Ted and looked at the officer. "Allow me to introduce meself. Yancy Curtis, a *close* friend of the family." Extending his hand, he smiled down at Jane in gloating satisfaction.

Color flooded her cheeks, and Jane yanked Ted away before he had a chance to reply. "You needn't concern yourself with a mere sailor," she said with a sniff as she led the redcoats toward the house.

Yancy almost laughed aloud. Let her carry on her performance, if it made her happy. . . . He, Dan, and Mr. Haynes made their way after the others. Then, uneasily, Yancy glanced toward the second-story windows, hoping Emily had tucked young Robert MacKinnon safely away.

❦ ❧

Seated with family members and guests in the parlor as they awaited final dinner preparations, Dan looked across the room at Ted Harrington, whose morose attention kept drifting toward the staircase to the upper floor where Susannah was still resting. He prayed fervently that her brother would not make her adjustment to the family any more difficult than it already was.

As he saw the lieutenant's gaze wander there one more time, the thought suddenly struck Dan that if Ted were to rush upstairs to confront his sister, he might in haste accidentally stumble upon the wrong room and discover the *Gaspee* fugitive. He cleared his throat. "So, Ted," he began. "Tell us more about Oxford."

"Oh, really, Dan," Jane sighed wearily from Ted's other side on the settee. She cast a scathing glance at Yancy. "Who wants to discuss a dreary old university? I'd far prefer hearing about London and all the fine parties."

Ted straightened. "Actually, Alex would be more suited for that sort of report than I." He gestured the invitation to his friend, seated in a wing-backed chair in the corner.

"Ah yes," Alex said, lounging back and stretching out his long legs. "The shops. The parties. 'Tis difficult to decide on which to elaborate first. But I shall start with the shops. After all, London merchants are renowned the world over for their vast selection of the most exotic and delectable goods available today."

Dan watched Jane's face soften with childlike delight. She would hang onto every captivating word concerning her two favorite subjects. He, on the other hand, had no problem whatsoever in completely dismissing the entire account from his consciousness—especially when Ted got up restlessly and strode toward the adjacent hall.

"I should like to go and greet my sister while my friend keeps you all entertained," he said to Dan. "I wonder if you would mind directing me to the proper chamber."

Dan noticed his father and Yancy exchange looks of apprehension, but he had little choice but to comply. "Not at all. I'll show you the way." Rising, he headed out of the room.

Ted turned to follow, but in the hall he collided with Emily, who was coming from the dining room. "I do beg your pardon," he said, stepping around her. "Most clumsy of me."

"My fault, I'm sure," she answered as Ted walked to the foot of the staircase. "Wait!" she blurted out, grabbing hold of his arm. "W-where are you going?"

"I wish to speak to my sister." He extracted his sleeve from her grasp and smoothed it with his other hand.

"No! You can't!"

"Emily," Dan said patiently, tapping her shoulder. "Of

course he can. I was just going to show him the way. Come on, Ted."

"But dinner is ready," Emily insisted. "You know how Mother hates for us to straggle in once everything has been set. *I'll* go get Susannah while you two bring the others to the dining room." Before either of them had a chance to argue, she darted past them both and ran up the steps, her orchid frock rustling as she went.

Catching Ted's eye, Dan shrugged incredulously after his younger sister and shook his head. "Sisters!" he said, rolling his eyes. But he couldn't help wondering if she thought him foolhardy enough to escort the redcoat right to the Scotsman by mistake. He led the way back to the parlor. "Emily says we've been summoned to the table," he announced.

Everyone rose, and Yancy immediately snagged Jane's arm.

"Kindly unhand me," she whispered through clenched teeth at his overly familiar manner. She tried to jerk away, but he held fast until she relented.

Dan had barely caught her faint words, but he was quite conscious of Ted's rigid posture at his elbow, the sharp set of his jaw as he regarded the sailor. The reason for the unusual tension that had been present since the arrival of the king's men now dawned upon him with unmistakable clarity.

The seaman strode confidently by with Jane stiff and mortified on his arm. His mouth tweaked into a grin at Dan.

"I'll be along in a moment," Ted announced as Jane passed, "after I speak with my sister."

"I'll save a place for you," Jane assured him as she was yanked along. "Right next to me."

Dan watched Ted with some reservation. He wasn't altogether certain he wanted to leave his wife entirely at her brother's mercy. At the moment the young man did not seem in the most amiable frame of mind. "I'll wait with you, Ted," he said, nodding to his father as the older man and Alex walked by.

Hearing faint footsteps at the top of the staircase, Dan turned toward the sound.

Looking rested and fresh as she secured a wayward wisp of hair, Susannah started down, one hand trailing along the banister. Catching sight of her brother, she stopped. She didn't appear to breathe as a look of apprehension came over her face, then dissolved into an expression of wonder.

Dan shot a furtive glance at Ted and saw the lieutenant's broad grin and open arms.

"Oh, my dear Teddy!" Susannah cried, almost running the rest of the way as her brother stepped forward and caught her in his embrace. "I can't tell you how marvelous it is to see you again."

"And you," he said. "I thought you'd never come down." Easing her away to arm's length for a second, he drew her close once more. "I've been a fool, Sue. I hope you'll forgive me for the thoughtless things I said, the way I acted. I let my duties to the Crown come between us, and it was wrong. So very wrong."

"All of that is in the past," she said with a watery smile. "We have a chance to start again. I'm just so happy to have you back—even if it did take the army to bring you to me!" She gave a teasing glance at his red uniform as she smoothed the fringe of a shoulder epaulet. "You do look rather wonderful."

"That's what I thought when I first saw you."

Amid their shared laughter, Emily glided down the steps and embraced them both. "I am so happy for you," she said, giving Susannah an extra hug.

Speechless, Dan watched the whole affair almost afraid to believe it. Even in his most far-fetched imaginings, he hadn't thought a reconciliation could transpire so smoothly or with such immediacy. Admiring his glowing wife as she smiled up at her brother, Dan remembered her telling him how close she and Ted had been before their parents had died. Now he believed it.

Feeling suddenly like an intruder, Dan switched his attention to Emily, who had done an amazing amount of growing up since he'd last seen her. Why, his youngest sister was even turning into a bit of a rebel.

"Well," Emily suddenly announced, "the other guests must surely be waiting for us. We'd better hurry."

❧ ❧

Susannah felt as though an oppressive weight had been lifted from her chest; at last she filled her lungs with a sweet breath of relief as the four of them entered the dining room where the others had already gathered.

The men rose politely, then resumed their seats as Dan pulled out a chair for Susannah next to his father's. When his wife was settled, he assisted Emily on his other side.

"We trust you had a pleasant rest, Susannah," Papa said with a kind smile.

"Yes, it was most pleasant, thank you." Giving him an answering smile, she turned her head to the other end of the table. "Mother Haynes," she said with a nod, then smiled at Yancy and Jane across from her, then on to Ted and Alex. "Oh, Lieutenant Fontaine. How good it is to see you again."

"Good day," he answered in a friendly relaxed tone, then transferred his attention to the hostess. "I must say, Mistress Haynes, as always, the hospitality of this home and its bountiful table are most delightful."

"Why, thank you," she gushed with a gracious smile. As she met Susannah's gaze, however, the warmth evaporated from it. "I see your color has returned. I presume you found the room satisfactory."

Dan covered Susannah's hand protectively as it rested on the lace tablecloth. "Thank you, Mother. We're both happy to be here. We have a joyous announcement to make concerning Susannah's delicate health, as you might have already guessed. We are anticipating the arrival of a wonderful gift sometime in December. Our firstborn."

"Yes, I suspected as much," his mother returned coolly. Her stiff smile vanished.

"We all think it's wonderful," Papa said, answering for everyone else as he lovingly squeezed Susannah's shoulder.

"It appears we have a great deal to be thankful for today. Shall we bow our heads?"

Susannah closed her eyes gratefully, ignoring the smarting tears that threatened to spoil her happy day. She also had much to be grateful for; surely God would enable her to bear the more difficult parts of whatever the remaining hours held in store.

"Almighty God," came Papa's voice, "we do so thank thee for thy wondrous goodness to us all. Thou hast brought all our travelers safely here and established them close enough to insure the opportunity for future visits. As we look with joy toward the birth of this dear new family member, we do pray thy blessing upon it. Grant thy mercy and protection to Susannah as she nurtures the new life within her. We are ever grateful for the abundant provisions of our table, and we ask a special blessing upon it, as well as continued safe journeys for everyone sojourning beneath the roof of our dwelling. Amen."

As they raised their heads, Susannah saw Papa give Emily a conspiratorial wink that seemed to contain an element of reassurance. She turned to see the younger girl trying to control a smile. What could be the explanation for this curious interplay?

"Shall we eat?" Papa said, lifting the platter of meat. He helped himself before passing it to Yancy.

Forking a slab of roast, Yancy plunked it onto Jane's plate, then took a second for himself.

Jane's eyes glittered, but she tossed her head and ignored him as she stared straight ahead with flushed cheeks.

Ted looked with suspicion toward Jane and the sailor, but Yancy appeared not to notice. He took his first bite of food and chewed jovially.

Feeling a nudge at her elbow, Susannah accepted the bowl of potatoes from Dan and spooned some onto her plate. But having intercepted several rather peculiar looks passing between her husband, his father, and the sailor, she could not escape the feeling that this occasion was more than just a simple gathering of family and friends. There was a strange undercurrent flowing among those present, one she did not entirely understand.

She looked at Dan, drawing little comfort from his reassuring smile. Could it be that he was being sent to Boston for a reason far beyond the mere saving of souls? And Ted was to be stationed there to put a stop to the city's rebellious activity. A nagging dread crept with cold fingers up her spine. With all her heart she wished that Dan would forgo his dedication to the patriots and concentrate fully on the ministry.

Yes, dear Lord, she pleaded silently, *please grant a special blessing and safe journey to us all.*

Emily watched a devious expression settle on her sister's face as Jane turned to Ted.

"I'm so pleased that you and Alex were still able to join us," the copper-haired girl said, "considering last evening's lawlessness." She tossed Yancy a smug look, then continued. "I was quite certain the two of you might have been enlisted to aid in tracking down the culprits responsible for the deed."

Emily stole a glance at her father, then began pushing food around her plate with her fork.

"I beg your pardon?" Ted's even brows drew together in curiosity. "I'm afraid I'm unaware of any sort of trouble."

"Oh, you haven't heard?" Jane asked in a candied tone, placing a hand lightly over her heart in feigned surprise. She looked around the table, obviously enjoying the stir she was causing.

Emily maintained her poise, but all the while she envisioned Jane's neck stretched over the chopping block like a chicken's.

"Daughter," Mama said, "don't leave us in suspense. We should all like to be informed of the situation."

"I'm surprised you haven't already heard," Jane said, a snide smile barely under control. "Some dreadful ruffians rowed out to the Royal Navy's *Gaspee* under cover of darkness and set it afire while it was mired helplessly on a sandbar." Heedless of the deadly glares emanating from various seats around the table, she continued, centering her gaze on Yancy. "Isn't that right, Seaman Curtis?"

"Merciful heavens," her mother replied. "Surely the Crown will not rest until the monsters responsible for such a despicable act have been brought to justice."

Alex's cool gray eyes drifted from one diner to another. "So that would explain all the whispers at breakfast this morning."

Ted put down his fork. "Exactly what details can you tell us of the incident?" he asked Jane. "What of the officers and the crew?"

She inclined her head toward the sailor next to her, her curls catching the glow from the candles that had been lit overhead. "Mr. Curtis, why don't you inform our honored guests what you told us? His account was so vivid, that one might even imagine he had actually been there. Isn't that—"

Papa slammed his glass down onto the lace-covered table. "Jane! I see we are running low on lemonade. I would like you to take the pitcher into the kitchen and refill it."

"But, Papa, couldn't you just ring for Tillie—"

"At once," he ordered.

Jane pursed her lips and snatched up the pitcher.

"Should ye need to go to the springhouse for it," Yancy offered in mocking challenge, "I'd be happy to assist ye."

Jane clenched her teeth and cast him a withering look. "I'd sooner ask help from a common scoundrel," she grated, then flounced from the room.

"Mercy!" Mama exclaimed. "What has gotten into her?"

Papa shook his head. "Well, now," he said in the ensuing silence. "On such a beautiful day, surely there must be other more pleasant topics for us to discuss."

No one broke the stillness. Everyone resumed eating, and the grandfather clock in one corner ticked loudly.

Emily cleared her throat and looked in desperation at her sister-in-law. "Have you and Dan settled on any suitable names for the baby, Susannah?"

"Not as yet," she returned with a gracious smile. "We have

a number of people whom we love dearly and admire. It's been most difficult trying to decide on a namesake."

"Oh," she answered breathlessly. "Our oldest sister, Caroline, confessed to having the same problem. Her husband's family is even larger than ours. They finally settled on names from the Bible, only all the good ones have been taken. So my very inventive sister decided to name them after places. Places, mind you, not people."

"Emily," her mother chided, "the little ones have perfectly fine names." She bit into a warm roll.

"I'm sorry, Mama, but it took me a while to get used to having nephews named Jericho, Philippi, and Kidron, and a niece called Bethany Blessing." She ended with a grin, and the others laughed as her mother glared sternly.

On her mother's other side, Alex's eyes twinkled with mirth. He quickly hid his chuckle behind his linen napkin.

Dan nudged Emily's leg with his. "The names may be a bit grown-up for the children just now, but they don't seem to mind being called Jerry, Flip, Kid, and Beth."

Jane swept grandly into the room carrying the full pitcher. With a flourish she set it pointedly before her father. A dollop of the pale liquid splashed from the lip. Resuming her seat once more, she took exaggerated care to insure that her skirt did not come in contact with Yancy on her left. She flashed a fawning smile at Ted on her right as she settled her gown about her.

"I do so miss my darlings," Mama said pensively, brushing a few crumbs from her bodice. She blotted the corners of her lips meticulously. "If only they weren't miles and miles to the north of us."

Jane looked across the table at Dan. "Will you and Susannah visit either Caroline or Nancy before you go to Boston? I'm sure they would love to see you. No doubt the children have grown at least a foot since the last time you were there."

He shifted in his chair. "I would like to, of course. But we'll be hauling all our household goods along with us, and a side jaunt would add needless miles to an already hard trip. Once we get settled, though, we'd enjoy scheduling a ride inland to visit them."

"Yes," Susannah added. "I'm so looking forward to meeting the whole family. Your older sisters do live near one another, do they not?"

Papa nodded in answer. "Caroline lives in Worcester, and Nan just a few miles beyond, on her husband's family's farm."

"Yes, Daniel," Mama added with a meaningful glare, her eyes reflecting the subdued green of her gown. "Nancy's husband has always been the dutiful, respectful young man. *He* chose to stay at home where *he* was needed."

"I say," Alex cut in. "What sort of planting do they—"

A loud crash sounded in the room above.

Emily's heart plunged to her stomach.

"Merciful heavens!" Mama said. "What on earth—"

Emily jumped up with an alarmed glance Yancy's way. What they didn't need just now was to have everyone's attention drawn to Ben's room. "I—um—opened the windows upstairs. It was becoming so stuffy. A curtain must have knocked over one of the lamps. Yes, I'm sure it's that. I'll go see." She took hasty flight.

"My," Jane said with unconcealed amusement, "today is certainly full of surprises. Wouldn't you agree, Seaman Curtis?"

Terrified that her sister would not be able to control her flapping mouth, Emily hesitated in the hallway. She ducked behind a philodendron and stared through the trailing leaves as she listened. *Please don't let Jane be malicious enough to give away the Scotsman's presence,* she prayed silently.

Yancy did not respond to Jane's thoughtless remark, much to Emily's relief.

But Papa did. "What do you mean, Jane?" he asked menacingly.

"Oh, didn't Yancy tell you?" came Jane's coy answer. "That is a surprise. It's just that he must leave directly after he has eaten. He's volunteered to assist the sheriff in the apprehension of the troublemakers who destroyed His Majesty's ship, the *Gaspee.*"

"Why, how very commendable of you, Yancy," Mama said.

"Yes, quite," Alex agreed. "Do let us know if there is some way in which we might be of service. A bit of sport would be most invigorating before we leave for Boston."

"Much as we would like that," Ted countered, "I'm afraid we shall have to forgo the pleasure. We're due in Boston the day after tomorrow. But no doubt we'll have ample opportunities to go *hunting* there."

Emily could just imagine the smirk on the lieutenant's face at the double meaning behind his words. Peeking around the plant, she saw Yancy stand.

The sailor shoved his chair back with his legs and bowed graciously toward the hostess. "If ye'll excuse me, I thank ye for this delicious meal, Mistress Haynes. 'Twas the best I've had in many a month. I appreciate the kind invitation to break bread with your delightful family. And Dan," he said, reaching a hand across the table and clasping his friend's, "I hope to see ye soon. Perhaps in Boston. In the meantime I'll return your hired rig to Providence. Good day to ye all."

"I'll see you out," Dan offered, "to help hitch up the horse." Rising, he laid a hand on Susannah's shoulder and left.

A chorus of good-byes followed them out, with Jane's the brightest of all.

At her eavesdropping post, Emily smiled sympathetically at Yancy as he passed by, and he winked.

Dan took hold of her arms and steered her toward the stairs. "I thought you were going to check on that pesky lamp," he whispered.

❦ ❦

Yancy hesitated on the sheriff's doorstep, wishing he had some other choice, but knowing he did not. Those two lobsterback friends of Jane's knew of the incident. The burning of the ship was bad enough, but if the authorities assumed the missing cabin boy had been murdered, they would track directly back to Dan Haynes and his family.

It was either the lad from the *Gaspee* or his friends. The reluctant breath he drew to steady himself did little to eradicate the feeling of being a cowardly turncoat. Lifting the latch, he stepped inside.

Both the sheriff and his deputy, Tom Coats, looked up from a stack of papers on the cluttered office desk.

"Well! Curtis," Deputy Coats exclaimed with a grin of recognition as he got up from one of the chairs. "Haven't set eyes on you since the last round of drunken brawls I had to break up. Giving the local gals a rest, for a change?" He bent with a snicker and nudged the stout sheriff. "This here's Seaman Yancy Curtis, pride of the eastern seaboard. Er, the taverns, anyways."

The sheriff gave a nod and studied Yancy over his spectacles. "What brings you by?"

Yancy swallowed, trying to clear his clogged throat. "I, er, that is . . ." He shifted his weight to one foot.

"Well, what is it?" the official prompted.

Yancy inhaled an uneven breath, then let all the air out in a rush. "I . . . was just over at the stables. The kid there says that an officer from the revenue cutter is accusing some of the local patriots of foul play. In regards to some cabin boy who's missing, I mean."

"Well, speak up, man," the sheriff bellowed. "Whatever it is you came in here for, out with it!"

Figuring that either one or both of the men before him had probably seen him in last night's parade anyway, Yancy decided it would be useless to deny participation in the event. But that didn't make what he was about to do feel any less treacherous. He had never given the Judas kiss to a comrade in his life.

Yancy looked from one to the other. "Aye, sir," he said flatly. "Well, it's like this. Last night, a lad did happen across me path. I thought it rather peculiar that he was dripping like a freshwashed sheet, but it seemed the decent thing to do to give the fellow some dry clothes." Even as he spoke, the words stung his conscience as if he were administering blows from a lash to Robert MacKinnon's bare back. "After that, he came with me to the Haynes place, where I'd been invited to dinner."

The sheriff's weasel eyes didn't waver from Yancy's face as he squinted across his desk. Finally he looked away with a disgusted shake of the head and slammed down the pipe he'd had clenched in his teeth. Tom Coats flinched. "Do you mean to tell me I've been badgered and harangued all morning by customs men and ship officers, all wanting to know the identity of the perpetrators of the fire and the death of the cabin boy, while you were blithely partaking of a leisurely meal out at the Haynes farm?"

Yancy only barely managed a nod.

The two men exchanged a knowing glance, then the sheriff rose and reached for the frock coat that hung on the chair back. "Well, Seaman Curtis, I think the matter would be best served if you'd take me out there now."

"Me? But I just came from there, me good man," Yancy hedged in desperation. "The Haynes family had no knowledge of the *Gaspee* burning, much less the lad. As it turned out, he didn't even stick around to eat with us."

"Yeah, well, we'll see about that, now, won't we?" Grabbing his pipe, the sheriff stepped from behind the desk.

❧ ❧

As he and his father escorted the two king's men around the property in the midafternoon mildness, Dan observed Ted's assessing glance over the prosperous farm. Many improvements had been made in the recent years as added income from the thriving business poured in. The grounds were immaculate, and the horses strong and vibrant as they pranced across the sectioned pastureland.

"Quite a nice endeavor you've got, sir," Ted remarked as they entered the stable.

"Yes, rather." Alex added. "Splendid. Splendid."

Dan's father tipped his head at the aristocrat with a good-natured smile. "I find it amazing that you, in particular, would find something admirable in these hardly grand settlements and colony properties."

Alex laughed. "I'll admit that the picture I carried in my mind of this country was one somewhat on the barbaric side. But since my arrival, I've grown to admire the natural beauty that is in evidence all around."

"My, that is quite a compliment from someone of your station," Father said. He studied the two young lieutenants for a moment, then looked back to Alex. "So you approve of my farm, then."

"Ah yes. It quite takes me back to Sussex County, in England, where my own father conducts a similar operation with thoroughbreds. Ted and I now ride two of our horses."

"Mm," Dan's father injected evenly. "I noticed their fine lines and muscle structure when Elijah and I unsaddled them earlier. Our Narragansett Pacers are not bred for fine looks or incredible speed, but rather for their smooth gait and riding comfort. With so few adequate roads in the Colonies, our good wives quite often must travel with their husbands on horseback instead of riding in a carriage, and for that reason, our breed has been quite well received. But another strain called the quarter horse has been developed for racing shorter distances, considering our lack of open lands. They're more heavily muscled than your fine beasts, of course, and measure a few less hands. But they're known to be quite swift and surefooted in our rough terrain."

"Hm," Alex said with a thoughtful nod. "I should like very much to see those animals run sometime."

"You'll have plenty of opportunities to do that, young man, I'm sure—once you're in Boston. Why, Dan will be only too glad to take you both to a few races, won't you, Son?"

Dan had a fleeting thought of Sam Adams and the Sons of Liberty and imagined their faces were he to escort two lobsterbacks to some public gathering. He wished his father hadn't cornered him with such a preposterous invitation. "Sure, I'd be glad to."

As Ted and Alex drifted down to the farthest stalls, Dan turned to his father. "I realize that having both Ben and me gone has placed an extra burden on you, Father. I've informed Reverend Moorhead, in Boston, that I'll require time away to assist you now and then. We haven't settled on how often yet, of course, nor when I'd start. In fact, I wouldn't even mention it to Mother until I know the particulars. I just wanted to mention it in case I forgot to tell you before we leave. I'll send word by post when I'm sure about things."

"That's wonderful, Son," his father answered, grasping Dan's arm. "The news will cheer your mother as much as it does me. She worries so about all of you—grown or not—since so many of you live elsewhere."

Dan smiled into his father's eyes. "God willing, Susannah and I will return here to live one day soon. I always miss you and the place, but never so much as when I return for a visit and see it all spread out before me."

Ted strolled toward them again, a faraway look on his face. "You certainly should count your blessings. You have all of this, plus parents to come home to."

"You're right," Dan said, placing a hand on Ted's shoulder. "I can only imagine the sorrow you and Susannah must feel."

Ted smiled sadly. "Would that I had appreciated my parents while they were still with us. They were kind and loving folk, well liked by everyone in our village."

Dan tilted his head. "They must have been, for I hear it in Susannah's voice whenever she can bring herself to speak of them."

Extending his hand, Ted clasped Dan's with a grin. "I want you to know how pleased I am that Sue is now within the secure fold of this family of yours. I shan't have to concern myself with her welfare henceforth."

❧ ❧

"Thanks, gals," Tillie said, a grin widening her dark face. "These old bones of mine get slower and slower all the time. It's grand to have help with the cleanin' up."

"It's the least we can do," Emily said, bending to bestow a hug to Tillie's plump rounded shoulders. "Mama says we need to practice taking care of things for when we're married and out on our own."

"At least at first," Jane said airly, hanging a damp dishtowel over the rod on the end of the sideboard. "Of course, *I* intend eventually to have servants." Patting her curls into place and straightening her frock, she brightened. "I think I'll go outside and check on Ted and Alex."

Watching her sister take her leave, Emily glanced nervously toward the door leading to the hallway and the stairs, where moments ago her mother and Susannah had gone up for afternoon naps. Mama had been so distant with Susannah that Emily couldn't help but feel sorry for her new sister. But in all likelihood, any young woman who had the misfortune of marrying a mother's favorite son could face similar difficulties. Especially when other dearly loved sons had died in infancy, as two of Emily's four brothers had. Hearing the two bedroom doors close, she breathed a little easier.

When Tillie left for the separate quarters she and Elijah shared, Emily took a clean plate from the cupboard and heaped it generously with leftover food from the noontime meal, then filled a glass with lemonade and carried them up to Rob.

She entered the room quietly and looked around. It appeared to be empty.

Stepping into view from the far side of the wardrobe, the Scot caught sight of the bountiful feast in her hands and grinned. "Looks like I'll na' be goin' hungry."

"I'm sorry I couldn't come sooner."

He shrugged off her apology and took a seat on the bed as she handed him the plate. He dug in without ceremony, wolfing it down as though he hadn't had a meal in days.

While he ate, Emily moved to the window to check on the whereabouts of the menfolk. She saw Alex in the distance, his booted foot propped on a pasture rail, absently patting a horse while he talked. Dan and her father appeared quite entertained by some animated dialogue he was delivering.

Off by themselves, near the rose-covered arbor, Jane and Ted were locked in a tight embrace, sharing a kiss. Emily felt warmth rise to her cheeks and stepped back a few inches. But curiosity overcame her; she took her original post and watched them kiss again. And again. *They must be in love,* she decided, wondering what that must be like.

Jane always seemed so dreamy and gushy after being with Ted, but that didn't seem to stop her from batting her big brown eyes at other available bachelors when the handsome lieutenant was not around. There must be more to love than that. Nan and Caroline—and even Susannah—had eyes only for their husbands. They didn't even appear to notice other men at all, not even one as gallant as Alex Fontaine. Emily flicked another glance at the British officer. With Robert MacKinnon hiding on the floor above the dining room, she had been so nervous that she had barely noticed the charming soldier who flirted casually with her at every opportunity. And she hadn't even missed his attention.

At least Robert wasn't a lobsterback. And he didn't seem the sort who would dally with any fetching young lady within his reach. He seemed different. What would it be like to be with someone like him . . . to kiss him? Her face heated at the thought. She took a step backward—and *bumped into him.* Too late she had felt his presence beside her. Had he also been watching the lovers?

"I-I'm sorry," she mumbled, skirting around him. Against her will, her eyes met his.

Emily felt as if she were drowning in the depths of Robert MacKinnon's gaze. She knew with certainty that he, too, had seen Jane and Ted out on the lawn. She looked away, wondering how to make a graceful exit.

Then the sound of rapidly nearing hoofbeats carried through the window.

Both Emily and Rob jerked back to the window.

"It's Yancy," she said with some relief. But she looked closer through the lace panel and stiffened. "Yancy . . . and the sheriff!" An awful feeling of dread tightened about her heart.

As Yancy rode onto Haynes's land, accompanied by the sheriff and Deputy Coats, he caught sight of Lieutenant Fontaine speaking to Dan and his father off to one side. Yancy's spirits sank. So much for convincing the sheriff to *accidentally* let Robert MacKinnon escape after his identity had been verified. The lobsterback would undoubtedly want to stick his nose into the matter. No telling what sort of pot he might stir up with the officials. At the very least, Rob would certainly have to be taken back and given a public flogging—if not worse.

As they drew near to where the three men stood talking, Yancy caught an uneasy glance from Dan and looked skyward with a helpless shrug. Mr. Haynes's apprehension was also apparent as the older man strode woodenly toward him and his companions.

At that moment Jane and Lieutenant Harrington also moved into view from beneath the rose arbor. Seeing her arm tucked securely in Ted's, Yancy felt himself nearing the boiling point. She had been trying desperately to betray Rob's presence and his own involvement in the whole thing. Now would be her best chance. He gritted his teeth.

"Yancy," Mr. Haynes said. "What a surprise to see you out here again so soon. Sheriff, Mr. Coats, step down. I'll have my daughter bring you out something cool to drink."

"Thank you kindly," the sheriff answered, "but I'm afraid we're here on official business."

❦ ❦

Rob felt the last hope vanish from his heart at the dismay so evident on Emily's face. "What'll we do?" she whispered.

Moving to see around her, Rob observed Yancy Curtis's bleak demeanor. Numbly, he searched for a place to hide, then cursed himself under his breath for being so stupid as to have trusted a stranger who had seemed friendly. He should never have been mindless enough to stay so near port when he could easily have been twenty miles away from this place by now.

Emily grabbed his hand. "Come, before they catch you."

Seizing his jacket from the chair, he followed her lead as she swiftly yanked him after her into an empty bedroom across the hall, then closed the door. Dashing to the window, she threw it open and sat on the sill, then swung her legs over it . . . and jumped.

Rob lunged forward in a useless attempt to save her, then almost smiled as he spotted her dangling from a sturdy limb and swinging hand over hand toward the trunk as though it were something she'd done a million times.

Her foot reached for a lower branch and touched down on it. Impatiently, she looked up and gestured wordlessly for him to follow.

Anticipating the hard ground fifteen feet below, not to mention the spindly branch not so easily within reach, Rob hesitated, but only for a second. If this little wisp of a lass in cumbersome gathered skirts could manage such a feat, pride would hardly permit him to do less. Breathing an unexpected prayer—which surprised even him—he leaped for the limb.

It groaned and bent precariously with the force of his weight as he latched onto it, and for a second he expected it to snap. But it held fast, swaying upward again. Cautiously, he made his way downward after Emily. When she dropped lightly to the ground, he followed.

Emily hunched low and took his hand. She led him swiftly toward the cover of the rows of staked peas in the kitchen garden.

❦ ❦

Jane called herself every foolish name she could think of. She should have informed Ted about the Scottish fugitive earlier when she had the chance; then her loyalty to the Crown would never be in question. But if she were to say anything now, he would think she had been part of the deception all along. Not that she especially wanted any actual trouble to befall that uncouth sailor, Yancy Curtis. She would never admit to a soul that she actually enjoyed the way she felt whenever he was around, especially since he always managed somehow to bring out the very worst in her. But wouldn't it be gratifying to see him squirm a little and have that sickening smirk of his wiped off his face?

After the others filed by them into the house, Ted rushed Jane along behind. "Undoubtedly, this is all some tasteless jest on your friend's part," he said. "Another attempt to ruin my visit, I'm sure."

Not wanting to have to answer the comment, Jane purposely missed the top porch step and stumbled.

He caught her around the waist and helped her regain her footing. "Forgive me," he mumbled. "I shouldn't have been in such haste." Opening the door for her, he motioned her inside.

Papa and the others were already tromping up the dark wood staircase. The hollow sounds made by their boots echoed through the house, filling Jane with apprehension. What if Yancy were to find himself in serious trouble? Quite possibly it could reflect back onto her family as well. She and her parents rarely spoke of the danger involved in rebel activities such as this one or the special postriding job once held by Dan—and now Ben. But an odd tension always hung in the air, despite their reluctance to speak openly of it. She shook off the irrational thoughts and stepped onto the top landing.

Ted followed after Alex and entered Ben's room just as the sheriff came out.

The law enforcer turned a dark scowl in Yancy's direction. "I shoulda' known this would turn out to be some wild-goose chase."

"No, Sheriff," Papa said wearily, sidling close and speaking under his breath, "I assure you the young man was under our roof. And if there's guilt to be placed on anyone, I am just as much at fault as Seaman Curtis for harboring him."

The man squinted as he looked at Papa's face and listened in earnest.

"It's just that I found the circumstances under which the lad had been impressed into service most unfair," Papa continued. "He was awaiting passage to America when they snatched him off the wharf and forced him to serve aboard the *Gaspee*. I couldn't help but want to aid him in some way."

"Well, Mr. Haynes," the sheriff retorted. "Much as I sympathize with the lad in some respects—after all, none of us agree with such unfair practices—still, there's nothing to be done about it. The boy must be caught to finish his time or be tried for desertion. That's the law. I must verify that the boy is alive, or else all the British will be dragged into the mess."

Just then Mama's door swung open and she appeared, still struggling into her satin dressing gown. Her hair was askew as she rubbed sleep from her eyes. "What in heaven's name—" Her gaze flashed quickly about, taking in the sight of so many strange men, and a flush colored her cheeks as she readjusted her attire.

"There's no cause for alarm, my dear," Papa said comfortingly, moving to her side and putting an arm around her. "The sheriff merely wanted to question a young man who was resting here today."

Her finely arched brows rose high in alarm. "A young man?" She turned to the deputy. "Tom Coats? Have you been hiding up here this afternoon?"

The skinny man with the leathery face grinned sheepishly and spread his hands, palms up. "No, ma'am. Weren't me. I come with the sheriff is all."

"I daresay, gentlemen," Alex announced, coming into the hall, "while we are all standing about, the deserter is undoubtedly making good his escape." He shoved open the door to Dan and Susannah's room and strode in, everyone crowding after him.

Clutching a light blanket to her chin, Susannah sat up with a gasp.

Dan was beside her in an instant, stroking her hair. "Terribly sorry, sweetheart. We've got a bit of a problem at the moment. We are trying to find a deserter we suspect may be hiding somewhere in the house."

"How dreadful," she murmured. "Well, it's quite obvious I was alone in here until you all arrived." But nonetheless she bent forward and lifted a corner of the blanket to search under the bed.

Jane met Yancy's eyes, but she could not decipher whether his look was one of sympathy or another of his usual taunts. She crossed her arms and averted her gaze. A sentence in the town jail just might do him some good. The lowlife had probably ruined any hope of capturing the man of her dreams. She glanced briefly at Ted Harrington.

Not even noticing her, Ted and Alex brushed past in their haste to get to the hall again. They led the charge into Emily's room.

Reaching the window, Ted glanced out, then turned. "Well, at least we see how the escape transpired. In fact," he said, his voice rising with excitement, "I can see which way they're heading." With a furious glare at Jane and Susannah, he and Alex were out the door and bounding down the steps before the boom of his voice had faded from the room.

Jane moved hesitantly to the window. To her astonishment, she saw her sister and the deserter climbing over a pasture fence in the distance. Her heart sank. It was true. Her own sister aiding and abetting a fugitive from the law. All was lost.

So much for her own chances with the handsome lieutenant now. How could she ever explain *this* away? With a family assisting not only rebels but fugitives as well, he would never give her another glance.

Mama nudged Jane aside with a cry. "Our little Emily is being kidnapped! Why, the cur is forcing her onto one of the horses! Oh, this is terrible. Just terrible."

Over her mother's shoulder, Jane saw Emily astride a horse as Rob hopped up behind her. They rode out the far gate in the direction of the dense woods beyond.

"Don't fret, my dear." Papa steered Mother to the bed to sit down, but the worry didn't quite leave his voice. "The foolhardy girl is merely helping the lad to get away. I'm certain she's in no danger."

"Well, stop them!" Mama cried. "She can't run off with a common criminal. She'll be ruined."

Susannah stepped beyond the bed, where Mama lay moaning with a hand over her eyes, and went to the window beside Jane. In silence they watched the last flash of the younger girl's lavender frock vanish on horseback into the foliage.

Already outside, the sheriff and his deputy had mounted their animals and could be heard riding off as the others hastened to the stables.

❧ ❧

Emily tried to calm her breathing as she stole a quick glance back toward the farm. But at the sight of the sheriff already in pursuit—*with* Yancy Curtis, who, up until now, Emily had considered a family friend and even an admirable patriot—a chill ran through her. She lifted her chin purposefully and turned her attention ahead. "I know a spot not too far from here where we can hide," she said, sounding far more confident than she actually felt. She gave Star a sharp nudge to his flanks and dodged through the trees.

Behind Emily, Robert tightened his grip around her waist. "Ah, lass. 'Tis best ye dump me off an' let me take me chances."

"I couldn't. Not yet. I know these woods." *And I thought I knew our friends,* her mind railed as the smart whip of betrayal goaded her on. She knew the gully, concealed below ground level, would be an effective haven. And no one knew of its existence but her. Without another backward glance she pressed on, drawing comfort as they approached the secret place.

❦ ❦

In utter defeat, Jane slumped down onto the bed beside her mother. Even if she could manage somehow to convince Ted she had been opposed to harboring the lad from the beginning, that smuggling, kiss-stealing flirt, Yancy Curtis, would no doubt confess everything. Ted would suspect she had not only kept silent, but had a dalliance of some sort with the sailor. Not only would the lieutenant question her love and loyalty then, but her family's as well. This was the absolute worst day of her life. All her shining dreams of being rescued from the tiresome sameness of dull farm life by her knight in shining armor crumbled about her feet. There would be no hope ever again of marrying Lieutenant Ted Harrington, of being whisked away from Pawtucket to someplace more exciting and being accepted by the aristocrats.

The whole thing was Yancy's fault, she decided, gritting her teeth. Coming here with that contemptible overconfident air of his, that gleam in his roving eye, and all the while involving her and her family in coddling a deserter. He would pay for his despicable acts somehow. She'd see to that.

She curled a finger around a fold of her gathered skirt, and a scheming smile slowly curved her lips. Perhaps the sheriff would be interested to know that Seaman Yancy Curtis was one of the burners of the *Gaspee.*

Grasping Star's mane tightly in her hands, Emily guided him down toward the streambed, where she knew the banks and overhanging trees would provide the best cover.

"'Tis best for ye to be gettin' back now, lass," Robert said from behind her on the mount. "I canna' expect ye to bring even more trouble upon your wee shoulders. I can go on from here."

"Can you?" Emily asked evenly. "You must know this country pretty well then."

"Na' a'tall," he admitted. "But I ken the direction we are headin' is north, and I trust your judgment."

"Shh," she said over her shoulder. "I can't hear if there's anyone coming after us." Coaxing the pacer to a stop, she strained her ears to listen.

"Please, lass," Rob whispered. "Ye must get down and go home. I couldna' live with meself should any harm befall ye."

Emily turned an incredulous look his way. "And leave you out here with one of our prize horses, lost and not knowing where to go to find safety?"

"'Tis for the best."

"The best? To add horse stealing to your list of other offenses? And what if you accidentally rode him into a hole and he broke a leg? You'd be caught and taken back in shackles. Is that what you want, truly?"

"Nay. But—"

"Then let me help you. That way neither of those fates will be yours. I happen to know where there's a good hiding place, a gouged out spot in the stream bank that's big enough for us and the horse. This time of year with all the vines and brush growing wild they'll never find us. They could ride right past us and never suspect we're there."

Rob let out a breath. "Weel," he said, dragging out the word, "I'll accept your help *if* when the danger has passed ye'll go back home. I canna' abuse your good family's hospitality by absconding with their youngest child."

Raising her eyebrows slightly, Emily turned. "I'll have you know I am not a child. I—"

Unmistakable sounds of riders crashed through the undergrowth above and shattered the stillness of the woods.

Emily tensed, only barely aware of the way Robert MacKinnon's hands tightened around her waist as she held her breath.

"Spread out," echoed the sheriff's gruff voice. "Holler if you see 'em."

Bending low over the horse, Emily felt Robert follow suit as she veered the animal to the stream and down the steep bank, continuing on for several yards in the winding creek bed.

"Over here!" the officer called. "I've found some hoofprints."

"There's more over here."

Emily's stomach knotted at the sound of Yancy's voice. Some friend he was. How could he be assisting the officials? But the realization that he was quite far from them—and in a direction they hadn't even taken, no less—slowly made its way into her consciousness. Yancy was trying to divert the search *away* from them.

Spotting the great hemlock that marked the opening to the secret cave, she appreciated more than ever the way its bared roots provided a natural lattice for vines and wild shrubs. "Come on," she whispered, sliding off Star.

Rob followed, crouching as she had, close to the bank. Emily pushed aside some hairy branches of a rhododendron.

Its vase-shaped white flowers gave off a fragrant perfume that seemed out of place at such a tense moment. As the opening to the cave appeared before her, she turned to the Scotsman and smiled. A wave of relief replaced the furrows on the young man's face.

Emily led the gelding into the opening of the small cave, checking behind to make certain Rob came also. Once they were safely inside, she slipped out again. Taking an old fallen branch, she brushed the surrounding area of all traces of their trail, then returned to the shelter once more.

Emily wiped her hands on her skirt, heedless of the new stains they added to her once spotless frock. Her mother would be mortified at the sight of her. But her "darling daughter's" *appearance* would be the least of the reasons for Mama's anger about now.

For several moments they stood in silence, hearing only the sound of their own breathing slowing to a more normal pace.

A twig snapped somewhere in the area. Then another.

Swallowing down her own fear, Emily nibbled her lip and swung a glance of reassurance to Robert. His eyes had widened. She patted his arm. "We're safe here," she barely whispered.

He opened his mouth to speak, but she touched her fingers to it and shook her head.

His expression relaxed, and his palm covered the hand that lay on his arm.

His touch felt warm, and for an instant Emily enjoyed the strength in his calloused fingers. Then, remembering herself, she quickly withdrew hers and looked away.

"Emmm-ilyyyy," her father's voice rang from far off.

She drew her lips inward and bit down on them to keep silent.

"See anything, Alex?" came Ted's voice ominously near.

Shocked that the two king's men had joined in with the search so swiftly, Emily felt a chill. Their horses had been unsaddled in the barn upon their arrival for dinner.

"Not yet. But when we sight them, they'll find out what

some real horseflesh can do. It should be a feather in our caps when we reach Boston."

Their laughs grated across Emily's nerves as she looked with some apprehension at Robert.

Appearing much more at ease than either of them felt, he lowered himself to the cave's floor and stretched out his legs. He reached up, clasped her hand, and gave an encouraging squeeze as he drew her down beside him.

Emily took a deep breath and smiled as the pursuing hoofbeats faded into silence. "It sounds like they've all gone. But they'll probably check with all the neighbors before they give up."

He gave a nod. "Sorry I caused—"

Loud splashes sounded from the creek as a horse plodded through the ripples.

Emily sprang to her feet and caressed Star's muzzle, hoping to keep him calm.

Her breath caught as the rhododendron branches were swept aside.

"Dan!" she gasped at the sight of his familiar face.

Robert jumped up beside her.

"I had a feeling I'd find you here," her brother said tersely, his gaze roving over the shaded enclosure and Robert MacKinnon before meeting Emily's.

"I forgot you knew about this place," she answered.

"*I* showed it to *you*, remember? A few years ago?"

"Are—are you going to tell?"

He smiled and shook his head, a warm twinkle in his dark brown eyes. "That isn't to say I approve, mind you," he said, adjusting his stance. "But I understand your desire to lend aid where needed." Dan looked again at the Scot. "I'm Dan Haynes, Emily's brother."

"Mr. Haynes," Rob said uneasily as they shook hands.

Her brother turned again to her. "Mother isn't exactly pleased about this situation, you know. She is furious at having been embarrassed before her distinguished guests. Says she'll neither forgive nor forget this incident for a very long time."

"I can imagine." Looking away, Emily felt warmth flood her cheeks. "And I'll be the one who must face the music, no doubt."

"Yes, well . . ."

Rob stepped forward. "I've been tryin' me best to convince your wee sister to leave me to me own fate," he began.

A look of understanding, even sympathy, crossed Dan's features before he turned and fastened his gaze on Emily. "Ah yes, I know what you mean. I do appreciate your effort."

"And if I had gone back, as he wished," Emily injected, "he would already be on his way to face the wrath of Lieutenant Dudingston!"

"Nevertheless, young lady," her brother stated, "you have no business placing yourself at risk."

"You would've done the same, and you know it." With an affirming nod, she stood her ground. When a grin began to lift the corners of her brother's mouth, she knew she had bested him.

"Very well. Stay here until nightfall. By then Robert should be able to manage an escape from the area without any trouble. Yancy and I will run the search party around until they tire of this sport and give up. Meanwhile, little sister, give our young adventurer the very best directions you can without sending him along any of the post roads. Send him to Caroline's. Philip is one of the Sons of Liberty, and he'll no doubt help him from there."

Emily flung herself into Dan's arms. "Oh, thank you. Thank you. I knew you would help."

Untangling himself from her embrace, he looked sternly at the Scot. "I don't know your character, young man, but I expect you to treat my sister with the utmost honor this afternoon while she is in your care."

Robert straightened. Placing a hand over his heart, he met Dan's eyes. "I give ye me solemn vow that no harm shall come to the wee lass. I'll treat her as I would me own baby sister and protect her with me very life, should that be necessary."

Emily crossed her arms stubbornly to stave off a sudden impulse to suck her thumb. *Baby sister, indeed!* She had a mind of her own and could think quite well for herself, whether or not her older brother and her newfound friend might agree.

"Well, then," Dan said with a nod, "I'd better catch up with the others. I'll be praying for your safe journey." With a smile at Emily he left, his footfalls and those of his horse diminishing into the stillness.

"'Tis a fine family ye've got, lass. Your brother is quite like your father, and no doobt we canna' go wrong trustin' his judgment."

Emily eyed the cabin boy who considered her a mere child. When it came right down to it, men really were all alike. Someone should inform them that even a slip of a girl was quite capable of putting two intelligent thoughts together.

The incessant ticking of the big grandfather clock echoed from the adjoining room. Susannah stared at a passage in Psalms.

To her right, Mrs. Haynes sat stiffly in one of the wine-colored wingback chairs, poking a threaded needle in and out of an intricate embroidery design. The somber lines of her face were tense and unflinching, while Jane paced back and forth near the window in the fading afternoon light.

Susannah looked up at her sister-in-law. For the tenth time the girl burst out onto the porch and peered beyond the pasture to no avail, then returned. "I do so wish—"

"Please!" Mother Haynes interrupted. "I have the most dreadful headache. Do try to keep still."

"Yes, Mama," Jane sighed. Turning, she hurried out of the room and came back with a lighted wood stick, which she touched to each lamp. "It's starting to get dark. Surely they'll have to come back soon."

Jane blew out the stick and tossed it into the empty hearth, which had been swept clean for the summer. "Do you hear something?" She ignored her mother's glare and rushed to the open window.

Mrs. Haynes set her work aside with a sigh and twisted her hands in her lap.

Susannah closed the worn Bible and replaced it on the lamp table as the definite sound of approaching horses carried from outside. Rising, she assisted Dan's mother to her feet, then allowed her to precede her out to see what was happening.

Jane was already at the arbor. Beyond her, Dan and his father were dismounting. Susannah and Dan's mother made their way down the porch stairs, but while the older woman went on, Susannah remained on the bottom step and waited.

"Where's Ted?" Jane demanded. "Why have you come back without him?"

"Now, Janie-girl," Papa said wearily as he brushed dust from his clothes. "I'm aware that today has been quite a disappointment for you. But if your young man really loves you, he'll calm down and come back."

"Oh, no he won't," she wailed. "He won't ever lower himself to come back here again." Angrily she jammed her knuckles on her hips and stepped up to her father. "It's all your fault, Papa. You're the one who insisted we keep that criminal here. And you knew very well how important it was to make Ted feel welcome. But no. You made us all appear as though we're as lawless as that rabble down at the wharf. You did this!"

Dan grabbed his sister's shoulders and drew her back, only barely preventing her from pummeling out her anger on their father's chest. "Oh, come now, Jane. Father was only doing what he felt was his Christian duty toward that unfortunate young man. I would have done the same thing."

Narrowing her eyes, Jane turned her pout on him. "Most likely you would have done even more!" she spat. "In fact, if it hadn't been for you, that rude Yancy Curtis wouldn't have brought that fugitive here in the first place. How *could* you invite that bounder of a wharf rat to share our dinner? Why,

I'll have you know he had the audacity to steal a kiss from me in our very own springhouse. Even after I slapped him, he continued to flirt with me the rest of the day. *And right in front of Ted,* no less."

Susannah barely suppressed a smile. For all his rough edges, Yancy Curtis had the sort of charm that could melt the eyelashes off a sea lion. Why he chose to waste it on Dan's spoiled, flighty sister was a mystery.

"Now, Jane, dear," her mother soothed, stroking her coppery curls. "Do silence that tongue of yours before you say something you truly will regret." As the girl appeared to quiet down, Sophia Haynes looked beseechingly at her husband. "Where is Emily? Why have you come back without her?"

Papa touched his wife's arm. "With all the pistols and sabers being waved about, Dan and I thought it best that she remain hidden until the search had been abandoned."

"Am I to assume that you actually found the bold, thoughtless child and then left her?" she interrupted, her anger sharpening her tongue.

He nodded. "Dan knew just where to look. He told her to stay put until after dark. I'm sure she'll be home in an hour or so at the most."

Mrs. Haynes paled. "You had the audacity to leave our little Emily alone and unprotected with that . . . that ruffian?"

"Now, Mother," Dan began. "He seemed quite trustworthy to me."

"*Seemed?*" she railed. "Have you both taken leave of your senses? The scoundrel deserted his post not twenty-four hours past."

Susannah met Dan's swift helpless glance. Despite the fact that dear sweet Emily was still possibly in danger, it was a great comfort that at least Dan had come home. Surely God would keep his hand on the younger girl and bring her back safely as well.

"The lad had just cause, Sophia," Papa said, putting an arm about her shoulders and starting toward the house. "As a mother with two sons, certainly you can sympathize with a young man who was kidnapped and forced into slave labor aboard one of His Majesty's armed schooners . . . taken thousands of miles from his own home and family and made an unwilling accomplice to the piracy of a peaceful coast."

She peered up at him. "That is one thing about which you and I will never agree, Edmond. It is quite beyond me how you can consider *smuggling* lawful—and anyone who tries to stop it a villain."

"You're right," he said cheerfully, hugging her against himself.

"Oh, Papa," Jane whined from his other side, "why couldn't you at least inform Ted that I had nothing to do with this whole awful mess?"

"I did, Janie-girl. But—"

She pursed her lips. "But that detestable Yancy Curtis has already spread his lies, hasn't he? He made Ted believe I would dally with the lowlife likes of him."

"Of course not," Dan said. "Ted and Alex already had the lust of the chase in their eyes. Yancy made a real point of keeping a safe distance from them. He knew his own blood could flow as quickly—and as red—as the young Scot's. But, Susannah, my love," he said, switching his attention to her as he reached the bottom porch step where she waited, "I'm afraid your brother has decided not to set foot on this farm again in the future. After what he considers such a blatant act of disloyalty, he feels that any effort to make amends will have to be on your part."

Susannah's smile vanished sadly at the news.

Dan stepped up and drew her into his arms. "I tried to assure him that you were in no way responsible for any of this, that in fact you had not the slightest knowledge of it at all. But he didn't seem to care. He felt that since you've aligned yourself with this family, you have in effect already betrayed everything which he holds dear."

The very thought stung Susannah's heart, and she could only nod in response. Earlier that day she and her brother had come so very near to regaining their closeness. He had all but forgiven her for having injured his standing in the military ranks by her indenturement. Their parents' death must have hit him extremely hard to have made him so rigid.

He hadn't been like that before. She tried hard to put from her mind his rantings over her having fallen prey to the overenthusiastic George Whitefield and becoming one of the "new lights" for the Lord. Ted considered her not only a fool, but a dissenter from the Holy Church of England . . . which, in his opinion, was just as treasonous as her becoming one of the troublesome rabble in the Colonies. Susannah shuddered, and she felt Dan's embrace tighten as he brushed a lock of tawny hair from her eyes.

"That girl is nothing but bad luck," Mrs. Haynes muttered harshly as she and Papa reached the steps and started up. She stared icily at Susannah. "First the Christmas ball. And now this. You haven't been in this house a single day, and we're beset with far worse calamity. I can only wonder what whirlwind of adversity you'll bring down on us tomorrow."

Susannah felt the color drain from her face. Her knees weakened, and tears rose to her eyes. She swayed against Dan's chest, which tightened to rock hardness.

"Mother!" he roared.

Papa extended a staying hand. "Let me." He turned to his wife. "Sophia, that was most unkind and uncharitable. You shouldn't shift blame onto that innocent child with your superstitious nonsense."

Dan filled his lungs and stepped toward his mother, his expression like granite. "Susannah and I will be leaving at first light."

"But Daniel! I didn't mean that you—"

His eyes hardened into glittering brown shards. "Father, if I might borrow the small wagon, I'll load our trunks tonight."

"Please," his mother pleaded, contrite and flushed with guilt. "Your father is right. I'm sorry for my thoughtless words. I'm just so distraught over Emily and all that has happened today I don't know what I'm saying. Susannah, dear, please forgive me."

Dan sighed wearily.

Barely able to hold together the fragments of her shattered composure, Susannah prayed desperately that Dan would not relent. She would pray for strength enough to forgive his mother for voicing her unkind thoughts in a reckless moment. But the woman had made her feel unwelcome from the moment she had arrived with Dan. The chill in the night air was nothing compared to the calculated indifference that had made her shiver all day.

"I brought Susannah to Rhode Island because I wanted her to know and love my family," Dan blurted out, as if unable to hold it back any longer. "I did not expect her to be treated with outright hostility. Considering her condition, I think she's had about as much as she can handle on her first visit."

And the last, Susannah added silently. It would be a hundred years before she would consider ever coming back to this farm.

Using a rope Emily had fashioned from braiding vines during their hours inside the shelter of the cave, Rob led the gelding toward the far edge of the woods. She had told him about a road and a bridge spanning the Blackstone River. If he could get across, his escape would be easier. He turned and stopped as he gazed down at her in the growing darkness. "I shouldna' be draggin' ye into this, lass. I'm as sure of that as I am that me own life isna' worth a drop of river water. Your family trusted me to return ye to them. They canna' help but be worried."

"I'm aware of that," she said, matching his low tones. "But I could hardly expect you to make it through this forest without taking a wrong turn and getting lost. I couldn't live with myself if I weren't certain of your safety."

Robby stared at her in wonder as light from the wedge of the rising moon found an opening in the branches overhead and frosted her hair in silvery glory. The lass was a treasure, the likes of which he had never known. Under different circumstances, he would have counted it joy to be able to spend time with her—time that might one day lead to something lasting and solid. But at the moment, thoughts in that direction were not even a luxury. They were completely out of the question. No doubt her close family already had other plans for the girl, plans that held far better prospects than he could ever dream of in this new land. The only thing left to him was to ensure her safety until she would agree to go back home where she belonged. And he would see to that even if it did cost him his life.

"Any second now," Emily said in a more normal voice, "we should come out onto the road. Once you've crossed the bridge, all you have to do is follow the river road until you come to Worcester. Anyone in town can tell you where my sister lives."

"Sounds simple enough, even for the likes of me," he quipped.

Favoring him with a sweet smile, Emily took his arm and stopped. "Keep hold of Star for a moment while I go ahead and make sure the road is empty."

Robby nodded gratefully and watched her walk away. The lass had barely a thought for herself. Her one concern seemed to be his safety, and the realization touched him deeply.

❦ ❦

Emily wished fervently that she had chosen a darker dress that morning. The orchid satin trim on the one she wore seemed to shimmer in the glow of the moon and mirror all the light it caught. Peeking from behind a tree at the very boundary of the forest, she took advantage of the unbroken view she had of the road. From the position of the stars, she guessed the time to be near midnight.

Her mother would be hysterical by now. She dreaded having to face her again. No doubt she'd be confined to her room for the rest of her life . . . if she lived through being skinned alive, that is. But just the same, she decided, squaring her shoulders, she had done the right thing—the Christian thing, as Dan and her father were so fond of saying. In time they would all agree that she had done the only thing she could have in all good conscience.

Looking up and down the expanse of empty road, Emily stood still and listened to the night sounds. The lonely hoots of an owl and the chorus of crickets and tree toads had always sounded charming from the sanctity of her own bedroom. But out here in the deep eerie darkness, they made her uneasy. She'd be glad when she returned home. Perhaps. She squinted in the direction of the bridge, but it was not in sight. Ducking back into the shadows, she stepped quietly along the boundary of trees until she could see the bend in the road. She knew the bridge would be just beyond that.

When the arched stonework finally came into sight, she noted with relief that it was deserted. Apparently, the searchers had tired of the bothersome chore. They could have easily positioned someone there. She smiled smugly.

Then a twig snapped from somewhere near the bridge.

Emily held her breath and froze. Directly across from her, just emerging from the trees, she could make out the barest silhouette of a red-uniformed figure astride a tall horse. It could easily be Ted Harrington or Alex Fontaine. She inched backward into the deeper shadows, watching to make certain that whoever it was hadn't seen her as well. When it became apparent that she hadn't been noticed, she sneaked back along the tree line to where Robert MacKinnon waited with the horse.

A faint shaft of light coming through the uneven canopy above lit upon the young Scot's face as she approached, and his expression brightened. He opened his mouth to speak.

She put a finger to her lips, then motioned for him to follow her deeper into the forest. When they had gone into the woods, she leaned close to him. "I saw a soldier up on the road," she said in a near whisper. "There might be more. Ted and Alex, or others I don't know. I was sure they would have given up on us by now and gone away, but they haven't."

"Then it's imperative that ye return to your family now, lass. I'll move on by meself. There's no sense involvin' yourself in this any longer."

"What?" she asked. "And how do you expect to get anywhere alone? You don't know these woods."

"That may be," he said confidently. "But I do ken enough

to get oot of sight if I hear someone comin'. Sooner or later I'll end up someplace safe."

"But you'll get there faster if I show you the way," she insisted. "If we keep to the woods, we can still get to Worcester. It'll be a little slower, but it shouldn't take us more than two days at the most."

"Us!" he hissed. "I'll na' hear of any such thing, and that's me final word. Wee Emily," he said in a quieter tone as he gently took hold of her arms and made her face him. "I must go on alone from here. Please believe me . . . 'tis better this way."

"Haven't you been listening to me, Robert?" Emily said boldly. "The searchers are still out looking for us. There's less than a slim chance of your ever making it to my sister's without being discovered or getting lost and starving to death. You need me to guide you."

Robby bristled at the thought of his being incapable of charting a course by the night sky. He'd learned a lot about the constellations and the movements of the stars since his capture. He let out a frustrated breath. "Now, this may come as a shock, lass," he said through his teeth, "but I'm quite capable of puttin' one foot in front of the other here in America just as I did back in me homeland. And whether ye realize it or not, the sun comes up in the east on the other side of the vast water and goes down again in the west, the same as it does here. As much as I thank ye for the way ye've been escortin' me thus far, what I truly need now is for ye just to give me the proper directions and be off wi' ye!"

She raised her chin. "You may be quite good at traveling through the tame woods of Scotland, but here along the Blackstone River they've been untouched by man. They're thick. Wild. And they hold all sorts of danger."

"All the more reason for ye to go home and be safe," he said rigidly.

"I'm not leaving, and that's that." Her whispered words came out in a hiss. Folding her arms, she stood rooted in place.

"Look," Robby's own voice edged louder. "I promised your brother I'd be sendin' ye back safely tonight after dark. And I keep my promises."

"So do I," she said, arching a brow. "I promised myself that I wouldn't leave you until I felt you were safe. And I won't."

"Ye'll na' be comin' wi' me."

"I will, and I am."

"Then I shall have to tie ye to a tree, and I wouldna' like to be doin' such a thing as that."

"Do it, and I'll yell my head off."

Neither spoke in the thick silence as each regarded the other.

"It's either me or the hangman's noose. Your choice," Emily said, pressing her advantage.

"Surely jumpin' ship isna' a hangin' offense."

"Perhaps. But when they throw in horse stealing, kidnapping—" She picked a small bit of dried leaf from her skirt and looked up again. "Housing and feeding prisoners is really a bothersome expense, you know. Now, shall we go, or would you prefer we continue this senseless debate until morning?"

Susannah yawned in the pale predawn light as she and the family awaited Dan's return from Pawtucket. It had been no more than an hour since he had ridden into the nearby village to find out if perchance Robert MacKinnon and Emily had been arrested during the night, but each minute had ticked by with plodding slowness. She cast a wary glance at her in-laws. After the all-night vigil, they appeared as haggard as she felt. No one had so much as changed clothes.

At the first sound of an approaching rider, Jane rushed to the door. "It's Dan!"

As one, Susannah and the others rose and hurried after the girl in grim silence.

Dan skidded his mount to a stop and swung down. "Emily hasn't been arrested, thank the Lord."

"Then where is she?" Mother Haynes wailed. "Do they know where the child is, at least?"

"No, there hasn't been a word." He wrapped the animal's reins around the hitching ring. "She must have felt the lad needed to be guided partway until she was sure he was out of harm's way."

"Oh, Edmond," she moaned, leaning against him as she pressed a lace handkerchief to her nose. "I simply cannot bear it."

He steadied her. "What do you mean, Dan? The sheriff planned to return to Providence at dusk. Surely Ted and his friend didn't continue the search beyond that hour."

"I'm afraid they did." Dan's darkly shadowed eyes met Susannah's. "They kept watch on the road in both directions most of the night."

"Ted!" Jane's voice brightened. "Did you actually see him? Talk to him?"

He nodded. "I went directly to Pidge Tavern, where they have rooms. They had just gotten back moments before I arrived."

"I would like to know how the rest of you can be so calm in the face of this disaster," Mother Haynes said woodenly. "A stranger—a criminal—has kidnapped my sweet, innocent baby. Heaven only knows what he might do to her." Her hollow eyes moved from one bleak face to the next before finally closing in tearful frustration. "Edmond, I want you to wake me up from this nightmare and tell me that none of this is happening."

"You'll never know how much I wish I could do that very thing, my dear," he assured her. "What I can tell you is that the lad seemed a decent sort, and he promised Dan that no harm would come to her. We must believe that."

"Mother Haynes," Susannah said, moving to her side and placing a hand on her shoulder, "we must trust God to take care of Emily. I've seen his hand at work in far worse circumstances."

The older woman lifted cold green eyes and stared.

"Worse?" she spat. "Is that right? Have you nothing better to do than rattle off some trite platitude, when our lives are in total chaos?"

Susannah stepped back and swallowed hard. She sought Dan's face.

His jaw muscles clenched, and when he spoke his voice was rough and hard. "I have little doubt that Emily has stubbornly insisted on escorting the Scot to Caroline's. After I take *my wife* to Boston, I'll go after Emily."

His mother raised her head, her eyes little more than angry slits in her creased face. "I suppose you *would* be more concerned over a bondwoman than your own sister."

"Sophia!" Papa bellowed. "There will be no more of that! Come, we're going upstairs. You're obviously in sore need of rest. And Susannah," he said, softening his tone, "I apologize for the misery you have endured since your arrival. It is not the normal treatment extended to either guests or family, I assure you. I only hope you will believe that and find it in your heart to make allowance. No matter what has transpired, you are in no way responsible. Godspeed, my dear."

Susannah's own emotional state prevented her from trusting her voice. She lowered her gaze and stood apart from the rest, feeling utterly forlorn.

Dan slanted a reproachful glance at his mother, then turned his attention to his father. "Emily and that MacKinnon fellow have only the one horse, which will slow them down. And since they will have to give every village a wide berth, I have little doubt I shall beat them to Caroline's."

Without waiting for a reply, he strode to Susannah and framed her face gently with his hands. "Come, my love. I'm taking you home."

She had tried hard to maintain her composure, but his tender gesture caused a tear to escape the corner of her eye. It fell into his palm.

Dan sucked in a breath, and it came out long and shuddering as he exhaled. He led her toward the barn without so much as a last glance at the rest of the family.

Halfway there he turned back to Jane, who still stood glued to the same spot. "If it wouldn't be too much trouble, I'd appreciate it if you would see to the horse."

"Certainly." Her tone was stiff and unyielding, but an instant later, Jane seemed to turn unaccountably cheerful. "Yes, I'd be glad to."

❦ ❧

Ted roused and turned over in sleep. Feeling that he was not alone, he rubbed his face groggily as someone shook his shoulder. He opened his eyes and tried to focus on his sister's face. She was always such a patient sort in the morning and had the same gentle touch as Mum, no matter how long he'd slept. Ah, he finally concluded, it was just a dream after all. A lovely one who looked quite like the delectable Jane. And she was sitting on his bed! It was too good to let pass. Without giving a thought to propriety, he caught her arms and pulled the wondrous illusion down toward him.

"Ted!" she cried as she pulled herself away and jumped to her feet.

The reality of her presence shocked him fully awake. He bolted to a sitting position. "Jane! What on earth are you doing here?" Remembering the events of the past evening, he narrowed his eyes in suspicion.

"I had to come," Jane answered. "I couldn't bear to have you thinking horrid untruths about me. Even at the risk of ruining my reputation, should Alex or the innkeeper see me, I had to assure you I had no part in the deceptions devised by my family. When I tried to protest my father's decision to take in the fugitive, he forbade me to tell *anyone,* even my own mother. And you shouldn't blame Susannah, either. She knew absolutely nothing of the matter."

Drinking in the sound of her sultry voice, Ted continued to regard her, even though he was not fully convinced.

Jane moved nearer and sat down beside him. She picked up his hand and pressed it to her cheek. "Please, Ted. Don't look at me so. I'd do anything to prove my love to you. Anything you say."

Pleasantly surprised to be the recipient of such a tempting offer, Ted gave Jane a meaningful smile. Up until now she had always kept him at a safe distance, regardless of her outrageous flirtations. Now here she was actually offering herself. Perhaps she truly did love him after all, as she said. As he did her. Hadn't he found his normally sensible heart tangled up in thoughts of the flighty Jane Haynes since the first time he'd seen her? Only to mask his vulnerability had he kept his true feelings imprisoned behind a wall of reserve. Still smiling, he reached for her.

"Oh!" She stood and backed away. "I wasn't referring to—" A rosy glow heightened her complexion.

He slumped against the pillow and arched a brow, trying to fathom this curious encounter.

"I've come with information . . . so you'll know that I side with you."

What was she up to now?

"You see, I . . . know where Emily is taking the fugitive. If you promise that no harm will come to her, I'll tell you where they've gone."

Ted regarded her steadily, ashamed of his hasty assumptions. He tapped his fingers absently on his thighs. It would be quite advantageous if he could report to Boston with the capture of the *Gaspee* deserter to his credit. But what if this were simply one more ruse to throw him off? No. Not Jane. She wouldn't willingly do such a thing, not if she loved him. Reaching for Jane's hand, he pulled her close to the bed again. "And just where might that be?" he asked evenly, expending great effort to maintain control of himself.

"First promise me you'll see that Emily gets home safely."

"Of course, my darling." Searching her dark eyes, he placed his other hand over hers and gave a reassuring squeeze. "I'm quite fond of your little sister—despite her rash ways." He increased the pressure. "Now, tell me. Where are they?"

Jane hesitated, looking for the briefest instant as if she were about to change her mind. Then she drew a breath. "They've . . . gone to my sister Caroline's. In Worcester."

Gingerly sitting down on the edge of the bed, Jane straightened her skirt. "I know you've said you'll never come back to our farm. And I understand that, truly I do. But nevertheless, you can't stop me from coming to *you.*"

"What are you saying?" Ted asked, hardly daring to hope.

"I'm going to convince Mama to let me go to Boston to stay with Dan and Susannah during your sister's confinement. How can she not agree? So, you see . . ." She smiled teasingly.

Ted's heart gave a wild lurch. "Ah yes." His earlier levity left him as he reached for her in earnest this time. Perhaps fate would look kindly upon his relationship with his beautiful Jane if they were truly able to spend time together. And from her announcement, that possibility loomed deliciously on the horizon.

❦ ❦

Watching the intense changes on Ted's face, Jane barely outmaneuvered his grasp as she giggled and jumped up. She backed toward the door. She had him right where she wanted him now. She would never give him what he most desired without the benefit of marriage. But she had managed to restore Ted's interest in her. "I'm sorry, dear heart, but I must hurry back before someone misses me. Mama would lock me in the cellar for a year were she to discover I'd gone to see a gentleman in his bedchamber."

She opened the door, then turned. "But in Boston we'll have plenty of time. Days and days."

"And nights and nights, my love," Ted called after her as she closed the door. "Nights and nights."

A shallow brook that ran along the wooded grove gurgled over smooth rocks in the creek bed, its ripples reflecting patches of light from the clear sky overhead.

Rob MacKinnon followed Emily's line of vision as she stared toward a farm a hundred yards away.

"That's it," she said. "Caroline and Philip's place. I'll go on ahead and make sure it's safe for you, then I'll come back. I shouldn't be long."

"Wait," Rob said as she took a few steps away.

She paused and looked back. The smudges on her face were more apparent in the daylight as she absently smoothed a tear in her lavender ruffles.

Rob had no doubt that he, too, looked somewhat the worse for wear after having navigated the wooded countryside for two days and nights. What on earth would Emily's sister think when she saw her? He kept his voice even. "If there be soldiers aboot, or any officers lyin' in wait—"

"But we haven't seen any so far, and we've been watching the farm for almost half an hour."

"Still, it isna' somethin' aboot which we're completely certain, ye ken. Ye must use every caution, lass. I dunna' want ye to sacrifice yourself for the likes o' me."

"What are you saying?" Emily searched his face.

"I want ye to promise me that if the worst should happen, and it comes down to where ye find yourself arrested, ye'll turn me in. Ye can say I forced ye to come wi' me, that I gave ye no choice. Ye canna' bring shame upon yourself or your family."

She observed him without expression for a moment, then a corner of her mouth curved upward slightly. Turning, she clutched her skirt in her hands and ran lightly through the meadow toward the road and the dwelling beyond.

Robby watched her graceful flight. A balmy breeze tousled her long curls and ruffled her dress until she looked like wild heather rippling in the wind on the open moors. When she stopped suddenly and turned, a jolt of alarm shot through him. But it changed to warmth with the gift of her smile.

Never in all his eighteen years had he seen such a glorious sight. He engraved it forever upon his mind; it would comfort him through all the lonely moments of life. A hollow ache filled his insides. What had he done? How had he allowed himself to abscond with this pure, innocent lass?

Sinking down to his heels, Rob leaned against a tree trunk and waited as his gaze followed Emily the rest of the way. He saw her reach up and smooth her hair; at once it brought back a tender memory of this morning, when she had undone her ribbon and released the tangled locks. He knew he shouldn't have dared such intimate familiarity—particularly since he had found himself sorely tempted in a number of ways already—but he hadn't been able to resist helping her finger-comb it into some semblance of order. Even before he touched it, he had known that the fine-spun flaxen halo would put the softest eiderdown to shame. Had she felt the tremor in his hands when he offered to retie the satin ribbon at the nape of her neck?

Robby took an unsteady breath and slowly let it out. This small agony could not begin to rival what he had felt during the chill wee hours of last night. While Emily had picketed the horse, Rob had scooped old fallen leaves into two piles for beds, and though it would have been wiser for them to share their body heat in the unseasonable coolness, he had placed them a discreet distance apart.

Emily had returned with her arms full of lace-trimmed petticoats. Without so much as a glance his way, she tucked one around each mat and spread another on top. As Rob lay down, the tantalizing fragrance that caressed his nostrils would have made sleep impossible had he not been so exhausted. He hoped his light jacket had kept her warm during that cold night. His own shirt-sleeves had been little protection, even with the petticoat over him.

Not once during the ordeal could Robby recall a single complaint coming from her. She possessed a stalwart courage admirable in one so young . . . and a lass, yet. Mentally berating himself for indulging in any wanton thoughts about the winsome beauty, he swallowed. Without so much as a thought for herself, her driving force seemed to be concern for him, that he escape being captured by the officials. The very least he could do would be to keep the promise he had made to her older brother and see that she came through the escapade unscathed.

He forced aside the memory of the smoky look in her green eyes when he'd awakened her in the predawn. It had almost been his undoing. He had found himself imagining the wonder of feeling her lips against his. To keep himself under control, he had flung himself away and spoken roughly to her about how they needed to be on their way. Rob closed his eyelids at the aching remembrance.

Just then his stomach growled. The two of them had found such meager fare since that last feast at the Haynes farm. Wild berries and water. Perhaps Emily would think to bring some food back with her when she came. Even a crust of bread would be heaven itself.

❧ ❧

Emily crossed the road and started up the lane to Caroline's house. Still trying to concoct a believable excuse for her present state of dishevelment, she discarded one ridiculous fabrication after another. *Hi, Carrie. I was just out for a walk and. . . . Hi, Sissie. Mama said you've been homesick lately, so I. . . .*

She clenched her fingers as she walked, knowing that the only logical explanation lay in the truth. And that, of course, was out of the question. She sighed and shook her head.

From down the road came the rumble of a wagon.

Emily leaped behind a stone wall and hunched down out of sight, assailed by a resurgence of fear that Ted and his cohorts might have thought to look for her and Robert here at Worcester. She peeked through a crack between the layers of rocks, and relief washed over her. It was just a family traveling toward town, dressed in their Sunday finery.

Today must be the Sabbath! Caroline and her family had probably already gone to service themselves. Emily breathed a prayer of thanks. At least by the time they returned, she might come up with a plausible explanation for having shown up on their doorstep.

Deciding it was wisest not to draw undue attention to herself, she stayed behind the stones and crept the remaining distance to the square, white clapboard house.

When she was close to the clearing, she stood and peered as far as she could in every direction to be sure no long-legged British horses were waiting outside. A quick check of the barn verified that she was safe—for the moment, at least. The family wagon was gone.

Emily hurried to the house and knocked tentatively on the door. When no one answered, she let herself inside. "Anybody home?"

Silence.

Her smile froze in place as she passed the walnut-framed mirror in the dim entry hall and took stock of the reflection that met her eyes. She hadn't once considered the effects that two days and nights of running and hiding would have on her. Mama would have the vapors if such a shockingly unladylike waif would dare claim to be her daughter. Small wonder that Robert MacKinnon could bear the sight of her for only the briefest moment before he would turn away with a strange expression on his face.

"Well, there's only one thing to be done," she announced

aloud, her voice a hollow echo in the vacant house. She mounted the enclosed staircase to the second floor and went into the master bedroom, where she opened the door of her sister's pine armoire. Considering each gown as she fingered through the selection, she finally settled on a cornflower blue muslin that looked serviceable, yet had dainty white lace trim on the bodice and sleeve edges. She held it up to her at the dressing table and nodded. Surely Caroline would forgive her for borrowing it.

Emily poured water into a basin on the commode and scrubbed her face and hands, then gave her body a quick wash before pulling on the dress. It seemed a bit loose, but one of Caroline's crisp white aprons would take care of that. She took one from a dresser drawer and tied it snugly around her waist.

Sitting down at the mirror, she took a brush and began to work the tangles from her untidy curls. A flush warmed her cheeks as she recalled Rob's gentleness earlier this morning when he had helped with her hair. How fortunate that she hadn't realized how unkempt she looked! He had been so close that she had felt his breath on her neck. A smile teased her lips, and she subdued it only by force. Robert MacKinnon had been nothing less than a gentleman helping a lady who needed assistance. She had better not read anything more into the situation. The family already had one avid romantic in Jane. It did not need two.

But Rob was, indeed, a gentleman of the first order. Why, he had even insisted she ride the horse alone, while he walked along beside her much of the way. Rarely had he ridden behind her. He had more than proven himself by his concern over her welfare, and not once had he given the slightest hint of having a dishonorable bone in his body. He had kept his word to Dan and treated her as if she were his own little sister.

Baby sister, she corrected with irritation. Perhaps nature had not endowed her generously, but still, she was no longer a child. Would no one ever realize that she was a young woman and regard her as an adult?

Well, she reminded herself with several more downward strokes of the brush, there *had* been that one fleeting second when Robert had awakened her. She had almost expected him to kiss her. Worse than that, she had *wanted* him to. But most certainly she had misread him, for he seemed touchy afterward.

What would it be like having a gallant young man, a world traveler at that, attracted to her? She allowed her mind a few leisure moments to consider his close-set blue eyes, the thick black hair smoothed back neatly from his forehead. Despite his youthful, almost skinny frame, his arms had surprising strength. His hands, too, though hardened from his duties aboard ship, were gentle whenever he touched her. His smile was easy and appealing, and his accent was more than pleasant to listen to, with its wonderful lilt. . . .

Emily pressed her lips together and straightened. What on earth was she doing wasting time daydreaming, when Robert was still waiting for her to return? It was time to rein in her foolish imaginings . . . after all, she was just a baby, remember? Hardly the feminine ideal. And Robert MacKinnon had far more important matters on his mind anyway.

Rising from the dressing table bench, Emily inspected herself in the mirror one last time, then left the room and hurried down to the kitchen to gather up some food for them.

❧ ❧

From a distance, as he sat waiting under the tree, Robby heard the unmistakable strains of organ music. There must be a church somewhere nearby. He stood and cocked an ear toward the sound. A smile spread across his face as he recognized the familiar melody, and he quietly mouthed the words:

Jesus, Lover of my soul,
Let me to Thy bosom fly;
While the nearer waters roll,
While the tempest still is high:

The hymn took him back to his last church service at home, when he'd stood beside his father and sung the same words with enthusiasm. Afterward they had climbed up the hill from the village to their wee stone cottage on the rise. The steep ascent had winded his father, and for the first time Robby noticed how much the older man had changed since Rob's mother had passed on. The realization that age had begun its relentless march on the once robust frame had shocked Rob, for he had been convinced with the carelessness of youth that time would never alter things.

Now his father had no idea of the fate that had befallen his son. He had gathered all the savings they could scrape together, and sent Rob off with a prayer and a hope for a better chance in the new land. Robby knew that in all likelihood he would never set foot again upon the Highland soil, nor would he see his father's beloved face in this life.

The parting had been rough, and he recalled it with a twinge of sad longing. "I'll be prayin' for ye, laddie," his father had said, clasping Robby's hand tightly in his. "Remember always to trust in the Lord. Keep close to your heart the things your dear mother and I taught ye. Trust in him, and he'll always see ye through, from the fading light of gloaming until the break of the new dawn . . . no matter how dark the night, or cold."

Father had no idea how true those words would be. Through the many lonely weeks aboard the *Gaspee,* even when it seemed the Almighty had forsaken him, he had still been aware of God's protection in the heavy seas. And in the dark and cold of last night, he had known the tender provision of sweet Emily's petticoats to see him through. He bowed his head. "Almighty God, I've been a faithless fool, thinking ye cared not a whit aboot me or me troubles through all these past dark months. Surely your hand has been upon me all the way, and even more so in the present deep valleys of danger. Keep me aware of your presence always."

The musical prelude to another hymn floated on the air, and even before the congregation began to sing, Rob recognized it. He smiled, and his mind added the rich, reedy flavor of bagpipes:

Be Thou my Vision, O Lord of my heart;
Nought be all else to me, save that Thou art. . . .

As he savored the moment, his eyelids started to close, but a splotch of blue caught his attention, and he looked up. Someone in a frock the same hue as the summer sky was crossing the meadow . . . and the *vision* was Emily. His heart pounded as he watched the youthful fluidity of her steps.

Thou my best thought, by day or by night,
Waking or sleeping, Thy presence my light.

The very sun seemed caught in her spun-gold hair. In that instant his months of darkness became light because of her radiance. Surely God in his goodness had ordained the steps of Robby's life toward this glorious morning and now was bringing this precious gift to him on the melody of a song. His being filled with wonder. The Lord had chosen for them to be together—not just for a few frantic days and nights, but for a lifetime. He knew it as certainly as he'd known anything in his life before. Jumping up, he ran out to greet her.

Emily's smile surpassed the sunshine itself, and without thinking, Robby grabbed her shoulders.

"I came as quickly as I could," she blurted. "Didn't you believe me?"

Realizing where his hands were, Rob removed them at once. "Forgive me," he muttered. "It's just that y-ye look so bonny."

She averted her eyes and blushed. Then her brows drew together in a slight frown as she grabbed his hand and tugged him back into the shelter of the trees. "We shouldn't be out in the open, you know."

"Aye," he said, wishing that he could stop smiling . . . or that he cared about being a hunted man.

Emily gave him a look of confusion. Setting down the basket she had looped over one arm, she took out a biscuit and handed it to Rob. "No one was home when I got to Caroline's. They must be at church."

He took a disinterested bite, reveling in the sight of her. She was much more than he deserved.

"Now might be the best time for us to go to the house," she began, "since the roads are empty."

With a nod he took another bite and chewed slowly. "I shall like meeting more of your family." He almost chuckled at the odd look she gave him. What a joy it would be to share his wonderful new revelation with her . . . when the time was right. Picking up her basket, he offered her his other arm.

Before they had gone two steps, Robby stopped. He pulled Emily back into the thicker growth and shielded her with his body as the sound of hoofbeats drew closer.

She peeked around him as the redcoats trotted past. "Ted," she whispered. "And Alex."

Emily held her breath as Ted and Alex rode by tall and straight and somber on their magnificent military horses. What must they think of her now that she had run off with a young man she had never even seen before in her life? Well, at least they wouldn't consider her a child any longer.

"I feared they might come," she whispered to Robert. "Ted has been courting my sister, Jane, since a year ago Christmas. No doubt she has spoken to him any number of times about Caroline and Nancy and where they live. I'm glad my sister was at church when I got there. At least she won't have to lie for us."

"Ah, sweet Emily," Rob crooned, putting his arms around her. "What have I done to ye? I dunna' ken how I ever let ye get involved in this mess for a worthless ship's rat like me. But I promise ye, everything'll turn out. Ye'll see."

She raised her head and met his gaze, feeling less optimism at the moment than she had since they had fled her bedroom two days ago.

Robert grinned at her tenderly. "I canna' say how I ken, lass, just that I do. As sure as we're standin' here, I ken."

Easing away from the warm comfort of his arms, she smiled. "And I don't know why I believe that, but *I* do." Emily looked from him to the basket she had brought. "Well, I'm certainly glad I brought all this food. It's quite a distance from here to Boston."

"*Boston!* 'Twould be like walkin' into the very lion's den!"

"Yes," she said with an even brighter smile. "And who better to be there with than Daniel? Dan and Susannah should arrive at their new home sometime later this week."

"But—" He stared in alarm and disbelief.

"Think of it, Robert. No one could possibly imagine you would be foolish enough to go there, of all places. We'd be truly safe. And if I know those two pompous lobsterbacks, they'll waste hours, maybe days, searching for us here before they decide to give up and press on. Come along. In a mile or so we should be able to ride the rest of the way up on the road."

❦ ❦

Star's rhythmic gait had a lulling effect upon Emily as the horse plodded steadily east along the road to Boston in the fading light. She relaxed and rested her head against Rob's strong back and mulled the day over in her mind. Her initial uneasiness that at any moment they might be overtaken by their pursuers had gradually lessened as the miles stretched out between them and Worcester. And now in the stillness of evening they rode in comfortable silence.

Robert had passed the hours by telling her clever stories about his boyhood and youth in the lush green countryside of Scotland. Emily could picture him running across the windy moors, climbing rocky slopes, being fearless and adventuresome. Though his family had not known the comfort and advantage she had taken for granted, his parents had been warm and loving and hardworking. They had instilled in their son a deep abiding trust in God that made Emily's own faith appear weak by comparison. And to think she'd thought him a heathen!

With her ear pressed against Rob, Emily heard him humming softly. He had sung hymns off and on along the way and had encouraged her to sing with him on any she knew. And in between, he would admire occasional farms they passed and talk about his dream of someday owning one of his own.

Now she closed her eyes and listened once more to "Be Thou My Vision," which seemed to be a particular favorite of his. Despite his skepticism about the power of prayer that he had voiced at home in Ben's room, Robert MacKinnon had kept the Sabbath by singing only hymns today.

She gazed up at the first star of evening. Only a few nights ago she had been brash enough to lament the fact that God had cursed her with being a girl and assigned her a tiresome life, when what she most longed for was excitement and adventure. How quickly God had granted her wish! She chuckled.

"What ha' ye to be laughing aboot?" Rob asked, placing a hand over the one she had clasped around his waist.

"I was just remembering something. It's been only a few days since I was complaining rather loudly to the Almighty because my life was so dull."

Rob broke into hearty laughter, and she joined in with his merriment.

As their mirth subsided, Emily stiffened. "Listen," she whispered. "I think I heard something. Someone's coming."

Guiding the horse off the road and into the bushes alongside, Robert reined to a stop and slid down, then helped Emily.

"C-could the news about us have reached Boston already?" she murmured. "Perhaps the authorities there have sent patrols out to hunt for us."

"It canna' be that, lass. Na' so soon," Rob said soothingly.

But at this time of night, whoever was galloping at such speed must have urgent reason to do so. Emily's heart pounded like the thundering hoofbeats that rapidly approached. As the rider passed, her eyes widened in recognition. "Dan!" she yelled, dashing out onto the road. "Dan!"

His horse, Flame, skidded to a stop, then turned and trotted back toward her. When he reached her, Emily's brother jumped down and grabbed her in a fierce hug. "Thank heaven," he breathed. "Thank heaven."

She felt him go rigid and looked up to see that Dan had spied Rob coming their way leading the weary horse.

"You're a little late getting my sister home, wouldn't you say?" Dan asked dryly.

"Wait!" Emily interrupted. "Don't blame Robert. I blackmailed him into taking me along with him."

Dan's expression of disbelief didn't waver his resolve for an instant. He took a threatening step toward Rob.

"He was ready to resort to tying me to a tree to keep me from following him, but I threatened to scream bloody murder."

"Is that true?" he asked Rob in clipped words.

Rob nodded. "'Tis a shame to admit it, but aye. 'Tis true. But I've not harmed her in any way, ye've me word on that. I treated her at all times with the same honor I would me own sister."

Sister? Emily railed inwardly. *He still thinks of me as a sister?*

"Why the troubled face, Emily?" Dan asked. "MacKinnon *is* speaking the truth, isn't he?"

She flashed an aloof smile, not about to let either of the blackguards so concerned about her welfare know how upset she felt. "Oh, he has always been a perfect gentleman," she said coolly. "Absolutely perfect."

"Well, then," Dan said, relief apparent in his voice, "you must realize what a muddle you've managed to get yourself into this time, Sis. I needn't tell you that Father is probably even yet combing all the countryside within a ten-mile radius of the farm. And Mother . . ."

That last word struck Emily like a blow. She had far greater problems than merely being considered a child by these two handsome men who cared about her honor. She could only imagine what punishment awaited her upon her return. "You came from Boston. Have you already taken Susannah there?"

"We thought it was best, under the circumstances."

"Oh. I must have really spoiled your homecoming."

"That's a bit of an understatement," he said evenly.

She compressed her lips into a thin line and looked away,

then back at her brother. "I'm sorry. I really am. I never thought—"

"Precisely," he interrupted. "If you had, you wouldn't be in this mess. But since you are, we'll have to allow God to work things out for the best somehow, in his own good time. I know that you're not completely at fault here," he added on a softer note.

"Amen to that," Rob said.

Dan regarded the two of them for a moment, then shook his head with an expression of finality, as though a die had been cast that would remain forever unchanged. Grinning, he clamped a hand on Robby's shoulder. "The two of you look like you could use a decent night's rest. There's an inn about a mile back the way I came. You'll be safe there. The owner's a sympathizer for the cause. Tomorrow morning we'll go on to Boston and decide what to do from there."

Scooping Emily up in his arms, Rob set her on the horse and vaulted up behind her. "Let's na' be wastin' time."

The following afternoon, Robby guided the gelding alongside Dan's horse, all too aware of Emily's absence while she rode with her brother. He had grown so accustomed to having her near during the past few days that riding alone made him feel as though something was missing. But having her alternate between the two horses did spare the animals somewhat on the journey.

He inhaled, and a whiff of a briny breeze filled his nostrils. Boston couldn't be much farther. He glanced at Emily and found her staring off in another direction. It gave him a chance to feast his eyes on the alluring vision she made. *Please may it be true,* he prayed fervently, recalling the wondrous revelation he thought he'd received in Worcester. But at the moment he couldn't imagine Emily's family permitting him, a fugitive without apparent means of support, much less any decent prospects, to court her. No doubt her brother would send her back to Rhode Island within a few days. It was a depressing thought. And these last precious moments were being wasted by not having her near.

Dan stopped his mount and held an arm out to Emily. "You'd better ride with Rob for a while."

Robby swallowed. Had he spoken his thoughts aloud, or had the Lord heard the prayer of his heart? In any event, he cheerfully gave Emily a hand up behind him and stilled his pulse as she slid her arms around his waist.

"We're almost to the Neck," Dan said. "It's the only way to reach Boston by land. We'll have to pass through a British post."

"Are ye saying," Rob asked, trying to keep the alarm from his voice, "that the citizens of the town must endure British interrogation wi' every coming and going?"

"I'm afraid so," Dan replied calmly. "When we get there, let me do all the talking. That Scottish brogue of yours is pretty noticeable. I'll introduce you as my sister's husband and say that we've just come from your farm outside of Roxbury. That's the village we just passed."

Rob's mouth went dry, and he swallowed as Emily's hold tightened a little. He patted her clasped hands comfortingly and kept the pace steady. *Her husband . . . could it ever be?* He let his mind dwell on the words Dan had spoken. The hope and dream of his heart, a reality? What a joy it would be to come home to Emily at night and sit with her before a crackling fire sipping spiced hot cider. He sighed.

But the fantasy vanished with the sight of the guard shack just ahead on the narrow corridor of land that was the gateway into Boston. Armed soldiers stood with their muskets at the ready, bayonets gleaming in the sun. Rob felt the first stab of actual fear since the day before. He felt as if he were about to suffocate.

Emily gave him a slight hug. "It's all right. Dan's used to this. He was a postrider before he was ordained by the Presbyterian Church."

He craned his head around and looked at her. "Your own brother, a minister of the holy Scottish church?"

She nodded and smiled.

With a grin at Dan, Rob relaxed a bit. "Then there's naught to worry aboot. Almighty God is surely at work here."

❧ ❧

Emily took her first good look at the busy port they were entering, with its landscape of hill and sea. She had heard that Boston was known for its scrambled lanes and crooked streets. Several side streets curved out of view as the horses' hooves clattered over the cobblestone pavement along busy Marlborough Street. She admired the lovely, well-attended homes and brick buildings, the neat shops, the abundance of maples, oaks, and elms so liberally sprinkled around. Wagons rumbled by carrying farmers and peddlers on their way to or from market. Emily returned the smile of a fashionable woman who passed in an elegant horse-drawn chaise. Finally they turned onto Milk Street. "Is that big church yours?" she asked Dan, noting a huge structure on the corner.

"No, that's the Old South Meeting House," he replied. "My church is a couple of blocks away, on Long Lane. Our house is down this street, though."

"Are there always so many people out and about?" she asked, trying to keep her voice calm as a British patrol marched by.

"Pretty much. This road leads to the wharves, Fort Hill, and Castle William, so it's never empty."

"We must be getting close then." Emily would never be so glad in her life to be indoors again.

"Right. That's it down there." Dan indicated a two-story white clapboard dwelling with black shutters and a gabled roof. "We were quite fortunate to get the place, actually," he said. "A recent widower in Reverend Moorhead's congregation had to go to Ireland to visit relatives and graciously offered his home to us for the year he'll be away. It looked comfortable, from what I was able to see of it. I only had time to unload our trunks before I started for Worcester."

"What about Susannah?" Emily asked. "I imagine she was as shocked by my behavior as everyone else."

He reached over and squeezed her arm. "My Susannah, as you'll soon discover for yourself, is both generous-hearted and fair. Naturally, she was concerned for your safety." Coming to the gate, he drew Flame to a stop. "Hm. Isn't that one of our horses tied to that post?"

Emily recognized the familiar markings. "Oh yes. That's the one Ben is using these days." She peered around at Robert. "He's my other brother. The postrider I told you about before. You were using his room."

Dan dismounted and secured his own horse. "I'm surprised he tracked us down so quickly." As Emily and Rob got off and tied the gelding, Dan rushed inside. "Susannah! I'm home! I've found Emily and the Scotsman."

Only a few steps behind her brother, Emily went in, followed by Rob. She saw Susannah fly into Dan's embrace.

Beyond them, Ben stepped forward, his square chin jutting out in rage. The ever-present grin was absent as he glared at Emily. Then he lunged at Robert. "I'll kill you, you filthy dog!" Grabbing the young man's shoulders, he rammed him up against the wall of the entry hall with surprising strength.

"No!" Emily screamed, trying unsuccessfully to pull the two apart. "Let him go. He hasn't done anything."

Dan finally managed to untangle them and pull his younger brother away. "Give it up, Ben," he said calmly. "Emily is unharmed."

Rob brushed himself off and straightened his clothing.

"Um, why don't we all go into the parlor?" Susannah suggested, forcing a smile. "We can have a bit of the tea that Ben so thoughtfully rescued off some remote beach."

Dan stared steadily at his brother. "Is it safe to unhand you now?"

His wide mouth in a grim line, Ben shrugged himself free and smoothed his sun-streaked brown hair. "I suppose." He shot a glance at his sister and Rob, who stood side by side. "For now."

Emily had never seen Ben so furious in her life. He'd always been a merry and adventurous sort, ready for fun, slightly mischievous. Now his eyes were dark with anger, his straight, even brows nearly touching in a frown. If her jovial brother was this livid, she seriously doubted that she could ever go home to face her father—or even worse, her mother. No telling how much more out of hand things could get. With great effort she managed to keep her knees from buckling as she followed the others into the parlor.

"Please, sit down, everyone," Susannah said, taking a seat on a silver gray velvet settee.

Everyone else remained standing.

"Sit!" Dan ordered.

Emily felt she'd be safest next to Susannah, so while the others chose places of their own, she sank down next to her sister-in-law and casually assessed the open-beamed room with its homey mahogany furnishings and sapphire brocade drapes. She concentrated her attention on a porcelain figurine on the mantel, a fragile Staffordshire that was similar to one of her mother's.

Dan cleared his throat. "Ben. It's good to see you again. Have you been in Boston long?"

"No," he rasped, a scowl still tensing his boyish face. "Just got here. From Providence. With news of the *Gaspee* burning." His attention shifted from Dan to Rob, and his eyes narrowed. "And a few other things."

"I see," Dan said. "You've spoken with Mother."

"Oh yes." He glanced back to Dan. "But not till half the citizens of Providence and Pawtucket got to me first. Do you know—any of you—what it's like to ride into town and find your baby sister's name being bandied about like she's nothing but a . . . a . . . ?" He zeroed in on Rob again. "That not only has she run off with a pirate from the *Gaspee,* but a deserting coward, at that? Fire and brimstone!"

Susannah's look of sympathy and her comforting pat on the hand kept Emily from blurting out exactly what she was thinking at the moment. Before she had formulated a more appropriate reply, Dan interrupted.

"I'm afraid you have a slanted picture of the event, Ben," he said. "Robert MacKinnon has treated our little Emily with the utmost respect. Nothing untoward happened between them. Isn't that right, Rob?"

Rob nodded soberly. "Precisely. I wouldna' do anythin' intentionally to bring harm to the wee lass."

Emily fought against stinging tears.

"Mother, of course," Dan began, "is a loyalist by nature. She was wholly opposed to our harboring a fugitive—even one who had been kidnapped off the docks in England and impressed into service. Robert had gone to Bristol, quite unsuspectingly, to book passage to America after he and his father had saved for years to afford the fare. You know, Ben, that you'd have done as much as any of the rest of us to help Rob yourself. He's as much a victim of British tyranny as we are."

Ben waved a hand idly in confusion, and his countenance lightened a measure. "Of course," he admitted grudgingly. "You know I've aided other deserters now and again."

"And," Dan continued, "we could hardly expect Emily to do any less."

Ben leveled his gaze her way.

"If I hadn't acted when I did," Emily said in her own defense, "the authorities would have caught him for sure. I knew I could get him away safely."

"Maybe," Ben answered. "But did you have to do it so publicly, Emmy? And then stay with him? How do you expect any decent man to ever come courting after this? Any chance of finding you a husband of any worth now is out the window, like so much slop."

Her mouth dropped open.

Robert cleared his throat pointedly, drawing everyone's attention at once. "The young lass's plight is my responsibility. I'm quite willin' to marry her and rescue her from the waggin' tongues. In fact, I couldna' do less, after all she's done for me. Me prospects may be dim at the moment, I ken, but I still ha' me savin's. Perchance it may even be enough to buy a partnership in a dairy or a wheelwright shop. I'd work hard and take good care of her. Ye've me word."

Emily felt herself turn beet red with mortification. How very noble of the braggart to sacrifice himself for her—and all without so much as a "by your leave," let alone any word regarding love! For the first time in her life she regretted her proper upbringing. She wanted to give them all a good earful—and would, as soon as they finished dividing her up.

Ben turned thoughtfully to Dan. "What do you think? Can we trust him?"

Dan scratched his head in thought, then nodded. "Yes. He's a good lad, and raised in a devout Presbyterian home to boot. This just may be the perfect solution."

Emily could not believe they were discussing the matter right under her nose like a business proposition, that no one had so much as considered that she might wish to have some say regarding her whole future!

"In fact," she heard Dan say, "it would be my great joy to perform the ceremony. My first official act as an ordained minister."

Emily sprang to her feet and glared at the lot of them. "How dare you!"

Emily's cry resounded throughout the house. Her eyes flooded with tears, and she clenched trembling hands to herself. "I'm . . . I've never been so . . ." With a strangled sob she flung a scathing glance around the parlor, then whirled and ran out of the room. Her footsteps echoed all the way up the stairs.

Rob shifted uncomfortably in his seat and met stunned expressions all around the silent room. In his haste to protect sweet Emily's honor, he had not only offended the lass, but also humiliated her in front of her own family. The realization almost stopped his heart.

Ben cleared his throat. "What was that all about, I wonder? We were all simply deciding how to set things to rights again."

No one spoke for several moments.

Finally, Susannah Haynes rose. "Perhaps you thought you were acting in Emily's best interest, but in truth you were discussing the girl's possible marriage as if she weren't even present. For a woman, you know, marriage is the most important decision of her life—with the exception of her commitment to the Lord." She crossed to a window and stared outside.

"But these aren't ordinary circumstances," Ben argued. "Surely even a willful brat like Emily can see that."

Rob thrust out his chin. "I'll thank ye na' to speak aboot

Emily in that manner. She's been heaven's own gift in me hour of direst trouble."

"Is that right?" Ben said, coming to his feet menacingly. "Well, she's my sister, and I'll—"

Dan held up a hand. "Come on, you two. Please. Losing your temper does no one any good." He turned to Susannah. "Sweetheart, I gather we've made a mess of things. Would you please go to Emily? See if you can persuade her to come back down and talk."

Nodding, Susannah walked toward the hall. "I'll do what I can."

Rob got up. "Perhaps I should be the one to go. After all, 'twas I who brought trouble upon the lass. 'Tis only right I set the matter straight. Gi' me a few wee moments alone wi' her."

"Well, if you're sure," Dan said, giving Rob a nod. "Emily is our first concern here. If you think you can say something to calm her spirit enough to see reason, the rest of us would be most grateful."

Rob nodded several times and backed self-consciously out of the room. As he bounded up the stairs two at a time, he wracked his brain trying to come up with the proper thing to say. Why on earth should someone as lovely and wonderful as young Emily deign to marry a homeless fugitive with dim prospects, one whom God just happened to drop into her lap? He turned his eyes upward and breathed a prayer for wisdom as he touched the top landing.

Trying to decide which of the doors might lead to the right room, he stopped breathing and listened. Muffled crying came from behind one of them. Quietly, he went to it and entered, closing the door after himself.

Emily lay curled up on the bed, one hand over her mouth, trying in vain to stifle the deep sobs that shook her.

The sight touched Robby deeply, and he felt all the more a criminal for having caused her such pain. Without thinking, he sank down beside her and took hold of her shoulders, drawing her into his arms.

"Let me go!" she cried, attempting to pull away. "Go away."

"Shh. Forgive me, sweet Emily," he whispered, holding her tighter. "Please, forgive me. 'Twould be fit punishment for me to die rather than be the cause of your suffering." Feeling a burning behind his own eyes, he gently brushed her hair away from her damp face and kissed her cheeks. "Forgive me, I beg of ye."

Her crying subsided a little.

Rob attempted a brave smile as he pulled a handkerchief from his back pocket and dabbed at her face while she struggled for control. The sight of her dark lashes spiked with tears brought a renewed stab of guilt. "How could I ha' been so bold as to think a lass as wonderful as yourself, dear Emily, would consider one so unworthy as meself? Ye had every right to be revolted."

Emily moistened her lips and opened them as if to speak.

He touched his fingers to them. "Let me finish before me courage flees. Ye must think me a simple-minded fool, but just as certain as we're here in this room together at this minute, I ken for a surety that almighty God intended ye to be me wife."

Her mouth gaped in surprise.

"And I canna' imagine any other who'd suit me better."

Confused, her back stiffened, and she met his gaze. "What does that mean—I would suit you?"

Rob filled his lungs, gathering courage enough to utter the words she could by rights throw back in his face. Were she to do so, it would inflict unbearable pain, he knew. "It means that I love ye." The statement came out in a near whisper.

"I beg your pardon?" she said incredulously. Drawing back, she gave him a baffled look.

"I said that I love ye," he repeated with force. "And I do. More than me own life."

Emily did not speak. She did not even move. In fact, she didn't appear to breathe.

"I canna' expect ye to believe that," he said in a rush, "much less feel the same for me so soon. But if ye'll but give me the chance . . ."

A shy smile curved her mouth as fresh tears brimmed. "Did you mean what you said? Truly? You love me?"

Relieved beyond words to see her tremulous smile, Rob blinked, and a tear of his own rolled down his face. He nodded.

Emily slid her arms around his neck. "I-I love you, too, Robert MacKinnon. I love you, too."

Rob closed his eyes for a second against the unbelievable wonder of the words he had dared not even hope to hear. A warm rush surged through his veins, and his heart constricted. He let out a shaky breath and eased her away slightly. Then, cupping her face in his palms, he brushed the tips of his thumbs over her eyebrows and searched the depths of her green eyes. Ever so slowly he lowered his mouth and let his breath intermingle with hers as he kissed her eyelids, her cheeks, and at last her soft lips. Were she to refuse him now, he would most certainly die. He almost faltered as he voiced the question. "Then . . . will ye marry me, sweet Emily?" Breathless, he waited the eternity it took for her to answer.

"Are you sure you want such a notorious maiden for your wife?"

He crushed her to himself. "I'd ha' none other."

❧ ❧

Susannah's eyes wandered to the tall clock and sighed. It was only five minutes since the last time she'd checked. How was Emily? Her fingertips tapped anxiously against her gown.

"Well," Dan said after sipping his tea, "no doubt Sam Adams was gratified to know our cause is not dead after all."

Ben nodded absently. "What is taking them so long?" He set his drink aside and looked curiously at it, as if surprised to find the cup half-empty. He shot one more glance toward the staircase. "I'm going up to see what's keeping them."

Dan shrugged at Susannah.

Just then they heard the upstairs door open and footsteps descending.

Rob and Emily came into the room shyly holding hands,

their faces glowing. Emily turned a demure smile toward the Scot.

One look at them, and Susannah was quite sure young Rob had convinced Dan's sister to marry him. "You've decided, then?" she asked, crossing to the couple. "You're quite positive? You shouldn't take such a serious step if you've the least doubt about it."

"Of course they're sure," Ben said, jumping to his feet. "Aren't you?" He flicked a quick look their way, then apparently satisfied, turned to Dan. "Well, let's get on with it, Reverend. I still have some stops to make."

"Now, wait just one minute," Susannah said in her no-nonsense tone. "A wedding is far too momentous an occasion to be rushed into on the spur of a moment. We must all bathe and change into proper clothes. Daniel, go stoke up the fire for bath water, then go to the candle shop for a dozen tapers or so. And flowers. We must have flowers." She fluttered a finger toward Ben. "There are lovely ones in the field just behind the house. Go gather some. Lots of them. And Emily—" Her tone softened lovingly. "—I think my wedding gown would fit you nicely with a little tuck here and there."

Dim evening shadows played over the vines that entwined the banister as Dan fastened a small bunch of flowers to the last sconce.

Rob pushed one more wildflower into place on the stair rail, then stepped back to admire his handiwork.

"Not bad, I'd say." Dan grinned.

Ben finished filling the candleholders. "Women. Why they think all this gimcrackery is necessary for one measly hour is beyond me." His callow features clouded with a disgusted frown.

"Ah, but ye canna' say it doesna' look bonny," Rob said. "And it's more than worth all this and more, if it but brings wee Emily a single moment of happiness."

"I still think it's stupid." Ben scrunched his face. "A lot of fuss and bother over—"

A knock sounded on the door.

The three stopped and exchanged guarded looks.

"Rob," Dan whispered, controlling his mounting alarm, "go to the kitchen. It might be the authorities." Once the Scot had hurried away, Dan opened the door, then stepped back in shock. "Father! What a surprise!" he exclaimed, meeting the older man's weary countenance.

Handing Dan his hat, his father stepped inside and closed the door. "Emily . . . I've been following her tracks forever. Is she here?"

Dan nodded. "And she's safe."

A deep sigh of relief issued from his lungs, and he relaxed his stance a bit. "Good. I've been out of my mind with worry. I tried Caroline's, but they were only sure from the few things that were out of place that Emily had been there and gone."

"What about Ted and Alex?" Dan asked. "Are they still around Worcester?"

His father nodded. "Still combing the countryside, bound and determined to find the deserter and bring him to justice. Caroline mentioned the possibility that Emily might have come here, so I took the chance she was right."

"Well, good." Dan clapped him on the back. "Your timing couldn't be more perfect, Father. We're just about to have a wedding."

"A wedding?"

"Yes. My first official act. I'm about to unite my baby sister and Robert MacKinnon in marriage."

"You can't be serious!" His father's face went ashen, and he wobbled a little. He rubbed his temples between his thumb and forefinger. "This is all too much, Daniel. I cannot take it in. Our little Emily?"

Rob entered quietly and approached them. "'Twas the only way we could think of to protect Emily's honor, what wi' the past few days, and all."

Father raised a hand. "But, young man. I—"

"I love the lass, Mr. Haynes. I'll do me level best to take care of her and provide for her."

"And just how, exactly, do you plan to do that?" Father challenged. "If you don't mind my asking, of course. I'm concerned about my daughter's future here."

"Don't worry, Father," Dan insisted, putting a hand on his father's sleeve. "I know of a place just a few miles outside of the city. Susannah and I will be able to keep in close touch with them. Rob had been apprenticed to a wheelwright, and there's a man I know who might give him a position there. And Rob still has all the money from his passage," he added, seeing that his father still looked skeptical.

Father ran his fingers through his thinning hair and shook his head. He looked from one to the other, then searched Dan's face. "Have you talked to them both, Dan? Do they know what they're doing? Are you happy with it? I must know that, at least, before I can begin to give my blessing to this arrangement."

"Quite. I feel sure that Rob will work hard to make a good life for Emily. And they love each other. They really do. Isn't that what's most important when two people consider uniting their lives?"

He kneaded his jaw in thought for a moment before answering. "Well, then, much as I hate to admit it, this might just be for the best after all, considering the gossip that's running rampant. And you cannot begin to imagine the various forms of torture your mother has awaiting my little girl at home."

At the mention of his mother, Dan's anger flared—a poor way to begin his life as a minister, he knew. He sent a prayer heavenward for a more forgiving heart.

With an assessing glance around at all the decorations in evidence, Father arched his brows. "I had hoped one day to be a part of the plans for my youngest daughter's wedding, but it seems you have the matter well in hand and have done all the preparations without even consulting me or your mother. And you *will* have to answer for that, I'm sure."

Dan nodded slowly, then grinned, his anger no longer

ruling him. "It's not that we intentionally wanted to slight either of you, Father. But we have Emily's good name to consider above all else."

"Yes, I can see that," he answered as tired lines etched his face. "But if you can stand the thought of waiting just a while longer, I'd appreciate the chance to wash up. And I'd like to have a word with my daughter before you take her away from me."

❦ ❦

Emily tried to still her trembling hands as she stood before the mirror. The elegant satin wedding gown clung appealingly to her slight frame, the blue ribbon belt accenting her small waist and youthful curves. But just looking at herself was causing her knees to get weaker by the minute.

Susannah fastened a circle of flowers atop Emily's head, then stepped back to admire it. "I must admit, you look rather lovely, don't you think?"

"I think I'm going to be sick," Emily murmured grimly.

"Oh, now, let's have none of that," Susannah said with a comforting hug. "It's not the end of the world, certainly."

"But you don't understand," Emily whispered. "I don't . . ." She fluttered a hand in helplessness. "I don't know anything about . . . about . . ." Her cheeks flaming, she sank to the dressing table bench and covered her face with her hands.

"Oh, now," Susannah soothed. "Most brides feel exactly the same way, I assure you."

"Did you?" Emily asked, raising her head.

Susannah nodded. "It's really quite natural. But I knew that Dan loved me, as I did him, and that he was the man God had for me. And now when I look back, I see that my fears were completely unjustified."

The younger girl looked only slightly mollified.

"Emily, dear," Susannah said with a smile. "Robert truly loves you. What else really matters? Why, I'm certain that if the truth were known, he is at this very minute having a few misgivings of his own to sort through. After all, he's taking upon himself the responsibility of providing for someone other than himself . . . you and all your children to come. But when he takes one look at his beautiful bride, all of that will vanish like the dew of morning. You'll see."

A wistful smile curved Emily's lips. "I hope you're right. I do love him so."

"Then put aside your fears and leave things to God. This is your very special day, and we're going to make it one you shall always have to look back on with joy."

Blinking away tears of relief, Emily rose and hugged Susannah.

A rap sounded, and the door opened.

"Papa!" Emily gasped in alarm. Her mind began to reel. Had he come to take her home? Did she want to go? Would he let her marry Rob? That was what she wanted, wasn't it?

He smiled gently and crossed the room. "My, my. Just look at you. Haven't you grown up in the last few years." He opened his arms to her.

Emily plunged into them, laughing and crying at once. "Oh, Papa. I thought—"

"Shh." Comfortingly, he pressed her close and stroked her back. "I've been downstairs awhile, and I've had a chance to talk to Dan and Rob. They've allayed many of my fears. Even if I dislike having to part with my little girl so suddenly, I think you've all made a wise decision."

Easing away a little, Emily smiled up at him. "You do? I'm very happy, Papa. Robert has been wonderful to me. He's kind and brave. And don't you think he's about the handsomest man you've ever met?"

Papa chuckled. "Precisely. And I hope you feel as beautiful as you look, my darling." A fleeting sadness touched his eyes. "Sounds like my little tomboy has fallen in love."

Blushing, Emily smiled. "Someday when you really get to know him, you'll understand why. He's a fine Christian, too, and he loves me. We've both come through a fiery test unsinged. I know God will keep his hand on us."

"Even my baby's faith in God has strengthened through all

of this," Papa said with amazement. He raised her chin with his finger. "Be happy, sweetheart. No father could ask for more. Now," he said, offering an arm, "I believe everything is in readiness. Shall we go?"

Emily took a deep breath as he led her out onto the landing of the stairs. On their slow descent, her eyes took in the bowers of beautiful summer flowers and the amber glow of dozens of candles, and she blinked back tears of joy. There across the wide hall stood her brother Ben, satisfied and subdued, looking preoccupied and eager to be on his way. Beside him was the man of her dreams, straight and splendid in one of Dan's suits, his black hair slicked back and still damp. As he caught sight of her, his face and eyes displayed his love more eloquently than if he had spoken it aloud.

At the bottom of the staircase, Susannah pressed a nosegay of summer roses and daisies into Emily's hands, then walked gracefully to the front as Papa followed, escorting Emily to Rob's side.

Dan stepped forward and opened a black leather book. "Dearly beloved . . ."

Indescribable peace flowed through Emily's being as she heard them, and her trembling stopped. She smiled into Rob's eyes and waited breathlessly to repeat the vows that would make her Mrs. Robert MacKinnon for all time to come.

The summer breeze did little to ward off the heat and humidity as Dan and Ben rode along busy Marlborough Street on their way home from Cambridge. Dan nodded and waved a greeting to one of his church members as they passed the man's home. Then, taking out a handkerchief, he wiped his forehead.

"I sure hope you know what you're doing," Ben said. A look of worry added uncharacteristic maturity to his face. "Setting up the newlyweds so close to Boston. They're only a stone's throw from here." The sun glistened upon strands of his golden brown queue as he shook his head.

"Don't worry, runt," Dan answered. "I've known Sean Burns for years. He's a good man, one we can trust. And he'll look after them just like they're his own."

"That may be. But the man's a wheelwright with a shop right on Main Street. What if folks get too curious? Or what if Fontaine or Ted should venture in sometime with a broken wheel, and there stands our Emily?"

"I don't think that'll happen." Dan guided his horse closer to the edge of the street and took advantage of a long patch of shade from a stand of birch trees fronting a row of small brick houses. "In the first place, Emily is smarter than that, and in the second, Burns is as loyal to the cause as Sam Adams himself. Besides being a Scotsman, I doubt anyone would consider it odd for him to take in one of his *relatives* from the old country."

"Just the same," Ben said, "I'll feel better about it once MacKinnon gets to eating regular and fills out some—and that mustache he's working on comes in."

Dan tossed his younger brother a grin. "Relax, will you? The matter's well in hand."

"I guess. Especially if the rest of us keep Janie's lieutenants busy in town."

With a chuckle, Dan nodded in agreement.

Ben's tanned cheeks rounded with a grin as he nudged his tricornered hat back an inch and checked the position of the sun. "Listen, I'm cutting my own time pretty close. I still have some dispatches to deliver, so I'd best not come for supper. Mind giving Susannah my regrets? Old Sam is sure to be at Faneuil Hall by now, and Dr. Warren might be there too. I'd better head over that way."

"Sure, kid. We understand. It's been good to see that freckled mug of yours around for a little while." Dan grinned, then grew serious once more. "Oh, be sure to let Mr. Adams know that I've returned from college with a letter from President Witherspoon full of news from the middle Colonies."

"Will do. Can't say it was much of a surprise to me that you were sent here—even with the shortage of Presbyterian posts in Massachusetts."

"What do you mean?"

Ben cocked his head. "Well, Dr. Witherspoon seems as eager as anyone in Boston to rid ourselves of the British."

"Yes," Dan admitted. "But I haven't agreed to do anything except write a report on the local political happenings once a month, though I'm sure he hopes for more from me."

"So do I, Brother—if becoming ordained hasn't robbed you of your commitment to the cause, that is."

Dan looked straight at him. "We all do what we must. My first loyalty now lies in the ministry where God has called me. But whenever possible I'll seek some way to aid the patriots as well. I'll keep my eyes and ears open as usual."

A military wagon approached Dan's turnoff on Milk Street. The two rode steadily onward with practiced nonchalance.

"A pity things didn't work out for Susannah with her brother," Dan said. "She was hoping so much for a reconciliation. But it may be for the best."

"Hm?" Ben muttered. "How's that?"

"You know. The situation between the locals and the regiments quartered here is still quite strained."

"And it's bound to get worse. Could even pick up—especially if you preach freedom from lobsterback tyranny the way other local ministers do."

Knowing Ben was trying to corner him, Dan only smiled. "We'll see."

❦ ❦

In her bedchamber, Jane pushed a needle impatiently through the pillowcase she had been embroidering for her hope chest. Some good it would do her now. At this point, she only had a slightly better chance with Ted than she would have had if they'd never met. How would she ever be able to get him to see beyond her family and look at her the way she wanted him to?

Pressing her lips together, she held her work at arm's length and examined it before starting another flower petal. He still cared, of that she was certain. He had to. After all, he had said as much . . . and even more. She smiled at the remembrance of those few stolen moments in his room at the inn.

The front door squeaked open, and her mother's voice carried from below. "Edmond! You're back!"

Jane stabbed the needle into the material and tossed the stitchery onto her bed, then dashed downstairs.

"Have you news of Emily?" her mother continued.

"Yes," Papa began gravely. He stopped as Jane flew into his arms. He gave her a hug, then released her. "Janie-girl. You're here, too. Good." He looked from one to the other and breathed out slowly. "There's something I must tell you both."

"You've found her?" Jane whispered. She watched a look of apprehension settle over Mama's face and fought against her own feeling of dread. Papa's silence and unreadable expression did little to calm her fears.

Mama's eyes closed, and she pressed trembling fingers to her lips. "It's something dreadful, I just know it, or my baby would be with you."

"Now, don't immediately expect that what I have to say is bad," he said gently. Putting an arm around her shoulders, he turned her toward the parlor. "I just think you need to be sitting down before I explain it." Steering her toward her favorite chair, he motioned with his head for Jane to follow, and they all took seats. Papa took a deep breath as though trying to decide where to begin.

Jane and her mother exchanged foreboding looks.

"Well," Papa started. "I don't quite know how to tell you this, but there's no way around it. I've just gotten back from Boston."

"Boston?" Mother echoed. "But you said you were going to Caroline's."

"That's right. I did. I followed Emily all the way to Worcester. But by the time I arrived there, she had already been there and left."

"Well, what did Caroline say?" Mama asked. "Didn't she have any news?"

"Not really. Apparently, Emily had gone into her house while she and Philip were at church. She borrowed a clean dress and took a few staples from the pantry, then was gone before Caroline arrived home from service. Undoubtedly, Emily knew Carrie would be questioned by Lieutenants Harrington and Fontaine. So I continued my search and went on to Boston."

"Oh, Edmond," she moaned, casting an anxious glance at Jane before looking back to him. "I have a terrible feeling that this story is going to get worse."

Jane had the same conviction herself, but she was too afraid to ask more questions.

Papa's brows knitted together as though he were trying to find just the proper words to say. Then he looked at Mama. "They're . . . married." The word hung suspended for a second. "I attended the wedding myself."

"What?" Mother gasped. She paled, then turned an angry red as she closed her eyes and went rigid. "I simply cannot accept this. I won't. It's a cruel, thoughtless hoax."

"Emily? Our Emily? Married?" Jane whispered. "To the fugitive?"

"Yes. It's a long story. Suffice it to say that under the circumstances, we all agreed it was the best course to take."

"Under the circumstances?" Mama echoed woodenly. "He ruined her."

"No, no, nothing like that," Papa assured her. "But he was concerned about her reputation—"

"Reputation," Mama repeated in the same flat tone.

"—as was everyone else in the family," he finished. "After talking it out, the decision was made to salvage what remained of Emily's good name by eliminating all possible scandal. Dan performed the ceremony two nights ago."

Mama rose stiffly and turned away, clenching her fists. Her knuckles whitened. "Daniel wed them, did he? Need I wonder whose idea that was? *That woman,* again. She has been the ruination of this family, Edmond. I shall never, *never* forgive her as long as I live."

Papa stood and touched her shoulder, but she flinched and drew away. "I might have known you would jump immediately to the wrong conclusion, Sophia," he said quietly to her back. "It is beyond me why you must always place blame—whether justified or not. And believe me, in this instance there *is* no blame to be placed. Not on anyone. Susannah least of all."

"So *you* say," she sneered as she swung around and faced Papa. "All I know, Edmond Haynes, is that I am completely appalled at the things which have transpired under our roof during the past unbelievable week. Her first and *only* week here." She placed a hand against her cheek and shook her head. "The rest of you shouldn't surprise me either, considering the mess you've been stirring up in these Colonies—you and all your free-thinking radicals here in Rhode Island. Not one of you has any respect whatsoever for order and decency. And now this family, Edmond—*all* of us must pay the price for it. Our youngest daughter more than anyone. I cannot even take it in. Married! To a penniless fugitive, no less. A criminal." Her shoulders sagged in defeat.

Jane watched the exchange in mute horror. She had never seen her mother so upset.

Mama threw out her hands. "Well, what could I have expected? My own parents warned me not to marry any son of this cursed colony. But I would not listen. Oh, no. And now my poor baby is chained for life to some good-for-nothing Scottish whelp. And you simply let it happen."

A muscle twitched in Papa's jaw as he took her lashings in stony silence. When he spoke it was with supreme control. "Do you actually believe I would have stood by and allowed that wedding if I hadn't been completely convinced that Emily and Robert were very much in love?"

"In love!" Mama spat, arching her perfect eyebrows. "Those two *children?* Really, Edmond. You are so naive."

"Not so naive, my dear Sophia, as you are blind."

Mama did not appear to have heard the barb. "And you just handed your daughter over to a rascal. What a fool I married." Whirling around, she stormed out of the room and went upstairs, leaving a heavy disquietude in her wake.

Papa stood staring after her for several moments, then bolted up the steps.

Jane brushed her tongue over her dry lips. She couldn't have heard such vicious remarks coming from her mother's mouth. They weren't at all characteristic of her, not even considering the last inescapably trying week. It must have been too many things occurring at once. Surely that would account for her mother's sudden need to strike back.

But what would happen now? Would Mama insist on leaving the farm to escape the humiliation she'd suffer in front of everyone who knew her here in Pawtucket? Where on earth would she go? Philadelphia, perhaps, where she had family. And, of course, she'd probably expect Jane to go. They had both always longed to live there. Jane gave herself a mental shake. No, that couldn't be. It would present one more obstacle in her own plan. Ted was in Boston now.

With a sigh, she got up and went to the kitchen. Perhaps a pot of tea would help the situation. She'd take it upstairs and do what she could to help Papa smooth things over. Filling the kettle with fresh water, she put it over the coals.

Emily . . . married. Could that be possible? She was only a little girl. A child. Jane shook her head at the bizarre thought, then grew serious. *Her baby sister had wed before she had.* As if all the rest of the scandal the little imp had caused the family of late were not enough, now Jane would become a laughingstock on top of everything else. "Well, not for long," she muttered determinedly between her teeth. "Not for long!"

Angrily, she prepared the tray. When the water boiled, she poured some into the pot and carried the tea upstairs.

Her parents' door was ajar as she reached the top landing, and Jane could see them sitting on one side of the bed. She sighed with relief at the reassuring sight of Papa's arm around Mama and her head leaning on his shoulder. Mama looked up with moist eyes as Jane entered.

"I thought perhaps you might like some tea to drink." Jane set the tray down on the bedside table next to her mother.

Papa smiled. "Thank you, sweetheart. That was most thoughtful of you. You're becoming quite the young lady these days. So grown-up."

"Too grown-up, actually," Jane said grimly, twisting one of the bows on the pocket of her frock.

"Why, what do you mean?"

She grimaced. "Now that Emily—my baby sister—has married, I don't know how I'll ever face anyone ever again. People will think I'm an old maid, that no one has ever offered for me."

With a gentle smile, Papa shook his head. "I'm sure that won't be the case, Janie-girl. Why, you know there are several eligible bachelors in the area who would fall at your feet in an instant. We've mentioned more than one match to you already."

She pouted, retying the bow she had pulled loose. "Mama," she said suddenly, "I would like to go to Boston. I must. Please say I can. Please."

"No, dear, not this time," Papa said.

"But why?" she cried, plopping down on his other side. She leaned forward to see her mother. "Please, you both know how very much I've wanted this, how very hard I've been working to that end. Surely you above anyone wouldn't deny me this chance—especially now that Emily has made me the object of sport." She searched their faces pleadingly.

Mother's expression eased. "I think the tea must be finished brewing by now. I do hope it's strong. We can all use a cup, I'm sure. I'll pour." She filled three cups in the ensuing silence and handed them around. Taking her seat again, Mama sampled her portion. She swallowed and closed her eyes as though she held the first perfect cup of tea in years. Then she opened them and looked at Jane. "I'm afraid your young lieutenant has made it quite clear, my dear, that due to our *rebel* leanings he has no further use for this family. And considering that your sister, too, is now hunted by the authorities, perhaps you would best turn your attentions elsewhere."

"Yes," Papa added. "Even Widower Jones, with the huge apple orchard east of us, mentioned you just the other day. Remember? I told you about it."

Jane nearly choked. "The man has five children, Papa. Five! Is that what you'd wish for me—becoming a drudge to some other woman's brood? Don't I deserve a chance to make my own happiness in this life?" She sought her mother's face again. "Please, I beg of you, Mama. Let me go to Boston. I've hardly asked for anything in my whole life before now. I could stay with Dan—he'd be sure that no harm came to me. I'd have the chance to set things right again with Ted and Alex and get them to forgive us. I just know I could."

Papa regarded her evenly. "Jane, we have done absolutely

nothing wrong. I refuse to have any daughter of mine crawling on her knees to the likes of them."

"What does that mean?" Jane challenged. *"The likes of them?"*

"You know precisely what it means," he answered. "Redcoats. Uppity redcoated puppets of the Crown. Charming as Lieutenants Harrington and Fontaine appear to be, you must never forget that they represent the opposite of what this colony believes in. What *we* believe in."

Her face contorting with rising anger, Jane stood and trudged over to a chair by the window. She flopped onto it and stared outside wordlessly, her china cup cradled in her hands.

Mama got up and carried the pot over to her. "This tea is excellent, my dear. Have a little more to calm yourself." She filled Jane's cup, then met her daughter's eyes. "I think that for now—" She emphasized the last word slightly. "—we should all remain where we are until things die down. Perhaps in the future there will come a time when things are somewhat less *heated,* shall we say. In the meantime, Jane, perhaps you might give some serious thought to forgetting this awkward alliance."

Never, she thought to herself. *Never as long as I live. I'll find a way to come to you somehow, Ted, my darling. I promise.*

October arrived cool and crisp, painting a glorious mixture of red, yellow, and orange across Boston and the surrounding countryside.

Dan had just completed a pastoral call to a church member who was ill. As he came from the brick town house, a plume of gray smoke from burning autumn leaves next door swirled upward. The familiar smell blended with the pungent salty tang ever present in the air, and a wave of autumn nostalgia washed over him.

At the edge of the walk Dan gazed in the direction of the harbor, then took out his watch. Two-thirty. He had plenty of time to check in at the Bunch of Grapes Tavern for news of any possible arrests in the *Gaspee* incident.

The British government had wasted no time in responding to that recent offense against the Crown—especially since Rhode Islanders had attacked British vessels on two previous occasions as well, in '64 and '69. Royal officials knew that if Great Britain were to retain any respect at all in the tiny colony, this latest flagrant act of rebellion had to be punished. But so far there had not been a single arrest.

Nothing had come from the accusations made by Aaron Briggs, the disloyal indentured servant. His masters, John and Joseph Brown, had indeed been leaders in the affair, but the betrayal had been foiled. Signed affidavits from four upstanding citizens, whose word held far more weight than a mere slave's, had provided the Browns with an alibi.

Tucking the watch back inside his fob pocket, Dan headed toward the tavern. If nothing else, at least he might get to hear one of the new ballads relating the story.

As Dan turned onto Mackerel Street, he saw three redcoats enter the British Coffee House, an establishment that was frequented by Crown sympathizers and that was set across the road from the Bunch of Grapes. The sight of the officers reminded him of Ted and Alex, and he sighed with relief. At least Emily and Robert were safe in Cambridge. Ben had been correct in assuming that soldiers would be hesitant to venture far from their posts when they were already unpopular enough with the locals. And even though Dan would have enjoyed taking Susannah to visit Emily much more often, he suspected that Alex Fontaine was monitoring his and Susannah's movements.

Reaching the tavern, Dan grasped the iron latch and entered the smoke-filled room.

"Shiver me timbers," a familiar voice called out. "If it isn't Dan Haynes."

Dan's eyes made a swift adjustment to the dim interior, and he caught sight of Yancy Curtis's uneven grin. The loose-jointed sailor strode up and whacked him on the back.

"How ye been, mate? That little barnacle ye been expectin' attached itself to your hull yet?"

"No," Dan laughed, "we're still waiting. But we're both doing fine. Haven't seen *you* in a while, though. Not since that little episode in the summer."

"Aye. 'Twas time to weigh anchor for a bit, ye might say. Let things cool down."

"Daniel," a voice called from across the room.

Dan turned to see the prominent silversmith, Paul Revere, seated at a side table with the always impeccably dressed and distinguished John Hancock. The brawny Revere gave a nod, and a jovial smile spread across his plain, honest face. "Bring your friend over here. We'll buy you both a drink."

"Looks like it won't strain their coffers," Yancy quipped under his breath.

Dan chuckled as he and Yancy joined the two men.

Settling down after greetings and handshakes, Revere waved a square, work-worn hand toward a serving girl, who appeared at once with tall glasses of ale.

"What brings you by?" Revere asked, lifting his drink in a salute before sampling the contents.

"Just trying to keep up on the latest events," Dan confessed.

"Same here, friend," Hancock said, wrinkling his high forehead as he idly made intertwining rings of moisture on the table with his glass. "Same here."

"Not a single arrest so far," Revere said wryly, his wide-set eyes twinkling. "The king's illustrious Royal Commission has not succeeded in bringing even one responsible party to justice in the *Gaspee* affair."

"Governor Wanton of Rhode Island has issued a proclamation offering a reward, of course," Hancock supplied, "as you probably know." He relaxed his soft, manicured fingers on the tabletop. "But it doesn't appear as though he's pursuing the matter with any great zeal."

"Well, think of it!" Revere said. "The man is caught between the two factions—on the one hand, the 'Charter Privileges' of the colony of Rhode Island, and on the other, the responsibility to enforce British law. It was most fortunate indeed," he added with a grin, "that no one questioned to date has a single recollection whatsoever of the affair."

"And I, for one, want it to stay that way," Yancy piped up.

Dan nodded. "I would hate to think of the ramifications if the Crown took someone from Rhode Island all the way to Britain for trial, as they intend. Not only would the accused be tried in a hostile court, but it would be an absolute infringement on our basic rights granted by my colony's charter—and yours, too, I'll wager."

"And 'twould lead to more than a fire on a single vessel," Yancy added. "I think we'd be settin' a wee spark to the whole Royal Navy!"

"That would be a warming sight, indeed," Revere said, chuckling. "No wonder the commission has all but disbanded. I seriously doubt that any more will ever come from the incident."

"Still," Hancock added, "Paul and I have no doubt that Sam Adams will use that infringement on our liberty to the best advantage."

"Hear! Hear!" Revere smiled. "I can barely wait for another one of those public letters he's so fond of penning. His way with words convinces even the most doubtful heart to side with the Colonies against tyranny." He drained his glass and got up. "Well, gentlemen, I must attend to a few pressing matters at my shop. Feel free to walk along if you have a mind to, John." He winked at Dan. "I think there's a counting house on the way."

Hancock laughed at the jibe about his wealth and rose also. "It's been most pleasant talking with you again, Daniel. Yancy."

"I should be on my way also," Dan replied, standing.

Yancy joined the group as they walked outside for another round of handshaking and good wishes. Then Revere and Hancock took their leave.

"So, mate," Yancy said, cocking his head. "Whatever became of the young Scot I so carelessly aided, then turned coat on?"

"Actually, he, uh, married my youngest sister."

"Ye jest!"

"I'm afraid not. Seems little Emily took it upon herself to be his guiding light through the dark night. And a few more that followed."

Yancy's mouth gaped, and his sun-bleached eyebrows nearly touched the red curls on his forehead. He punched a freckled fist into his other palm. "Ye mean that sea rat—"

"No. Not at all." Dan fought to control a snicker. "The lad was a perfect gentleman the whole time. Our Emily couldn't have been in better hands. But as it all turned out, since the two of them had disappeared together for days, it was the only way we could salvage Emily's good name. I married them myself, in fact. But they'd grown so fond of each other by then, I could have done no less anyway."

Yancy shook his head in wonder. "What a tale. Guess I'd better not be settin' foot too near your mother for a spell, eh? It'd be sure to set off a nor'easter that would level the eastern seaboard!"

Dan laughed heartily. "You could be right. I've been steering clear of the farm myself."

"What about that other fair maiden we both know?" Yancy asked evenly. "She ever marry that lobsterback she was all but glued to last summer?"

"No, not yet. Ted didn't exactly endear himself to my family with that overbearing, offensive attitude he has toward the lot of us rebels. My parents have forbidden Jane to see him."

"Well, at least somethin' good came out of the entire mess, then. Perchance I'll sneak by there one of these days and see if I can spot her from afar, make sure she's farin' well."

"Why, Yance. If I didn't know better, I'd say you're starting to think about settling down yourself."

"What? Me, drop anchor? Not as long as I can still climb a mast!"

"And keep a few tavern maids happy, from what I hear," Dan said teasingly. Then he sobered. "Just remember, my friend, you *are* talking about my sister."

"Aye, mate. I'll not forget."

Dan checked the time, then slid his watch into his pocket. "Say, Yance, you're always welcome to come share supper with us when you're in town. We live just over on Milk Street. But it's only right to warn you that if you should happen by on a Sabbath, you could run into Ted and his other puppet friend. I believe you made a rather *sterling* impression on them when last they saw you."

"Nay, I'd best be off. But thanks."

Dan clapped him on the arm. "As you say. I just wish I didn't always have the feeling that the two lieutenants are keeping tabs on me, waiting to catch me at something."

Susannah ushered the stout young British infantryman to her front door.

He bowed graciously. "I shall accept your kind offer again one day, Mistress Haynes, if you're certain it would not be an imposition."

"Not at all, Corporal. I'm most glad to be of help." With a smile, she opened the door.

Ted was just coming up the walk, and he stepped sideways to allow the freckled, fair-skinned lad to pass.

The younger man put on his military hat and gave a sharp salute, then waved to Susannah before striding to the street.

Ted returned the salute, then cast a suspicious glance toward his sister. "What, pray tell, was all of that about?"

"Nothing, silly. Come in." Placing a hand to her aching back, Susannah made her way to the one chair in which she still found a measure of comfort. She sank cautiously to the cushion and spread her loose cobalt skirt about herself.

Ted took a seat on the settee. "I would still like to know what a strange British soldier was doing at my own sister's home in the middle of the afternoon."

Susannah smiled brightly. "Corporal James is not some stranger. I know him from the Presbyterian Church on Long Lane. The poor fellow asked if I would be kind enough to write a letter for him to his sweetheart back home, which I was more than happy to do."

"Well, it isn't necessary for the lad to impose on you. We have chaplains who take care of that sort of thing, you know."

"Oh, come on, Teddy," Susannah said, tilting her head. "I'm certain it would be difficult for a young man to have another gentleman be a party to his private thoughts, especially when they concern one's betrothed. Nevertheless, I *am* very pleased to see you. Might I offer you some hot cider?"

He whisked a glance over her swelling abdomen and colored slightly. "Thank you, no. I wouldn't want you to be waiting on me just now."

"How sweet, Teddy."

"How are you, Sue? Still taking care of yourself, and all that?"

She nodded. "Of course. Dan hardly allows me to lift a finger about the house. He even has one of the young girls from church come by one afternoon a week to help out. How is Alex?"

"Fine," he said with a chuckle. "Alex is dining with the general. Having Lord Hillsborough for a cousin has nearly as many disadvantages as it has benefits. Perhaps now that Hillsborough has resigned, Alex's own star will dim. But so far it hasn't." He looked around. "Dan is not at home, I take it?"

"He had an errand to run, actually."

"Hm." Flicking a piece of lint from his ivory military trousers, Ted raised his gaze. "By way of Faneuil Hall or the Bunch of Grapes, perchance?"

Susannah grimaced. "Today is the Sabbath, Teddy. Being a minister does entail a variety of duties. I'm quite sure that he'll be coming back soon, though. But what about you? Has Jane been able to spirit any further letters out to you of late?"

A smile spread across his face, and he visibly relaxed. "Oh yes. She is still determined to convince her parents to allow her to come to Boston. I must admit, I rather hope she succeeds. I'm not at my best during long separations. In any event, Jane feels that if Dan would intercede on her behalf and ask his parents for her assistance here during the remainder of your confinement, they might possibly relent."

"I'm aware of that. She has written Dan and asked as much. He's promised to request that she come in December, my last month. So do try to be patient," she pleaded. "Both of you."

He grinned. Resting an elbow on the armrest, he cupped his chin in his palm. "According to Alex, I have become tiresome and dreary these past four months. He says that not only have the local maidens been remarking about my lack of attention to them, but the rest of the gentry—what there is of it—is growing reluctant to extend further invitations to me. And I suppose they're quite right, the lot of them. I am as depressed as I am dull. If Jane does not come for the holiday season, I'll—"

The front door opened, and Dan came in. He hung his cloak on a peg in the hall, then straightened his brown tweed frock coat before entering the parlor. But his smile of greeting took on a forced quality when he noticed Ted sitting in the room.

"Oh, good, darling," Susannah breathed, "you've come. Our dinner is getting cold. And as you can see, we have a guest."

"Sorry I was detained, sweetheart." He crossed to her and kissed her cheek, then helped her up. They led the way to the homey dining room with heavy moldings as dark as its cherrywood furniture.

"Do please be seated," Susannah said. "I shall fetch another place setting." She hurried off.

"So, how've you been, Ted?" Dan asked, pulling out a chair and sitting at the head while Ted chose another spot along one side.

"Quite good, actually. Susannah's looking rather well."

"Yes, isn't she? Approaching motherhood has put a glow in her cheeks."

"And how about the rest of your family?" Ted asked casually. "Any word from Emily or anyone?"

In the adjoining kitchen, Susannah gasped. That sort of blatant question would have sounded more natural coming from Alex.

"Now, that would be a welcome relief, wouldn't it?" Dan answered smoothly. "The way we've all been worrying about the girl—"

Susannah could imagine her husband's expressionless countenance as he skirted the truth. Smiling, she took another "King's Rose" patterned bowl and more silverware from the open cupboard. But the ensuing silence gave evidence that her brother had been only slightly appeased. She carried the dishes to the table and returned to the kitchen.

"By the way, Dan," Ted remarked, "I just happened to

notice you a few days ago outside the Bunch of Grapes in a deep discussion with that silversmith, Revere, and John Hancock. I was sure Seaman Curtis was part of the group as well."

"Is that right?" Dan asked.

"Quite. And since you're my brother-in-law, I feel somewhat obligated to warn you that Admiral Montague is a member of the investigating commission, and he plans to get to the bottom of that *Gaspee* affair one way or another. He feels that your sailor friend is a definite suspect—as are the rest of those radicals who insist on stirring up constant trouble in Providence as well as Boston. It might behoove you to keep your distance from them. They are all being watched quite closely."

Susannah hurriedly poured the stew into a tureen and carried it to the table, hoping to get back in time to keep things from getting out of hand. She looked from one to the other as she ladled stew into their bowls and served them.

Dan steepled his fingers and leveled his gaze at Ted. "I don't imagine watching any of us should require *too* awfully much effort, do you? Since the Crown has sufficient *brave* soldiers quartered in Boston to watch practically every man, woman, and child in town."

Sinking to her seat, Susannah expelled an easy breath. "Dan, sweetheart," she asked, flashing her brightest smile, "would you please ask the blessing on our food and thank almighty God for bringing a beloved member of our family to our table as well?"

Susannah gazed through the kitchen window at December's dreary barrenness. The snow, which only days ago had turned the city into a magical fairyland, now lay in shrunken patches of dull gray-white, exposing fields of dead weeds and mud. Chill, damp air drifted through the edges of the sash. With a shiver she rolled a kitchen towel and pressed it along the sill, then continued with the task at hand, peeling potatoes.

"Hello, my love," Dan whispered from behind her, his warm breath feathering a few loose hairs below her chignon as he slid his arms around her. His hands came to rest on her swollen belly.

Suppressing a giggle, Susannah leaned back against him.

"How is our little one doing today?"

"As active as ever. I wouldn't be surprised if he should turn out to be a splendid drummer boy."

"Or a sweet little girl," Dan teased, nibbling her ear. "Lovely and soft as her mama. One who'd grace the fancy little clothes you've been working so hard on. I'd like that."

Susannah's mind flashed to the last pair of articles she'd finished and tucked in the bottom of the drawer, beneath the other baby things . . . a burial shroud for her and another for the babe, just in case. Her dearest friend, after all, had died in childbirth, and . . .

Forcing aside the chilling reality with as much of a smile as she could manage, Susannah turned in her husband's embrace and put her arms around him. The love radiating from his dark eyes filled her with warmth. "Oh, Dan, it's so very hard to wait, is it not?"

"Mm." He planted a kiss on her nose, then raised his head and searched her face. "What is really hard is watching you spending so much time on your feet lately."

"Then why not sit down and have a cup of tea with me?" she said. "I've been brewing some, and it's surely ready."

"Only if you allow me to wait on you, for a change." He steered her to a chair, then crossed to the sideboard.

Susannah lowered herself gingerly to the hard seat and watched as Dan returned with the teapot. Two cups also dangled from his fingers.

Removing one at a time, he set them at her place and his, then poured the tea. "I shouldn't have let you talk me out of it."

"Out of what?" she asked innocently. Absently she placed a hand over her abdomen and shifted in her seat.

"Hiring a servant girl for this evening."

"I'm quite sure that Jane will prove to be sufficient help once she settles in."

Dan looked skeptical. "If she doesn't, we'll pack her straight back to Pawtucket, since her primary reason for coming, supposedly, is to make things easier for you. But still, I should have hired a girl for tonight, at least. With Jane arriving, plus Emily and Rob—oh, and Yancy. I think I forgot to mention him. That's far too many people for you to be serving, don't you think?"

"Yancy will be here too? I thought he was off sailing the high seas again." She took a sip of tea and let its comforting flavor soothe her weariness.

"I ran into him earlier this morning. You know him; he's forever asking after Jane. When I mentioned that her coach would be coming in late this afternoon, right away he wanted to know if Ted would be meeting her. I guess Yance can't resist an element of danger. I informed him that Emily and Robert would be sneaking in for a quick visit with her before Ted even hears of her arrival, and Yance sort of invited himself."

"He is one of a kind," Susannah said.

"Well, I must take most of the blame. I extend some rather broad invitations to him whenever he crosses my path. He was bound to accept one sooner or later. In fact, he could be here any minute. He asked to go with me to meet the stage."

"Oh, Dan, I do hope all our juggling of people doesn't come crashing down upon us. Jane might easily have told Ted when she would arrive in Boston, you know."

Dan covered her hand as it lay between them on the table. "Don't be overly concerned about that. That sister of mine has been constantly writing to us about her dull, tiresome lot in life. I doubt she would have risked encountering my parents' wrath by trying to sneak another letter past them now that they've finally relented and permitted her to come."

"I do hope you're right."

A sprightly rap sounded on the door.

Dan grinned. "Sounds like trouble has arrived. Must be Yancy."

❧ ❧

Jane pulled her fur-lined pelisse closer about her as she peered out the window of the crowded coach. For the past several hours, the endless chatter of the other passengers and the incessant whining of the cranky toddler beside her had set her teeth on edge. The sight of the busy city at dusk as the carriage drew toward the lights could not have been more welcome. She sincerely hoped to find Ted waiting at the station. Surely either Dan or Susannah would have told him she was due to arrive. Straining to catch a glimpse of a red uniform in the fading light, she nibbled at her lip.

It had been nearly a month since his last letter, and from the tone of that one and the two preceding it, she knew her handsome lieutenant had become quite impatient with the whole affair. But he had to still care for her, he just had to. Especially after all the chances she had taken for him—including the betrayal of Emily, her own sister. But she never allowed herself to dwell on that discomforting thought. She dismissed it at once rather than let it spoil this long-awaited day.

Jane's glance rose to the top of the coach, and she smiled in anticipation. Her trunk held three ball gowns that she had succeeded in concealing from Mama's prying eyes. And now she was here. Boston, glorious Boston. She *would* accompany Ted to all the Christmas parties, no matter what. Dan would not be able to prevent it. And by all that was holy, Lieutenant Harrington *would* propose marriage this time, she'd see to that. Even though Ted and Dan didn't particularly get along, there had to be a way. If she had to, she would resort to running away as Emily had.

The coach slowed, and Jane's mind jerked to attention. On the platform a short distance away she could make out Dan standing beside a handcart. And someone was with him! Her heartbeat increased as she took a second look. The other man had on civilian clothes. That was against military regulations, wasn't it?

He removed his hat, and a shock of bright red hair reflected the light from a nearby lampstand.

Yancy Curtis! For the briefest second, Jane smiled. But then disappointment took the fore as she searched frantically for Ted. He wasn't there. Just that Yancy Curtis! Her face flushed with anger as he stepped forward and opened the door.

"'Tis an honor to welcome ye to our city, me fair Miss Haynes." With a satisfied smirk, the sailor offered an arm.

Peering down her nose at the uncouth ruffian as she accepted his assistance, Jane looked beyond him with supreme indifference and spotted her brother. "Oh, Dan," she said with every ounce of sweetness she could muster, "the two trunks on the end are mine."

Yancy's mouth twitched with obvious mirth as he and Dan hefted the heavy luggage down and into the cart. Then he dusted his hands and returned to her side, offering his elbow once more. She rolled her eyes and took it, and they joined

Dan, who had begun pushing the cart down the street toward his house.

"Say," Yancy said cheerfully, "'tis a pleasure to set me eyes again on your bright face. Many's the lonely night the very thought of your smile lightened me drab existence."

With concentrated effort, Jane pretended not to listen to any more of his ridiculous prattling, especially with Dan snickering in the background. Instead, she clenched her teeth and stared straight ahead. But she could not ignore the pleasantly solid feel of the sailor's muscled arm as they continued on.

Finally, they reached the tidy white house, and Susannah flung the door wide as they mounted the steps. She walked out to hug her. "Jane! We're so happy to have you here at last. Do come in. How was your trip?"

Even as Susannah's kiss warmed Jane's cheek, she hoped her sister-in-law did not think she'd taken pleasure in arriving on Yancy's arm. She sent a quick glare his way before smiling at Susannah. "It was a little tiring, but at least the coach didn't have any problems along the way."

"I've some tea on in the kitchen. Let me show you up to your room. You can freshen up and have a rest, and I'll bring you a tray." Leaving the men behind, she lumbered up the stairs. "Emily and Robert will be here for supper. They must wait until after dark, of course, and use extreme caution not to be discovered, but they're most anxious to see you again."

Stunned, Jane stopped halfway up the steps. "Doesn't that sort of skulking about make you feel just a little guilty, Susannah?"

Susannah paused and regarded her evenly, then continued on to the landing. Opening the guest room door, she motioned Jane inside. "I pray you'll be comfortable here."

Jane unfastened her thick cloak and draped it over the cheerful counterpane on the double bedstead. She turned, unwilling to be ignored. "Your own brother is an officer of the Crown. Yet you seem to think nothing of betraying him."

"One does what one must. I happen to think family concerns take precedence over unjust governmental rules."

"*Ted* is your family," Jane countered. "And speaking of him, I was hoping *he* would be at the station to meet me, instead of that dreadful Yancy Curtis."

Susannah smiled as if Jane had just said something quite humorous. "Dan and I thought it would be wiser to allow Emily and Rob a chance to visit with you before we informed Ted of your arrival."

Jane could barely control the irritation in her voice. "So once again, my feelings and desires are trodden underfoot for our poor little Emily. Will it never stop? She's the one who made her bed. It's high time for her to lie in it."

Susannah gently squeezed Jane's hand and drew a steadying breath. "I understand how you feel, dear. Truly I do. It's difficult to be separated from someone special. But it meant so very much to Dan for all of you to have one night together. On the morrow you'll have more than enough opportunity to be with Teddy. You'll see. Won't you try to enjoy this evening for Dan's sake? We're both so delighted you've been able to come."

"I don't even know that Robert MacKinnon—the criminal," she pouted.

"Well, then, you shall be pleased to find out what a kind and considerate young man he is. He, too, is part of the family now, and he and your sister get along superbly. They're really quite sweet together. If only you'll give them a chance, you'll discover that for yourself."

Jane shook her head. There was no arguing with Susannah's logic. But still, the truth of Susannah's words didn't dull the sharp edge of her disappointment. Jane only wanted to be alone with her misery. "Would you mind terribly if I lie down for a while?" she asked. "The trip was quite tiring. Almost as unbearable as having to put up with that scoundrel, Yancy."

Susannah smiled. "Not at all. I'll bring you a cup of tea, and then you shall have a nice rest. But just remember, Jane, Yancy is Dan's friend, and he's an invited guest who'll be having supper with us this evening. For Dan, won't you please—"

"Oh, all right. I'll try," Jane grumbled. As the door closed behind Susannah, Jane sank down onto the bed and looked at her surroundings. The fire in the small hearth lent a warm glow to freshly painted apricot walls and crisp white woodwork. The carved mahogany bedstead and matching armoire were fine pieces of workmanship, as were the dressing table and bench. The rust shade of the curtains was repeated in the multihued counterpane. Mother would have approved—if it hadn't been Susannah's home.

When a few minutes later her sister-in-law brought hot tea, Jane found it delightfully soothing. She sipped it slowly while Susannah took her leave. After swallowing the last bit of it, she lay down and closed her eyes.

❧ ❧

Sometime later Jane awakened to a bustle downstairs. *Emily and Robert must have arrived!* she thought, jumping up with more excitement than she cared to acknowledge. She splashed cool water on her face and gave a quick touchup with the hairbrush, then went down to see the imp of a sister who dared marry before *she* had.

Entering the parlor, Jane spied Emily at once and flew to hug her, then stepped back and took a closer look. Emily had on an indigo muslin dress with hand-crocheted lace trim, and her blonde hair was brushed smoothly back and tied at the nape of her neck with a black velvet ribbon. "Well, I guess I can't call you squirt any longer. You look all grown-up."

The younger girl blushed daintily under Jane's scrutiny. "I'm wearing my hair different now. That's probably it."

"Aye," Yancy quipped from beside them both. "If 'twas asked of me, I'd have to say it makes ye look older. Older than Jane, in fact." He chuckled as Jane raised her chin and glared at him.

"Well, come and say hello to your new brother-in-law." Her younger sister grabbed her hand and tugged her across the room, where Rob sat in an overstuffed chair. "Robby, love," she said with a smile. "You remember my sister, Jane."

"Aye, that I do." He rose, bowing slightly. "'Tis a pleasure."

Noticing grudgingly that the young Scot looked quite attractive now that his lean frame had filled out a bit, Jane nodded and took a seat nearby as Emily reclined against the arm of Rob's chair. She hated to admit it, but her little sister and her husband did look sweet together, just as Susannah had said. She fought against a twinge of jealousy. "So, where are you two living?"

"Not far from here, in Cambridge," Emily answered. "We've got a charming little room of our own over the shop of the wheelwright Robert works for."

Susannah and Dan entered at that moment, and Jane wondered why they looked concerned. But as she thought about it, she realized that up until Emily so freely imparted the information about where she lived, neither Dan nor Susannah had mentioned a word of it, not even in letters to Papa and Mama. Had they suspected her all along?

"Supper is ready now," Susannah announced, "if everyone would please come to the dining room."

Jane allowed Yancy Curtis to escort her to the table and draw out a chair for her. As he took the seat next to her, she purposely ignored the way the wavering candlelight glowed against the seaman's rowdy curls. For her brother's benefit she would be polite and pleasant. While the others took their places, she concentrated on the pretty arrangement of dried flowers that adorned the center of the lace-covered table. Then, following her brother's lead, she closed her eyes and bowed her head.

Dan asked the blessing over the meal, then passed the meat platter to her. It brought back memories of their last family gathering, when Yancy had taken the liberty of serving her plate in a deliberate attempt to taunt Ted. But it was the heathen's cocky grin she detested most, she decided as his arm *accidentally* brushed hers for the third time. Men like Seaman Curtis weren't interested in finding love at all. They merely enjoyed the sport and challenge of snagging some unsuspecting female and taking whatever liberties they could. Ted was not at all like that, thank heaven. He truly loved her. She was sure . . . almost.

"Aye, there was I," Rob was saying as his voice broke into her musings, "face-to-face wi' that giant of a red man. His long hair was plaited in two sections and tied wi' strips of leather. I dinna' ken whether to run or stand me ground, such was his girth as I stumbled upon him."

Jane found his brogue easy to listen to and noted the twinkle in his clear blue eyes as he told of his first encounter with an Indian. She watched Emily lean forward, completely enthralled with her husband's words as she gazed upon his angular face.

Jane had to admit that he looked appealing. He wore a neat homespun shirt of tan cambric with his brown wool breeches, and he now had a full mustache, the same rich black as his hair.

"His arms were like the mainmast of a great ship," Rob continued. "I'd no doubt he could snap me in two wi' little effort. Then I spotted the mean knife he'd strapped at his belt, so I stepped verrrry carefully around him . . . as he snored on the floor b'fore Mr. Burns's hearth. Seems the fellow thinks not a whit of walkin' into any odd hoose in the middle of the night to sleep off a jug of hard cider." He sat back and popped a crust of bread into his mouth as everyone laughed.

"I remember just the Indian you're talking about," Dan said. "Came across him myself now and again. His tribe cast him out, some years ago. He's a great worker, though. Can swing an axe for hours at a time—but only if he's of a mind to. He's just as likely to up and disappear whenever the notion takes him."

Rob chuckled, then turned his attention to Susannah. "Emily and I do appreciate this fine meal. 'Tis a delight to share time wi' the family again." He nudged Emily.

"Oh yes," she added, blotting her lips on her napkin.

"Robby and I . . . we, um, have something to tell all of you." She cast a look downward at the tablecloth.

Jane saw a huge grin spread across Rob's face before she looked at her sister again.

The younger girl blushed and slipped a gaze shyly in Susannah's direction. "It seems that your new baby will have a little playmate, come summer."

"Aye, a wee bairn," Rob supplied.

"You're with child?" Susannah cried, squeezing Emily's hand. "Oh, how simply marvelous. I couldn't be happier."

Jane sat in stunned shock, the rush of congratulations and good wishes rumbling around her as if from a great distance. She managed to force a smile. "I'm very happy for you both," she said as she rose. "Congratulations, Emily, Rob. Now, if you'll all excuse me, I'm afraid I haven't quite recovered from the headache that began during my trip. I need to go upstairs and lie down for a while."

"Of course," Susannah said, her tone filled with concern. "Is there something I might get you?"

"No, nothing, thank you. I'll be fine. So nice seeing you again, Emily. Perhaps we'll find another chance soon." Exiting the room, she started up the staircase. With each step she became more morose as the laughter and good-natured teasing at the table continued with hardly a break. No one really cared about her. *Dear little Emily* was a new bride. *Dear little Emily* was going to be a mother. How very sweet for the dear child. But did anyone care that Jane had been relegated to the odious position of spinster? No. That was far too much to expect.

Going into her room, she flopped down on the bed. No one cared about her or her happiness. It was painfully obvious that she would have to find fulfillment for herself, with no help from her family at all.

At least Ted still cared. If only he had been here this evening, she would have known the joy of being loved, of being special to someone, too. She had waited all these interminable months to come to him. Why should she be forced to endure one more day of it?

She shouldn't. *She wouldn't.* After all, he lived just over on Water Street, a short walk from here. He had mentioned the fact in his letters and described its location. No doubt she'd be able to find the address without a problem. All she had to do was sneak out without anyone noticing . . . perhaps once they all retired for the night. She knew Ted would be thrilled to see her again—no matter how late the hour.

The tinkle of crystal and silverware drifted upward from the dining room as Jane stood at the top of the stairs with her arms folded. She could not quite hear the conversation taking place around the table except for the occasional prominent name. *Hillsborough. Admiral Montague. Adams.* They were involved in yet one more endless political discussion. As another round of laughter erupted, she tapped a foot impatiently upon the hall rug. She could have been to Ted's and back by now if she had gone the moment the idea had dawned in her mind.

She paced the landing, then stopped. Everyone in the family was so wrapped up in eating and visiting that no one would even notice if she were to steal out right now. Pressing her lips together in defiance, Jane retrieved her warm cloak from the bedchamber and threw it about her shoulders. Then she tiptoed down the steps and slipped out the back door, her fur muff clutched in one hand.

The bitterness of the December night chilled her face immediately. She flipped the thick hood over her hair and hunched deeper into the warmth of its fur lining as she struck out determinedly.

The night was still as she hurried across several adjoining backyards, then came out once again on the street. She avoided patches of old snow and gave wide berth to the glow streaming through the windows of various houses along the way.

A dog barked.

Startled, Jane flattened herself against a wall until the animal quieted again. This time when she moved, she made no sound. Her eyes darted up and down the street to make certain no one was about, then she dashed to the other side and on to the corner, thankful for the broad spaces of darkness between the street lamps.

Keeping her distance from the dim circles of lamplight, she finally reached Water Street. Not sure in which direction she should go, she headed toward the harbor, where after determining the house numbers of several dwellings, she smiled. Ted's residence was just a few doors farther.

Reaching a narrow, two-story brick building that bore his address, she heard high-pitched laughter and spied a soldier at the corner draping himself around a wench. Jane took a few calming breaths and knocked. Even though the house was shrouded in darkness, she hoped Ted would still be up. He had to be. After a moment she raised her hand to try once more.

Just then the door opened, and a plump woman clad in a warm flannel night robe and sleeping cap appeared. Barely stifling a yawn, she lifted a lamp and studied Jane coolly.

"Please forgive my intrusion," Jane said tentatively, "but I must see Lieutenant Harrington."

A graying brow rose high and vanished beneath the woman's ruffled cap. "'Tis not a decent hour to be callin', young lady."

"I cannot help the time, Madam," Jane insisted. "But I have an important matter which I must discuss with him at once. It's most urgent."

The sides of the woman's thin mouth sloped downward with disapproval. "Even if he was in—which he's not—I wouldn' be lettin' the likes of you in to visit him this time of night. Now, be off with you."

Jane's shoulders slumped. "He's not here?"

"Not for at least another hour or so."

Effecting an extremely polite smile, Jane flared her eyes in innocence. "Then, might I please wait inside for him? In the parlor? I have an urgent message. One he'll be most upset about if he doesn't receive it."

"Tell me, then. I'll pass it on to him."

"It's a family matter. Very personal. Now please, I cannot be expected to stand out here in the cold and the dark all that time."

The woman inhaled slowly, then shook her head in disbelief. With a shrug she turned away, leaving the door open as if she knew Jane would follow. "As long as you don't expect me to keep you company." After ushering Jane to the unlit parlor, she gave a disdainful glance over her pudgy shoulder and went back upstairs.

In the diminishing glow of the woman's lantern, Jane grabbed a lighting stick and touched it to the last glowing embers in the fireplace. She lit a table lamp, then chose a seat, taking in at once the plain furnishings and serviceable draperies of the room, the faded rug that covered the center of the plank floor. She snuggled into her cape and sat back to wait.

Finally, after what seemed hours, she heard laughter and the tromping of approaching boots. The door swung open, admitting Ted and Alex on a burst of cold night air.

Jane sprang to her feet.

A shocked look registered on Ted's flushed face as he saw her. His crooked grin widened as he removed his hat. "Well, if you aren't a most pleasant sight to behold. My beautiful Jane."

"Hello, Ted. Alex," she whispered, a flush rising in her cheeks.

In three strides Ted crossed to her, the uneven smile on his mouth still in place as he pulled her into his arms and claimed her lips.

Jane felt dizzy, but whether it was from the undisguised passion of his kiss or the ale on his breath she wasn't altogether certain. Wobbling slightly as he released her, she purposely avoided looking at his friend.

Alex leaned around Ted with a smirk she could not miss. "I say," he said teasingly, a spark in his mischievous eyes. "What brings you here on your own, and at such an unearthly hour? I should think you'd be concerned about endangering your reputation and virtue."

"*My* virtue?" Jane snapped coldly. "Certainly *I* am not the one at risk. *I* haven't been out in the taverns tippling half the night."

"Of course," Alex said, as if remembering his manners that instant. "I beg your pardon." The sincerity in his tone soothed Jane's ire as he unfastened his military cape and draped it over his arm. "I shall depart and leave you two alone." With a click of his heels and a bow of his aristocratic head, he made good his word and went upstairs.

As his footsteps grew faint and then stilled with the closing of a door on the second floor, Ted smiled broadly and reached for Jane.

She took a step to the side, effectively eluding his grasp.

Sobering, he drew himself together. A muscle flinched in his jaw as he met her eyes. "Sorry. For a brief moment I actually presumed you'd left that hotbed of traitors you call your family and come to me . . . at long last, I might add."

Jane crossed her arms and looked up at him. "I've written you numerous times about the difficulties I've had in trying to come here, Ted. Far more often, in fact, than you have sent any word my way. I checked with my friend, Belinda, in Pawtucket, a hundred times. Every week when we were at church—and other occasions as well, when I made countless excuses to go and visit her. But there was rarely ever a note from you."

"Which was due to the fact that I had about given up on you," Ted finished flatly. "After all, I've done my part. I secured a transfer to this pest hole, just as you asked. And what have I received for my effort? Nothing but betrayals and insults."

"Oh, Ted." She blinked back a tear of frustration. "It's not my fault. Can't you see that?"

He stared for a moment, then took off his cape and laid it on the settee near the archway.

She watched his movements. It seemed forever since she had gazed upon that compelling squared face of his, with its firm mouth, its hard-set jaw. She had missed it so. She missed being locked in his embrace, hearing his whispered words of love. When his blue eyes found hers once more, she felt liquid heat course through her. "I've been disappointed by my family, too. You'll never know how I begged Dan to inform you that I'd be arriving today. But no, he would not deign to do even that one small favor for me."

"And my own sister is still against me," he added, his expression easing as if in understanding. "She did what she had to do, when there was no one around to help her, and I no longer hold that against her. But she'll never understand how much *I* needed some important mission of my own after our parents died."

"I know exactly how you feel. But you can trust me, Ted. Truly. Haven't I already proved that?" She reached for his hand.

He evaded her touch. "Still, if you cared as much as you say you do, you'd have come months ago, as you promised. All this time I've been waiting for you, you've no doubt been entertaining yourself with others who would beg for your favors. That sailor, Curtis, perhaps."

Jane's lips constricted at the mention of Yancy's name. "You're wrong. Very wrong. I've been completely faithful to you. I have."

"Does it really matter, I wonder?" He raised his hand and idly studied his fingertips. "I fear I can't align myself with you, Jane. Both of your brothers consort with anarchists. Susannah, my own dear sister, has yet to admit her part in hiding Emily and that *Gaspee* deserter. And you, my love, make your bed with that same enemy. What future could there be for us?"

Jane bristled at his remarks. She straightened her spine. "Oh, for heaven's sake, Ted. None of this is my choosing. You know for a certainty that I do not agree in any way with their politics. Do you imagine for one moment that I am pleased they'd rather entertain my bratty sister and her fugitive husband this evening than you?"

Ted gripped her upper arms. "The two of them are at the house right now? Emily and MacKinnon?"

A rush of guilt flamed Jane's face at her blunder, but she fought to quench it. After all, no one cared a whit about her or her feelings. Hadn't that been evident for months? She nodded, slowly meeting Ted's eyes.

One side of his mouth curved upward in triumph. He pulled her close, wrapping his arms around her. "For how long?"

"Until early tomorrow morning," she whispered. A heaviness settled in her chest, nearly suffocating her. This was her family. Her own family. How would they feel if they knew what she had just done? With the greatest effort she gathered the ragged edges of her conscience together, shielding herself from the awful, sickening truth. She couldn't let herself think about it.

Releasing Jane, Ted looked toward the staircase and took a step in that direction. "I must awaken Alex at once."

"No!" Jane's heart thudded hard. She grabbed his arm, holding him back. "Please. Wait until I've gotten home again and have had time to get to bed. They mustn't know I was the one who told you. I don't know what they'd do to me. Most certainly they would never allow me to see you again."

"Quite likely you're right," he admitted.

"And there's something else."

"What might that be?"

"It cannot be either you or Alex who comes to make the arrest."

"How can you ask that?" He gritted his teeth in frustration. "I want that satisfaction more than anything. It will be quite a feather in my cap."

"Please, Ted," she begged. "Please. Since last summer my family has ruined everything for us. Don't let them spoil the holiday season as well." Rising to tiptoe, she slid her arms around his neck, loving the smooth, rich weave of his uniform beneath her fingers. "I've brought all my ball gowns," she said with a hopeful smile. "You don't have to be concerned about my being from Rhode Island. You can introduce me as the niece of Landon Somerwell, my mother's cousin from Philadelphia. He's widely known in the Colonies and the most loyal Tory ever."

As Ted's gaze darkened in speculation, she could tell he was weakening. She pressed on. "I've waited so long, Ted. Please, do this for me, won't you?"

Releasing a pent-up breath, Ted drew her close and rocked her in his arms. The pounding of his heart matched hers as he eased her away and searched her face, then kissed her gently, tenderly. "I must admit I've missed you, my love. I was counting the days and hours until you would chance coming to me. It seemed the moment would never come."

Jane smiled into his eyes.

"Well, at least I shall escort you home," he began as he reached for his cape.

"Oh, no. You mustn't," Jane said pleadingly. "What if someone should see us together? I'll go alone."

Ted eyed her for a moment, then frowned. "I can't say I relish the idea of sending you off by yourself at this unholy hour. Nevertheless, I see the prudence of your decision." He steered her toward the door and opened it reluctantly. "But use every caution as you go. There are always common soldiers patrolling the night streets, and they're not always of the highest caliber in character. I would have no harm befall you. I shall give you one hour."

Nodding, she reached to touch her lips to his once more, then pulled her cloak securely about herself and put her hands into the fur muff as she stepped out into the biting cold.

As the door closed behind her, an exhilarating lightheadedness made Jane want to dance all the way home—dance as she would soon be doing, night after night . . . with Ted. Quelling the impulse, she hastily made her way out onto the street and headed for Dan's.

Before Jane had gone even the length of the block, the fine hairs on her neck rose with alarm. Clutching her wrap tighter, she strained her ears and quickened her pace.

Footsteps sounded behind her and also picked up speed.

Icy shards of fear pricked at her heart, and she started to run.

Too late!

A strong, hard hand clamped on her arm and jerked her to a stop. The motion spun her around. Falling against her assailant, Jane opened her mouth to scream, but the cry never surfaced. Her voice failed her as she met the livid face of her pursuer.

"My, such a touchin' scene, back yonder," Yancy Curtis grated with sarcasm, his breath rising on moist white mist.

Jane wrenched free with a huff and straightened her cape, then took a step backward. "You frightened me nearly to death. What are you doing skulking around in the night, anyway?"

"What am *I* doin'?" he challenged, his thick reddish brows arcing on his forehead. An incredulous chuckle rumbled from deep within his chest.

She could not meet his eyes. She pursed her lips haughtily and tried to step past him.

Yancy blocked her escape. "I happened to see ye sneakin' out, before, so I excused meself. Thought I'd find out what little errand made ye absent yourself from your lovin' family."

"I needed some air," she lied. "I thought a walk might help my headache."

"Aye. Especially when ye ended up in a nest of lobsterbacks, eh?" His eyes glittered dangerously in the darkness, and his gaze never wavered.

Jane knew her face was red from shame, but she was not about to let this infuriating sailor get too smug. "I only wanted to let Ted know I had arrived," she said smoothly, "since Dan hadn't the courtesy to attend to the matter for me."

"Aye. And ye had to pass information about a certain young couple him and his cohorts have more than a casual interest in. Don't try to tell me ye never mentioned who all was present at supper. Voices carry clear as a ship's bell on the night air. 'I'll give you one hour,' the rascal said. I heard every word."

"You didn't," she whispered. She had really done it this time. Dan would send her back to the farm on the morning stage once Yancy related the whole escapade to him. And then he'd never allow her to set foot in his house again. Ever. She swallowed a huge lump in her throat and fought back a growing feeling of nausea.

The seaman kept staring at her without expression, as if considering a variety of methods by which she might be properly humiliated and punished. "Never in me life have I known a lass like ye, Jane Haynes," he said, his tone rife with both threat and disdain. "You've got a wonderful family who've provided a good home, a sheltered life. And love. Yet you've no qualms whatsoever about causin' them trouble. 'Tis hard to fathom."

Jane studied her feet. She would have bolted, only she knew she'd not get far before he grabbed her again . . . and did heaven only knew what horrible things to her.

"What ye need most is to be horsewhipped," Yancy continued. "'Tis a sure bet ye were spared a few well-deserved licks when ye were a lass. If 'twas up to me, I'd set it to rights now."

With a sniff, Jane switched her attention down the deserted street. She would never let him know she felt the least remorse. But, certain that Yancy Curtis was capable of carrying out his threats—and even worse, no doubt—she shivered. She had to clench her teeth tightly to keep them from chattering. Jane wished desperately that Ted would come even now to her rescue. But she had only left his place moments ago.

"'Tis lucky for ye that Susannah's time is upon her and she has need of ye right now," Yancy said, the wavering light from a street lamp on the next corner matching a deadly gleam in his eyes. "So I'll save your little behind this once. I'll not tell on ye."

"What?" Jane gasped, lifting her eyes to his. Had she heard right? He would *help* her?

A devilish smile played across his mouth. "For a wee price, ye might say. One that'll be named later. Count on it."

Her mouth gaped in shock.

Without warning, Yancy grabbed her and kissed her hard. Then, just as abruptly, he let her go.

Jane barely kept her balance. In reflex, she placed her fingertips to her tingling lips. "You . . . you . . ."

"That's the first payment, shall we say," he mocked. "I'll collect the rest later. Ye'd better waste no time in slitherin' back to bed."

Fighting hysteria, Jane turned and ran the rest of the way without once looking back. What horrid plans were churning about in that rascal's twisted brain? What would he do to her? And when?

Yancy leaned against the side of Dan's darkened house and turned up his collar against the icy breeze blowing in from the ocean. After tugging his knitted cap more firmly over his ears, he rubbed his hands together and blew into them, then stomped his feet to get the circulation going. He looked up toward Jane's room, wondering how long it would take the little *turncoat* to undress and get to bed, as Dan and the rest of the family must have done during her absence. How in the name of providence that girl could justify the willful betrayal of someone in her own family, he had no idea.

He frowned and shook his head. He'd give her a few more minutes, but no more. It was getting colder all the time.

When he was positive his toes were freezing solid, he checked the narrow street for passing redcoats, then strode to the back door and pounded on it. If Dan had fallen asleep, it would take him a while to hear it. He thumped on the door again.

Finally, a dim light gleamed from the kitchen window, then drew nearer. The door opened. Still tucking his sleep shirt into his breeches, Dan blinked in surprise. "Yance. What are you doing back here?"

"I've some urgent news, mate."

"Well, come in. You look half-frozen." Turning, he set down the oil lamp, then crossed to the hearth and stoked up the fire.

Yancy entered and shut the door. He followed Dan over to the fireplace and held his hands out to warm them.

"What's amiss?" Dan asked as he poured the dregs of left-over evening tea into a mug and gave it to him.

Yancy gulped a mouthful of the strong, hot brew, then held the cup between his stiff hands. "Just overheard somethin' passin' the British Coffee House on me way to the Bunch of Grapes. Thought ye'd better know, so I came right over here."

Apprehension furrowed Dan's brow as understanding dawned. "Don't tell me."

"Aye. Someone was sayin' he spotted a young couple of Emily and Robby's description go into your place a bit ago."

"And I'd imagine they'll waste no time getting here. Come on." Rushing past Yancy, Dan bounded up the stairs and knocked on a bedchamber door. "Emily! Rob! Wake up, you two."

Instantly, the Scot was at the door. "What is it?"

"Soldiers. Someone informed on you."

Inside the room, Emily gave a little cry and jumped up.

"Get dressed and out of here, now!" Dan continued. "But don't light a lamp. We don't want it to appear as though anything unusual is going on."

Emily scrambled around in the dimness, gathering whatever she could and stuffing it into a satchel.

"Dunna' worry, love," Rob said, already throwing off his nightshirt and grabbing his clothes. "I'll na' be lettin' harm come to ye. I promise."

Susannah stepped out into the hallway holding a candle as she looked from one grim face to the next. "Dan, whatever is the matter?"

Jane, too, opened her door and came out. She rubbed sleep from her eyes and feigned a yawn.

Yancy gritted his teeth at her theatrics as she met his eyes, then innocently shifted her attention to Dan.

"Help Emily, will you?" Dan told his sister. "She and Rob must get out of here, and fast. We've only got a few minutes before the soldiers come." Shoving his hands into his pockets, he paced the hall nervously.

Without protest, Jane rushed into the room and gave Emily a comforting hug. Then she helped the younger girl fasten the buttons on her dress and shoes. In an unguarded moment, a look of guilt crossed her face, but when she caught Yancy's eye, it vanished as quickly as it had come.

The pair threw on their coats, and Rob grabbed the bag they had brought with them. With a quick look about the room, he and Emily started out into the hall.

"Listen," Dan instructed as they all clattered downstairs. "Head across the field behind the house and keep going over Summer Street and through the next field. Pond Street's just beyond that. It'll take you to the main road. You'll know when your horse's hooves hit the cobblestones. Once you get that far, you should have a good lead."

Rob nodded and squeezed Emily's hand.

She gave him a brave smile, but her chin quivered as she blinked a few times.

"Say, mates," Yancy said lightly. "Maybe if I hang around, the lobsterbacks'll decide 'twas me and Jane the informant saw before." He swung a knowing glance her way, and she immediately looked elsewhere.

"That might work," Dan said. He turned to Rob. "Soon as it's safe, I'll come to Cambridge and let you and Emily know just how good this little ruse of ours was."

"Nay, not Cambridge," Yancy warned. "I wouldn't be stoppin' there. Now that the word's out, I'd keep goin'. Go on up to Salem, Robby, and catch a coastal packet outta there headin' south. It'll stop here in Boston, but nobody will expect to find ye on a ship comin' *into* port—will they, Jane?" he added with a stern glare her way. "Then ye can take it on down to Philadelphia," he continued. "'Tis a good size city, and easy to lose yerself in."

"Yes, that's ideal," Dan said. "From there take the stage to Princeton. We've some wonderful friends there at the coaching inn. Jasper and Esther Lyons. They'll look after you until we can make other arrangements. Let's see. You'll need funds to tide you over. We'll pool all we can find." He shot a meaningful glance around, and everyone dispersed.

Within moments, Rob's coat pockets were stuffed with the money gathered from various rooms and purses.

Yancy watched as Susannah wrapped a thick knitted scarf about Emily's neck, then kissed her and Rob. "May God be with you," she whispered.

Everyone else followed suit, bidding hasty good-byes in a round of hugs and kisses.

"Godspeed," Dan said. "I'll go to your place in a few days and pack the rest of your things. We'll see about sending them on to you as soon as possible."

"Thank ye—all." With a grateful smile, Rob tugged Emily's hand and pulled her after him as he hurried out to the horse shed.

Susannah moved to Dan's side at the door and slid an arm around his waist as they watched the two family members ride away into the cold night.

Drawing her close, Dan gave her a reassuring smile. "The Lord will look after them. We can trust naught but him now." He closed the door and turned, then held out a hand and clasped Yancy's. "Thank you, friend. We owe you."

"'Twas me pleasure. The least I could do for a mate. Hope I got here quick enough." He slanted a glance at Jane.

Uncharacteristically silent, she lowered her eyelids and transferred her attention to the other side of the room.

"We'd deem it an honor if you'd stay the night, Yance," Dan said. "You can have the room Emily and Rob were in."

"Might be best," Yancy admitted. With a wink, he snagged Jane's hand and headed up the steps, holding tightly enough to keep her from tugging free. He smiled ruthlessly at her.

"Perhaps," Susannah suggested as she and Dan also started slowly upstairs, "we should first make sure that Emily and Rob have left nothing incriminating behind that the authorities might find."

"Good thinking, sweetheart." Dan kissed her cheek.

As the others went into the recently vacated bedroom, Susannah held her candle high to enable them to conduct the search.

Yancy bumped purposely into Jane and chuckled at her look of irritation as they hurriedly picked up any items that appeared out of place. He ignored her scathing glares and even answered them with a triumphant grin, knowing she dared not say a word. He barely contained his jubilation and, in fact, was beginning to enjoy the heady feeling of having her in his power for a change.

Suddenly Susannah latched onto Yancy's arm and held tight.

"I think it is time."

Dan looked up from over near the bedside table. "Time? For what, sweetheart?"

She took several deep breaths, then relaxed. "I've been having small pains all evening. I thought at first that it was just all the excitement, and I didn't want to be a bother. Now I'm quite certain that our baby is about to be born."

"No!" he gasped. Dan made a dash for the door, stopped and looked back, then came to her. "Let me help you back to bed, love." He gestured to Yancy. "Light the lamps, would you? And, Jane, put some water on to boil."

"Why?" she asked.

"How should *I* know?" he grated. "It's what the midwives always say, isn't it? I suppose we'll soon find out. Get going."

Dan took Susannah to their own room, helped her into bed, then covered her gently and bent to kiss her cheek.

She moaned and clutched at her abdomen. Her face twisted in pain and apprehension. "Dan, I-I hope it all goes . . . well."

He took her fingers in his and let her clench hard until the discomfort subsided, then gave her hand a nervous pat of encouragement before releasing it. "We'll be praying for you, my love." Uneasily, he looked at Yancy and motioned with his head toward the door. "I think I'd better run out for the midwife."

"I'll go, if ye'd like."

"Better not. We still need you here, remember, in case the soldiers come. I'll try not to be too long." He left the room at once.

Yancy stood gawking at the empty doorway. "But—what should I be doin'?" he called out after Dan, who was already halfway down the steps.

Without stopping or turning, Dan shrugged. "Just be at hand, in case Susannah needs anything." Grabbing his greatcoat from a peg by the door, he pulled it on and left.

Yancy swallowed as the front door slammed shut. His pulse picked up, and he glanced nervously toward the bed. What sort of things would a birthing woman need, anyway? He'd never been within fifty miles of one—at least one that he knew about. Perspiring, he tugged at the neck of his shirt.

Susannah moaned again and doubled over.

He swallowed. Where was Jane? Being a woman, she'd probably have some idea what to do—or not do. Clearing his throat, he crossed to Susannah and patted her shoulder until she relaxed once more. "I, er, better go see if Jane needs help. Will ye be all right?"

She nodded and gave a wan smile.

Scuttling backward like a crab, Yancy bumped into the doorjamb. He felt heat rise up from his neck to envelop his entire face, and he flashed an awkward, embarrassed grin. Then he wasted no more time, exiting the room and leaping down the stairs three at a time. At the bottom, he stopped until his pulse rate had returned to near normal, then he drew a deep breath and swaggered out into the kitchen.

Across the room in her indigo velvet dressing gown, Jane had one kettle of water already heating over the fire and was lighting some extra lamps as he entered. She looked up with a guarded expression.

"I'll, er, fetch some more water," he blurted, seizing an empty bucket.

A loud pounding sounded from the front door.

The soldiers! He had completely forgotten about them!

Jane's eyes widened, and a sheen of tears glistened in her eyes as her face paled in terror. "What should we do?" Unconsciously, she moved nearer, as if seeking reassurance . . . or absolution. Yancy wasn't quite sure which.

Even with the realization that Jane must now be regretting her thoughtless betrayal, Yancy had no time to delight in the way she stood willingly within his reach at last. He shook his head in frustration. Who could begin to imagine the extent of the trouble the minx had brought upon their heads this night? Filling his lungs with a hearty breath, he winked at her and grinned. "Company. Shall we see to them?" He offered an elbow.

She looked up uncertainly; her lips parted.

With a huff, he put an arm around her shoulders. "Come on, me darlin'. You've got another performance to put on." He drew her reluctantly along to the front door, then stopped and nudged her into a strained smile.

"Open up, in the name of the king!"

Yancy let go of Jane, who skulked back apprehensively against the wall and chewed her lip. He pressed the latch and opened the door with a flourish. As he did so, a bitter December gust stirred the hall draperies. "Ah, gents. So nice of ye to be stoppin' by this eve."

"Step aside," the officer in charge commanded. He and his detachment tramped in, cold air floating around them as they stood in a cluster of red and black. The last man shoved the door closed.

"I must say," Yancy said, manufacturing a look of purest relief. "This is a service I'd never guess the king's men performed. 'Tis a wonder. A real wonder. But we need all the assistance we can get, so you're most welcome, indeed."

"Cut the jabbering," the officer in charge demanded with a scowl. "Where are they?"

"Right this way, gents. Upstairs." Yancy motioned with an arm in the direction of the steps and led the way. "How long have ye *been* in the midwife business? I'm real glad your trainin' included birthin' babes."

As a body, the men halted. The last one bumped unceremoniously into the soldier in front of him.

"What did you say?" the officer asked, stunned.

"Aye." Yancy grinned. "We're about to become uncles. All of us."

The faint blush of dawn tinted the eastern sky as Dan paced the plank floor of the kitchen. Lines of worry creased his brow. He raked his disheveled chestnut hair with one hand. "Why is it taking so long?"

Jane filled a platter with scrambled eggs and biscuits and set it on the table near Yancy, too weary to bother avoiding his eyes or to keep up the games of challenge he seemed intent upon continuing. "Why don't the two of you try to eat a bit?" she asked, turning to her brother as she sank onto a chair. She, too, was exhausted and concerned after their all-night vigil.

From the second floor another of Susannah's cries shattered the quiet.

Dan tensed and looked in the direction of the stairs. "I don't think I could swallow." He took a few steps forward and leaned against the doorjamb with his hands in his pockets. Light from the hearth played across his back. "Childbirth brought her to me. Will it now take her away?"

Rising at the end of the table, Yancy crossed to his friend and touched his shoulder. "Don't think that, mate."

Jane looked from one tired face to the other. Both men had stubble on their jaws; she probably also looked the worse for wear in her wrinkled dressing gown, her unbound hair streaming about her shoulders. She got up and took her brother's hand, tugging him gently to the bare wood table.

With surprisingly little pressure, she nudged him down onto a seat.

"Perhaps some coffee," he murmured.

"And a biscuit," she added, trying to sound motherly. "At least that much. You'll need strength to hold that new little babe when it comes, won't you?"

Dan forced a smile as she filled a mug. He took a sip but didn't appear to taste it, and he merely stared unseeing at the platter of food.

Jane took her seat and sent Yancy a concerned look, hoping he might come up with some words of wisdom or comfort for Dan, but he only shrugged and shook his head. As much as could be expected from a no-account seaman, she decided, watching grudgingly as he took a huge helping and began wolfing it down. A thought came to her and she voiced it, hoping to encourage Dan. "I don't think this is unusual. I once heard that a birthing can take as much as two or three days. Especially when it's a first child."

With a withering glance, Dan propped both elbows on the table and rested his head in his hands. His eyes closed.

Jane knew her brother was praying again. Even though it seemed as though his pleas were falling on deaf ears, she knew it gave Dan a measure of comfort. And who knew, perhaps God *would* help her brother. After all, Dan had sacrificed a lot for the Almighty. He had given up a prosperous future to go into the ministry.

The clock in the dining room chimed seven times, and Jane sighed with frustration. This had been an interminable night. Even the coming daylight seemed to have brought little change.

A few more minutes passed, the heavy silence punctuated by low cries from upstairs and the audible ticking of the tall clock in the next room.

Yancy cleared his throat. "I think I might go down to the wharf and see when the next packet'll be comin' down from Salem." Gulping the last of his coffee, he pushed his cup away and unfolded his lanky frame with an ostentatious stretch.

Dan stared blankly at the sailor.

"If I sign on," he explained with a meaningful glance toward Jane, "I can see that Robby and Emily have safe passage to Philadelphia, and then on to Princeton."

Ignoring the redhead's not-so-subtle warning against any further betrayal on her part, Jane stood and walked to the hearth for the coffee pot.

"I'd almost forgotten about them," Dan said in disbelief as Jane refilled his mug and then hers. "I've been so wrapped up in things here." He gripped Yancy's forearm. "I'd be most beholden to you if you would see to those two for me. Someone needs to look after them, especially now."

A grin of undisguised relief softened the sailor's weather-beaten face. "Then I'd best be on me way." Getting up, he strode to the door, took his coat from a peg, and pulled it on.

Jane knew that it was not possible for a coastal packet with her sister and Rob to arrive before tomorrow, even if they had found one sailing on the next tide. And Yancy knew it, too. He just wanted a convenient excuse to get away from the tension of this household. It wasn't as if the rascal were of any actual help. Ted, on the other hand, would be most welcome. For a brief moment, she desperately wished she could feel the strength of his arms about her, her cheek resting against his firm chest. A smile tugged at her lips, and she let out a wistful sigh.

For the unbearable minutes it took for Yancy to leave, Jane struggled to keep her composure. But as the back door finally closed behind him, she turned to her brother. "Dan, don't you think someone should inform Ted that his sister is even now on her childbed?"

Dan looked as though the thought had not yet occurred to him.

Hurried steps prevented his answer as Mistress Brown, the midwife, came downstairs and into the kitchen.

"Is it—has the baby—," Dan sputtered as he came to his feet.

The heavyset woman shook her head, stirring a frizz of

salt-and-pepper hair beneath her ruffled mobcap. "'Twill be a while, yet. Your wife's not quite ready." After blotting her round nose on a handkerchief, she replaced the cloth in the pocket of her white linen apron.

"What? Are you mad?" Dan asked incredulously. "Of course she's ready."

The midwife's plump hand pushed him back down. "Her *body* ain't yet ready to have the babe." Without ceremony, she took the seat Yancy had recently vacated and lifted her brows at Jane. "Girl, bring me a clean plate, would ya'? May as well have some victuals while I have the chance."

Dan released a ragged sigh. "How on earth can Susannah bear much more of this? It's been so long already."

Mistress Brown's head bobbed back and forth. "She's havin' a hard time of it, but then birthin's a hard business. Somethin' a man don't think about till it's right upon him." Taking the plate Jane had brought from the cupboard, she scooped a generous portion of food onto it. "With you bein' a preacher, 'tis likely your prayers will get listened to quicker than most, I'd say," she said, voicing aloud what Jane had thought earlier. "Pour me some coffee, girl."

Closing her eyes in exasperation, Jane obeyed. *Do this, girl, do that,* she echoed silently. *I might as well be a bondservant myself.* Grudgingly, she filled a pewter mug.

Plate in hand, the midwife started for the stairs.

With a huff, Jane followed with the coffee, catching up with the woman in the hall. She noted absently the few curious stains dotting the apron that protected the midwife's gray and white striped work dress. The round face leaned nearer. "Be sure and keep him busy down here," she whispered, motioning with her head toward Dan. "From the look of things, I fear 'tis goin' to get a whole lot worse before—"

"Before things get better?" Jane finished with dread.

The white cap bobbed with her nod. "I just pray they *will.* I truly do."

An icy feeling clutched at Jane's heart as she watched the woman ascend.

"What did she say to you?" Dan asked, coming up behind her.

Startled, Jane jumped. A flush spread over her face as she searched for an answer that wouldn't alarm him. "She, um, said she always feels better about a birthing when she knows someone is praying all the while." She swallowed.

Dan kneaded his temples and peered up toward the second floor. "Does she actually think I'd be doing anything else?" With a sigh, he sagged against the banister. "I've recited every prayer I ever learned, every Bible verse I know with a promise. Over and over I've come back to the same one."

As the midwife opened the door upstairs, a pitiful moan drifted out. Quickly, Jane took Dan's arm and led him back to the kitchen. "Which one is that?"

"Huh?" He glanced back upstairs.

"The promise," she coaxed gently. "Which one was it?"

"Oh. The one from Romans, about all things working together for good to them that love God."

Jane nodded, attempting a smile, but it vanished as Dan gripped her shoulders.

"Oh, Jane," he said desperately. "If it comes to losing Susannah, I'm afraid I won't be able to accept that. There's no way in the world that her death could bring any 'good.' No way at all." Releasing her, he turned away in despair.

A sudden chill shook Jane's body. Dan had always been so strong, especially in matters regarding his faith. To see him doubting now added to her own fear. Reaching for his hand, she drew him to the table and made him sit down, then took the chair opposite him. "We just have to wait this out. And trust the Lord," she added for good measure. "Everything will be fine, Dan."

His sable eyes revealed his inner torture as he raised them to her. "Will it? Julia, Susannah's best friend, died in childbirth shortly before Susannah arrived in the Colonies. And Duncan Grant's wife succumbed to childbed fever just last month. Do you have any idea how I feel right now?"

Jane fell silent as he continued.

"I feel like Jesus did on that last night in the Garden of Gethsemane, when he said, 'My soul is exceeding sorrowful, even unto death.' On that lonely night, too, Jesus pleaded that if it were possible, God would let that cup pass from him—that deadly cup of crucifixion."

Drawing a fortifying breath, Jane nodded. "I know, Dan." She grappled to find the words to ease his pain. She had never been one to listen to the tiresome dronings of a Sabbath sermon. But she knew her brother did and that he needed whatever comfort God almighty would bestow on him about now. "Still, Jesus did find the strength to face what God had destined for him," she continued. "And you above all else should know the importance of that sacrifice." Her own words surprised her.

"Yes, you're right." Dan sighed wearily and slumped forward, dropping his head on his propped hands for a moment before looking up again. "But you're forgetting one very important factor. His death meant life for every believer. Tell me, Jane. Who could possibly benefit if Susannah were to be taken today? What measure of good would come from that?"

Jane searched frantically for an answer. If only she had paid attention at church once in a while, or even at home when Papa read aloud from the Holy Scriptures. Surely there would have been some wise saying she could pass on now when her brother needed it most. She reached across the table and squeezed his arm. "Dan, tomorrow, when you hold your precious babe in your arms, you'll forget all this. I promise."

He stared at her with glazed eyes.

Oh, how she wished it were all over with, that she could put it all out of her mind and get on with living! Certainly Ted, if he were here, would be able to help her forget this unpleasantness.

Her eyes widened. Dan hadn't answered her before. "Dan," she said quietly, "Ted should be notified, don't you think? After all, Susannah is his only sister, his only family. And despite this family's rebellious behavior, he still loves her very much. He shouldn't be shut out at such a crucial time. Why don't I go outside and pay some lad to fetch him?"

Dan raised his head, haggard lines shadowing his face. "Of course. Ted. By all means, he should be summoned."

Hope surged within her, and Jane did not try to hold back her smile. "I'll go and compose a note for him at once." It was entirely possible that Ted had already heard about Susannah from the soldiers' report the evening past. But even if he had, he might have thought the entire matter just a ruse. He most certainly would have come if he had believed Susannah was giving birth. Taking a sheet of paper from the secretary in the parlor, she sat down and dipped the quill into the inkwell.

A few hours later, Jane stood at the big kitchen hearth inhaling the delicious aroma of chicken and sage as she stirred a boiling pot. Mrs. Brown, the midwife, was probably right. A little broth *might* help Susannah in the difficult process of giving birth. Jane flinched as another moan carried down from the bedroom. Perhaps her sister-in-law would also be glad to know that Ted would be arriving—if and when he ever did.

Jane wondered if Ted had received the hasty note she had written earlier that morning, or if his duties had gotten in the way of his coming. Surely he would respond to the news that his sister had been in labor since last night and still had not given birth. But just to be certain, Jane had told him that she had another piece of news to give him upon his arrival as well.

She swept a critical glance over the jade morning gown she had changed into after putting the soup pot on to boil. There hadn't been time to dress her copper hair properly, but she hoped it looked becoming, brushed and shining and pulled back off her face with a matching satin ribbon.

A knock sounded from the front door.

Jane's heart skipped a beat, and she almost dropped the long wooden spoon. She tore at the bow of her apron with fumbling fingers, then flung it aside. Taking a deep breath, she rushed into the hall. Near the stairs she barely glanced at a half-asleep Dan slumped on one of the steps midway up.

He started to rise.

"Don't bother," she said breezily. "I'll answer it." If only that bossy Mistress Brown would permit Dan to visit his wife for a short while, she'd have some precious moments of privacy with Ted. She lifted the latch and opened the door.

"Jane," Ted said with a polite, preoccupied smile. He stepped inside and hung his cloak on one of the hall pegs. "How is she?" he asked, looking right past her.

"I'll get to that in short order," Jane said. "Come with me to the kitchen." Seeing his perplexed expression, she lowered her voice to a whisper. "I must explain about last night. It wasn't my fault." Turning, she took a step away.

Ted stopped her with a hand on her shoulder. "Not now, Jane," he said with a sigh. "How is Sue? Your note said she'd been in labor since last night?"

Jane nodded.

"But that's over twelve hours. What has the midwife said? Do you think she'd let me see my sister?"

From the deep concern on Ted's face, Jane realized she would have to allay some of his worries before he'd even begin to listen to her tale about the previous evening. She attempted a smile. "According to Mistress Brown, it's not terribly unusual for a first child to be a long time coming."

"But still, many hours have passed since her labor started, and she wasn't even due for another two weeks. Do you think there might be something wrong?" His blue eyes gazed intently at her.

Jane shrugged a shoulder. "No, not really. No one has said anything yet to indicate there's a problem. Come along and sit down for a while." Taking his hand, she began leading him toward the kitchen.

Ted stopped abruptly and jerked his hand away. "How can you be sure of that? Susannah's own best friend, Julia, died in childbirth a few years ago, and she was a strong, healthy young woman. Full of zest and life. How can we be certain the same thing won't happen to Sue?"

Above them a pitiful cry of pain came from the bedroom.

From the middle of the staircase, Dan came to his feet. Ted sprinted past Dan and up the stairs, and Dan, as if shocked into motion, followed instantly.

"Wait!" Jane called. "You can't—" But her words had no effect whatsoever. She threw up her hands and went after them. When she reached the bedroom, the two men were already at the bedside.

Mistress Brown harrumphed and rose from the rocking chair, wagging a plump finger. "You men must get out of here this instant."

Paying the woman no mind, Ted knelt beside his sister. He took Susannah's limp hand in his, then brushed a lock of damp tawny hair from her flushed face. "How are you doing, Sis?" he asked gently.

Jane could not see the loving smile he bestowed on her sister-in-law, but she could imagine it, and for the flicker of a second she felt jealous.

"Teddy." Susannah tried to smile. "You've come, too."

He nodded. "As soon as I heard. How could I not?"

Her eyes glistened with tears. "I'm glad. I wanted to tell you I love you, that I've always loved you, no matter what." She paused. "I'm afraid, Teddy. I can't help thinking of Julia—" Her breath caught, cutting off her whispered words. She closed her lashes, gripping her swollen abdomen with her free hand.

Pacing the side of the room like a palace guard, Mistress Brown shook her head. "A birthin's not a place for menfolk," she groused. "I'll let you stay, but only for a minute. Ya' hear?"

No one responded.

She raised her close-set blue eyes to Jane. "That broth ready yet, girl? I need to get Mistress Haynes to try takin' a bit, get some of her strength back."

In silent irritation, Jane gritted her teeth and left the room as the midwife settled her bulk once more into the rocker.

❧ ❧

Ted sighed, barely aware of Jane's departing footsteps or of Dan standing just behind him. He studied his sister's flushed face with rising alarm, fighting back his own fear. She had never looked so dreadful. Even their mother, after her worst attack of asthma, had never looked this bad. Susannah's normally glossy hair lay dull and matted, her eyes glazed in pain. The ribbon at the throat of her sweat-stained cotton nightdress had been loosened, and he wondered idly if it helped make her more comfortable.

He ran a finger over her cheek and smiled. "I love you, too," he said. Never before had he voiced the words to her. But at the moment, he had a strong conviction that it was important for him to say it, and for her to know. How could he have wasted so many months, so many years, allowing some inane laws of Parliament to separate them, when she was all the family left to him on this earth, and now her life was dangling in the balance. "The two of us must stick together, little sis. I know that now. I'm sorry I've been so—"

Susannah smiled weakly and pressed a fevered hand to his cheek as she looked beyond him to Dan, then back.

Ted knew it had pleased her to hear how he felt. He opened his mouth to say more, but was stopped as his sister drew in a hiss of breath through her teeth.

Her face contorted as she gripped his hand and squeezed. He knew she was using all her strength, but Ted felt alarmingly little pressure. Dark misgivings coursed through him. It was torture to watch her trying to endure the pain, and when she moaned again, his throat clogged with unshed tears. A tear trickled from the corner of her clenched eyelids, and her groaning rose to a cry that wrenched his heart. Finally, as the pain subsided, she relaxed, panting.

A nudge on his shoulder caused Ted to look up.

"'Tis best ya' go now, and leave us to our work," Mistress Brown said. "She's in no shape to be entertainin' anybody."

With a nod, Ted rubbed the bridge of his nose and stood, shifting from one foot to the other as he gazed at Susannah's now quiet form. He glanced at Dan, who wedged past and leaned down to kiss her forehead.

"Now, shoo," the midwife said. "Be off with ya'."

Wishing he could take upon himself the remainder of his sister's torment, Ted exchanged a guarded glance with Dan, whose furrowed and shadowed face bore grim evidence that he was shaken to the core. Ted put an arm around his brother-in-law's shoulder and turned him toward the door, only then catching sight of Jane, who stood mutely watching from the doorway.

"Jane, girl," Mistress Brown called. "Don't you leave. I might need your help."

Ted saw Jane's silent desperation in the look she sent his way. The bowl of broth shook in her hands as she obediently crossed the room to the bed.

The midwife put a pudgy arm under Susannah's upper body and raised her to a sitting position, then gave the pillows a few fluffing punches. "Come on, now, missy," she coaxed in a motherly voice, "we've some nice broth for you. It'll give you strength." She glanced up at Ted and Dan. "Pray that she keeps it down."

Ted exhaled sharply. From Jane's white face, he could tell she had never before been exposed to the frightening realities of childbirth, and he found himself wishing somehow that she might have been spared. But at the moment Susannah needed all the help available. With a last glance toward his weakened sister, he led Dan downstairs.

Taking a seat in the parlor, Ted sank back against the sofa just as another whimper filtered down from the bedroom.

Dan sat on a hard chair by the window and slumped forward, staring at nothing.

A second cry followed quickly, then became a scream.

Ted jumped up. "I need to *do* something!" he said, feeling more completely useless than ever before in his life. "I'll go get some wood."

"It's already been done," Dan said flatly.

"Water, then. I'll get water."

"Done."

"Logs. Have all your logs been split and stacked?"

Dan looked up, as if cheered suddenly by the very thought. "No. What do you say we get at them, Brother?"

"Capital idea . . . Brother." With a sound slap on Dan's back, he grinned, and they headed for the back door.

Outside, light tentative snowflakes danced on the wind and swirled softly downward. Ted and Dan removed their outer coats and worked in their shirt-sleeves, taking turns splitting or stacking wood.

Even through the noise they made, there was no mistaking the piercing screams from upstairs that came with increasing regularity.

Ted cleared his throat. "I used to stay outdoors quite a lot when I was a lad," he blurted out, trying desperately not to think about what his sister had been enduring for all these hours.

"That right?" Dan swung the maul, slamming it into a wedge. A log fell away in two halves. He picked one of them up and quartered it.

"Yes. Our mum was always sick. Sue was the one who stayed with her. I offered to, but they wouldn't allow it. It was for the best, I suppose. I had no idea what to do, and it made me feel trapped to be in that dark, stuffy room too long." Ted picked up several pieces of split wood and added them to the woodpile, rambling on almost without a break. "Father never ceased praying for her. By the hour, he would kneel, praying her through many a crisis. But another spell always came, and each one seemed worse than the last."

"Must've been hard on you and Susannah." Dan positioned another log on the block and pounded in the wedge.

"The doctors didn't hold out any hope, actually. None of them. And Father tried them all. He'd spend his entire yearly stipend, feeling any sacrifice more than worth it if it would help Mum."

"He must have loved your mother deeply."

"Yes. I, on the other hand, have only ever thought of myself," Ted admitted. "My own dreams. What I wanted out of life. Next to my father's example, I was a worthless chap."

Dan met his gaze. "In a lot of ways, my father is similar to yours." Handing Ted the maul, he stooped and gathered some split wood.

"It was quite a shock," Ted said quietly, leaning on the handle as if it were a cane, "to lose them both so suddenly. A bridge gave way beneath their phaeton."

"Yes, I know. Susannah misses them immensely."

With a nod, Ted set a log in place and gave the maul a practiced swing. "I was actually quite bitter, at first. I thought it rather cruel of God to take them like that. Especially a most trusted servant. But later I realized that at least they had gone together. They had suffered so much together, and now they are both at peace. When I thought about that, it seemed—I don't know, merciful. Proper. Does that sound strange?" He bent for the wedge.

"Not at all."

"Sometimes I regret that I never told my father I loved him. After he died, I went off to Oxford—purely out of duty, I'm afraid, to make it up to him. But my heart wasn't in the tedious studies. And I knew I could never be the pastor he was. I'd not measure up in the least. I couldn't sacrifice myself that way."

Dan searched his face, but didn't respond.

Positioning another log, Ted shrugged uneasily and shifted his stance. "I've never told these things to anyone before. I can't say why I've told you, except that I've such great respect for you."

With an understanding smile, Dan stacked the wood he held on the pile, then put a hand on Ted's arm. "Sounds to me as if God never called you to be a minister."

"I don't understand."

Dan tilted his head. "If a person has the call, it's something that comes from deep inside, yet is not of himself. It's a desire given by God that cannot be denied and that comes with the strength to serve, no matter what the cost. Without it your ordination from Oxford would have been of little benefit. Even, perhaps, a detriment. Did you ever consider that?"

"Never." A frown drew Ted's eyebrows downward. "I've felt only that I was disappointing our father. And, of course, Susannah was quite upset."

"Well, it's time to put those feelings to rest. Remember how in the twelfth chapter of First Corinthians the apostle Paul wrote of the various spiritual gifts at work in the church?" At Ted's nod, he went on. "Well, each of us must pray to God in faith and ask him to reveal which particular gift, or gifts, he has given to us to use expressly for his glory. I'm sure that when you discover yours, he'll give you the desire and strength to fulfill your purpose."

Ted considered Dan's words, wishing desperately that they were true. But still he felt the weight of wrong choices pressing him down. "But what if it's too late?" he asked in all sincerity. "What if I've gone too far to turn back? I'm a soldier now. I belong to the Crown. If only I'd been faithful to my heritage, the way Sue always has, instead of wanting to strut around like some vain peacock and give orders."

Another cry issued forth from the second-floor window.

He cast an uneasy glance upward. "Surely if God is truly good, he must show *her* mercy, at least. If for no other reason than for our own father's sake, he must bring her safely through this."

Releasing a deep breath, Dan also looked in the direction of the upstairs bedroom, then back. "God is Susannah's heavenly Father, Ted. He loves her and wants what's best for her even more than her earthly father did. More than you or I do."

"Do you actually believe that?" Ted asked, leveling his gaze straight at Dan.

Dan paused, then smiled, and a look of relief came over his face. "Yes, I do. I truly do. And not only that, but I believe God loves you just as much, if you'd just let him close enough to show you. Talk to him."

"It's . . . been so long."

"Then he'll be all the more glad to hear from you."

"Think so? Even after turning my back on him?"

Nodding, Dan reached for Ted's hand.

Ted sank to his knees on the blanket of soft new snow. Strangely at peace, he bowed his head.

"Dan, Ted," Jane called from the back stoop. "Get up out of that snow before you come down with a chill. And come in. Now." Without further word, she returned inside.

A vague coldness, which had nothing to do with the season, clutched its icy fingers around Ted's heart. He and Dan sprang up and ran into the house, where Jane was busy at the hearth.

"What is it?" Dan crossed the kitchen and took hold of her shoulder, turning her around. "Jane. Tell me. Please."

She blew a bedraggled wisp of copper hair away from her eyes and put her other hand on her hip. "It's over. Finally. This has been, without a doubt, the absolute worst day of my entire life."

"Oh, no," Dan moaned. "You mean she's—"

"Merciful God," Ted whispered in prayer. "Don't let it be." Not Sue. Not his only sister.

"Don't be a goose," Jane said, reaching for a pail of water. "I didn't say it was *your* worst day; I said it was mine. The baby has come at last. It's a boy."

"A boy," Dan breathed in amazement. "I have a son!"

Profound relief washed over Ted as he and Dan all but tripped over each other trying to be first through the door in their mad dash to the hall.

"Stop! Wait!" Jane cried.

"What?" her brother asked in vexation, one foot poised

midair above the first step. "Is something—" His shoulders sagged at once, and the color fled from his face. "Oh, no. Susannah. My wife. How is she?"

Coming their way lugging the hot-water bucket, Jane rolled her eyes. "You two, being men, are fortunate enough to get to wait down here in comfort while *I* clean the horrid mess up. Let me by." Shoving past them, she lugged the heavy bucket upstairs, talking nonstop as she went. "Of course, once I have everything all nice and tidy—if indeed that is even possible—then we'll send for you. In the meantime, take off those muddy boots. I have enough to do without you tracking up the kitchen."

"Hold on a minute, Jane," Dan commanded.

Even Ted had to restrain himself forcibly from going after the girl and throttling her just to get her to stand still for a minute.

She stopped with a huff halfway up the stairs and turned, looking down at the two of them, her chest heaving in consternation, her dark eyes glinting. "What? Can't you see I'm in a hurry?"

"I don't care about that. I want to know about Susannah."

Jane pursed her lips. "The midwife seems to think Susannah will be fine. Personally, I can't imagine how, after all the . . ." She gave a shudder. "But Mistress Brown must know best."

Dan nodded and released a pent-up breath.

Feeling at least two stones lighter, Ted breathed easier at the splendid news. Then the realization hit him that he was now an uncle.

"Jane, girl," called Mistress Brown from the bedroom. "Where are you with that water? I told you to hustle."

"Jane, girl," she mimicked with a pout. "My mistress awaits," she muttered as she tromped up the remaining steps.

Dan turned around, his hands in his pockets, and shot a grin at Ted.

"I must say, old chap, congratulations are in order, are they not?" Ted chuckled.

Dan looked dazed. He shook his head in wonder and began to laugh. "For both of us!" Then he grabbed Ted in a bear hug.

❧ ❧

Before returning downstairs, Jane donned a fresh gown of larkspur blue and a clean, crisp apron, then brushed her hair. Now that all the excitement was over, she assured herself, certainly she'd be able at last to spend some time with Ted.

Dan's voice drifted from the kitchen as she descended. "I'd feel honored to name our son after both of our fathers. If Susannah agrees, of course."

Entering the room quietly, Jane found the two men relaxed and sitting at the table. All traces of the mess they had brought in on their boots had been mopped up.

At the sight of her, they both sprang to their feet. "Is it time?" they chorused as one.

"Yes," she announced wearily. "You may go in now. One at a time. Dan first."

The words barely left her lips before her brother bounded gleefully away. She wondered if his feet even touched the steps on the way up to the bedroom. The thought brought a smile, and she turned it on Ted. "Well, at least now we can concentrate on each other for a while."

Ted smiled vacantly in return.

"Mistress Brown says Susannah will have to remain in bed for two weeks," Jane gushed, allowing her gaze to linger on the appealing angles of Ted's face. "Isn't that wonderful? That will extend my visit at least that long, but I'm hoping it might stretch into another two beside. And if I have anything to say about the matter, Dan will hire someone to come in and take care of Susannah and the chores, for the most part, then you and I can—"

"Are you quite certain my sister is going to be all right?" Ted asked impatiently.

"Yes, of course." She frowned in irritation. Why, he hadn't been listening to her at all! "I told you that before. Unless she gets childbed fever, the midwife expects Susannah to recover fully. Now, tell me, Ted, what invitations have you received? Has the governor sent you one?"

A baffled expression crossed Ted's features. "I beg your pardon?"

"The Christmas parties, the balls. Have you gotten any invitations yet?"

"I'm afraid Alex would be more attuned to that sort of thing than I am." With a sidelong glance, he stood and walked out into the hall, looking up toward Susannah's room.

Jane stared after him. What was the matter with him? She had toiled hours and hours up in that birthing room with the midwife, taking barely a moment even to go to the privy. And all that time, all she had thought of was the British lieutenant downstairs and how much she wanted to be with him, to talk to him.

When the sound of Mistress Brown's heavy tread on the stairs carried to Jane's ears, and then Ted's voice asking if he could go up to Susannah, her anger doubled. She gritted her teeth and marched into the hall.

"Not just now, lad," Mistress Brown was saying. "Give the two of 'em a few minutes more. Then you can go up." She turned to Jane. "I'm headin' on home to get some sleep. I'll send my daughter over to look after the missus and the babe until I come back. I want you, girl, to see to Susannah until my Liza comes. The difficult delivery took its toll, and the poor gal will be needin' help for some time before she recovers."

Jane's lips parted in dismay.

"Then," the midwife continued, oblivious to Jane's reaction, "get some rest yourself. Tomorrow's gonna be a very busy day for you—as will the next few weeks."

"But-but I don't know the first thing about babies," she stammered.

"Mercy! Then it's high time you learned, wouldn't you say?" Without ceremony, she retrieved her wool cloak and threw it over her weary shoulders.

Ted put an arm around Jane and gave an affectionate hug.

Elated that he had finally taken notice of her, Jane smiled up into his clear blue eyes.

"You'll find that our Jane's quite a clever sort," he said to Mistress Brown, who was halfway out the door. "She'll catch on in quick order." Then he bent and placed a kiss at her temple. "Won't you, my pet?"

It was all Jane could do to muster a weak smile. *Pet,* was it? Well, that certainly was an apt name. She felt like a pet, all right—a pet dog! Fetch this. Get that.

❦ ❦

After the midwife had made her way out of the bedroom to give Dan time alone with Susannah, he stared down at his wife in the golden candleglow, and his heart almost burst with joy. If he lived to be a hundred he would always remember the heavenly smile she had bestowed upon him when he came to her bedside. Pale and utterly spent, it must have taken the last fraction of energy she possessed to look up at him and smile, for she had drifted off to sleep almost immediately. Now she lay serene and fragile, looking like an angel in her fresh nightdress, her tawny hair brushed and rippling over the lace-edged pillow cover. When he had kissed her cheek, he could do no more than whisper that he loved her; he could not trust his voice to speak anything more.

His eyes moved to the wee babe in the cradle next to the bed. Could it be possible? A son! Loosening the blue flannel blanket slightly, he marveled at the miracle. The child was so tiny, so perfect. He had miniature fists, unbelievably small, a cap of velvety brown hair like fine-spun silk to the touch, and a mouth that was a sweet replica of Susannah's. The wee garment she had embroidered so lovingly months ago, one of dozens, almost swallowed him up. Dan's chest swelled with gladness and gratitude. He knelt on the floor between his wife and son. Then, placing a hand on each of them, he bowed his head, and a prayer of thankfulness flew swiftly to heaven from a heart too full for words.

❦ ❦

Jane trudged downstairs the following afternoon carrying an armful of laundry. There seemed no end to the things she had to look after: a bedridden patient, a newborn babe, cooking, cleaning, enormous piles of washing. She simply had to convince that miserly brother of hers to hire a servant to help out. It wasn't fair that he had left everything to her. When would she ever be able to spend time with Ted? After all, she had come to Boston for a few reasons of her own. And even though this city wasn't quite so large or grand as Philadelphia, it did have quite a selection of interesting shops she was eager to visit. There were several Christmas gifts she wished to purchase. She particularly wanted to find something special for Ted.

Stepping onto the bottom landing, she heard men's voices in the parlor. *Ted!* It had to be! Dan should have called her. Instinctively, she reached up to her hair to make certain it was neat, even though she had checked it in the hall mirror a hundred times already today, hoping that her handsome lieutenant would call. Leaning over her bundle, she peered into the room. Then she let out a disappointed breath. It was only some stranger talking to Dan. She took a step away, but was arrested by a curious singsong voice. The newcomer seemed to be making a recitation of some sort. She moved nearer, but remained out of sight while she listened:

Seventeen hundred and seventy-two
In Newport Harbor lay a crew,
That played the parts of pirates there,
The sons of freedom could not bear.

That night about half after ten,
Some Narragansett Indiamen,

Being sixty-four, if I remember,
Which made this stout coxcomb surrender;

And what was best of all their tricks
They in his britch a ball did fix.

And set the men upon the land,
And burnt her up, we understand;
Which thing provokes the King so high,
He said those men shall surely die. . . .

Jane grimaced as the voice droned on in seemingly endless verses. Men and their rhymes. Why must they forever seek to glorify their lawlessness? It had already been months, and the authorities had yet to ferret out the culprits responsible for burning the *Gaspee.*

Dan chuckled when the last stanza came to an end. "No self-respecting Rhode Islander would turn in a fellow citizen for taking long-overdue action against a villainous pirate. And since the Crown intends to breach our freedoms and rights even further by carrying our citizens off to England for trial, my neighbors will be even more determined to shield the participants. And well Governor Hopkins knows it."

So you think, Jane railed silently. She was sorely tempted to go in there and tell them exactly what she thought of their principles, but she knew it would do no good. With a shake of her head, she flounced off to the kitchen. If it weren't important for her to encourage a friendship with Ted's sister to further her own cause with the lieutenant, she'd have washed her hands of her whole traitorous family. With the exception, of course, of Mama—the only one of the lot with the good sense to want to lead a gracious, civilized life.

Just as she dropped her burden of soiled sheets into a big basket, a knock sounded on the front door.

Rushing out into the hallway, Jane saw Dan already approaching the parlor doorway. "I'll get it," she said pointedly. "Most likely it's Ted. *Lieutenant* Ted, remember?" She sent a meaningful glance beyond her brother. "I'd suggest you sneak that other traitor friend of yours out the back door while I answer this one."

Dan's eyes narrowed. "I think it's time you and I—"

The man reached Dan's side and placed a hand on his arm. "Prob'ly for the best." With a wave, he brushed past them both and headed toward the kitchen.

Dan continued to glare at Jane. "We will talk later." Then he followed the other man.

Taking a deep breath, Jane fairly flew to the front door and opened it. "Ted!" she cried, drinking in the sight of him and his friend in their splendid red uniforms. "And Alex. How wonderful of you to come by. I've been thinking about you all day."

Ted gave her a peck on the cheek. "Dreadfully sorry I couldn't get here sooner, but I'm afraid I was on duty until now." He removed his cloak, then turned to her as Alex followed his lead. "That *Gaspee* nonsense has all the locals talking up their *victory* with renewed vigor," he said bitterly. "We've been kept quite busy."

With a lazy grin, Alex tipped his head. "Ah yes, old chap. But if they've a mind to carry on with more foolhardiness, we'll be *obliged* to squelch it, of course."

Jane listened to their brave comments and smiled. What a pleasure it was to hear rightly placed sentiments for a change.

"How is Sue today?" Ted asked suddenly.

"She's doing well," Jane answered evenly, annoyed that already his attention had shifted so quickly to his sister. "In fact, the only person who isn't doing fine around here is—"

"Marvelous!" Ted cut in. "Might I go up and visit her, then? And my nephew, of course."

"Be my guest," came Dan's voice as he strode into the hall from the kitchen. "I'll even go up with you. Can't seem to get my fill of looking at the two of them." He nodded to Alex. "Lieutenant Fontaine. Do make yourself comfortable. We'll be back shortly."

Jane watched their selfish grins as they deserted her yet again. No one seemed to notice her anymore or appreciate her unceasing labor, day and night. Nothing mattered to either of them but Susannah and the baby.

"I see they've gone off and left us," Alex said smoothly. "Or might I say, left you. And this, after you've come all this way in the dead of winter, just to be passed over for a sister and a whelp. Pity, that."

Alex understood completely. A slow smile curved Jane's lips, and she turned to him. Had he always been so thoughtful and perceptive? And those clear gray eyes that danced in admiration across her green frock . . . not to mention the rest of her. How could she not have noticed them before? Or those fine aristocratic features? Here was someone who was always of the same mind as she when it came to parties. And after all, the holiday season was upon them. "Why didn't I fall in love with you instead of Ted?" she asked impetuously, gliding into the parlor with a gesture for him to follow.

"That is something I've asked myself on many a sleepless night," Alex said, taking a seat quite near the one she'd chosen. A teasing smile widened his generous mouth.

Jane laughed lightly, not altogether sure she had read his expression correctly. But how very pleasant it was to hear gallant words again. He couldn't possibly be serious, but she thoroughly enjoyed pretending even for a few minutes. The initial flicker of conscience that he was actually flirting with her—and she with him—vanished like a vapor. "How nice to have someone who truly understands me," she said.

"And why should I not?" he asked. "You're not so unlike the young ladies of class who moved in my circle as I was growing up."

She blinked and smiled through her lashes at him.

"You've the air of an aristocrat about you," he added. "One of the few I've come across in these provincial Colonies." Another of his bold looks washed over her. "One who would have no difficulty holding her own in my world."

"Ah, such charm and wit," she gushed. "And always just the right words to bring me out of my doldrums. I'm surprised you're not beating off all the young ladies of Boston with that saber of yours."

He grinned rakishly. "Perhaps I find nothing of interest in the lot." He raised an eyebrow suggestively.

Jane felt a rush of warmth in her cheeks and looked away. Getting up, she moved to the window and fingered a lace panel as she stared out. "Who, um, might be the fortunate belle who will be receiving your lavish attentions during the round of Christmas affairs?" She gazed back coyly over her shoulder.

With a deep sigh, he smirked. "Boston, I fear, is a rather strict little country town . . . unlike your enlightened Philadelphia."

She nodded in agreement, then returned her attention to the snow-covered scene outside. "But surely there are those who still have the good sense to want to make up for the rebel hooliganism. And what better way than having the great honor of entertaining Lord Hillsborough's relative during the season of peace and good will? After all, your mother's cousin was colonial secretary for years. He was responsible for the presence of the regiments stationed here to protect the commerce."

"Actually," Alex said, coming up behind her, "I've received a number of invitations to date."

Jane held her breath, trying not to betray her pleasure in his nearness.

"Of course, I wouldn't dream of attending without my friend, Ted. Or the fairest of maidens," he added in a whisper.

Her heart began to beat crazily.

"I shall arrange to have Captain Bidwell and his wife chaperon you to the functions, if you like. Even if Susannah were well enough, I don't believe either she or her husband would be welcome, considering his questionable political leanings . . . if you know what I mean."

"Oh! That would be wonderful!" Jane turned and impulsively threw her arms around him, giving his cheek a light kiss.

Alex's hands went to her shoulders, and his smoldering gaze locked with hers.

Jane swallowed and stepped back, uncomfortable with the

lingering hunger in his expression. She eased out of his grasp with some difficulty. Then, as she watched, he cocked his head and resumed his customary nonchalance, returning to his seat.

Jane turned and gazed unseeing through the lace curtain. Her pulse still beat erratically at her throat, and she found it hard to breathe. Suddenly, she understood why Alex Fontaine had never seemed to have a particular lady friend. He had been waiting for an opportunity with her! She found the knowledge a bit provocative—and, considering the way in which Ted was presently ignoring her, ever so interesting.

A sudden gust of wind splattered a handful of snowflakes against the windowpane and rattled the shutters of Susannah's bedroom as it howled by.

"Merciful heavens!" Jane said, crossing to look outside at the snowdrifts that had begun to pile up against every structure within sight. "Listen to it blow."

"I have been," Susannah said. "At a time like this, I'm most thankful we've been provided with this sturdy house."

Jane smiled at the beautiful picture of motherhood Susannah made as she serenely nursed her baby. Both the babe and his mother were gaining strength with each passing day, it seemed. Already in the few times Jane had held tiny, warm Miles Edmond, she felt a tangible attachment to him. She couldn't help but wonder what it would be like to hold her own sweet baby in her arms one day—a new life that she and Ted had created and brought into the world.

Shaking off her reverie, she moved to the commode and picked up the towel that had covered Susannah's breakfast tray. She folded it and used it to stay the chilly draft that seeped past the windowsill.

"I wonder if Emily and Robert are warm," Susannah mused. "I do hope they'll soon be safely tucked in at the Lyons' Den in Princeton. Some of my most treasured hours were spent at the hearth of Esther and Jasper Lyons." Her smooth brow creased with worry. "Rob and Emily have been on my mind all the time, of late. I've been praying for them constantly."

"Me, too," Jane confessed, pricked with yet another twinge of guilt for the way that her youngest sister and the Scot had been rudely awakened and forced to flee Boston in the dark of night with little more than the clothes on their backs. And all because of her. Now Emily was cut off from nearly everyone she held dear and might even be forced to endure the birth of her child without the comfort of family around to sustain her.

But Jane could not allow herself to dwell on that thought, and she immediately replaced it with another. She found it odd that Ted had never questioned her about them. It had been days. But it was probably only a matter of time until he did. She returned her attention to Susannah. "Are you sure you and the baby will be all right alone while I attend the church service this morning?"

"Why, of course. We shall both be happy knowing that a member of Dan's family will be there to see and hear him. You'll be the first, dear Jane. I'm only sorry that baby Miles and I cannot go as well. I so hate to miss it—especially now. Dan will be filling the pulpit at Long Lane Church while Reverend Moorhead is away visiting his children for the holidays."

"But no doubt he'll have many other opportunities to present the sermon there, and you'll be able to go then." Picking up the tray, Jane headed for the door.

"I'm so thankful for Teddy's change of heart," Susannah said as Jane stepped into the hall. "Aren't you? I was quite pleased when he mentioned he wanted to attend also. It's an answer to prayer."

Jane looked back and gave a crisp nod. "Yes. It was a surprise to me." *If nothing else, it would be interesting,* she added silently, *having him attend service with the rebellious Presbyterians.* Though what the lieutenant would think of Dan's traitorous leanings—should her brother proclaim any from his pulpit as did so many other local pastors—remained to be seen. It might tax the tentative friendship that seemed to have been developing between him and Dan over the past several days.

"I'll be leaving, then," she said over her shoulder, "if you're certain there's nothing else I might get for you."

Susannah shook her head. "You've done so much already."

"I'll try not to be gone long."

"Enjoy the service. We'll be fine."

Jane left the room, trying to contain her eagerness to go out. Despite the bitter cold snap, even a short time away from her tiresome duties would be a treat. Her arms ached, her back ached, and she had to use balm every evening to keep her hands from chapping from the unaccustomed task of doing the laundry. It felt ever so good to be wearing her velvet Sunday frock of deep violet with its hand-crocheted ivory lace trim. She brushed a hand down the rich nap of the gown that molded itself to her body.

Entering the kitchen, tray in hand, Jane found Dan at the table having coffee with another young gentleman. It took a second glance before she recognized Ted in civilian clothes and without his military wig. Her gaze assessed his snuff-colored satin breeches and dark brown frock coat with its embroidered satin waistcoat. A frilly white cravat adorned his throat, and his dark brown hair was tied back in a neat queue.

"My goodness," she said with a laugh. "I wasn't certain it was you at first. You look positively dapper."

"I thought it best," he said with a grin, "to blend in with the masses this morning—particularly when they're mostly Scotch-Irish."

"How clever. The troublemakers will be far more likely to give themselves away if they're unaware of your identity."

"Jane," Dan scolded. "This is the Sabbath. Do try to think and act in keeping with the holy day."

Jane cut a glance back at Ted.

"Actually, I'm rather looking forward to hearing what they have to say," the lieutenant admitted. "I've yet to understand the colonists' hostility toward my country, and I've been trying to sort through it all."

"It's not as hard to comprehend as you might think," Dan said, refilling their mugs from the coffeepot at his elbow. "I'll be only too glad to enlighten you on the matter."

"Carry on, then." Ted grinned.

"Imagine yourself in our place, Ted, as one of our forefathers who came here for the freedom to worship almighty God as his conscience dictated. England had washed her hands of us, for the most part. Picture yourself clearing the land, putting up a dwelling, planting the crops—all the while protecting your family and your home from hostiles. Then at last you and your neighbors start up a few businesses and begin trading with others around you, until your little settlements grow into prosperous townships. You develop a democratic system which serves quite well in a land where a man is judged by his accomplishments rather than by his heritage. Can you see what I'm saying?"

Ted nodded and took another sip of his coffee.

"Well," Dan continued, "so could Great Britain, I'm afraid. But for far different reasons. Suddenly all those troublesome radicals they were so eager to be rid of a century and a half ago—so eager that they casually gave charters granting more freedoms than we'd ever known—began to look like a new, untapped source of revenue. Little by little the Crown began to revoke our rights and institute taxes . . . taxes which were vastly unfair, since we received no benefit from them whatsoever."

Busy folding diapers and baby clothes at the other end of the table, Jane listened uneasily, wondering how much of Dan's explanation Ted would allow before he exploded in anger. After all, the mother country did have the best interests of the Colonies at heart, and the lieutenant had been sent here to enforce British rule.

Stroking his jaw with his thumb and finger, Ted thought for a moment. "That's not the way we heard it, actually. Rather, we were told that you colonists were most ungrateful and refused to pay for the French and Indian War, which was fought to protect you. What say you to that?"

Dan gave a hint of a smile. "That's what the Crown would have you believe. But the fact is, we weren't in need of protection until the British and the French started fighting over territories to the west of us and stirred up the Indians."

"Is that true?" Ted asked.

"True as I'm sitting here," Dan answered evenly. "The two European powers *paid* various tribes of Indians to make war for them."

Frowning, Ted straightened in his chair, but he didn't interrupt.

"Quite a number of our people were burned out and killed, simply because the rulers of England and France were squabbling over territory thousands of miles away—territory they had not so much as set foot upon, let alone had a right to. Needless to say, not only were we not happy about the damage to us wrought by their warring, but then to have the British demand that we foot the bill for it! You can see—"

"If you ask me," Jane interrupted nervously, "most of these settlers sound like children who've been running wild while their parents were away. And now they resent being turned into the civilized, grateful offspring they should have been all along."

Dan merely stared at her without response as the grandfather clock chimed the hour. "Well, looks like it's time for us to go." Getting up, he led the way to the hall and grabbed his greatcoat from its peg. "I'll just go tell my wife and son good-bye," he said, dashing up the stairs.

Ted turned to Jane and took her hands in his. "My, you look lovely this morning. A veritable feast for my eyes. I might decide simply to sit and look at you all day."

She smiled at his gracious compliments and felt herself blush.

"I know I've been neglecting you since you've arrived in Boston, and I beg you to forgive me. But I'm rather glad we'll be together this morning and have this opportunity to enjoy your brother's success." Taking her fur-lined pelisse from where it was draped over a hall chair, he put it around her shoulders, planting a light kiss beneath her ear as he did so.

Jane felt a tingly glow down to her toes and leaned her head back against Ted's chest. He could be so sweet when he put his mind to it.

❧ ❧

In a flowing black ministerial robe, Dan stood behind the imposing pulpit of the somber Presbyterian Church and read the text for his sermon from the eighth chapter of the Gospel of John. After he had finished, he looked out over the congregation. "'And the truth shall make you free,'" he repeated. "What a precious promise. One which has become quite significant in these times in which we live."

Ted's mind pondered the thought as his brother-in-law's voice continued in the background. *Freedom.* The word was on everyone's lips. The colonists spoke of little else, no matter where he and Alex traveled. The rebels seemed more intent on being free than on bowing gratefully to the wishes of a generous benefactor who had enabled them to cross the wide sea and establish a new land. How could that be? His gaze wandered to other worshipers within easy sight. Some dressed in grand style, others in threadbare but serviceable attire. Yet all sat side by side in common dignity.

How different from the way things had been in England, where the highborn and the wealthy purchased the more prominent pews, the tradesmen the lesser, and the peasants huddled in the back. At home the classes had little to do with one another and moved in distinctly separate circles. The attitude here in Massachusetts was one of equality for all. In truth, he had to admit that the concept had merit. It had succeeded quite admirably in the new world—at least until the Crown stepped in and started taking over. By what right *did* Britain impose her own systems and restrictions upon people she had virtually sent packing decades ago, people who simply wanted to coexist to the betterment of all?

The very question shocked Ted. When had he begun to

comprehend this other side of the issue and to relate to the thinking of the colonists? He cleared his throat and shifted on the hard seat of the chilly sanctuary. Beside him, Jane sat composed and intent upon her brother's sermon. Perhaps he should do the same. Looking forward once more, he opened his mind for whatever further thoughts Dan might express on the matter.

"But bondage does not always come from outside," Dan was saying. "Sometimes it's just as much from within. When we choose to serve sin, we put ourselves in bondage to the one whom God calls the father of sin and the father of lies. When we give ourselves to God, and purpose to serve him, only then do we know the true meaning of freedom."

When the service ended and the benediction had been pronounced, Ted and Jane made their way to the door, where Dan shook hands with the departing members.

"'Twas good of you to come to worship with us this morning, my good man," said a stout gentleman at Ted's elbow. "John Burns is the name." He extended a puffy hand.

"How do you do," Ted answered, grasping it. "I'm Ted Harrington, the pastor's brother-in-law."

The man's eyes crinkled in a jovial smile. "That makes you all the more welcome here. We hope you'll attend regularly. Always a pleasure to see new faces among us."

"Not always," a cool voice added flatly from Mr. Burns's other side. A rail-thin man with a long, craggy face stood there.

Ted felt Jane's fingers tense in the crook of his arm.

"It took me a while to recognize him," the man continued, "seeing as how he's usually sportin' a different manner of dress. Whole different color, too. Red."

Mr. Burns's face paled, and he looked taken aback as his mouth tightened into a grim line. "Why, I had no idea. Have you the gall, sir, to come spying on us—and in church, yet?"

As his voice rose, a handful of other people came near, their eyes blazing.

Dan stepped at once into the melee. "Gentlemen, gentlemen," he said quietly. "It's the Sabbath, and we're in the Lord's house. Can we not speak in brotherly love to one another? Accusations and angry words will keep us forever at opposite ends in this difficult situation."

"Oh, is that right?" a voice demanded. "And just how much kindness or brotherly *love* will it take on this side of the water to make one smidgen of difference to the king or his cronies?"

"You tell him, Nathan," another urged.

"I think quite enough has been said already," Dan answered with a dispersing motion. "Let us depart in peace to our homes."

Ted watched the men as they turned reluctantly and left with a few disparaging backward glances at him. A few days ago, he would have been just as obstinate as any man here today, and he could easily have matched anyone's arrogance. But somehow now, with his renewed faith in God and the determination to follow Christ, he felt none of those old reflex emotions. Instead he felt patience and understanding, tempered with something else. . . . Wisdom? Could almighty God have deemed him worthy of such a high gift? Even the possibility filled him with awe.

"How perfectly horrid those men were," Jane whispered. With a shiver she swayed against him slightly. "I cannot wait to go home."

Ted put an arm about her shoulders and gave a comforting hug, appreciating her concern. "Don't worry, sweetheart. Somehow I understand how they feel, . . . and I can't say I blame them for it."

She looked at him, puzzled.

He smiled down at his beautiful—if a bit high-spirited—companion and led her outside, where a brilliant sun shone over the pristine landscape of the city. He filled his lungs with the refreshing fragrance of new snow and wood smoke and started walking his lovely lady back to the parsonage.

Crisp, light snowflakes danced on Boston's night wind. Blowing over the snow-packed road like gossamer veils of white dust, they frosted the tops of old snowdrifts and accumulated up against fences, buildings, and stark winter trees as the skids of Captain Bidwell's well-appointed phaeton shushed along in the quietness.

Inside the carriage, Jane adjusted the fur lap robe and tried to contain her excitement. The first Christmas ball, at last! She'd thought the day would never arrive.

"I truly hope you have an enjoyable evening, Miss Haynes," said the distinguished captain, resplendent in his fringed and corded dress uniform.

"'Twould be hard for the child not to, Thomas," his beaming wife said at his side. "There'll be dozens of young bachelors present and lined up to dance with such a lovely belle. She'll not have a moment to herself."

Jane smiled politely at the prosperous-looking couple opposite her, her chaperons for the evening. Mistress Bidwell's gold brocade gown, what she could see of it in the opening of the woman's luxurious velvet cape, was of the very latest fabric from Paris. She sighed and switched her attention to the brightly lit homes and fine shops along the way, unable to keep from wondering if Ted would continue to be attentive this evening as he had been in recent days. She hoped fervently that he would not get so caught up in another one of those tiresome religious conversations with Dan that he would arrive dreadfully late, if at all.

The bells on the horse's harness stopped jingling as the phaeton drew up on North Square before the large, three-story, columned home that belonged to the governor. Breathless, Jane accepted a hand from the coachman and stepped out, admiring the immaculate mansion. She allowed the Bidwells to precede her through the gate and on to the stately front door.

Within moments they were ushered inside and relieved of their cloaks. Jane drank in the opulence of her surroundings with delight. As elegant as any mansion in Philadelphia where she had attended similar balls, the entire downstairs exuded holiday finery. Banisters and pillars were entwined with evergreen and ribbons, and the entire house emanated the festive scent.

In the ballroom, huge arrangements of green boughs and holly adorned the long mirrored walls, accenting rich, scenic tapestries. A thousand candles glowed from crystal chandeliers in the high-ceilinged room, creating dazzling rainbows among the prisms of rich jewels and spangled gowns. Jane felt blissfully radiant as the sparkling sequins sprinkled liberally over the midnight blue bodice and hooped skirt of her ruffled satin gown reflected the flickering lights.

"I wonder if Lieutenant Fontaine has arrived yet," Mistress Bidwell whispered, leaning near.

The captain straightened and craned his neck as he peered over the throng. "Alas, I've not caught sight of the lad's face. But 'tis certain he'll be here."

Not about to correct the couple's misunderstanding, Jane returned Captain Bidwell's smile. Let them assume Alex would be her escort. They had treated her with obvious deference thus far, no doubt because of his illustrious family connections. Though he was a mere lieutenant, Alex might possibly have more clout than anyone else at the party—with the possible exception of the general himself or Governor Hutchinson. Her lips twitched at the humorous thought.

Alex's cousin might not be secretary to the Colonies at the moment, but that could change with the arrival of the next ship from England.

"Well, my fair lasses," Captain Bidwell said, offering one arm to his wife and one to Jane, "allow me to introduce you both around." He ushered them across the polished floor toward another cluster of guests.

Aware of numerous admiring glances from some of the young men in attendance, Jane lowered her gaze coyly. When they reached the other side of the room, the introductions had barely been completed before the opening notes of a minuet sounded from the string quartet.

"Excuse me, Miss," said a tall, dark-eyed lieutenant at her elbow. "Might I have the honor of this dance?"

"And I the one after it," said a second voice from her other side.

Jane almost laughed with delight. "I'd be happy to accommodate both of you gentlemen," she gushed. "One at a time, of course." Placing her hand on the first young man's arm, she allowed him to lead her onto the floor, where they joined a line of other paired dancers.

The officer fairly beamed at Jane as he turned to face her.

All the drudgery she had endured over the past week fled from Jane's mind as she curtsied gracefully to her partner's bow, then began the familiar pattern of steps.

Half a dozen dances later, Ted and Alex had yet to arrive. But Jane was far too well attended to mind very much. After sipping citrus punch with a well-mannered officer named Lieutenant Stark, she returned to the floor on his arm, and they joined a dance in progress. As they swung toward each other, she couldn't help but notice how the young man's olive complexion glowed in the bright candlelight. A warm smile graced his face and lit his hazel eyes. Jane reveled in his admiration and wondered when she had last enjoyed herself so much.

Near the end of the dance, Jane caught sight of Ted and Alex as they entered the room. They both smiled and tipped their heads at her, then proceeded to join Captain Bidwell and his wife, who stood with the elegant Governor Hutchinson.

"Ah," her partner said gallantly as the music stopped. "Pity our dance had to end so soon. I was only just beginning to appreciate being the envy of all, with the loveliest maiden in the Colonies on my arm."

"Why, how very sweet, Lieutenant." Jane tilted her chin a fraction. "But would you mind terribly escorting me over to my friends who have just arrived?" She inclined her head with a significant gaze in Ted and Alex's direction.

Lieutenant Stark's eyes followed, and he stiffened slightly. "Of course," he said politely, though his smile was suddenly absent. Without further word, he accompanied her to her two gentlemen. "I do thank you, Miss." With a slight bow, he walked away.

Jane barely stifled a giggle at his sudden change. Obviously, he was loath to have Alex think he had taken even the slightest liberties. Nevertheless, he, like so many others, had showered Jane with more flattery and attention than she had dreamed, and she had loved every moment of it. She turned a brilliant smile on Ted.

His answering gaze was both admiring and appreciative. "May I have the honor of the next dance?" he asked, bowing over her hand and kissing her fingers.

"I'd be delighted." Jane glided out onto the floor with him as the string quartet began the opening measures of another piece.

"You look magnificent," Ted whispered, bowing. "Absolutely ravishing. No one else present can compare with you this evening."

Jane curtsied to the man of her dreams as her heart fluttered in pleasure. "Thank you. I was so glad to see you come." Stepping into position, she felt his hand close over hers, and her whole being swelled with joy as they began to execute the intricate movements.

During the dance, Jane glanced toward the sidelines, where

Alex conversed with Captain Bidwell. The younger man's eyes were fastened on her as he talked, and when Ted's back was turned, Alex's mouth curved into a flirtatious grin. Jane blushed and looked away at once, reminding herself that Ted was the one who had truly stolen her heart. But a tiny flicker of pleasure flowed through her with the heady knowledge that even Lieutenant Fontaine, the most eligible man in the room, was interested in her! A small part of her hoped Alex wouldn't mention to the captain that Ted was her beau. As she glanced his way again, she met his storm gray eyes and knew for a certainty that he would not.

The dance ended with the announcement of an intermission to follow.

"Thank you, my lovely lady," Ted murmured with a warm smile. Taking Jane's hand, he led her over toward his friend.

"I say, old chap," Alex said as they approached. "I've a dreadful thirst. What say we find something in the other room to quench it?"

"Splendid thought." Patting Jane's hand, Ted eased her in the direction of the punch table. But when he saw how crowded it was there, he deposited her safely near the wall while he and his friend ventured into the mass.

Jane purposely kept her eyes off Alex, but she was more than aware of every stolen gaze the lieutenant managed. She felt warmth steal over her cheeks as she concentrated on several richly adorned gowns among a cluster of young ladies who giggled behind their fans. She swept a glance over her own attire and lifted her chin. Thanks to Mother's dressmaker, she was every bit as fashionable as any woman present—and as daring.

"Easy, gents," a loud voice said from near the punch bowl. "Enough crowding. We wouldn't want to cause another Boston Massacre, now, would we?"

A round of laughter followed the remark.

"Tell you one thing," said a burly officer on the edge of the gathered throng. "If it had been me in charge back in '70 there truly would have been a massacre!"

"That so?" said a short, dandified gentleman in satin and velvet. His loose wig slipped askew as he raised his head, and he straightened it with a smirk.

"Most assuredly," the bigger one answered. "The square would've been flooded with blood—from the whole mob, instead of a mere handful." He puffed out his chest and guffawed.

"That's the sort of talk that keeps the trouble pot stirring," Ted said evenly as he waited to be served.

"You don't say," a voice piped in from the other end.

Ted nodded. "I believe that if we would simply take the time to learn why the colonists feel the way they do, perhaps many of the animosities could be resolved. Or, at the very least, lessened."

A moment of awkward silence followed.

"Hmph," the burly officer finally scoffed, elevating his bushy eyebrows. "Everyone who came to these northern Colonies was a dissident—or an ignorant pauper. It's impossible to reason with the likes of them."

"Have you ever tried?" Ted challenged.

"I'm not entirely sure I know what you mean, young man."

Everyone within earshot stopped talking and turned to listen.

Undaunted, Ted continued. "Imagine you're a big dog, allowed to run at will in the woods and play freely from the time you were a pup. One day your master informs you that, since you're all grown up, it's time to begin earning your keep. He hitches you to a cart and makes you work the rest of your days for him. After experiencing total freedom your whole young life, how would you feel now, being fettered and forced to obey your master's every command?"

Appalled at the spectacle Ted was making of himself, Jane looked helplessly to where Alex stood.

"Well, that's a dog for you," she heard Alex say jokingly, one side of his mouth curled in distaste. "They never know what's good for them. Come on, old man. The fair damsel awaits."

By the time they emerged from the crowd, cups of punch

in hand, both Ted and Alex wore rather false-looking smiles. Jane took a sip of hers—anything to keep from blurting out something quite unladylike as they made their way to a quiet corner. But once there, she turned to Ted, aware of heat rising to her cheeks. "Honestly, Ted. How could you?"

"How could I what?" he asked smoothly.

She expelled a huff. "You know very well. Make a fool of yourself. And in front of your own fellow officers, at that. I can't believe it."

"My sentiments exactly," Alex said, raising his glass to his mouth.

Ted looked from one to the other, then settled on Jane. "I'm sorry that you seem to care more about being popular than about what's right or wrong. Or what's just and unjust, which is closer to the truth."

Jane slapped her fan closed. "I take that as an insult. And I'll be even more sorry if I have to listen to one more distasteful remark from you." Pursing her lips, she turned her back to him.

"In that case," Ted said, "perhaps it would be better if I were to excuse myself."

"Yes, perhaps it would," she said icily, piercing him with a look.

Ted returned her glare, and a muscle twitched in his jaw. He thrust his empty cup at Alex. "Would you mind, old chap, thanking the captain and his good wife for accompanying Jane here this evening, and see that she's taken safely home for me?"

"My pleasure," Alex answered.

Without another word, Ted stalked away, saber-straight.

Jane watched him go in disbelief and shock. He must have been bewitched during this past week somehow—by his sister, by Dan, even by that baby. Jane didn't know exactly how, but that was the only answer she could find for the complete change in Ted. She watched him pace impatiently out in the foyer while the attendant went to find his military cape.

"I say," Alex said in mocking amusement. "What exactly

happened on the day Susannah's baby was born? Ted hasn't been himself since."

Turning his way, Jane raised her eyebrows. "I've been wondering the same thing myself, but haven't the slightest idea. They did name the child after Ted's father—and from what I've heard, the Reverend Harrington was practically a saint. Perhaps Ted is feeling guilty for not following in his father's footsteps."

Alex cocked his head. "Perhaps that's all it is. I shouldn't want to have to—"

Jane glanced toward the entrance at Ted, who had just retrieved his cloak. He flung it about his shoulders and started out the huge door without so much as a backward glance.

"Oh, my!" Jane cried under her breath. "There's something I must say to Ted before he leaves." Deserting Alex, she hurried after Ted and managed to catch him just as he reached the bottom step. "Ted!" she called from the landing. Her breath created frosty vapors on the cold night air.

He strode back, waiting in silence, his face devoid of emotion in the glow of the porch lamps.

Jane attempted a carefree smile. "I know things aren't exactly as they should be between us at the moment," she began.

He brightened measurably, but did not reply.

"But you must promise never to tell Dan or Susannah that it was I who aided you in your search for Rob and Emily." She nibbled her lip nervously as she rubbed her arms against the cold.

A look of disgust came upon him as he peered at her over his nose. "You've nothing to fear on that account, Jane," he said flatly. "Not from me, at any rate." Wheeling around, he strode off.

Jane drew a huge breath of relief. Turning, she swept back into the governor's mansion.

Alex met her gaze as she entered the ballroom, and something flickered in the depths of his steely eyes. He smiled.

The meaning of his expression was not lost on Jane. Yes, she assured herself. Lieutenant Alex Fontaine was a far better catch than Ted Harrington ever was. How could she not have seen it before? Even if her heart didn't do flip-flops every time he looked at her, Alex was everything she had ever wanted . . . wasn't he?

Ted's only advantages, both financially and socially, were due to having Alex for his friend. She must never forget that. And if Ted continued on in the self-destructive path he seemed to have chosen of late, even that would disappear. Had she been smart, she'd have chosen Alex in the first place. She might have been married and living in style by now, instead of acting the slave for her brother and living in dread of the day when that uncouth Yancy Curtis returned to collect his pound of flesh.

Jane favored Alex with her most flirtatious expression.

Obviously pleased, he crossed the room to collect her.

❧ ❧

Later that week, as Jane busily rinsed out another pile of baby things in the kitchen, she refused to think about the fact that Ted was upstairs visiting with Susannah. Forcing her thoughts elsewhere, she concentrated instead on the fancy dinner party she had attended last evening with Alex.

The prominent customs official and his family had been eager to fawn over Jane during the gathering. After all, she was the lady of the most influential lieutenant, was she not? Even yet she could hear them gushing flattery by the cartload, obviously hoping to secure further advantage for themselves by a favorable word from Wills Hill's cousin. Still, it had been quite pleasant. Who cared if it hadn't been Ted she'd been with, or that she'd felt just a little empty without him? That would pass in time.

The sound of persistent knocking sounded from the front door.

Drying her hands, Jane put her idle thoughts aside. Perhaps someone else was making a social call on her, extending another invitation. She pressed the latch and opened the door, but disappointment washed over her at the sight of a man in the garb of a postrider.

"Letter, Miss," he said. His face was flushed from the cold weather, but he managed a wan smile through thin, chapped lips. "Ben asked me to drop it by, since I was headed up this way."

"Thank you," Jane said with reservation as she accepted the letter. No doubt it was one more treasonous dispatch. She closed the door abruptly.

"Who was that?" Dan asked, coming downstairs.

Jane shoved the thing at her brother. "One of your questionable postrider friends brought it by."

"Thanks." Dan's dark brows dipped into a scowl, then flared as he opened it and scanned the message. "It's from Father," he said. "He and Mother are delighted with the news of the baby. Mother, it seems, is finally beginning to accept Susannah, because it says they're sorry we won't be able to spend the holiday with the rest of the family. They expect you before Christmas Eve, however. A good sign, don't you think?" He grinned.

"Quite," she said with a pout. One week was pitifully inadequate for her to establish any solid relationship with Alex Fontaine. Would she even manage to light a spark of loyalty in his heart?

Reading further, Dan laughed and looked up. "They had word from Emily and Rob when the packet they were on stopped at Newport. Emily mentioned that Yancy was escorting them safely on to Princeton. I'm sure Mother found the news most welcome."

"Yes. I'm certain she did." Jane grimaced as the seaman's name echoed in her mind. But realizing that the rat was hundreds of miles away was some comfort. At least she didn't have to worry about Yancy Curtis. Now, if only a big storm would come up on his return voyage and sink his ship—perhaps maroon him indefinitely, or for a few years, at least, on some remote uninhabited island. . . .

She had to smother a giggle.

"Well, I'm glad to see you're looking more cheerful," Dan said. "I thought for a minute that the news of going home would have depressed you, since by all indication you seemed to be enjoying yourself here."

Jane nodded slowly. "I have been. Truly. And in fact, now that Alex and I are beginning to discover one another through different eyes, becoming special friends, well, I'm not exactly looking forward to having to return to Pawtucket at all."

Dan squeezed her shoulder with brotherly concern. "Jane, I'm sorry you and Ted are no longer friends," he said compassionately. "He's really a fine fellow. Susannah and I would be most happy, especially now, if you two were growing closer."

"Well, you can both forget it," Jane announced with finality. "Ted may be a fine fellow in your estimation, but I'm afraid I see him as quite the opposite." She met her brother's dark eyes. "By the way, what was it, exactly, that you two were talking about outside the day the baby was born? He's been different ever since. What changed him so?"

"He didn't tell you?"

She shook her head.

"That surprises me," Dan said. "It's the most wonderful news, actually. Ted rededicated himself to the Lord that day. He's decided to follow God in a much closer manner. Nothing could have pleased me more. Don't you feel the same way about it?"

Jane couldn't have felt less enthusiasm. "So, you've managed to convert him into another one of your overenthusiastic 'new lights.' Hmph. I certainly hope he comes to his senses, and soon. That anarchist 'freedom in the Lord' nonsense will ruin his army career. See if it won't."

"That's what we're hoping," Dan announced with irritating glee.

"Well, just don't expect me to be a party to it." She turned and stalked back to the kitchen.

"And we're all praying for you, too, Jane," he called after her.

Clenching her fists at her sides, Jane ground her teeth together. How dare her brother think she needed prayer, when he was nothing but a traitorous, corrupting rebel! How dare any of them?

December 1773

Jane ran her fingers pensively over several gowns in her ornate walnut armoire, then turned, perplexed. "It's just so hard to decide, Mama. Only two carpet satchels. Really. I'll be taking next to nothing. I can't go to Boston for this holiday season without any number of changes. Alex receives so many invitations, and I'm hoping at long last I'll get him to propose."

Her mother looked up from folding undergarments on Jane's canopied bed. "I'm sorry, dear," she replied, setting a neat stack on the pink-and-ivory counterpane. "But it's for the best."

"But why won't you and Papa simply allow me to take the stage again, as I did last year? It'll be dreadful having to accompany Ben and ride along on horseback."

Mama added a few lace-edged handkerchiefs and an apron to one of the piles, then crossed to the window of Jane's second-floor bedchamber. She parted the ruffled curtain panels and looked out at the chilly grayness of December. "Nothing you may say will change our minds. Since this dreadful tea business has tempers flaring again worse than ever, it's neither wise nor safe for you to travel unescorted, no matter what the occasion." Tugging her knitted house shawl snugly about herself, she walked to Jane's commode and opened a silver-inlaid jewelry chest.

"Yes, I know all about that nonsense over the British East India Company," Jane said with a pout. "But what has all of that to do with me? If I arrive in the city with so few gowns, Alex will think we've become paupers."

"That may be, Daughter. But you know if it were left entirely up to me, you wouldn't be allowed to go at all—especially now that that dreadful tea company ship has arrived. All of Boston is in an uproar. They will never allow it to be unloaded. The one thing Boston merchants abhor more than a new tariff is a monopoly, especially one legislated by Parliament."

Jane sighed. "But I have no intention of venturing anywhere near that old harbor. And you promised I could go. I so want to be there for the baby's first birthday celebration. I'm sure Miles must be quite the little man by now."

"Hey, Sis," Ben yelled from downstairs. "If you don't hustle your backside down here, I'll leave without you."

"Oh, no you won't," Mama informed him with matching force. "Your sister will be only a few minutes more. Be patient. And I'll have no more of that crude mouth, either."

Jane cast another frantic glance into her armoire and selected three day gowns and her fanciest party frock, then carried them to her bed, where she began folding each of them carefully. She handed the first one to her mother to be put into a satchel, then started on the next.

Mama reached across for the second gown. "Why don't you just tell me which others you would like, dear, and we'll send a chest along by stage. Will that do?"

With profound relief, Jane dashed around the narrow bed and grabbed her mother in a hug. "Oh, thank you, thank you. Today, then. Promise you'll send Papa into town with it today."

Her mother broke into a smile.

"Wonderful!" Jane led the way to the clothes cupboard and threw open the doors. "I'll show you which ones I'd most like to have. Now, let's see. These three newer ball gowns definitely, and—" She pointed to two other dresses. "—those on the end."

Her mother nodded, then raised her clear green eyes to Jane's and sobered. "You know, Daughter, if you hadn't been so insistent that Ted transfer to Boston, you and he might very well be married and living in Philadelphia by now."

Jane returned to her task at the bed and stuffed the third gown into a satchel, then fastened the closure. "I'm surprised to hear you say such a thing."

"Why is that?"

"Well, I thought that you, most of all, would be in favor of an alliance with Alex Fontaine. After all, he is the one with the wealth and the family connections which you've always regarded so highly, not Ted. I, for one, am rather sorry I ever became so infatuated with Ted in the first place." She met her mother's steady look. "And now he has ruined his friendship with Alex, not to mention any chance at all of furthering his career. Surely I've told you how Dan has turned Ted into the same kind of tiresome provincial thinker he and Father are."

"Jane! Really!"

"Well, it's true, Mama, and you know it. How often have I heard you complain about being buried here on this farm in Rhode Island?"

Silver strands glistened among the auburn as her mother slowly shook her head, and a deep flush heightened her fair coloring. "I do admit having been guilty of that, I'm sorry to say," she answered softly. "Your father may be an old stick-in-the-mud when it comes to getting out and about with people of quality. But I wouldn't trade the sincere love he and I have shared over the years for anything, not even for a place at any court in the world. And I wish for you that same kind of sincere love as our other children have."

Jane tucked her chin. "Surely not all of them! Why, Emily ran off with an absolute stranger. And a penniless one at that."

Mama smiled sadly. "I felt the same way about it for a while, too. But although Robert didn't have connections or even plausible prospects when he first arrived, he did have some savings. I must give him credit for that. And Emily's last letter announcing the birth of their little daughter, Katie, was full of love. I'm only sorry that the child arrived earlier than expected, and too quickly for you to go and assist her, as you did with Susannah. Robert is making a place for himself in Princeton as a wheelwright. They seem to be quite happy."

"Well," Jane said disgustedly, "there's still the matter of Dan's match. You were opposed to that marriage from the very beginning. You were very clear about your feelings last year when they visited, if you recall."

Mama's composure faltered, and her eyes swam with tears. "I know," she whispered, pressing her handkerchief to her nose. "And I've never forgiven myself for that."

Jane's eyebrows rose in surprise.

"I've been a fool," Mama rasped. "A stubborn fool." She cleared her throat. "Just this morning Mrs. Simpson stopped me at the butcher shop. Seems she'd just returned from spending a month with her daughter—who just happens to live on Long Lane, across the street from Daniel's church."

"That old biddy?"

"Oh, she means well. She can't help being a gossip, I suppose, or the way she's always sniffing about for the latest tidbit to pass on."

"What did she say, exactly?" Jane asked, suspicious.

Her mother took a deep breath and slowly exhaled. "Mostly she spoke of Susannah and the way the entire congregation at the Presbyterian Church adores her every bit as much as they respect Dan. Why, if you must know, the *old biddy,* as you put it, couldn't find a single unkind thing to say. She reported that Susannah and Daniel simply dote on each other and the baby. And my daughter-in-law keeps an immaculate house, bakes bread for the unfortunates who stay at the almshouse, and even writes letters for the illiterate."

"My goodness. What a surprise," Jane said sarcastically. "Papa, Ben, and I have all told you any number of times that Susannah is a very loving person. She's gone out of her way to make me feel quite welcome each time I've visited. In fact, if it weren't that Ted could pop in at any given moment, my stays there would be almost perfect."

"I know," Mama admitted. "You've all been right about her all along, while I've remained the worst kind of fool. But when someone like Mrs. Simpson relates that sort of information—a woman who likes nothing better than to keep things in a stir—I must take stock of my attitude toward the girl."

She sighed and bit her lip. "Of late I've begun to feel so ashamed of the way I've treated Susannah that I haven't even been able to say my nightly prayers for the burden of it. As you recall, I even kept your father from attending our grandson's dedication, even when Susannah and Daniel both were willing to put it off indefinitely to give us time to travel at our convenience. And your father dearly wanted to go. Even worse, we've now missed the entire first year of the child's life. He doesn't even know his own grandparents."

Jane watched a variety of emotions cloud her mother's refined features as her gnarled hands twisted the fragile handkerchief. For a fleeting second Jane wondered if her own tapered fingers would one day grow crooked with age. She shook off her idle musings as her mother continued.

"I do hope Susannah will find it in her heart to forgive me. I doubt I shall ever forgive myself." She pulled some folded papers from her apron pocket and held them out to Jane. "I must make amends with her somehow. Would you please give this to her for me? I've apologized as sincerely as I know how. And I've invited—pleaded, really—that they join us and the rest of the family for Christmas this year."

"I'm sure Susannah and Dan will both be delighted. No doubt they'll try to come, if it's at all possible, considering his church duties." Noting her mother's relieved expression, Jane tucked the letter into her own skirt pocket.

"I might as well tell you . . . I've invited her brother also."

Jane's heart plummeted. "Mama! It's difficult enough facing the possibility that I might see him every time I go to Boston, without having him come here as well."

"Well, Ben says he doubts Susannah would come without

him. Especially now that he and Lieutenant Fontaine are no longer spending their free time together."

"You certainly can't blame Alex," Jane chided. Taking her prayer book from the commode, she slipped it into the bag. "He's so lighthearted and entertaining. All Ted wants to do is sit around discussing the Holy Scriptures—when it isn't even the Sabbath! Ted never apologized for his dreadful conduct at the ball last year, either. And he never says he's pleased to see me or even compliments me anymore, no matter how much time I spend trying to make myself look especially pretty." She grimaced. "But he notices, I know he does. When he thinks I'm not aware, he watches me with the deepest longing in his eyes." A sly smile curved her lips. "I'm glad he's unhappy! He deserves to be as miserable as he's made me! Taking the side of Boston's riffraff, shaming me in front of—"

"Hurry it up, Jane," came Ben's call again. "Figs and fiddles! We were supposed to get an early start. Remember?"

Jane walked to the door. "I'm almost done." Quickly, she returned to the bed.

Wrapping a pair of Jane's kid slippers in a piece of cloth, Mama added them to the other packed clothing, then looked up. "I know how you feel, my dear. But I've been listening to your father and his friends of late—really listening, for the first time in my life. I'm finally beginning to realize that there is true merit in most of the colonists' grievances, and I understand how they feel."

"Oh, no. Not you, too, Mama," Jane moaned. She shook her head, and a rust-colored curl worked loose. She tucked it back into place.

Her mother nodded. "Governor Hutchinson and his pack of friends and relatives in Boston may side with the Crown, since they're all receiving generous salaries from Britain. But the merchants are all rallying with the rest of the townsmen in opposition to the newly granted monopoly given to the British East India Company. They know that allowing one monopoly to pass will only lead to others and destroy the free trade that's made Boston so prosperous. And then there's that despicable nuisance of a tea tax as well."

"Is there no place on this continent," Jane began wearily, "where I can be free of all this tea talk? It's maddening! I'll tell you one thing. By the end of the holiday season, I fully intend to be engaged to someone who will take me away from all of this. If it doesn't happen to be Alex, then it'll be one of the other officers. There are any number who've shown considerable interest. Even if they lack his high connections, they are all quite well set up, nonetheless."

Mama let out a troubled sigh, and her expression grew grave. "Oh, Jane, my dear. Forgive me, I've been so remiss. I have wronged you terribly . . . far worse than I ever did Daniel's wife, I fear."

"What on earth do you mean?"

Mama looked deeply, lovingly, into Jane's eyes. "I have led you to believe that high social position should be your utmost goal in this life. It was something I, myself, truly believed at one time. But only recently have I begun to understand how completely wrong those convictions are. True happiness comes from building a life with the man you love, the family you raise together, and the faith you both share in God."

"You and Papa have never shared a faith," Jane said with a hint of accusation in her tone.

"That's where you're wrong. We do. We simply do not always agree completely on the proper way to express it. After all, he is a Baptist, and I am an Anglican."

Jane opened her mouth to speak, but not soon enough.

"Please, please, dear—before it's too late, listen to me, I beg you. Everyone in my family felt sorry for me, their poor Sophia, when I rashly eloped with your father. Poor Sophia, forced to live in this lawless backwater of a colony, while my sister, Phoebe, married into titled gentry in Virginia. For years that has been thrown at me. Well, I picked up a letter from Phoebe this morning while I was in Pawtucket. She announced that she will be coming for a visit at Christmas, alone. As usual. Again she wrote how much *she* envies *me* for having a loving husband, a close family. This from a woman positively dripping with jewels and the latest fashions, who has never lacked for anything. Yet I doubt she's known a moment's joy in years. Whatever you do, Jane, don't ever marry a man you don't love. No amount of prestige or fortune is as precious as real love."

Jane dropped her gaze at once to her hands. "I l-love Alex," she forced herself to say. She toyed with the lacings on the front of her cobalt traveling gown as if it were suddenly important they be tied just so.

"No, you don't," her mother challenged. "No matter what your lips say, your eyes tell the truth. It has always been Ted you truly love, and those feelings will never go away. Should you forfeit that love to marry the cousin of one of the most hated men in all of America, you may also be forced to forfeit your family and all your friends. Of late I have heard much talk of open rebellion against Great Britain. The flame which has been kindled in the minds and the hearts of people throughout these Colonies may soon flare into a passionate blaze."

"Last call," Ben shouted from the stairs. "You're gonna slow me down enough as it is! Get movin'!"

Leaning near, Mama kissed Jane on the forehead. "Think about all I've said, won't you? There's plenty of time to consider my words during your ride to Boston. Your future happiness may depend upon the choices you make on this very trip. I shall be praying for you, my dear. Do nothing in haste which you might regret later." Closing the last carpet bag, she took it and headed out the door.

Her head buzzing, Jane took the other bulging carpet bag and followed.

❦ ❦

Exhausted and chilled to the bone, Jane would have liked nothing better than to crumple into a heap and die when Ben mercifully announced they'd be stopping for the night at an inn near Dedham. It was one of the few complete sentences he had said to her since they left the farm a little before noon. The harried pace at which they had been traveling had prevented all but the most basic conversation. For that, however, she was most grateful. Knowing she and her brother saw eye to eye on very few matters, not the least of which was her *consorting with redcoats,* she had determined not to discuss anything controversial along the way.

Nor would she have dared to voice a single complaint. He had let her know in more ways than one what an inconvenience it was to have her tagging along. She had gritted her teeth and ridden in sulky silence. If she did manage to marry Alex and sail off to jolly old England, she certainly wouldn't miss her younger brother's scowl one whit.

Ben slowed his horse and waited while she guided hers alongside. "This is it," he said. "The Brass Caldron." Swinging down, he reached up and helped her off with very little effort. "Go inside and warm yourself at the fire. I'll take care of getting us some rooms and a meal."

"I'm forever in your debt," she mumbled, forcing her stiff limbs to carry her toward the inn.

The unassuming fieldstone inn sat back a few yards from the road in the shelter of a stand of pine and elm. Welcoming lamplight streamed from its small windows. She stopped inside the door, and the comfort of a fire at the far end of the long smoky room drew Jane like a magnet. She worked off her dismal gloves and held her hands out, her fingers stretched wide. Brightly burning candles in wrought-iron wall sconces lent an orange glow to the sturdy, dark furnishings.

Jane noticed that a few tables were occupied by other warmly dressed travelers who conversed and chuckled over mugs of ale or hot cider, but beyond that she paid little attention to her surroundings. She concentrated on thawing herself out as she waited for Ben.

At last he strode through the door and stood near the entrance, talking with the innkeeper. How could her tall younger brother look so fresh? As a postrider he was forced to cover this many miles every day as a matter of course, yet he appeared as though he'd been out for a short afternoon jaunt. She grudgingly conceded that he had done a lot of maturing during the three years since he had taken over Dan's old duties. He spoke and walked with confidence and assumed whatever responsibilities came his way. But what did he carry in those saddlebags, anyway? Dangerous, incriminating letters, to be sure.

It was no secret that the British were becoming more aggressive than ever in their efforts to stop smuggling and other rebellious activities. If Alex were to find out that Ben's innocent-appearing postriding duties were merely a cover, a ruse to hide his traitorous affiliation with the Sons of Liberty, Jane knew he would never ask her to marry him.

Unfastening her cape, she opened it to allow the welcome heat to penetrate her body. She tried to put her brother's rebellious ways out of her mind as various snatches of conversation drifted her way.

"What do you suppose we'll end up doin' with that rat-infested *Dartmouth,* anyway?" a hoarse voice rasped.

Jane glanced over her shoulder. A cluster of nearly a dozen men occupied one of the long, wooden trestle tables across the room. All of them were clothed in the attire of tradesmen. Not wanting to stare or appear to be nosy, she cocked an ear in their direction but kept her face turned toward the fire.

"Well," a second voice said, "the docking of that revenue cutter should make old Sam Adams happy. I can see him rubbing his hands together now. Especially since word has it that two more tea tubs, the *Eleanor* and the *Beaver,* are lurking just outta sight, waiting to come into port as well."

"Why should that make Adams happy?"

"Don't you see?" the second man answered. "For months now, he's been wanting something to happen that would unite the Colonies again. Pit them against the Crown. The devil ships are just what he's been waiting for. See if they ain't."

Jane straightened as Ben came toward her and motioned to a table.

"The girl will be right along with our supper. Whatever it is, it smells pretty good. Hungry?"

Nodding, Jane smiled and sat down opposite him. "Starved. I had no idea riding horseback brought on such an appetite."

"Sure does. Sometimes I—"

"Come, now!" the raspy voice bellowed, interrupting their conversation. "The *Dartmouth* will never be allowed to unload."

Ben shifted in his chair as steaming bowls of venison stew and a plate of biscuits were placed before him and Jane. He shot a casual glance over toward the loud customers as the tavern girl poured fresh coffee into his mug, then his sister's.

"She will if Captain Rotch pays the fool tax on the cargo," the other voice announced, determined.

"Ha. Now, who do you suppose is about to let *that* happen, I ask? Even with our tea stores as low as they've been since the boycott, it's not likely."

"Yes, and the Committee of Correspondence has already started inviting committees and other citizens from the nearby towns to join us in protest. Oughta be one fine mob that sends the rotten ship back where she come from."

"Aye. I hear the tea agents are cowering up at Castle William," another man piped in. His fist slammed down on the tabletop in emphasis.

A round of raucous laughter followed.

Jane grimaced. "Mama was right. Sounds as if I truly will be arriving in the midst of a crisis."

Ben shrugged in nonchalance, but soon his attention wandered back to the talk on the other side of the room as he ate. "We only had ten more miles to go," he muttered after a while. "We should have kept on."

"What do you think will happen?" she asked nervously. "Will they send the ship elsewhere?"

"Won't do any good if they do," he answered. "The people in New York and Philadelphia won't brook any of that stinkin' tea, either."

"But how will they prevent it from unloading? After all, Boston is overrun with British troops."

Ben snorted. "You mean those fine upstandin' lobsterbacks who were sent here to *protect* us?" He shook his head as a gleam of merriment settled in his light brown eyes. "Time for you, dear sister, to take stock of where you stand."

"What do you mean?"

"Soon, very soon, the British—all of them—will be gone from our shores, even if we have to start a bonfire as big as Hades and throw them in one at a time." Ben's straight, even teeth flashed in a broad grin. "I can almost hear those pigs squealin' now. And, sister Jane, anyone with connections to that villain who sent them here in the first place will be a prime target."

Jane's appetite vanished. "I think I'll retire now." She rose and looked down at him. "Which room will I be occupying?"

Early the next morning, guiding her pacer alongside Ben's, Jane caught sight of the guard shack that dominated the narrow neck of land leading to Boston peninsula. She knew from the tight set of her brother's square jaw that he had seen it, too, but he made no comment. She followed his lead and tried to act naturally as they approached.

"Halt, in the name of His Majesty," a stern redcoat ordered as he came outside, his rifle ready. "State your reason for entering Boston."

"Family business," Ben offered. "I'm escorting my sister to our brother's home for a short stay."

The soldier opened his mouth as if to challenge Ben, but when he noticed Jane, recognition registered on his scowling face.

The corporal must have seen her on Alex Fontaine's arm at one time or another, for never before that moment had she seen a redcoat snap to attention so instantly.

Ben flung Jane a look of disgust. Nevertheless, relief and even a touch of pride flowed through her. Because of her high connections they would not be subjected to further harassment.

"Good day to you," the soldier said as he stepped aside. "But keep your wits about you and get off the streets without delay. There's trouble abrew."

"Oh?"

"Aye. Rebel crowds've been loitering about with a lot of big talk. The whole city is on the verge of treason. Use every caution."

"Why, thank you, Corporal," Jane said with a bright smile. She drew her cloak closely about her and nudged her horse into motion.

Once out of earshot of the soldiers, Ben's countenance became smug, and his gaze darted about as if in search of rebel mobs. But as his attention veered to Jane, he sobered. "Guess we'll take a short cut. Come on," he said, turning onto a narrow lane.

"Why? What's the hurry?" Jane grumbled, much preferring the wider main street. "We won't have any trouble. The soldiers know me."

"That's the point. Do you think I want to be seen with the *special friend* of one of the king's puppets?"

Ben's words cut Jane deeply. Where was his loyalty? After all, she was his sister. Then, recalling her own betrayals, a stab of guilt pricked at her heart. But the prodding of conscience didn't last long. After all, everything had worked out fine for Emily and Rob. They were safe and happy. And Jane couldn't help it that Alex had taken a liking to her. Besides, she had met the lieutenant through Susannah's own brother.

Upon reaching Dan's, they stabled the horses, then carried Jane's two bags to the rear entrance. Ben knocked, then opened the door himself, admitting them both. "Anybody home?" he called while Jane removed her cloak and gloves.

"In the parlor, runt," Dan yelled. "Come join us."

"Always room for one more, mate." The voice was unmistakably Yancy's.

Jane took a backward step before she regained her composure.

Ben didn't lose a moment, however. He hung up his heavy coat, then went immediately to join the men.

Jane had not seen the blackmailing sailor for a whole blessed year . . . she wished it had been ten. She smoothed her dress, straightened her shoulders, and debated whether or not to follow her younger brother.

"Good to see you, Ben," another voice said pleasantly. "We're discussing a tea party, down at the harbor."

"Aye," Yancy added. "Mates from as far north as Maine have come for it. How 'bout you?"

Hmph, thought Jane. *That useless tea talk again. Always tea—even at the expense of daily business.* Tightening her lips, she walked in behind Ben and saw that several men were seated around the parlor. No one spoke for a minute. She looked at Yancy's usually jovial face, but it bore not even a hint of a smile of welcome.

Ben turned and motioned toward her with one arm. "This, gentlemen, is my sister, Jane."

They all rose and inclined their heads.

Even as she smiled, Jane wondered why her brother—who a moment ago hadn't wanted to be caught with her—now suddenly wanted everyone to know who she was.

"She's come to attend the usual round of holiday parties with Lieutenant Fontaine. Of the Fourteenth Regiment," Ben added with intentional emphasis.

The spontaneous grins suddenly vanished, and Jane watched a few surreptitious glances being exchanged.

"Hello, Sis," Dan said, giving her a hug and steering her toward the empty hall. "Susannah's upstairs, rocking the baby. She told me to send you up the moment you arrived."

Knowing she had just been given the boot, Jane acquiesced and went up the steps. If nothing else, at least she was spared a confrontation by that vulgar Yancy Curtis, and she was grateful for that. If there was one thing she did not need, it was to have to endure his suggestive remarks in front of others. Reaching the second-floor landing, she tapped softly at the nursery, then opened the door. "Susannah? It's me, Jane."

"Oh. How delightful. Do come in." Susannah sat in the rocking chair near the hearth.

Jane had to admit that her sister-in-law was the picture of

motherhood in her blue muslin gown and white apron, a knitted shawl around her shoulders. Baby Miles, who seemed to have doubled in size since Jane had last seen him, dozed contentedly. His silken curls peeked out from a satin bonnet, making fragile coiled shadows on his mother's arm. His mouth made little sucking motions in his sleep. "My goodness," Jane whispered. "He's gotten so big."

"Do you think so?" Susannah looked down at him. "I suppose Dan and I hardly notice, since we see him every day. And it's been months since your last visit. But he's still an angel, and walking about already. Let me put him down so we can have a visit." She rose and carried the sleeping babe to his bed, then covered him up with a warm woolen blanket. "When he wakens," she said, smoothing her hand over his round bottom, "I'll show you how clever he's becoming."

"I'd like that. You're looking well, Susannah. Motherhood seems to agree with you."

"It has made me quite happy, I'll say that. We're so pleased you've come, Jane. Might I get you some tea after your long trip? It won't take but a moment. I have the water on already."

"I would truly love some. You have no idea how bitter it is out. I feel chilled to the bone. It's much colder in Boston than it is back home."

"Well," Susannah said, crossing the hall to the guest room, "you'll find your room toasty warm. I had Dan put on extra logs." Opening the door, she gestured for Jane to precede her. "Go sit down by the fire, and I shall bring you some fresh tea. Ben keeps us supplied, despite the present turmoil."

Jane didn't need to be coaxed. She sank gratefully onto the needlepoint-cushioned rocking chair near the hearth and admired the familiar homey furnishings as she took a few relaxing breaths.

A few minutes later, Susannah's return startled Jane. She had dozed, although it seemed that she had only closed her eyes a second ago.

Susannah set down the tea tray on a table beside Jane's chair. After filling a delicate china cup, she offered it to Jane, then poured a second for herself and sat down on the bed. "You look tired. I'm certain the ride from Pawtucket must have been exhausting."

"Yes. Ben isn't one for leisurely jaunts through the countryside," Jane answered tersely. "I could barely manage to keep up. I won't care to sit on another horse for some time." She sipped her tea.

Susannah chuckled. "Well, we're just glad you arrived safely. How is your family?"

"They're all fine. Oh, by the way, Mama sent you a letter." Reaching into her dress pocket, Jane extracted the paper and held it out.

Apprehension clouded Susannah's fine features, then just as quickly disappeared as her fingers closed around the offering.

"You needn't worry," Jane assured her. "You might find it a pleasant surprise. Mama's actually had a change of heart. A virtual miracle, if you ask me." She took another gulp. "I, um, couldn't help but notice Dan's having a meeting of some kind downstairs. Has Yancy Curtis come merely for that purpose?"

"He arrived in port a few days past. Why do you ask?"

Jane shrugged. "He's always such a bother. He disturbs me, though I can't imagine why."

"Yancy's a singular sort. But he always treats me with the utmost courtesy. Of course, Dan thinks the world of him." Raising her cup to her lips, Susannah took a drink. Her gaze fell upon the letter that she had laid on the table.

"Oh, forgive me," Jane murmured. "Of course you'd like to read Mama's message. I'll be quiet while you do." Getting up, she refilled her cup, then sipped it slowly while Susannah unfolded the letter and scanned the contents. Thus far Yancy must have kept the dreadful secret, Jane thought. But what would he demand in return?

Moving nearer the doorway, she could barely hear the voices from the parlor. It sounded as though they were bidding one another good-bye. Somehow she must see Yancy alone. Clearing her throat, she went back to the tray and set down her cup. "I'll just take this downstairs for you while you read in private."

Jane hurried downstairs just as the men were going out the front door. Taking a deep breath, she swallowed her pride. "Pardon me," she called after them, still clutching the tray. "Mr. Curtis."

He, along with the others, stopped and turned.

"May I speak with you?" she asked.

A look of resignation settled on his weather-lined face, then he grinned and shrugged at the others.

They returned disconcerting smiles as they departed with Ben.

"Mr. C-C-Curtis," she stammered. "I was asked by a lady friend in Providence to pass a message on to you if I happened to see you in my travels."

"Aye?" He gave a crooked grin. "'Tis always me pleasure to hear from a lady."

Jane flinched inwardly. Surely the despicable lout didn't actually think she'd be delivering word from one of his string of flirtations! She raised her chin and looked at Dan, still standing in the parlor doorway with a frown on his face. "It's private." Turning, she walked toward the kitchen, uncomfortably aware of the gangly redhead following a step behind. Setting down the tea tray, she busied herself putting fresh leaves into the pot, then, with elaborate nonchalance, added more water.

"Well?" Yancy challenged.

She looked up. Gone was the old spark that once had twinkled in his merry blue eyes. In its place was a hardness—not only on his face, but in his countenance as well. That unnerved her even more. "It's been a year."

"Aye. And not an idle one for you, I hear tell."

She hated that accusative tone of his. "Nor for you, I would venture."

Yancy stared woodenly without blinking. "So, what's the message?"

"Message? There isn't one. I just wanted to speak to you

alone." She anticipated an offensive remark like the ones he had always made before, or even a wicked smile. But there was neither.

"What do ye want, then?" he asked.

"Want? Nothing. Exactly nothing," she said, pursing her lips.

"Then we're even. I'll have nothing to do with someone who flaunts herself on the arm of that lobsterback cousin of Lord Hillsborough's. 'Tis a surprise that Dan or his wife'll still take ye in."

His tone chilled her. The words were like icicles shattering one by one upon the plank floor.

He turned and started to leave.

"Wait!"

Yancy stopped. Slowly, he met her gaze.

"I must know if you plan to keep silent about that little matter last year," she pleaded, angry with herself for the anxiety in her tone.

"Do ye speak of the night ye gave the Judas kiss to your own sister and her husband?"

Jane flushed under the glare of undisguised contempt in his eyes.

With a silent huff he grimaced. "Good day to ye, Miss Haynes." He then stalked off.

Jane felt dirty. Guilty. And the feeling frightened her. But gradually those sensations dissipated, overcome by the indignation that rose to the surface. How dare that lowlife brute dismiss her so rudely! Why, his total worth could be measured by the rags on his back. Why should she care what some shiftless gypsy sailor thought, anyway?

❧ ❧

A loud pounding on the front door downstairs awakened Jane, and she bolted upright in her bed. She must have slept the entire afternoon away! She swung her legs to the floor.

The knocking sounded again.

In her undergarments, Jane moved to the window and

peered out. All she could see was a flash of red as the uniformed man stepped inside. Could it be Alex checking to see if she'd arrived? Her heart beat wildly; she lit a lamp from the coals in the hearth, then pulled on a fresh gown. Grabbing a silver brush, she quickly arranged her hair and awaited the summons. But it never came.

Still the voices continued below.

If it was Alex, what could he and Dan possibly be talking about? The lieutenant had never attempted to conceal his feelings about the Boston clergy or their seditious rabble-rousing sermons. If he had his way, he would arrest every one of them and shut all non-Anglican church doors for good.

Jane made her way swiftly downstairs, but slowed at the sound of Dan's voice.

"Britain's single gift to New England was to leave us to ourselves," her brother said. "When we needed help in fighting Indians, in feeding and sheltering ourselves, none came. I'm aware that your soldier friends would truly like to believe that the French-Indian War was fought to save us from the savage hordes, but we had long since made peace with the Indians in these parts. It was a war over disputed territory between France and England, nothing more."

Jane hesitated as Dan continued.

"And, as I've said before, not only did the Crown expect us to volunteer and fight in it for Britain's gain, but afterward it was also declared that we should pay for it. And now, this England—which never built a single bridge to ease our way when this was a hostile land—wants to tax us without so much as a 'by your leave,' and *that* in order to replenish her depleted coffers."

Sucking in a breath, Jane debated whether to join them. Obviously, Dan must have offended Alex. The Fontaine family had more than likely participated in making those very decisions.

"Well, whether you feel they've a right or not," a rich baritone voice answered, "they have the might to enforce their will upon the Colonies."

Jane's heart thumped a joyous beat. *Ted!*

"I'm sure you're aware, Dan," he went on, "that most soldiers stationed here in Boston would relish nothing better than to knock some heads together."

"Did you notice," Dan asked, "that you said *they,* and not *we,* before?"

A moment of silence followed. "When my enlistment ends two years from now," Ted said quietly, "I've decided to leave the army."

Without taking time to let his words register, Jane chewed an inside corner of her lip. She should either join them or go into the kitchen; even now she could hear Susannah moving about, preparing dinner. But Jane had missed the sound of Ted's resonant voice. Surely she could listen just a little longer, let it ease the emptiness.

Dan said, "I know Susannah would be very disappointed should you return to England. And so would I."

"I've not told anyone as yet," Ted replied. "It seemed only right for you to be the first to know, since you're responsible in part. I've decided to take up my theological studies once more—at Harvard or your Nassau Hall, in New Jersey. I want to become ordained, as you are."

"That's quite a step. Do you feel this is what God is calling you to do?"

"This time I know it for a certainty."

Dan released a whoosh of breath. "That's wonderful. Wonderful! I'm thrilled to hear it. Susannah will be, too." He jumped up and rushed to the doorway. "Susannah! Sweetheart!"

Jane looked to the left, then the right, wondering which way to go. She didn't want to appear as though she'd been eavesdropping. When she took a step, Dan bumped into her. "W-what is it?" she asked, looking past her brother to oncoming Ted's handsome face.

A look of surprise and joy flashed over Ted's features, but she watched it calm into a gently smiling nod of greeting.

"Whatever is it?" asked Susannah, coming from the other direction. "Is something amiss?"

"No, my love," Dan said, grabbing her hand. "Everything is absolutely right. Perfect, in fact. Ted says that when his term of enlistment expires, he's going to return to college for his ordination."

Susannah's eyes misted as she stared at her brother for a moment. "Oh, Teddy, Teddy," she cried, rushing into his arms. "You couldn't have given me a more perfect Christmas gift. Papa would have been so pleased. So proud. Oh, but God is good, is he not? This wondrous gift after the one I received this morning."

She eased from Ted's embrace, and everyone looked at her questioningly.

She gave a bright smile. "Mother Haynes has written apologizing for rejecting me in the past. She's asked my forgiveness. And she humbly, and quite beautifully, pleaded that we join them for Christmas Day. It is all so marvelous."

Ted grinned and grabbed her in a hug. "I'm so happy for you, Sis. I know how often you've prayed for just that."

Jane watched the tender exchange with a twinge of bittersweet longing, wishing that she could have been the one he held in his strong arms. It seemed forever since she'd been in his embrace.

"Mother has asked that you come as well, Teddy. She wants you to feel as much a part of the family as any of her other children."

"Other children?"

"Her exact words," Susannah said with a smile.

Jane's heart sank to the lowest level it had ever reached. More than ever, she felt the outsider. Even her own mother, on whom she'd always depended, had lost her good sense—along with everyone else in the family. And now Ted, too, would be one of them. She had never felt so alone in her twenty-one years, especially when Ted's clear blue eyes sought hers for apparent approval and acceptance. It was more than she could bear. How could he have let Dan convince him that becoming a minister was better than the promising career Alex had so generously offered?

Whirling around, Jane made a dash for the stairs, but her flight was interrupted by a rap on the door. She stopped and took a breath to calm herself, then reached for the latch.

A young lad stood there. "Message for Miss Haynes."

"Thank you." Accepting the note, Jane clutched it to herself for a moment. Then, her lips pressed together, she unfolded it and read Alex's handwritten words:

> *My dear Jane,*
>
> *Due to the extreme unrest rampant in the city, I am afraid I will be on duty this evening and therefore unable to come by to welcome your return. I shall send my phaeton for you in the morning for services at the Anglican Church. Tensions are quite high, but I shall join you unless something prevents it. Afterward we have been invited for dinner at Captain Bidwell's. Until then, I remain, your devoted servant,*
>
> *A. F.*

Crumpling the note in her clenched hands, Jane glanced back toward Dan and ground her teeth. Because of him and those lawless friends of his, Alex would be unable to come tonight. Once more her plans were ruined, just as they had been on every other important occasion over these past two years. It was all Dan's fault. His and the rest of her family's.

The black phaeton maneuvered the narrow, winding streets, the leather of its three-quarter bonnet creaking with the movement. The rhythmic clopping of the horse's hooves danced off the multistoried buildings, town homes, and business establishments along the way to Captain Bidwell's house.

Alex lifted Jane's gloved hand and pressed it to his mouth, the glint in his steel gray eyes matching the hue of the last leaden clouds in the sky. "A pity," he murmured, "that we must be on display in this cursed open carriage. After counting the minutes until I could see you again, I should liked to have greeted you properly." He lowered his arm, her hand still captured in his grasp, and rested it upon his knee.

Jane felt herself blush under his suggestive gaze. Quelling a measure of uneasiness, she favored him with a bright smile. "Why, how gallant, Lieutenant."

"And quite true," he said, his eyes still holding hers. "I've not accepted the last half-dozen invitations for the simple reason that I could not bear to attend without you."

How easily he could remedy that problem! Jane told herself. Yet not once during the past year had he come close to proposing marriage. But surely after such promising statements, a proposal would soon be in the offing. And there was no conceivable reason why she should not grow to love the look of him as much as she did Ted.

Searching his face, Jane could not deny a certain attractiveness in its long, refined aristocracy, the generous mouth that curved into a rakish grin. The rich black military cape he wore contrasted with his clear complexion.

"Dreadfully sorry I was detained earlier, and therefore late for the church service," he apologized. "But despite my low rank, I'm sure that my having such an illustrious cousin has necessitated my presence at all meetings concerning the bothersome revenue cutter, *Dartmouth.* I suppose they intend to use me as a proverbial scapegoat, just as they did old Wills, if the matter is botched."

"I really don't see what all the fuss is about," Jane said with a pout. "Duty doesn't prevent Ted from having time to visit at Dan's at least once a day."

A muscle jerked in Alex's strong jaw, and his expression hardened. "I'm quite sure you are aware that, for obvious reasons, Ted Harrington is no longer privy to crucial military concerns."

The statement was heavy with innuendo, and Alex suddenly seemed far from his usual carefree, reckless self. Jane regretted the possibility that Alex and Ted's close friendship might have suffered irreparable damage because of their recent differences. "But, surely you must still consider Ted loyal."

Alex looked away in his typical, aloof manner. "One never knows. The past several years have seen quite a number of desertions in the ranks."

"Not among the officers, I would venture."

"I'm afraid I'm not at liberty to say. Good heavens," he said with a disgusted shake of his head. "Even I am now using that dreadful word."

"I beg your pardon?"

"Liberty!" he spat. "'Tis bandied about at every turn here in Boston. 'Liberty Tree,' 'Sons of Liberty,' even 'Daughters of Liberty.' I've grown quite sick of it."

"I once heard it said that liberty is a kindled flame which, like lightning, catches from soul to soul. One would think it was the start of another radical new religion rather than a rebellion."

Alex's cool eyes met hers. "All I have to say on the matter is that the flame had best not get out of hand and set any of our ships—the *Dartmouth,* in particular—afire."

Jane wasn't sure she liked the sudden turn of the conversation . . . or Alex's overbearing attitude. Nor did she appreciate being put in the middle of things. Just yesterday she had caught her own brother and his friends discussing the fate of that vessel carrying British East India Company tea. She sighed.

Renewed pressure by Alex's hand caused her to look up at him again.

"But you, my little Rhode Island rebel, have proven your loyalty more than once. I trust *you* implicitly." His mouth softened and lapsed into his familiar devil-may-care grin. As mischief sparked in his eyes, he guided the horse to the side of the street, then reined to a stop. "Perhaps this is as good a time as any," he said, lightly brushing a few stray hairs from Jane's cheek and then draping an arm on the back of the leather seat behind her.

"For what?" Jane whispered, looking up through the fringe of her lashes.

"You must know by now that I'm quite taken with you," Alex said, not releasing her gaze.

Jane felt herself turn quivery inside from his scrutiny. She could barely breathe and didn't trust herself to speak. She mustered a little smile.

"So much so," he continued, "that last spring I listed the countless advantages of a marriage to a loyal American in one of my reports to Cousin Wills—he does like to keep track, on the chance he may be reinstated."

"And?" she said almost inaudibly.

Alex raised his straight, dark brows and let out a breath. "I mentioned only your mother's connections and that I had met you in Philadelphia. But, alas, I'm afraid he took it upon himself to check further. He's discovered that you're from

Rhode Island. He sent me a most disappointing answer. I received it just this week."

Jane's cherished dreams crumbled to ashes. All the time she had invested in Alex was now for naught. Would nothing in life ever go her way? Only by sheer force of will did she manage to hold back the tears that sprang to her eyes. She switched her attention to her fur-lined muff and avoided his gaze.

Alex reached over and raised her chin with his fingers, compelling her to look at him once more. "No need to be disappointed, my sweet," he said gently. "When I want something I always find a way to get it."

Was this ray of hope a reality? Did she dare to believe what he seemed to be saying?

"I've spoken to the chaplain," Alex continued matter-of-factly. "He's agreed, for a price, to marry us at once—and antedate the contract by a month so it won't appear as though I disregarded my cousin's wishes."

"A-are y-you asking me—?"

"Yes, my darling," he said, pulling her close. "I'm asking for your hand, if you will do me the honor of becoming my wife."

The idea ran mad circles around Jane's heart, but her relief was far from complete. "Of course I'll marry you, Alex. But what about your family? Would they accept me after Lord Hillsborough's disapproval?"

"In time, of course. How could they not? Look at that glorious face of yours. Why, you're quite breathtaking. I shall be the envy of all far and wide."

Jane's mind reeled. Her dream of a wealthy, exciting life was on the verge of coming true. All she had to do was reach out and take it.

"However," Alex suggested meaningfully, "should you happen to be privy to any advantageous information—anything that you feel might assist us in handling this messy tea-ship business—I'm certain your welcome would be hastened immensely."

Jane tried to convince herself she had not heard correctly.

Alex couldn't be asking her to *spy* for him! But she could not ignore his voice as he continued.

"If you save the day for me now, my sweet, you'd be the belle of the season next year when we return to London. I'd probably have to resort to purchasing one of those Indian tomahawks for the express purpose of keeping my gentlemen friends at bay."

She lost herself momentarily in the comical picture his words painted. "Oh, I do so dream of leaving all of this unpleasantness behind." She tried to sift through her thoughts. "We'd have to wed in secret, of course. My family would never agree to such a hasty ceremony."

"Then you agree? Splendid!" He grabbed her and gave her a resounding kiss.

Even with her lips pressed to his, Jane could not ignore the fact that her heart did not flutter or ache with sweet longing, as it did when Ted kissed her. *As it used to,* she amended. Alex had merely forgotten to mention that he loved her, that was all. He was just caught up in the moment, particularly because it was the Sabbath.

The Sabbath! She pulled away. "Alex! People are watching us!"

He grinned devilishly. "What of it? A husband can't kiss his own wife? Why, when we get married in just a few days, our official papers will state that we've already been married an entire month!" Laughing, he picked up the reins and snapped them over the horse's back.

The carriage started into motion again, and Alex dodged a group of local men who turned mutinous looks his way as they crossed the street.

Jane struggled to contain the conflicting emotions that raged inside—joy and fear, thrill and dread, happiness and uneasiness. She tried to speak casually. "My goodness, what an unusual number of people out and about for the Sabbath, even for Boston. Wouldn't you agree?"

Alex snorted with disgust. "And all of them disturbed about having to pay *less* for their tea, of all things. Can you imagine?

No one shall ever credit Bostonians with possessing much sense."

It was not so much the price of the tea that the colonists protested, but the principle of the threepenny tax per pound. And Alex knew it. But Jane held her peace. Coupled with the tax was the fact that the British East India Company had been granted exclusive right to land tea in America, and *monopoly* was the foulest of words to the trade-minded New Englanders. Still, in Jane's opinion, there was far too much ado over a few dried leaves.

"I shall arrange our wedding for this coming Friday," Alex said, interrupting her thoughts. "I trust that will be acceptable to you. And I shan't tell a soul save the chaplain. It could not possibly serve my cause to do so. I wouldn't want someone knowing a particular wedding date, should my cousin inquire. After all, one never offends one's primary benefactor, and all that sort of rot."

A disconcerting thought nagged at Jane's consciousness as the phaeton continued on its way. She seriously doubted Alex would even consider marrying her if it were to cost him anything. But he *was* placing his future at risk for her. She did not allow herself to dwell on the fact that he actually expected her to spy for him. No, not just for him. For the two of them. But what about the sacrifices she would ultimately have to make? Surely any effort to secure her dream would be worth the price, however dear. Even if it meant the loss of her family, her friends, and her country. She tightened her lips. Whatever she would be called to do, it would be ultimately for them, for their success and happiness. It would be worth it. It had to be.

Jane's musings turned to her family. Emily had unselfishly sacrificed everything—her home, her name, her dreams—for Robert MacKinnon. The picture of her younger sister, a child-bride with a wee babe already, rose to her mind. Emily had found happiness. But the reality of having thoughtlessly betrayed her unsuspecting sister still left a sour feeling in the pit of Jane's stomach. Dan, too, had forfeited his place in the family and their good wishes, all for Susannah. But Dan and Susannah were so much in love. And amazingly, so were Emily and Robert.

Love. It had played no small part in Jane's own girlhood dreams.

With a sigh she stared unseeing at the passing scenes as her mother's warning played in her mind. *Don't ever marry a man you don't love. No amount of prestige or fortune is as precious.* But Jane was after more than mere love, much more. And she would have it all.

I will learn to love Alex, she told herself. *I will. I'll make myself love him. And I'll be the best wife he could ever have.* Impulsively, she took his hand in hers and stretched to plant a determined kiss on his cheek.

❦ ❦

The setting sun washed the rooftops and hills of Boston with liquid rose. The sky above appeared as a great glowing dome that reflected the same delicate hue upon lingering snowdrifts as Alex helped Jane down from the carriage at Dan's house.

"Won't you please come in for some tea?" she ventured.

He trailed a fingertip along her chin as his mouth twitched. "I think not. 'Twould not be wise for me to be seen visiting the local clergy, especially one connected with the rebellious Presbyterian sect." Softening his statement with a tender kiss, he gave her nose a tap. "Soon, my darling, we shall flee all this petty unpleasantness and take up the glitter and glamor of London's high society. How does that sound?"

Jane forced a smile. "Lovely. I cannot wait."

"Nor can I. Take care." With an answering smile, he kissed her lightly, then climbed aboard the phaeton and drove off.

Watching until Alex was out of sight, Jane realized with some chagrin that she had wiped away the touch of his lips with her glove. But she would come to desire him, truly she would. It would just take a little time. Purposefully, she walked up the steps and entered the front door.

As usual, a heated conversation met her ears. Hanging up her cloak, Jane craned her neck and noticed Ben, Dan, and a handful of other men gathered about the parlor. On the edge of the circle sat Susannah, looking worried.

Ben barely acknowledged Jane's arrival as he slapped a rolled-up newspaper into his palm. "No wonder Seth Parker looked so smug in his print shop in Philadelphia when he gave me that envelope to deliver to Sam Adams. This stinking article was in it! And now here it is for all to see. Well, the men who work down on the docks and on the ropewalks won't stand for being called cowards any more than I will!"

"Now, Ben," Dan said in a placating tone, "this will all be resolved. Just give it a chance. Certainly Governor Hutchinson will soon see the wisdom of sending the *Dartmouth* and its enticing cargo back to England, along with the other two ships."

"When?" Ben challenged. "It's already been here almost a fortnight. Time's running out. By law, if the *Dartmouth* doesn't set sail, it must pay customs fees by the seventeenth of December or have its cargo seized. That's only four days from now. Either way, the tea's going to have to be unloaded."

"I declare," Jane said with a sigh as she moved into the room. "One would expect you to give that bothersome matter a rest—at least on the Sabbath."

Dan frowned at her, then turned his attention to their brother. "If you'll just read a little more of the article, Ben, you'll find that a mass meeting has been called for tomorrow. We're going to demand an explanation from Captain Rotch as to why he hasn't made good on his word to return with his ship to England."

"Right," another man piped in. "And if this meeting's half as well attended as the last one, thousands'll show up."

With a nod, Dan went on. "For lack of room, we've had to switch from Faneuil Hall to the Old South Meeting House up at the corner. And even with that, people are still left out in the street. The town *will* do something—with or without King George's lackeys. Mark my words."

"Thousands?" Jane asked anxiously. This was a far more serious crisis than she could have imagined.

"At least five thousand, I would estimate," Dan answered. "All of them extremely angry men, I might add."

Jane glanced at Susannah, then back at her brothers. "Well, don't either of *you* go there. What if it becomes violent, as it did nearly four years ago? Surely no one's forgotten the Boston Massacre. And Ted—what about him? He and Alex will be ordered to stop you. People could get hurt again. Killed."

Susannah rose and moved to her side. "It's ever so easy to allow your imagination to run off that way. But let's not get ahead of ourselves. Or ahead of God's grace." She looked pointedly at Dan. "I think it would be wise for you to lead us in prayer. I'm sure Sam Adams, Doctor Warren, Mr. Revere, and all the others could use the Lord's wisdom. And," she added, sliding an arm around Jane, "so could the governor and the military as well."

Dan grinned, slightly embarrassed. "You're right, of course, my love. How easy it is for us all to forget to trust the Lord."

As Jane watched the men bow their heads, she followed suit. But even as she did, she couldn't help feeling that her brother's prayer would have far more power if she weren't there. Certainly almighty God would reject any sort of plea from her. She had given herself neither to prayer nor to humility, as the Scriptures instructed. Not for years . . . if ever.

The peacefulness of Monday morning was shattered by the tolling of the bells at Faneuil Hall and Old South Meeting House. Loud, steady bongs resounded for miles on the crisp winter day.

"Merciful heavens," Susannah whispered, staring out the window of her bedchamber.

Jane caught the anxiety in her sister-in-law's tone. She gave little Miles the stuffed bunny his mother had made, then rose to join Susannah. The baby sat contentedly on the rug, chewing on a gray flannel ear.

The sight which met Jane's eyes indeed looked ominous, and her pulse beat erratically in her ears. Milk Street fairly crawled with men bundled up against the bitter cold. All of them streamed in the direction of Old South Meeting House, which, it had been reported, would accommodate a far greater gathering than would Faneuil Hall, the usual assembling place for discussing city matters. All the shops within sight appeared empty, and Jane could see other women across the way peering out the upper-story windows, just as she and Susannah were doing.

Susannah reached for Jane's hand and held it tightly, as if gathering strength or comfort.

For a moment, as they stood gazing out upon the townsmen, Jane almost felt that they truly were sisters. She didn't care to think about what an organized rebellion might mean to people they knew and loved . . . on both sides. She herself had mixed feelings about it.

Stretching up on tiptoe, Susannah glanced in the opposite direction down the street, toward the icy bay that glittered in the thin morning sunlight. Then she settled back on her heels again. "Dan says that the tea agents consigned to receive the East India cargo have retreated to Castle William on the point, in fear for their very lives."

"Oh?" Jane leaned to see around Susannah. Her view of the castle was blocked by tall buildings, yet she could recall its stalwart presence from the times she had been down to the harbor.

"Yes. It's one of the fortifications used by the soldiers to guard the harbor. Apparently, the agents have refused the delegation's demand to submit their resignations over this tea business and have gone there instead, hoping to find sanctuary. I fear we are bound to have trouble now."

Jane agreed, but she tried to keep it from showing. "I hope it doesn't come to that." Down on the corner of Milk Street and Long Lane, however, she could already see the gathering of scarlet coats outside a printer's shop.

"I suppose all that is left for us to do is wait and pray," Susannah said, stooping to gather Miles in her arms. She disentangled his chubby fingers from one of her golden brown curls and returned to her post at the window. After a moment she turned to Jane. "Did you have an enjoyable time with Alex yesterday?"

"Yesterday?" Jane repeated as the momentous conversation suddenly came to mind. Strangely, the thought of the long-awaited marriage proposal brought no elation, but rather a feeling of grim finality. "Yes, we had dinner with the Bidwells, and it was quite pleasant. The captain's wife is a gracious hostess." She checked the corner once more to see if the soldiers waiting there had been joined by others. They hadn't, and neither did they appear to be trying to stop people from going to the hall. They merely lounged against the building watching the crowd. Her relief, she knew, would probably be short-lived. All too soon an officer could appear and issue an order, and—

"Is Ted supposed to be on duty today?" Jane asked suddenly. "Do you think he'll be sent if trouble erupts?"

Susannah shrugged. "I rather doubt it. He's been placed in charge of night patrols on the north end."

"Thank heaven," Jane breathed.

"Yes. It's marvelous the way God works things out for our good, just as he's promised. When Teddy first received those orders a few weeks past, he considered them punishment duty. I'm afraid his relationship with us has greatly damaged his standing."

Alex's remark about Ted no longer being privy to confidential military decisions resurfaced in Jane's memory. "It surprises me that he hasn't been ordered to stay away from here entirely."

Someone passing the house waved, and Susannah lifted her hand with a smile. "The authorities have no actual proof against Dan, since he rarely preaches at the Long Lane Church. And the other Presbyterian congregations he serves are so small that they meet mostly in individual homes. There's little likelihood of his sermons ever being overheard."

She paused. "Besides, Dan isn't quite as ready with angry accusations as are some of the other pastors—the Reverend Cooper, for example, of the Brattle Street Church. From the reports I've heard of him, I'm surprised he hasn't been arrested."

Jane put a hand on her sister-in-law's shoulder, and Susannah turned to meet her gaze. "Please, Sue, do encourage Dan not to become reckless like the others. For both your sakes . . . and this sweet baby's." The sight of the cherub's innocent face suddenly seemed infinitely more precious to her, and Jane fought back tears as she leaned near and hugged them both.

Would there have been a sweet little angel for her and Ted by now, if things had not gone awry as they had? For a fleeting second she envisioned herself in Susannah's place, having a dear babe in her arms, nestling it against her breast. . . .

Susannah gave a teasing smile as she handed the child to Jane. "Did you notice that you were concerned about Teddy's welfare a moment ago, but not Alex's?"

Immediately, Jane felt the warmth of a blush. She pressed her face against the baby's softness.

"When will you come to your senses?" Susannah asked quietly. "You've been in love with my brother for quite a long time. But I don't imagine he'll wait for you forever. And it's unfair to expect that of him."

Ted? Waiting for her? The very concept rendered Jane speechless. Her sister-in-law must be mistaken. Ted was distracted, moody, at times barely civil . . . and he knew about her betrayals of Emily. She tried to sort through her confusion. "A-Alex . . . asked me to marry him yesterday," she finally managed.

Susannah's chin rose. She searched Jane's face. "What was your answer?"

"I . . . said I would."

With a sigh, Susannah took Miles from Jane, then moved to the rocker. She absently smoothed a wispy curl that peeked from beneath the edge of the baby's embroidered cap. "We shall all miss you terribly."

All of a sudden, Jane's arms felt profoundly empty, and so did her heart—almost as if Susannah were abandoning her even as she spoke. But in a way, they all had abandoned her, hadn't they? Her family had far more important concerns than her happiness, and no one bothered to hide it. The thought inflicted pain, even though Jane was aware that as Alex Fontaine's wife she would never be permitted to associate with Dan and his little family again. Or Ted. Ever. For the rest of her life. A terrible heaviness settled over her, stealing her breath.

"Well," Susannah continued as she rocked the baby, "I do hope, for your sake, that the wealth and position you'll have as Alex's wife will somehow replace the love you will forfeit when you leave us. We shall pray for you."

"No!" Jane blurted out. She had grown increasingly disturbed by people flinging that irritating phrase at her.

"I beg your pardon?"

"I . . . I mean, I'm not quite ready to tell anyone about the proposal yet. Please don't say anything. Please."

With an understanding smile, Susannah nodded. "I see. No need to rush into anything, is that it? I suppose that's wise. I shan't say a word."

"Thank you." Certain that her eyes betrayed the truth, Jane turned away. It wouldn't do for Susannah to guess that the secret engagement would last a mere five days. She cleared her throat. "I'll, um, go down and do the breakfast dishes and tidy up."

❦ ❦

As she busied herself applying oil to the wooden stair rail, Jane became aware of renewed noise from outside. This time, however, it sounded different—it was far more loud and jubilant. Hordes of men returning from the meeting hooted and laughed until even the neighborhood dogs joined in with barking and yipping.

Setting down the cloth and the tin of linseed oil, Jane hurriedly wiped her hands on her apron and ran to the parlor window. She saw her brothers break away from the unruly parade and head toward the house. "Susannah!" she yelled. "Dan and Ben are home." Eagerly, she raced to the door and flung it open as Susannah rushed from the kitchen, her hands white with flour.

The men came in wearing the broad grins of victory, their faces glowing.

Dan cocked his head at his wife. "Well, it isn't likely there'll be trouble today, at least."

"Oh, Dan," she breathed. "Truly?"

He nodded, slipping off his coat and hat and hanging them on a peg. "Captain Rotch has agreed to go to the Customs

House for a sailing clearance. He and a committee appointed to accompany him will report back tomorrow."

"Praise be!" She looked visibly relieved.

A few taps sounded on the door, and Ben reached to open it. "Right on time," he said. "Come in, Yance."

Yancy Curtis again? Would that ruffian be her curse for the rest of her life? Skulking back against the wallpaper, Jane watched as the leggy seaman and two other roughly dressed characters started to follow Ben into the parlor. The strangers tipped their hats at her and Susannah as they passed. Cold air wafted in from the open door.

But Yancy's merry grin flashed at Susannah alone. He completely ignored Jane, not even acknowledging her presence as he strode by.

She felt humiliated, as if he had slapped her in front of everyone. No doubt the hateful cur was still waiting for some opportune moment to announce her horrid secret to the world—at a time when it would, she was certain, do her the most harm. Well, two could play that game.

"Come along, Jane," Susannah said pleasantly. "I could use a bit of help kneading the bread in the kitchen."

Still glaring daggers at Yancy's bony back as he leaned against the wooden parlor chair, Jane barely heard Susannah's voice. It should be quite simple to catch him in one of his traitorous deeds . . . and what a joy to be the one central to accomplishing his downfall. "I'll be along in a few minutes," she answered with a sweet smile. "I've nearly finished oiling the rail." She went to the stairs and retrieved her cloth, then began rubbing a portion of the banister.

As her sister-in-law returned to her task, Jane moved within earshot of the spirited conversation, hoping to overhear something incriminating—anything. After all, the hooligan did make lawlessness his calling in life. She could use that blackmailing scoundrel to make herself a heroine in the eyes of Alex and his family. How very perfect—and not in the least distasteful as betraying her own family had been. That was one thing she doubted she could do again—not even to secure an exalted place in Alex's eyes.

"Well, you're all aware that Boston is low on tea at the moment," Dan was saying to the others.

Jane had to stifle a yawn. She had heard this same conversation a dozen times before. Didn't *they* ever tire of it?

"Well, the governor is still stalling. If Captain Rotch is not allowed to leave port, the tea will be unloaded, and he'll be required to pay the tax. That's the law. And even if every one of those hundred and fourteen chests *is* locked in a warehouse, the tea will find its way out and into the shops because of the shortage. You know it as well as I. That's what Hutchinson is counting on."

"I have a remedy for that, mate," Yancy offered. "Fact is, that's what I came to town to arrange."

Jane perked up. *Please let it be illegal,* she wished. She held her breath.

"A few leagues north of here there's a ship hiding in a little cove with a cargo of Dutch tea aboard. All they need is the word, and they're ready to sail in," Yancy went on. "Couldn't ask for a better time, could ye? With the whole town's attention on Griffin's Wharf and that cursed cutter *Dartmouth,* some other fair vessel could easily slip in, say, to Gee's Shipyard, out on the north end."

"Which one is that, Yance?" Ben asked.

"Closest one to the mill pond," he answered. "If ye could round up some men and a freight wagon, I could ride up to where she's anchored and pilot her in on an eventide. By Wednesday night, for sure."

Jane's pulse thundered in her ears. He wanted to drag Dan and Ben into his scheme! She moistened her lips, hoping desperately that neither would participate. It was Yancy's hide she was after. His alone.

"Hm," Ben muttered. "I'm afraid I've been asked to be available twenty-four hours a day until further notice. But I might know some fellows who'd be more than willing."

Jane very nearly laughed for joy. But as Dan cleared his throat, she froze.

"I, too, will have to decline," Dan said. "Now that I have a son's welfare to consider as well as our own, I made a solemn promise to the lady of the house to refrain from smuggling."

Jane sank down on the bottom step in relief as a round of guffaws rang out.

"And," he continued, unruffled, "I cannot break it."

"Don't worry," said one of the other men as they sobered. "Won't be no problem to round up a bunch of *bachelors* eager to help out. Just name the time."

"Aye, mate. That's what I was wantin' to hear." Yancy took a deep breath and let it out slowly. "I need to borrow your horse, Dan. That is, if your good wife will let ye lend it out."

The men in the room chuckled at Dan's expense.

Unable to contain her own smile, Jane tiptoed to the kitchen.

You may laugh now, Able Seaman Curtis, she thought. *But you've just opened the door to your own jail cell.*

27

Jane survived the remainder of Monday somehow, fervently hoping Alex would contact her or send his phaeton for her, but to no avail. The hours dragged by and lengthened into night. Finally, in desperation, she went to bed.

The following day was the same—interminable hours helping Susannah with the multitude of daily chores. When at last Tuesday afternoon gave way to evening, Jane banished herself to her bedchamber rather than pace and fidget before Dan or Susannah's observant eyes. She would see Alex on the morrow even if she had to go to him! That decided, she climbed into the fluffy feather tick and pulled the blankets and counterpane up to her chin. But sleep did not come until long past the hour her brother and Susannah retired.

Wednesday dawned cold and rainy, just like the two previous days. But shortly before ten o'clock, the bells at Faneuil Hall and the Old South Meeting House again summoned the townsfolk.

Jane and Susannah watched as the crowds poured along the street in the falling mist heading toward the hall on the corner of Marlborough Street.

"Today," Susannah muttered, "we should find out whether or not Captain Rotch secured a sailing clearance."

"Mm." Jane feigned indifference by turning from the parlor window and going back into the kitchen, where she and Susannah had been seeing to the morning duties.

Susannah followed and soon was busy washing and rinsing a small bundle of soiled baby clothes.

Jane fumed as she swept the floor. There had to be a way to get to Alex. Then she noticed the half-filled milk pitcher sitting on the table. Checking quickly to be sure that her sister-in-law's back was turned, Jane moved nearer and knocked the container to the floor. It clanged against the planks, splattering milk in a wide white puddle. "Oh, no!" she gasped.

Startled, Susannah looked over her shoulder, one hand pressed to her heart.

"How clumsy of me," Jane said innocently. "It somehow got in the way of my elbow as I was sweeping." Seizing a rag, she immediately began mopping up the mess. "I'm sorry."

"Accidents will happen," Susannah said. "It couldn't be helped. I'm sure Dan will be more than happy to go to the milk barn for us when he comes home from the meeting."

"Nonsense. We need it for the soup. As soon as I clean up the floor, I'll run out for some more myself. After all," Jane offered graciously, "it *was* my fault."

"Well, if you're that determined. We could certainly use it."

Within minutes Jane grabbed her cloak and the covered milk bucket, then hurried out. The rain had stopped.

Nearly deserted, the puddled street seemed eerily quiet for a Wednesday. Hesitant to appear at British military headquarters unless it was unavoidable, Jane turned up her hood against the dampness and hastened in the direction of the house where Ted and Alex were billeted.

Even as she approached the unassuming dwelling, bitter memories assaulted her—memories of that night a year ago, when she had sneaked there to see Ted and had betrayed Emily. *For the second time,* she reminded herself, fighting off the familiar twinge of nausea the thought always caused. Thank goodness they had escaped. But that Yancy Curtis! He had probably helped them merely to have something more to dangle over her head, to torment her, destroy her. Simply because she preferred a British officer to a cloddish seaman.

She would suffer no qualms of guilt by turning in that insufferable man.

Jane walked purposefully to the door and set down the pail before giving a few sharp raps.

It opened almost at once, and the dour landlady stood before Jane. This time, however, she wore a serviceable, olive work dress, white cotton apron, and dust cap. Recognition flicked in her small hazel eyes. "Yes?" she asked, drawing her mouth into a prune-sized circle.

"Good morning, Madam," Jane began politely. "Would Lieutenant Fontaine perchance be at home?"

The woman's eyes squinted with her curt answer. "He's gone to his headquarters. Left some hours ago. Would there be anything else?"

"No. Thank you," Jane added as the woman shut the door in her face. She stood there for a moment, thinking.

Susannah had said that Ted had been assigned to night duty. Her gaze drifted upward to the second-floor windows. In all likelihood, he was up in his room even at this moment, asleep. If only there were some hope of reconciliation, some way to make amends for all that had come between them! But she knew that the deepest, most secret desire of her heart was futile. The paths they had chosen led in opposite directions. So be it. Inching up her chin, she stooped and grasped the handle of the pail, then took her leave.

Walking out onto the street, Jane glanced in the direction of the British headquarters and stopped. Much as she disliked the thought of having to go there in order to find Alex, it appeared she would be forced to do just that. She would just have to hope that no one she knew saw her. She took a deep breath and continued back toward Milk Street.

Jane had gone a scant two blocks when she spotted Alex standing with another officer at the corner. Their attention appeared to be directed toward Old South Meeting House at the end of the street.

As Jane drew near they both turned her way. "Good day," she said breezily, lightly swinging the pail in one hand. "Why, what a surprise to see someone I know on my way to the dairy."

"The dairy?" Alex's steel gray eyes made a slow circuit of admiration over her.

"Why, yes. I've been sent to fetch milk. I seem to have gotten lost, but I'm going in the right direction now, am I not?" She met his gaze boldly, certain he would offer to assist her, since only an idiot could actually get lost when her house was on the same street as the dairy.

"Quite," he returned. "But I should be most happy to accompany you. There's a number of ruffians lurking about."

She gave him her very brightest smile. "Oh, how very thoughtful, Lieutenant. I'd feel ever so safe in your company."

Alex nodded to his companion, who returned a sly, knowing grin, then reached for the milk pail and carried it as he and Jane started for the dairy. "I've missed you," he said.

"Have you? I wondered, since I haven't seen you in days." She regarded the tidy yard of a particularly well-kept brick town home as they walked by its iron gate. The shingled roof was coal black from the rain, as were the skeletal trees beside the house.

"Why would you doubt it? You know I've been assigned special duty of late, what with the current state of the town's temper." A ribald grin flashed her way as he took her arm. "But all of that will be behind us when Friday comes, of course, and you become my bride. The waiting is intolerable, don't you think? Hopefully, the next two days shall pass quickly."

Jane could not control the stubborn flush that heightened her coloring. She was certain that his manner would appear official to a casual observer, yet she felt imprisoned by his proprietary attitude. She had a fleeting image of herself as a dried butterfly . . . a creature that had once spread its lacy wings and fluttered about in the sunshine, but now was mounted under a sheet of glass. Was it really only two days until she would actually be united to this tall, aloof British aristocrat? Somehow she had managed during the week to block that small detail from her mind.

"I do hope you're as pleased about it as I," Alex went on.

"Of course." With a superficial smile, Jane added another lie. "I can think of little else."

He beamed down at her. "Splendid. I shall send the phaeton for you at three o'clock Friday afternoon, then."

With a nod, Jane managed another smile. Then she stopped and put a hand on his sleeve. What she had to do must be done quickly, before she changed her mind. "Alex?"

"Yes, my sweet?" His eyes made another meandering trip over her face.

"Do you remember telling me that if I were to hear anything . . . useful . . . it would help my standing in the eyes of your family?"

He sobered at once. "Yes, of course."

Jane swallowed hard. "I . . . I know something which might be of importance. I heard it the other night."

"Yes?" His features took on a granite-like hardness.

The frenzied beating of Jane's pulse throbbed in her ears. "It has to do with smuggling. Tonight. Somewhere on the north side of the city at a place called Gee's Shipyard. Do you remember Dan's friend, Seaman Curtis?"

Alex's mouth curled wickedly at one corner. "Is he not that uncouth fellow who was at dinner two summers ago in Rhode Island? The one with scruffy red hair? Who could forget him?" A curious laugh rumbled up from deep within Alex, unlike any sound Jane had heard him utter.

A sudden sharp gust of wind rustled through her skirts and cloak, making her shiver, and she felt goose flesh rise on her legs and arms.

"It's poetic justice, don't you see?" he said gleefully. "That day at your family's farm, Ted wanted to wring Curtis's scrawny, no-account neck for flirting so outrageously with you. And now—" His dark eyebrows drew together devilishly. "Now Ted may have his chance."

"W-what are you saying?" Jane asked as a tremor went through her.

"Why, it's perfect. Ted has night patrol on the north end. I cannot wait to see his face when I tell him. And if there's the slightest bit of soldier at all left in him, he shall have the ideal opportunity to prove it."

Jane had to fight to subdue the trembling that shook her from the very core of her being. "Y-you won't tell Ted that it was I who informed on Yancy, will you?" she whispered.

His eyes narrowed to suspicious slits.

"Oh, please, Alex," Jane pleaded desperately. "Tell no one but a trusted superior, and let him give the order to Ted. Otherwise my family will know I told. You do understand, don't you?"

"Of course, my darling." Alex's tone was patronizing, but his expression eased somewhat, and he brushed gloved fingertips along the curve of her jaw. "But remember, very soon you shall have a whole new family."

❧ ❧

As the afternoon waned, so did Jane's spirits. The noon hour came and went without Dan's return from the meeting, and the hush along the street seemed ominous, menacing. Jane and Susannah sat at the table alone, maintaining what seemed a mandated silence. Susannah hurried through her meal, then went up to the baby. But Jane did nothing more than rearrange the food on her plate with her fork. Finally, she dumped the entire meal into the slop bucket. She did all the dishes by herself so that Susannah could spend some extra time with the baby, but it did nothing to ease her guilt. Every nerve in her body felt raw and exposed, and the fine hairs on the back of her neck and arms stood on end, as though a summer electrical storm were gathering overhead.

Passing the hall looking glass, Jane was almost surprised that accusatory words were not emblazoned on her forehead for all the world to read. *Guilty. Turncoat. Witch.* What on earth had she done? What if something happened to Ted?

Reaching the parlor, she shoved the poker idly at the burning logs in the hearth, sending a burst of glowing sparks in wild flight up the chimney. Never in her life had she felt so uneasy, so afraid, or so responsible for causing trouble. She needed something to take her mind off the inevitable clash at Gee's Shipyard—a conflict that she had set in motion. Noticing Susannah's sewing basket, she rummaged through until she found some socks to darn—tedious work that Mama had always used for punishment.

From up the street a horrific racket split the quiet. Hideous yelling and bloodcurdling screams spewed forth, a sound like the war whoops of hundreds of Indians.

It sent chills skittering along Jane's spine as Susannah came running down the stairs.

"What is it?" her sister-in-law gasped.

Together they went to the window and peered out, but could see nothing. In frustration, they opened the front door and stepped onto the stoop.

Mobs of men ran and danced and leaped past in the falling rain.

Jane felt lightheaded with fear. Susannah, however, sighed and smiled. "Something's happened—and surely it must be good. It seems to be some sort of celebration."

But she was wrong. Dan emerged from the crowd and came up the walk toward them. He ushered Susannah and Jane inside, then closed the door and bolted it. He hung his rain-slicked cloak, and it dripped tiny puddles onto the plank floor.

"Whatever is amiss, Dan?" Susannah asked in a small voice.

"The customs officials and the governor have refused the *Dartmouth* permission to leave the harbor," he answered gravely.

Jane stepped nearer. "Then what is the celebration about?"

"It's hot blood flowing, that's all. People have grown impatient with all the talking and the waiting. Now it's settled."

"What is?" Susannah asked.

Dan sighed heavily. "They're going to take some decisive action."

"What kind of decisive action?" Jane asked, clenching her cold fingers.

"Oh, you needn't concern yourselves about it," he answered with a twinge of bitterness. "Either of you." He shot Susannah a look of frustration. "*Once again* I did not volunteer."

"You're a man of the cloth, Dan," she said. "The ministry is now your first priority. Surely they wouldn't expect you to—"

"What's settled is settled," Dan interrupted. "And they've got far more volunteers than they'll ever need anyway."

"For what?" Jane's voice sounded strange even to her own ears.

Dan looked sternly at her, then at Susannah. "It's best you don't know. Take my word for it."

Dan's fingers drummed impatiently on the kitchen table, adding to the distant roar of gathering men that had been growing louder since the gray day had turned to night. He finished the last of his coffee. For the tenth time he got up and went to the back door, opened it, and peered out.

Watching her brother, Jane tucked her skirts firmly about her legs as one more blast of cold air stirred around them. A piece of cake lay untouched before her. She fought the impulse to join Dan, to see if anything was happening down at the harbor. All over town the bright glow of lanterns and torches lit up the sky as though it were day.

"Still raining," he muttered with a sigh as he came back inside. "You know," he said, turning to Susannah, "I promised to check in on some of our flock this evening. I probably should do it."

His wife eyed him doubtfully. "Odd that you never mentioned it before."

"Yes, well," he sighed, then went to look outside once more.

"Daniel," Susannah murmured in defeat, "why don't you just go on? You'll drive us mad if you don't."

"Truly?" He came back to life, rushed to her chair, and planted a kiss on her cheek. "I love you, sweetheart! And I'll be careful. You have my word." Before she could respond he dashed away.

Jane watched as her sister-in-law's gray-blue eyes followed

Dan's flight. *Her eyes are like Ted's,* she thought, and her heart clutched as Susannah tossed her head in resignation—another of Ted's mannerisms.

"Honestly," Susannah said with a dubious smile. "There's simply no changing a man, is there?" Lifting her cup to her lips, she took a sip of coffee, then set it down. "The very first time I saw Dan he was breaking the law."

"Oh?" Jane responded with mild interest.

"Mm-hm. He and Yancy were smuggling something off the ship that brought me from England. Paper, if I recall correctly. Yancy and another sailor were dressed in the most gaudy women's clothing I'd ever seen. It was actually quite comical, now that I think back." Shaking her head, she chuckled.

At the mention of Yancy's name, Jane closed her eyes and tried to imagine the ridiculous spectacle. Then she stopped breathing and sprang up. "Dan is on his way to meet Yancy?"

Susannah tipped her head and gave a puzzled frown. "Yancy? No, I don't believe so. Yancy left a few days ago. I'm quite certain Dan's leave-taking has something to do with that meeting today. Something about the *Dartmouth* affair. I just pray that Dan keeps his promise and doesn't do anything rash." Casting a glance heavenward, Susannah reached for the dirty dishes on the table, then rose.

Dread of a far more certain doom that might be taking place at Gee's Shipyard at this very moment gripped Jane. The cup and saucer she held rattled in her fingers and slipped from her grasp. She froze in place as the two pieces shattered and flew in all directions.

Her shoulders slumped dejectedly. "I'm terribly sorry. I don't know what's come over me," she whispered as she stooped to gather the broken china. "I'll clean it up."

"Nonsense. There's enough for both of us," Susannah said good-naturedly, dropping into a stoop to help.

"Ouch!" Jane dropped a jagged chunk as if it were on fire. She lifted a bleeding finger to her lips.

Susannah came to help her and guided her to a seat. "Jane,

you've been far too jumpy all day," she said. "First the milk, and now this. Why don't you just sit in this chair while I finish? Then I'll make us a pot of tea. Would you like that?"

Fighting tears, Jane could only nod.

Susannah kept her hand on Jane's. "You know . . . you've been heavy on my mind of late, and I've been praying rather earnestly for you. I feel quite burdened to ask you something. Would you mind awfully if I did?"

Jane drew in a ragged breath. Could Susannah have heard of her latest act of betrayal? She met her sister-in-law's gaze.

"There was a time not so very long ago when you wanted nothing more than to marry my brother. You journeyed often to Philadelphia to see Teddy. You arranged for the two of us to reconcile, to make things right in the family—for which I shall be eternally grateful. And you even convinced him to transfer to the Fourteenth Regiment to be near you. You must have loved him quite deeply, despite the fact you knew he had no wealth to speak of."

As Susannah recounted the events that had led to her ultimate loss, Jane's melancholy increased.

"I was just wondering what it was about my brother that made you love him, poor as he was."

Jane averted her gaze until she stopped the tears threatening to fill her eyes. How could she evaluate all the intricate facets that made up the shining gem known as love? Her throat tightened, and she swallowed a great lump. "I . . . loved everything about him. He's really quite handsome, you know, and has some enchanting habits—like tilting his head and looking earnest just as he's going to speak. I liked the way his eyes shined when he looked at me." She paused. "And I can't explain it, exactly, but there seemed to be a manly strength about him I felt I could trust."

Susannah regarded her silently.

"I know you probably thought he was being mean and stubborn when he wouldn't speak to you," Jane went on. "But, Susannah, he did believe he was in the right. He often agonized over his decision when he was with me."

"Yes, we've discussed it. But what bothers me now is quite a different matter." Her sister-in-law paused for a moment, then went on. "I'd like to know why, for no apparent reason, Alex's fortune would make you suddenly turn away from Ted and all that you shared together."

Jane ran her tongue along her lips, and a tear fell from the corner of her eye as she blinked. "I wasn't the one who changed my mind. Ted turned from me! And from Alex."

Susannah brushed a lock of copper hair away from Jane's face. "Oh, no, Jane. Teddy didn't turn from you. He turned *toward* God. That should have only deepened your love for one another. Unless perhaps you felt left behind because you weren't going in the same direction. Did you ever consider that?"

The last of Jane's inner defenses collapsed under the weight of guilt and despair that had been building up inside her for some time, stealing her sleep, making her days unbearable. Susannah's caring face blurred beyond her tears. "You're right," she sobbed. "I'm not. I'm selfish—and willful . . . and evil. I'm beyond redemption by now, after all that I've done to hurt people."

"Of course you're not, dear," Susannah said. "Not if you're truly sorry. God's forgiveness is available to anyone."

"N-not to m-me," Jane said with finality. "You don't know what I've done. The spiteful, hurtful things I've done to this family."

Susannah took hold of Jane's shoulders. "Jane, no sin in this world is too great for God to forgive. Or too small. Why, look at King David in the Old Testament. He not only took another man's wife, but he also had the woman's husband killed to hide his own sin. But when he repented, God forgave him completely."

"Yes," Jane said bitterly. "But at the price of his son's death." Drawing a shaky breath, she began wringing her hands as she turned her eyes heavenward. "Oh please, dear God, don't make anyone else pay for the horrible things I've done."

In her mind, Jane envisioned Yancy being confronted by

Ted. What would happen? What if Yancy resisted—fought back? What if one of them was killed? She jumped up. "I have to go out! There's something I must stop—if I'm not too late." Running to the door, she grabbed a cloak and ran outside into the night, oblivious of the questions Susannah called after her.

She dashed through muddy puddles to the stable, taking time only to put the bridle on the horse she'd ridden from Pawtucket. Then, climbing onto a rail, she hiked her skirts and slid onto its back.

Jane rode toward the north end of town, giving little thought to the clusters of men loitering about all along the way. Whatever they were discussing or waiting for in the drizzle did not matter in the least.

The horse's hooves clattered into the night as Jane sped over the cobblestones. Clutching the reins tightly, she felt hot tears mingling with the cold raindrops that streamed down her face. "Oh, please, almighty God, please don't sacrifice Ted or Yancy as Bathsheba's husband was. I promise I'll never do anything bad again. I'll confess my betrayals to anyone who'll listen to me, and I'll take the consequences. But please save them. I beg you."

❦ ❦

A satisfied grin spread across Yancy's face as he watched the Dutch schooner slip quietly away from the dock and rapidly disappear into the darkness. From his perch atop a wagon loaded with chests of tea, he waited while the remaining few trunks were put aboard. Things couldn't have gone more smoothly. Not a soul was left at this end of town to take notice of this little operation at Gee's Shipyard. Every patriotic man on the Boston peninsula knew where the most excitement would be taking place this night.

"That's the last of it," one of the dripping men boasted as he wiped off his hands and grinned.

"Aye. This'll take care of Boston's low supply for quite a spell," Yancy quipped. "'Twas good of ye all to help, even with the tea party of the year taking place. We're beholden to ye. Now if ye'd like to make haste down Griffin's Wharf way, I can finish here. No sense missing it."

"I appreciate you taking the wagon back to Hancock's warehouse for me," another voice said. "I'm kind of worried, what with my hotheaded baby brother in the thick of things down there. He was one of the few chosen to do the actual deed."

"Me pleasure, mate. Thanks again. Meet ye at the Green Dragon later. To celebrate!"

The half-dozen men laughed and punched one another playfully, then hastened out to the rain-slicked streets amid ribald comments and good-natured chatter.

Yancy snapped the reins, and the work horses plodded in a slow turn toward Hancock's. He couldn't have picked a more fortuitous night for an unloading, if he did say so himself.

❧ ❧

Ted eased his hold on the horse's reins and flipped up the collar of his military cape against the cold, wet mist as he rode ahead of four foot soldiers coming out of Hunt & White's Shipyard. What a miserable night to be on duty up at this end of town. Anyone with any sense would know that if there was to be any action, it would take place at the harbor to the south. But his orders said to search all the deserted shipyards in this area for a suspected smuggling operation.

"I, for one, think we're wastin' our time," one of his soldiers muttered to another as they marched along behind Ted's horse. "Not even the mice are out here on Lyn Street."

"How many more to go, Lieutenant?" a stocky young private asked.

"We're to check them all," Ted replied, slowing his mount's pace so as not to get too far ahead.

"Wonder why?" the third said. "We'd be of more use at the Green Dragon or the Bunch of Grapes. You can bet the rabble are planning something for tomorrow. Maybe even tonight."

The fourth man snorted. "Aye. Looks like a wild-goose

chase, if you ask me. I'd like to get in one wee shot at them swaggerin' ropeworkers. Or, better, take one of their billy clubs away from them and deliver a few stout taps to some heads."

"You know," the first said, "we could cut across North End and head toward Griffin's Wharf. Way out here, we're almost a half hour march away, if trouble does break out."

Ted turned in the saddle and glared back at them. "Look, men," he said wearily. "We will stick to our orders. The informant was reported to be most reliable. Now keep silent, or you'll warn the culprits off."

Nudging the animal to a slightly longer stride, Ted considered how much better off he really was out here on the fringe of town. No telling what he might do if he were put in the position of having to shoot someone, as the soldiers had been forced to do when some unruly townsmen mobbed the king's men in front of the Customs House in '70. He had gotten to know quite a number of the locals during the past year, and more than likely, every one of them had been at the recent town meetings.

Traveling along the road that lined the wharf, Ted heard, then made out, a large wagon lumbering out of Gee's Shipyard. His pulse picked up, and he squinted against the spray of misty rain. Drawing his saber, he administered hard pressure with his knees to send his horse into a charge, cutting off the path of the wagon team.

His men ran after him.

"Halt!" Ted commanded, centering his attention on the driver. His gaze met a cocky half-smile. *Yancy—Dan's old friend!* A sinking feeling went through him.

As two of the foot soldiers grabbed the halters of the big work horses, Ted rode slowly back to the wagon bed and lifted the tarp with the tip of his sword. Tea! It would have to be that cursed tea! Circling his mount up beside the team once more, Ted took hold of a halter. "Go search the yard for the other culprits," he ordered his subordinates. "And seize the ship if it's still docked."

The men sprinted off to do his bidding.

"Too late, mate," Yancy said almost soberly.

"By all that's holy, Curtis, couldn't you have limited your smuggling activities to Rhode Island?" Ted asked. "You've put me in a very unfortunate position."

Grinning mischievously, Yancy said nothing. He merely shrugged.

"I'll not enjoy having to inform Dan of my part in your incarceration."

At the loud clopping of a rapidly approaching horse, Ted wheeled his mount to meet an ambush. He reached for his pistol. But a lone horse slid to a stop. Ted's jaw dropped open. *Jane!* Never in a million years would he have expected to set eyes upon her out here.

She slid down from her pacer and threw herself at the wagon, clutching the edge of the seat with her fingertips, her face streaked with tears. "Oh, please, forgive me, Yancy. I'm so sorry. I didn't mean it, I swear."

"What are ye sayin'?"

Jane sobbed. "I'm the one who told on you. For spite! I've been so wicked; I know that now. Please forgive me."

At first Yancy looked dumbfounded. Here was Jane, compromising herself before an officer of the Crown.

Yancy cleared his throat. "Go home, Jane. Now."

Ignoring him, she turned to Ted. "And I've been dreadful to you, too. All the while you were drawing closer to God, I've been more concerned with my own frivolous pursuits. Pursuits I considered far more important. I've foolishly cast aside the beautiful love you offered me. How could I have been so willful, so very wrong? Not only are Emily and Rob in hiding all because of me, but now Yancy, too, will pay for my betrayals. Please, Ted, I beg you. Let him go. Do what you wish to me; I deserve anything you would mete out. But please, let him go free."

"You know I cannot," Ted said. "It's my duty to prevent contraband from entering this port."

"Fine!" she cried. "Keep the wagon, then. But don't arrest Yancy."

Despite the awful circumstances, a deep joy filled Ted's heart. Jane had finally come to her senses. More than he had ever desired anything in this world, he wished he could comply with the first unselfish request ever made by the woman he loved. He gazed through the icy drizzle toward the darkened shipyard beyond them, looking for his dispersed men, who even now followed the orders he had given.

Jane gathered the reins of her pacer and led it beside the wagon seat. "Let Yancy take my horse and go," she begged on a sob. "Please."

Ted saw the seaman rising cautiously from the seat, and his grip tightened on the saber.

Yancy eyed it and hesitated.

Ted took another long look at Jane. From the sincere expression in her eyes, he knew this selfless act could come only from her return to God. He found it impossible to ignore the significance of that realization. With a last furtive glance at them, he slowly sheathed the sword.

Jane let out a huge breath of relief.

"I think not!" an all-too-familiar voice announced in distinct, measured syllables from the side of a nearby warehouse.

Swinging around in his saddle, Ted saw Alex and another officer ride out of the shadows. He knew at once that they'd been hiding—and in such an advantageous spot that they had undoubtedly overheard the entire encounter. What was worse, Ted realized Alex and the other lieutenant had been spying on *him,* to see if he would fulfill his duty as an officer of the king. Jane must have given Alex the exact location of the smuggling operation—information that had been withheld when he had received his orders earlier this evening.

A great desolation settled over him. Her change of heart was of little consequence now. It was too late. For all of them.

Lieutenant Fontaine, sitting tall in his saddle, drew his magnificently strutting horse to a stop a few feet from Jane. He looked with disdain down his long aristocratic nose at her. "I am most disappointed in you, my sweet. Most disappointed."

29

From his position on his horse, Ted saw Jane's eyes grow wide with fear. She moved close and clutched his leg. Her sodden cloak hung limp and heavy on her lithe body. She looked for all the world like a pathetic street urchin, trembling in the rainy darkness.

He heard the sound of two long blades sliding from their scabbards. Alex and the other officer had become the enemy.

Lord, help us, Ted prayed silently. *All of us.*

In one swift, fluid motion Yancy sprang from the wagon onto Jane's waiting pacer. With a sharp whack on the animal's rump, he galloped off, heading down along the shoreline.

"After him!" Alex commanded, wheeling his steed around.

The second officer spurred his mount into a gallop, taking up the chase.

Seizing the moment, Ted reached down and pulled Jane up behind him, then charged his horse into Alex's. Giving Alex a hard shove, he knocked his old comrade to the ground. Without a backward glance, he galloped inland, taking Prince Street, which led to the center of town. It would be only seconds before Alex would remount and follow them.

The cold air magnified the sound of the horseshoes striking against the cobbles; Alex's pursuit would be a simple matter—not to mention the fact he and Jane were riding double. He had to think of some way to outwit his former friend.

With Jane's arms wrapped tightly around him, he cut across to Back Street, then turned onto Union. Suddenly, Ted had to rein in sharply. A throng of men crowded the wide thoroughfare despite the cold rain. Many of them held lanterns.

"What've we got here?" one voice grated. "Something sneaky and red, it appears to me."

"The wench on back is comely enough," another added with a leer. "Too good for the likes of a lobsterback." He reached for Jane's skirt.

She screamed and clasped Ted tighter.

He kicked out at the attacker and urged the horse into a trot, and the milling mob scattered before the animal's threatening hooves.

Ted noticed a narrow lane off to the side and veered into the pitch-dark alley. As the noise behind them gradually lessened, he slowed and looked back.

No one had followed.

He released a lungful of air. It would only be a matter of seconds before Alex, too, rode into the crowd. "Stay put," he whispered, dismounting. "And if I yell, you ride like the wind. I'm going back to the corner to see if Alex discovers which way we went."

"No," Jane begged softly. "I won't go on without you." Leaning down on her belly, she slid off. "You're in trouble because of all the horrid things I've done."

He grabbed her arm. "Jane, get back on the horse."

She tried to pull away. "No!" she rasped. "Don't ask that of me. I'm staying with you."

Having Jane in jeopardy was the last thing Ted wanted right now. But there was no time to argue. "Well, at least keep well behind me, then. I don't want you to get hurt." Creeping to the corner, he cautiously peeked out across the jostling group of townsmen, but saw no mounted soldier among them.

Just then Alex rode into view and was also forced to halt in their midst. His stallion pranced nervously, causing the nearest men to fall back.

Alex peered down his nose with a conscious air of superiority all his own. "I'm on the heels of a deserter of the king's army," he said imperiously. "Did any of you see him?"

The townsfolk snickered and ignored him, muttering snide oaths among themselves.

"I'll have an answer," Alex said more forcefully, "or I'll arrest the lot of you for obstructing an officer of the Crown."

A barrel-chested man in working garb moved forward, carrying a torch. From the look on his face, Ted thought he meant to toss it at Alex.

Alex must have come to the same conclusion, for his gloved hand went to the hilt of his saber.

The townsman took a step back and removed his tricornered hat. "Let's see," he mumbled. "Seems there was a young man in red who rode by a little bit ago. Had a young woman with him. That the one?"

Alex raised an eyebrow triumphantly. "Which way did they go?"

Ted edged farther into the dark lane. "Jane," he whispered. "Get back to the horse and ride out of here. Now."

"No!" She gripped his arm with trembling hands. "I cannot leave you here."

"Hm," the informant said, rubbing his jaw. "As I recall, it was—which way would you say, Clark?" He turned to the man beside him.

The thin bearded fellow scratched his grizzled head. "Seems to me it was that way," he said, pointing toward the Common, away from Ted and Jane.

"No, 'twasn't that way a'tall," a third said. "'Twas over that way." He indicated an entirely different direction.

Soon everyone was involved in the ruse, gesturing at all points of the compass as they shouted with ever-increasing volume.

Alex's features turned to stone, and he went rigid with fury. He jabbed his heels into his horse's flanks and bolted through the middle of the mob without regard for life or limb, scattering them at once.

They stared after him as he rode away.

Ted's jaw fell slack with relief as he watched Alex head toward Dan and Susannah's.

Jane slumped against Ted and clung to him. "They actually helped us!" she breathed. "I can't believe it."

"Nor can I." Ted knew that time was precious just now, but he could not stop himself from wrapping his arms around her and holding her close for a moment. She felt so small and fragile in his embrace. He was just as soggy from the icy rain as she was, but the rapid thudding of her heart against his sent renewed warmth through his whole being.

He eased her away slightly and smiled into her eyes. "For a very long time I've been praying you'd come back to me. And you did, this day. I'm very proud of you for what you've done."

"How can you say that?" Her words rang with confusion. "I've only made matters worse. I've turned you into a fugitive. You and Yancy. I feel so dreadful."

"Oh, I shouldn't worry overmuch about Seaman Curtis. I'm sure he's quite adept at eluding the authorities. I've no doubt he'll slip past them this time as well."

"I hope so. I truly do. But you, Ted!" Jane's voice caught. "They could hang you for treason." Sighing, she shook her head sadly. "Even when I try to make amends for my actions, it works against me. But after all the horrid things I've done, I suppose I deserve no less than that." As she raised a dejected gaze at him, her tears shimmered in the flickering light from the many torches out on Union Street. "Listen, I'll go to headquarters and tell them all of this was my fault, and—"

"You'll do no such thing," Ted cut in, crushing her to himself. This was the spunky, spirited lass he had seen the first time he had crossed her path three years ago, and it was good to know she was back to normal once more. He leaned down and kissed her forehead tenderly. "From now on, my Jane, if you're brave enough, we shall trust the Lord to see us through, just as he did a moment ago by sending Alex away."

"Do you really believe God had a hand in it?"

"As much as I believe that he returned you to me, whole and selfless."

Jane studied him in wonder. "Are you saying that even after all I've done, you can forgive me? Can want me?"

"And love you? Yes, my beautiful Jane. All of that and more."

Her knees gave way.

Tightening his hold, Ted felt suddenly stronger, as though he could protect her from whatever harm might lie ahead. She was worth any risk or challenge, worth any price required. He lowered his mouth to hers. It had been forever since he'd tasted her soft, full lips, and he wanted to savor them now.

Jane reached up and encircled his neck.

He deepened the kiss, wanting the sweet moment to last forever.

Someone nearby cleared his throat, then tapped Ted's shoulder. "'Scuse me, young man."

Ted jerked up his head.

"Might you be the deserter that haughty king's puppet was lookin' for?" asked the man who had thrown Alex off course.

Ted wrinkled his brow at the stocky townsman. "I must admit I am guilty as charged. I allowed a smuggler to escape this evening. Quite purposely, I'm afraid."

"And just who might it have been, if you don't mind me askin'?" the man's rough companion inquired.

"Yancy Curtis," Ted replied. "I couldn't bring myself to turn in a friend."

"Well, I'll be! He's a mate of ours!" The two nudged each other with broad grins.

"We need to get you off the street right away, young man. Come with me to my house," the first one said, indicating the direction with a tilt of his three-cornered hat. "You need to get out of that uniform right quick, then we'll have you on your way before an all-out search is organized."

"And I wouldn't waste no more time, if I was you, kissin' on that girl," the second added with a grin as he brushed at the sleeve of his worn wool coat. "You'll have to get off the peninsula tonight. By morning the whole place'll be crawling with lobsterbacks."

"We'd truly appreciate that," Ted said gratefully, hugging Jane close. "By the way, why are there so many people out on the streets tonight? You're not thinking of trying to burn the *Dartmouth,* are you?"

"No. We're just waiting around for some friends who went to a little tea party."

"Tea party?"

"Yep," added his pal, whacking his knee with mirth. "And the British are bound to be a mite upset for not bein' invited."

Ted turned a puzzled glance toward Jane.

"I expect it's no secret by now," the bearded one explained, looking from Ted to Jane. "Some locals disguised as Indians are aboard the *Dartmouth* and dumpin' all the tea smack into the bay. Ah, 'twill be a grand cup of tea they'll be brewin' for the fishes, I must say!"

"What did you say?" Jane gasped. "I think my brother is with them!"

Ted hugged her closer to him and gave the men a stern look. "I wonder if you have any idea of the dire consequences such an act will bring. The admiral will have the heads of everyone involved. Count on it."

"Only if they dare arrest those *Indians* while hundreds are watching," the heavy man said. "I, for one, don't know a single name. How about you, Clark?"

"Who, me? I'm home sleepin' right now."

"Well, don't presume to think the Crown will let Boston off as they did Providence over the *Gaspee* burning," Ted warned. "The king cannot afford another embarrassment like that one. Don't be surprised if Parliament closes down the port. They'll strangle your commerce, starve you out until some-one comes forward and names names. And that'll be just the beginning, I'm sure."

"No doubt they'll try," the one called Clark scoffed.

"Aye," the other added with force. "Just let 'em try."

"Well," Ted offered, "I suppose there's nothing left to say but may the good Lord help you all."

"That's just what we're countin' on," the thick-chested man said with a toothy grin. "But first things first. Let's get the two of you dry and on your way out of town. I have a brother up Lexington way who'll be more than happy to take you two in until other arrangements can be made."

Jane leaned around Ted and smiled. "My brother is the Reverend Dan Haynes, sir, the assistant pastor at the church on Long Lane. Would you be kind enough to get word to him about us? He'll want to know we're safe. And I'm certain he'll be happy to help out in any way he can."

"You're Dan Haynes's sister, Miss? Sure thing." He squeezed her shoulder reassuringly, then began leading the way with his companion.

Ted hesitated. He cupped Jane's face with his hands and looked into her eyes. "Are you quite sure you want to do this, my love? Become a fugitive with me? You'll lose everything you've ever strived for."

"Well then," she said with a dazzling smile as her fingertips caressed his cheek. "I suppose I'll just have to settle for the loathsome task of being with the man I love and adore. For the rest of this life and for evermore."

Ted could hardly breathe as he gazed down at her and saw the adoration that shone from her eyes.

Drinking in the glory of Ted's loving expression, Jane began to laugh softly.

"Whatever do you find so amusing about all of this?" he asked with a curious frown.

It took a moment before she could control her mirth long enough to answer. "Not too long ago I thought Emily had lost her mind for running off with a fugitive."

Ted began to chuckle along with her. "Didn't we all, my love. Didn't we all." With a lopsided grin, he bowed with a flourish, then extended his elbow her way. "Well, I find this a most opportune time for the two of us to take our leave, m'lady."

Not the smallest doubt remained as Jane threaded her hand into the crook of Ted's elbow. Happiness, in whatever measure life presented it, lay with the man she loved. Arm in arm, they followed the townsmen as the mist began to fall again from Boston's night sky.